THE HORSEMASTERS

THE
HORSEMASTERS

Cynthia Harrod-Eagles

This first world edition published in Great Britain 2001 by
SEVERN HOUSE PUBLISHERS LTD of
9–15 High Street, Sutton, Surrey SM1 1DF.
This first world edition published in the USA 2001 by
SEVERN HOUSE PUBLISHERS INC of
595 Madison Avenue, New York, N.Y. 10022.

British Library Cataloguing in Publication Data

Harrod-eagles, Cynthia
 The horsemasters
 1. Show jumping – Fiction
 2. Suspense fiction
 I. Title
 823.9'14[F]

 ISBN 0-7278-5588-3

Typeset by Hewer Text Ltd.,
Edinburgh, Scotland.
Printed and bound in Great Britain by
MPG Books Ltd., Bodmin, Cornwall.

Prologue

F or perhaps the ninth or tenth time John Newland hauled the big horse away from the jumps and sent him pounding round the paddock with a thunder like a runaway train.

The purpose of circling was to make the horse relax before attempting the jumps, but it didn't take an expert to see that it was growing more tense with every circuit. Newland must have known it by the feel of the horse, by the hunch of its back under the saddle and the crabbed stiffness of its movements.

It was a chestnut – that bright coppery colour children call ginger – but just now its coat was dark and oiled-looking with sweat. White foam hung in ropes like saliva from the corners of its mouth, and spattered its chest and knees. Where the reins touched its neck they had creamed up a lather. The eyes showed white, and the ears were flattened to the skull as it fought for its head.

As it passed the gate a flying gobbet of foam smacked on to the cheek of Newland's young sister, Mary, but she wiped it away absently, her frowning gaze fixed on the horse. There was no missing the similarity between brother and sister, but a difference of feature of a millimetre here and there had made Mary quite pretty in a pink-and-white sort of way, while John was gaunt-cheeked and plain. The groom, Jean, sitting beside Mary on the paddock gate, thought that the frown made her look particularly like her brother, though in his case the frown was usually a useful warning signal to employees.

Mary didn't notice Jean looking at her: with her fists

1

clenched between her knees, she was willing the horse to yield to John's mastery. Family loyalty – plus the awareness, beaten into her almost since her birth, that John was a brilliant horseman – made her side with her brother; yet she felt an intense sympathy for the distressed animal.

The ginger gelding had been labelled as 'difficult' when Dad bought him three months ago for John to ride; but in those three months Coppernob, as they had called him, had gone from difficult to impossible. He was a horse with enormous scope and power, and had a huge jump in him, but he was highly-strung and easily spooked. He also had a stubborn streak which made him unwilling to do what he was told, particularly when it came to repeating a lesson over and over to perfect it.

Newland had ridden him hard and concentrated on breaking his will. He tended to rush his fences and jump flat, and, to make him more careful, Newland had employed some of those devices that Mary so passionately hated – though, in this household, she hated in silence. Dad always backed John up, no matter what, not just because he was a male and Mary a female, but because he had 'taught him everything he knew', so he must be right.

The response to any breath of a different opinion was: 'The proof of the pudding, my girl!' How she had come to hate that expression in the course of her short life! But John was among the most successful and highest-earning showjumpers in the country. To him and to Dad – and indeed to all the staff on the Essex cattle-and-horses spread – being 'in the money' was proof incontrovertible that the Newland method worked. Pure silly sentiment, that's what Mary's misgivings were; or, more per-jorative still, anthropomorphism.

But this particular pudding was not eating too well. There had been a steady deterioration in the horse's condition and performance. John and Dad said it was simply a matter of applying more of the same pressure until he knuckled under;

but Mary believed she knew how he felt as he scrabbled his way round the paddock, setting his jaw against the bit and, whichever way he was faced, keeping his head turned towards the jumps. Jumping had become an ordeal to him, and seeing the hated fences, he wanted to get them over with as quickly as possible so that he might be allowed to go back to his box. The more he was prevented from getting on with it, the more tense he got; but his rider would not allow him to jump until he had calmed down. It was a vicious circle.

Another circuit. The ground was hard after two weeks without rain – full of bone, as horsemen say – and it seemed to shake as the big hooves slammed it. As they turned at the bottom of the paddock the ginger horse almost got out from under his rider with a sudden swerve. Newland jerked his head back, and he snorted with surprised pain. They were coming up the side towards the gate now, and the horse rolled his eyes towards it, longing for escape. To Mary it seemed like a desperate appeal. *Sentimental*, she rebuked herself; but the foam on his lips was tinged with pink, and suddenly she could bear it no longer.

'Why don't you take him over a jump, John?' she called. The sound of her own voice frightened her with her daring. But it wasn't a criticism, she defended herself inwardly and automatically. It was just a suggestion. 'It might settle him down: give him something to think about.'

For a wonder, Jean seemed to agree. 'Circling's just making him worse,' she said.

'He'll rush it,' Newland said irritably, circling the chestnut on the spot to keep him within talking range.

'So let him,' Jean said. 'Take him over the fixed poles. If he clouts that good and hard, it'll teach him a lesson, make him think what he's doing.'

'All right, I'll give it a try,' Newland said, without conviction.

Mary watched in apprehension, afraid her intervention had made things worse for the horse. To hit a fixed jump at speed

3

would hurt it quite a bit, and while no horse would do it twice, they had only nailed it up last night, so the chestnut would not know it was fixed. He would remember only that he had always before been able to scatter the poles with his forelegs.

'John, maybe it's not such a good idea,' she began hesitantly; but he was going away from her and didn't hear. In any case, it was already too late.

Being turned towards the jumps was what the horse had been waiting for. He snatched at the bit and raced for the nearest fence, a small brush, but his rider wrenched him aside and drove him at the poles. Newland tried with seat and hands to collect the horse, but he seemed oblivious to everything but the need to get the ordeal over. He was going too fast, galloping flat with his nose up, and Newland was belatedly apprehensive. The horse was out of control, its speed beyond anything he had experienced yet; but it was too late to stop. The only thing to do now was to give the jump everything they had.

They thundered down on the blue and white poles; the horse lowered his head a little, proof he was looking what he was doing, and all three people experienced a little flutter of relief. And then at the last second he seemed to try to check. Perhaps some instinct warned him that the jump was not right, or some delicate horse sense perceived a difference in it from yesterday. At all events, he checked, hesitated a microsecond, and then tried to jump anyway, hitting it at a half-rear. He slammed into it with chest and knees so hard that the entire structure, stands and all, went over, and the big horse came down head over heels, landing in a welter of twigs and flying legs.

There was an awful sound of snapping as the poles broke under its falling weight. Newland came off over its head, hit a pole painfully with his back and then felt something heavy crushing his foot. He yelled with pain; and then a blow on the back of his head stunned him.

Mary and Jean had started running as soon as the horse checked, foreseeing disaster. When they reached the ruin of the jump the chestnut was trying to get up, struggling in desperate silence to right himself. He was hampered by the saddle, which stopped him rolling over and clear of the debris of broken poles that had got between his legs. With a final heave he gained his feet, slipped on a rolling piece of wood, and at last bucked himself clear. Jean darted in at once to see to her employer, but Mary's instinct made her catch the reins as the horse came near her, to stop him hurting himself any further.

At her touch on the reins the chestnut flung up his head, eyes rolling, beside himself with terror. He was full of splinters, and bright blood flowed from a number of cuts on his legs; a chunk of flesh was out of his shoulder and the ginger skin hung over it in a flap like a triangular stamp; a cheek-strap had broken, so that the bit hung out of the side of his mouth; and the saddle had been wrenched almost upside down. This much Mary took in at a glance as she hung on to the reins, talking soothingly to the frightened beast, trying to advance a hand to stroke the trembling neck.

Jean, kneeling amid the wreckage beside John, called, 'He's knocked out. I think his arms and legs are all right but he might have broken ribs. Better not move him. I'll call for an ambulance. Can you hang on to the horse while I run to the house?'

Mary nodded, though Jean had not waited for her answer before springing away across the paddock. Mary was not worried about John: it never occurred to her that he might be anything but all right. John and Dad were both given constants in her world, all-powerful and invulnerable. It was the little people like her, like her mother, who had died seven years ago – like the horses – who got hurt. The ginger horse had stopped trying to pull away from her, and now she led him a few careful steps forward with the dual purpose of turning him so that the jump was out of his sight and seeing whether he was lame. It seemed hardly possible that he could have escaped serious injury, but though he walked hesitantly and stiffly, he put his weight evenly on his legs.

But he was a pitiful sight, trembling and sweating, his coat covered in blood and lather, splinters and flakes of paint. A fierce determination seized Mary that John should never ride this horse again. It was a ridiculous thing to feel, for she had no say in the matter – had never had a say in any matter to do with horses – and Dad and John could always shut her up with a bare frown or a sharp word. But, oh, *surely* some tactful, face-saving way might be found for John to admit that he could not handle the chestnut? Some clever argument that he would accept, some flawless piece of logic? She wished ardently that she had a ready tongue, that she was clever, even that she was a little more brave. But she was only stupid, useless, shy Mary, whose sole worth in the world was that she was the famous John Newland's sister.

'Poor Copper, poor old man,' she was murmuring all this while, gently stroking the chestnut's neck, trying to exude calm and love. Hurt, bewildered, afraid, the horse accepted her caress, listened to her voice; and perhaps some dim colt-memory stirred in him, for at last he lowered his head and thrust it under her arm, as a frightened foal will thrust its head against its dam's flank. Mary put her other arm over the chestnut's ears, and he stood there quietly, in the darkness and warmth that shut out a world which had become too much for him to cope with. And gradually, as Mary murmured to him, his trembling stopped.

One

D an Roberts and Polly Morgan were standing side by side at the front of the competitors' box at the Wembley ringside, watching the jumps being raised for the jump-off. It was the final competition of the Royal International Horse Show. Both of them had been eliminated in an earlier round so their interest was purely academic. They were lingering here mainly for the pleasure of each other's company. They were old friends.

Had they looked across at that moment they would have seen themselves on the television monitor. There was Handsome Dan, or Dan the Man – he had a number of sobriquets familiar to his large fan-club – filling most of the screen: a big man, with the well-developed arms and shoulders that came from his early career in the building trade, and the vigorous dark hair and saturnine good looks that made the groupies tremble. He made Polly, by contrast, look small and pale, though she was neither. She had an athletic figure, a smooth, healthy face – faintly freckled – and thick pinkish-gold hair in a trademark single plait behind, which hung down between her shoulder blades like a bell-rope.

The BBC, filling in time on *Showjumping Special*, had drawn some significance from their proximity. As Polly was seen to laugh, the commentator said, 'And there, enjoying a joke together, are this week's big winners, Polly Morgan, who won the Queen Elizabeth II Cup on Taggert, and of course the great Dan Roberts, always a favourite with Wembley audiences; Dan who won the King George V Gold Cup for the second time running on his great horse, The Iceman.'

It was lucky neither party could hear the other. Roberts would have been infuriated by the commentator's low, intimate tone and the free use of his Christian name, and Polly might well have been annoyed that greater importance was acceded to Dan's win than to hers. On the other hand, the commentator would have been at the very least disconcerted by the joke about the nun and the policeman Roberts was telling. It was fortunate that the cameras switched to another focus before he got to the end of the joke with its explicit gestures.

Polly burst into laughter just as the ring announcer gave the name of the first competitor in the jump-off. 'My God, but that's a terrible joke!'

'Not bad, eh? I got it from Howard.' Howard Meak, another leading showjumper, was an old friend.

'He should be ashamed of himself. Who's this coming in now?' Polly screwed her head round to see the tunnel entrance. 'Oh, it's the Belgian with the unpronounceable name. Well, he won't win.'

Roberts shook his head. 'I wouldn't write him off. He got through the first round against all odds.'

'I wouldn't go into the ring with a horse as badly schooled as that,' Polly said, watching the Belgian's bay canter in slow motion across the ring with its head pointing one way and its body the other.

'Schooling? Who gives a damn about schooling any more?' Roberts said with a sound of disgust. 'Strap 'em up and kick 'em on, that's the idea nowadays.'

'What do you mean, nowadays? When was it any different? There was always a lunatic fringe that relied on martingales and hardware. Not mentioning any names, but looking hard in a certain direction.'

Roberts did not turn his head. He knew she meant his life-long rival and occasional nemesis, John Newland; he also knew she was teasing him.

'Yes, but it used to be just a fringe. Now it's mainstream,' he said. 'And the final insult is Klaus Gunter Reiner and his bloody double bridle. No one in the history of the world ever show-jumped in a double bridle until him.'

Polly was wont to correct his wilder exaggerations, but she left this one alone, knowing he felt strongly about it. They watched the Belgian's round in silence, unbroken except for Roberts's grunt of disgust as the horse, wrenching its head an inch free of its rider's hands, managed to scramble over the heightened wall. The competitor left the ring with a clear round, and as he passed them, Roberts shouted, 'That's not a horse, it's a bloody contortionist!'

Polly shushed him vigorously. 'You shame me! Don't be so unsporting!'

'It's all right. He doesn't understand English.'

'The Beeb does, though, and their microphones pick up everything. Do you want another article in the Sunday supps about your rudeness?'

'Ee, ma lass, it's nobbut ma Yorkshire bloontness,' Roberts said broadly.

'Don't give me any of that ee ba goom bollocks,' Polly said sternly. 'You're about as Yorkshire as a Cornish pasty!'

'I forgive you that insult,' he said in his normal, flat, roughly midlands accent. 'But only because we ought to stick together – the anti-strap league.'

'Yes, and the others probably think of *us* as the lunatic fringe,' Polly concurred. 'Look at us – only one noseband per horse! It's unnatural!'

'Talking of which, here's a treat for you,' Roberts said, looking over her shoulder. 'Spotty John's coming in.'

'Unfair. He only has the occasional spot.'

'I know. It's just he's got that unhealthy look, as if he always ought to have them.'

9

'I know what you mean, though I don't know why I do. He's perfectly normal-looking, really.' The audience greeted John Newland's entrance with huge applause and cheering. 'Listen to them,' Polly marvelled. 'Why do they love him so?'

'You should know,' Roberts pointed out. 'You used to go out with the bugger.'

Polly shuddered. 'Don't remind me! It was long ago and I was young and foolish. And I think he was nicer then. Fame has definitely spoiled him.'

'Something has.'

'But why does the public still adore him? It isn't even as if he's handsome, hunky and charming.' More your lean and knobbly sort, she thought. He had a nice smile when he used it, but these days it was rarely seen, and never pointing in her direction. He had never forgiven her for breaking it off with him.

'Success breeds success,' Roberts said with a shrug. 'That's why it's so hard to beat a champion. Look at ice-skating: the world champions won every competition regardless of performance, because the judges didn't dare give them bad marks.'

'Well, at least you can't cheat in our sport,' Polly said. 'A clear round's a clear round. I do love this horse,' she added as Newland's 'first string', Apache, made short work of the jumps without the help or hindrance of his rider. 'He makes it look so easy. And John at least has the sense to leave him alone. Pity he doesn't belong to someone nicer, though.'

'I hear one of his horses will soon belong to someone nicer,' Roberts commented.

'What's that?'

'Just a rumour, but I hear via the grapevine that he's been having trouble with that big chestnut he brought over from France. He had a bad fall with it, broke his ankle.'

'He couldn't have. He's not wearing a cast.'

'Well, he broke something, anyway. I'm not a doctor, don't ask me.'

'Is that why he's been looking more than usually cross?'

Roberts nodded. 'He's putting the nag on the market. Lost his nerve, they say.'

Polly stared. 'Lost his nerve? That doesn't sound like John. He may be all sorts of a bastard, but I never thought him a coward.'

'Who knows? I doubt if even Newland is perfect. There must be *one* horse in the world that's too much for him.'

'I wonder what it's like. Have you ever seen it?'

'Don't think so,' Roberts said. By the tone of his voice she knew he had lost interest in the subject. Chris Campbell was in the ring now on her little horse Sunny, and Dan, in his expansive way, was almost as friendly with Chris as with Polly.

It occurred to her, as she watched the round, that it was almost ten years since Chris and Sunny had come on to the scene – in the juvenile classes when Chrissie was only fifteen. Ten years! They were getting old, she thought sadly, she and Dan – yes, and John Newland, the horse groupies' matinee idol. Well, at least Dan had been married, though he was divorced now. John's name had not been 'romantically linked', as the tabloids said, with anyone since she had been on the brink of getting engaged to him all those years ago. Blimey, that had been a close call! She crossed her fingers to take off the bad luck.

She had fallen for John Newland in a weak moment, when still trying to make her way in the showjumping world and feeling something of an outsider. She had gone into the sport as a way both to escape from, and to prove herself to, a father who had never made any secret of his disgust that she was a girl rather than a boy. It had not answered, of course: 'I'll show *you*!' ploys rarely do. Her father, a successful company director, had regarded showjumping as 'a girls' game', and treated her successes with an aggressive lack of interest. He had died – in harness, of an early heart attack – without ever having given her the approval she craved.

It was in the earliest and most painful days of the struggle that John Newland – already famous and much run-after – had made a play for her, and she had been flattered and grateful enough to fancy herself in love. It was fortunate that her eyes had been opened in time to his real nature. Dan Roberts – admittedly not an unbiased source – said he was cold as a dead snake.

'Good round,' Roberts said now, as a burst of applause met Sunny's last, safe landing. He eyed Polly sidelong. 'Are you driving back home tonight, Poll?'

'No, tomorrow morning,' she said. 'Why?'

'I'm staying over, too. Fancy going out to dinner somewhere? Somewhere a bit posh? I'm fed up with egg and chips and sandwiches.'

She noted his eager stance, his brightness of eye, the closed, enigmatical smile that drove horse-loving girls everywhere crazy. Dan Roberts was an exceedingly good-looking blighter – and he knew it, more was the pity. 'It's a bit late, isn't it?' she observed.

'Not if we go now.'

'What, leave before the end of the show?'

'Bollocks to the show. Newland can have my balloon and cracker. Let's go and have a right proper blow-out. My treat.'

'OK. Sounds good to me.'

'And then we can drive up together tomorrow,' he added as they passed through the collecting ring.

The way he said *tomorrow* held a world of significance. What, she enquired silently of herself, did it suggest they might be doing together in between? But he flirted as automatically as he breathed, and she was used to discounting his riper innuendoes. She liked him, there was real liking between them, but she would have to have been made of stone not to feel a little flutter of something sexual when he turned the full battery of his charm on her. It was all just in fun, of course, but if ever he made a serious play for her – well, she didn't like to think how she'd stand up to that sort of temptation.

For the moment, of course, he was just polishing up his reputation. Wasn't he? She met his eyes and one of her eyebrows climbed her forehead, but his face gave nothing away.

They were not the only ones to leave early: already there were horseboxes on the road, transporting tired horses home to rest before the next big fray. As they crossed the tan they were watched by another ill-assorted couple who were following their horses back to the stable block.

Since Alison Neave was a tall, well-built girl and Michael Baker a slender young man, they were much of a height and weight. Both had short, brown hair – Alison's, in fact, rather the shorter of the two, since she had recently indulged, for reasons of practicality, in a ferocious haircut. Wearing a crash cap under hot lights made the head sweat, and washing your hair every day was a pain, she felt, unless you could just shake it dry and walk away. Michael, being fairly new to celebrity, was going through a period of personal vanity. His hair was one of his good points, according to his older, married sister, and he wore it full, expensively styled and discreetly highlighted.

They followed the shining rumps of their horses, walking unconsciously in step. Their ill-assortedness came from the fact that Alison was the daughter of an earl, whose horses grazed over more acres than they could crop in a year, while Baker was a scrap-dealer's son from West London. He lived with his father in a dreadful little flat above the mews stables in which his horses were kept, living in all year round like riding-school nags, except for holidays when they were turned out in a two-acre field the Bakers rented, out in Isleworth. Theirs was something of a spartan life. If Dad ever found out what he had paid to have his hair done, he'd get a right old mouthful, Michael knew.

Some children who had managed to get past the gateman ran up asking for autographs, and while they were signing they saw Dan Roberts and Polly Morgan leaving.

'I don't blame them,' said Baker. 'That's enough, now, kids. Go on, buzz off.'

'Who, for what?' Alison asked as they walked on.

'Those two, for leaving. The show's been a real let-down this year. So badly attended.'

'Was it? I didn't notice. I thought it was sold out from Wednesday onwards, anyway.'

'I don't mean the audience, God love 'em, I mean the competitors. For an international, there weren't many foreigners about, were there?'

'Four Germans,' Alison counted. 'Two French. Three Belgians.'

'And Sean McNally, the one-man Irish team. Not very impressive, was it?'

'Well, don't sound as if you blame me for it! Who did you expect?'

'Where were the Americans? Where were the Australians?'

'They never come. It wouldn't be worth their while, when the prizes are so small.'

'But they used to come when the prizes were even smaller,' Baker said. 'When the International was at White City. I was looking at some of Dad's old programmes last week.'

'You could be right,' Alison said, not knowing about that. 'But everything was different then.'

'Exactly my point. The show had prestige. It was the best competition in jumping. It didn't matter about the prize money – it was like winning Wimbledon. But how can you stage a big competition in a ring the size of a backyard?' he grumbled. 'So they don't come. They go to Dublin, but they don't come to Wembley.'

'They're not the only ones to miss it,' Alison said, catching something of his gloom. 'Come to think of it, where was Robin Peters? Keith Arnold? Howard Meak?'

'Ah, now Howard Meak I can tell you about,' Baker said. 'It's a bit of a juicy story. It seems . . .' He caught sight of his groom just ahead listening with anticipatory interest, and stopped. 'I'll tell you later,' he concluded.

'Oh good, I like a bit of scand,' Alison said.

He bent his head closer as they turned into the stables. '*And* I'll tell you why John Newland is selling that big chestnut of his.'

'You are a sink of gossip,' Alison said admiringly. 'Is there anything about anyone that you don't know?'

'I'll let you know when I find out.' He clapped his hands sharply, making the grooms jump. 'Come on now, girls, let's get these horses clothed up and boxed before the pubs shut.'

At the back of the collecting ring, Chris Campbell was making a telephone call, her free hand pressed over her right ear to cut out the voice from the tannoy, which was babbling about tickets for the next show.

'Howard? Yes, I can only just hear you. It's noisy here. No, I'm still in the collecting ring.'

Her voice was light, and it was hard to compete with the rest of the bedlam. Everything about her gave an impression of being faint and frail: she was small-boned, slender, with a little, pointed face, and short curly hair of that rare true blonde colour that goes with blue eyes. The sight of her on a horse raised fears in strangers for her safety: she looked so young, and her little wrists were surely too fragile to hold such a powerful beast?

It was illusion, of course: she was older than she looked, and a great deal tougher, and though everyone agreed that she was 'too nice' for a competitive world, she had a single-minded tenacity of purpose that did very well in place of that missing touch of malice.

'No, I got second. Weren't you watching? Oh. John New-land, of course, who'd you think? We both went clear but he was two seconds up on me. Oh yes, like a dream – as always. Why weren't you watching? Oh. Mm. Mm. I see. P'raps I'd better ring off, then. I wish . . . oh, never mind. What? Yes, lots of people asked why you weren't here. All right. Well, give me a ring when you can. I've got to go . . . they're calling me.'

She rang off as her groom, Lesley, came towards her leading Sunny and carrying her black coat, which she had shrugged off because of the heat. She slid into it, hastily buttoned herself, and cocked her leg for Lesley to boost her into the saddle. She bent to feel the girth while the groom whisked the rug off Sunny's quarters, and the little horse arched his neck and mouthed the bit in pleased anticipation. He was tired, Chris knew, but he would go again if required – would jump off until he dropped, if she asked him. If only people were as kind as horses!

'Shall I take the phone?' Lesley asked. Chris had forgotten she was holding it, and handed it over, meeting her groom's sympathetic eye. There wasn't much Lesley didn't know about her life.

'Did you get through to him?' Lesley asked, folding the blanket over her arm.

'Yes, but he couldn't say much. *She* was in the next room.' She sighed, turning Sunny towards the ring entrance. 'Why are all the good ones married?'

In the Beaumont Arms, Tom Emmerson – 'Gentleman' Tom Emmerson, as the media always called him – ordered another whisky and poured the second half of his bottle of dry ginger into it. He didn't particularly like whisky with dry ginger, but the mixer slowed down his drinking rate: he was inclined these days to bolt his whisky, which had the dual disadvantage of being expensive, and of giving him hiccoughs.

He counted the money out on to the bar top, and then in sudden panic dug into his inside pocket. Thank God, it was still there! The twenty-pound note, the blessed, God-sent score which he had found at the back of the stands. How long was it since he had been able to drop a twenty and not notice the loss? Well, perhaps he should be grateful that there had ever been a time.

He looked at his reflection in the glass behind the bar, what he could see of it through the bottles and optics. Seedy, that was the word. He'd been quite good-looking once, in that old-fashioned, soft, fair, upper-class way. A nice, clean public-school boy. Hah! Gentleman Tom, indeed! That was what had sold him down the river, of course. Born with a silver spoon in his mouth – which was all very well until the silver spoon turned into an incubus and sucked the life out of you.

If he had been born working class he might have had a proper job instead of trying to live on investments at a time when interest rates were at an historic low. He might have been living in a nice cosy council house, instead of trying to maintain the draughty ancestral pile, a fifteenth century timber-framed manor house in Kent that sucked up money like a giant bionic sponge.

He thought of the prize money he had won this week. If he had started off in the black, or even at zero, it would have covered the week's expenses at least. As it was, to a man who was overdrawn on his overdraft to his extent, it was almost worse than useless. Debt breeds debt. It seemed to be the only living, growing thing in his life. In the red, he thought with ironic amusement. Like those red-legged flamingos that live on the caustic salt pan where nothing else can survive, the only thing that survived around Tom Emmerson was a flock of scarlet debts.

But it had been a good week for the horses. Buccaneer had jumped well: he was going to be a good young horse. He had something of the style of Sunavon, dear old Sunavon who was grazing out his peaceful and deserved retirement back home in Kent. Those had been the days of his glory, when Sunavon was in his prime. Olympic Gold Medalist, twice winner of the King George V Cup, alongside historic horses like Italy's The Rock and the USA's Nautilus – only Foxhunter had won it more than twice. He was a horse who would go down in the annals of fame and take Tom's name with him. He had been a glorious animal, a flamboyant golden stallion with a mouth like silk and a heart as big as a house. And in those days Tom's wife had still been around: dear Tilly, beautiful Tilly – silly Tilly.

She had left him. She had never really liked his sort of life, not once the thrill of being the lady of the manor had worn off. She had married into a position and a custom that demanded more from her than she was willing to give: she resented the constant calls on her time – unpaid – that village life made. She resented even more the lack of privacy, the goldfish bowl, the constant gossip of the Aga set, the way everything she did and said was discussed and referred back to her as someone else's property.

Everything about country life repelled her. She disliked hunt meets and point-to-points, dog shows and flower shows. She hated the rank-smelling animals that bellowed and groaned, copulated, suffered and died without modesty all around her. She shrank from the fields and woods full of cruel nature that rolled almost up to her windows. She loathed the mud, the cold, the rain; and oh, the awful inconvenience of living in a five-hundred-year-old timber-framed house, miles from a tube station, a gym or a decent beauty salon!

So she had left him. In the inaugural year of the New York Horse Fair she had gone there with him and come back with a journalist who'd been covering it for *Horse and Hound.* They'd divorced, but by the time the decree came through the journalist was history and she'd set up with a well-known fashion de-signer, whom she'd eventually left for a very rich man with his own PR agency. And so on, always looking over her current man's shoulder in case she was missing something better. The last thing Tom had heard, poor old Till was living in France with a man who wrote semi-pornographic books. He felt sorry for her. She wouldn't like France at all, poor cow: her scribbler didn't even live in Paris, but somewhere in the Dordogne, and it was well known that French farming was far dirtier, smellier and crueler than in Britain.

He had finished his whisky. He was the same way with food – always bolted it down. Not for hunger, but from a sort of nervous tic. He envied people who could linger over a meal. He could if he had company, but never when he was alone. The bar door opened and admitted Alison Neave and the young Baker boy, and he swung round on his stool, eager for company.

'Hullo, come and join me, what will you have?' he said quickly, so they shouldn't go off in a huddle together.

'Hullo, Tom. Didn't expect to find anyone here,' said Alison.

'Aren't you going back tonight?' Baker asked. 'I'd have thought you were near enough.'

'I haven't got mains electricity,' Emmerson said quickly. 'I don't like getting back after dark. What'll you have?'

Baker accepted the excuse without probing the logic. 'Oh, well, thanks. I'll have a pint, then,' he said.

'Ali?'

'The same, thanks.'

They joined him with apparent pleasure, and began to chat about the show; but Emmerson, in his deep lack of self-confidence, had seen a glance pass between them, and his heart sank. They thought he was a nuisance, he translated it to himself. They were only being polite. They thought he was just an old nuisance.

By noon the circus was settled in to its new quarters on the open ground beside the stadium in St Denis. It was not exactly a place of rural tranquility: the traffic thundered by on the Boul Ney on one side and the Périphérique on the other, bracketing them in bedlam. But it was nicely placed for the Porte de la Chapelle Metro station, which was important for the punters. No point in having a circus unless the audience could get to you.

The Englishwoman had joined the circus in Barcelona as a

groom, and the usually suspicious circus people had accepted her surprisingly quickly. She plainly knew her business, and the six black liveries and the two grey rosinbacks responded to her with instant trust.

It was generally agreed that she did not look much like an Englishwoman. There was something both arresting and exotic about her appearance; gypsy blood, perhaps, they thought. Her hair was of a very dark shade of red approaching henna, thick and wavy; she wore it tied back when she was working, but let loose it came down to her shoulder blades and stood out around her head like a massy, living frame for her face. That face was a smooth oval, expressing little; her eyes, which should have been blue with that hair, were dark – not just brown, but almost black. And, amazingly with that hair and those eyes, her skin was quite unfreckled: it had an almost translucent quality, like eggshell china.

Though friendly enough, she spoke little, never volunteering anything, which appealed to the instinctive reserve of a people within a people. They did not like newcomers to put themselves forward. But as a result no one knew anything about her. She spoke an unaccented, colloquial French, but had also enough Spanish to get by in Barcelona, and knew a few words of Romany. The Kiskoros acrobat troupe were sure she was no Englishwoman at all, but Hungarian; the Flying Maryinskis said on the contrary she was plainly Russian, and of the Old Blood. But any questions put to her she evaded with a smiling blandness, and the circus people would not press, despising that kind of curiosity. Besides, it was much more fun to speculate: the truth might turn out to be disappointing and much less romantic than their imaginings.

On that first night at St Denis, when the animals had been tended, she sought and was granted a few hours off. There would be no show that night, so she had nothing more to do until the last feed and water round. One of the men was going into central Paris, so she hitched a ride with him. He dropped her on the Rue Reaumur and she made her way through the backstreets to cross the river by the Pont des Arts. Among the book stalls that lined the *quai* on the Left Bank was one that sold current English newspapers and magazines. Here she bought a week-old *Horse and Hound* and retired with it to a tiny café on the corner of the Rue du Pontoise. She ordered a *pression* and a *croque-monsieur* and settled down to read.

There was nothing in it about the International, of course, but there was plenty to interest her. In particular there was a profile – as they were called these days, though profiles seemed to probe such personal depths they were more like full-frontal nudes – of John Newland. He was bragging, she noticed, about how he was going to win everything at Wembley. As if dear old Apache couldn't have gone round just as well without him! Or better. In the years in which she had been grooming for showjumpers, what with the frequency she had moved and the frequency with which the horses changed hands, there weren't many top jumpers she hadn't met. Meaning the horses, of course. She knew the riders too, but on the whole liked the horses better. You always knew where you were with horses.

She was about to turn over when the last paragraph of the article caught her eye – a footnote, more or less, to something in the main story. John Newland was selling the new horse he had brought over from France earlier this year. Coppernob was what the reporter called it, but that was only the name the Newlands had saddled the poor beast with. The big ginger horse had been jumped in France under the name of Le Chiffre.

Le Chiffre. He hadn't always been Le Chiffre either, of course. Years ago, in another of his incarnations . . . Her mind drifted.

The waiter came by to clear her plate and see if she wanted anything else. She started guiltily, coming back from her reverie, and he raised a placating hand. No hurry, mademoiselle. He did not mean to press her. In fact, it was a quiet time of a quiet evening, and she looked rather decorative sitting there.

Good for business, he thought. No one wants to enter an entirely empty café: that's one of the mysteries about human nature.

She resumed her thought train. So, Newland was selling the chestnut. Now, why would that be? It must mean he couldn't handle it, mustn't it? Was there more to it than that?

Perhaps it was time to go back. Circus life was all right, and she had enjoyed the change, but she had been with it for over six months. It was long enough to be gone from the scene. She would not like to lose touch.

She wondered who would buy the chestnut.

Yes, perhaps it was time to go back. She finished her beer and stood up, swinging her bag on to her shoulder, and walked out into the hot, neon-lit, petrol-fumed Paris night.

Two

R oberts was home before nine o' clock in the morning. It was to be a rest day for the two horses who had been at the show – The Iceman and Freddo – and, having fed them, he turned them out and then went in to snatch a quick bite to eat before starting his own day's work.

He cooked himself bacon and eggs over the calor-gas burner in the lean-to that served him for a kitchen, and took it into the living room to eat while he opened the morning's mail. Bills, predictably, and junk mail. And a letter from his ex-wife. He chewed more slowly as he read it.

He and Peggy had known each other all their lives, had gone to the same school, had started 'going out' together when they were both fifteen. Even then he had been good-looking, and girls had been chasing him since he was not much more than twelve. Why he had picked out Peggy was a puzzle to his contemporaries, because she was quiet and only moderately pretty. Roberts hardly knew himself. Perhaps it was because she *didn't* chase him. Perversity? Or security? He could be sure Peggy was exclusively his, and he valued loyalty – in others, at any rate.

He had left school at sixteen and started work on a building site, where he'd been taken under the wing of the head brickie and taught the trade. His father was a plumber and had been disappointed that Dan didn't want to follow him, but Dan had always been a rebel and the very fact of being expected to do something was enough to make him do the opposite. But bricklaying was a good trade, too – a brickie need never be out of work, his dad had said. Roberts had quite enjoyed it. Laying bricks was soothing, and you had something to show at the end of it. Even now, if he felt the stress of the life getting to him, he could find relaxation in building a wall.

But the call of horses was always strong. It puzzled his family, since none of them had ever so much as been astride a horse, but from boyhood he could never pass a field with a horse in it without stopping to make friends. There were always apple cores and bits of bread in his pockets when he went for a walk, just in case. So he had started to work with them, first in his spare time, helping at a stables in the evenings and at weekends. But it wasn't long before the horses were the greater part of his life, and the bricklaying was a part-time job that subsidised his real love. His father said anxiously that if he was not careful he would lose his 'proper' job, but Roberts had said not to worry, he could charm the foreman all right. He had always been good at getting people to do what he wanted.

Meanwhile Peggy had got a clerical and typing job in the office of the local shoe factory, and since they had been going out for long enough for everyone to assume it was inevitable, they had got married. She had not been best pleased about the way horses were replacing his 'proper' job: to her, riding was either a hobby for rich people's kids, or something to do with the Turf, and therefore dangerous, unreliable and in some undefined way a bit seedy. When Roberts had started riding other people's horses for a fee, she had annoyed him by calling him a jockey: she couldn't and wouldn't learn the proper terms for anything in his equestrian life, and to the end of their marriage had believed that a pony was a baby horse.

He looked up from the letter and stared around him a little blankly. The room he sat in was fifteen feet long, twelve wide and five foot six high. The wavy stone floor was only partly covered with a threadbare carpet and the wavy ceiling was supported by sagging beams on which even the accustomed struck their heads. At one end was the inglenook in which, during winter, Roberts kept a good fire burning; beside it was the door to the lean-to; at the other end was the open staircase to the upper floor.

Upstairs two tiny rooms led off either side of the stairhead. They were even lower-ceilinged than the living room, had one tiny window apiece, set at floor level because of the length of the thatch. There was no form of heating except for the fire downstairs; and no mains sewage – the privy was a sentry-box affair at the end of the nettle patch he called a garden. Beside the lean-to kitchen was a lean-to bathroom with an electric water-heater and a hand-held shower over the bath. Electricity was supplied by the generator that served the stables. The only gas was the calor-gas by which Roberts cooked.

The stables – extensive and with every mod con – were the reason he had bought the cottage; the cottage was the reason – the final reason – why Peggy had left him. She had got used, in the end, to his way of life, and occasionally even felt proud of his growing fame, though she never trusted the money side of it, and never stopped hinting that he ought to get a real job. Being on the telly and having kids ask for your autograph was all very well, but you couldn't do it for ever, could you, and then what would you do for a pension?

She had got used, though with more of a struggle and infinitely more pain, to what she called his 'philandering'. Roberts was a handsome man, and fame has a glamour in its own right. Add to that the oft-told story of his 'humble' beginnings, and it gave him a macho sort of charisma that women found irresistible. Every area of celebrity has groupies hanging around its fringes, and horses in particular seem to exert a strange attraction over the female sex. Roberts liked women, enjoyed sex, and being away from home so much presented him with huge opportunities. He felt it was to his credit that Peggy only ever learned about the tip of his infidelity iceberg; but find out she did, and there were rows, tears, bitter silences – all the paraphernalia of marital strife. Still, he had never wanted to leave her. He was fond of her, appreciated her good qualities, and it is axiomatic that an unfaithful man needs a faithful wife. He was loyal to her in his way – in his heart of hearts, as she might have said. And she was the last relic of his early life, a reminder of his roots. He never saw any of his relatives any more.

In the end – much to his surprise – it was she who left him. She had stood for his absences and his sleeping around, but it seemed that the home is closer to a woman's heart: when he had moved them out of the modern brick box on the raw new housing estate which she loved, and into the sagging, comfort-less cottage with the palatial modern stables attached, she had cried *enough*, and left him. Quite kindly, but very firmly, she had left him and never come back.

He had been hurt and offended that the house had mattered more to her than he did, and once the first shock was over, he had dismissed her from his conscious mind. But there were times when he still missed her. Most days he didn't notice the lack of comfort in the cottage – he didn't really spend much time there anyway – but today he found himself listening to the silence, even observing the dust drifting down through the bars of sunlight coming in through the window. Peggy had been in the background of his life for so long there were still times he half expected to hear her bustling about. With the prompting of her letter, he could hear her voice in his mind, running on quietly with her commonplace bits of news and comments. Her letters were just like her; and she wrote to him still kindly, as if they were the childhood friends they probably ought to have remained. When he missed her, he told himself that it was a good thing she had left him. He was not the same person he had been when they married, and when he had changed and moved on, she had not changed with him. If she had not gone, sooner or later he would have found her a drag and a handicap, and then he would have hated himself for those feelings.

Peggy had eventually remarried, to a motor-mechanic called Kevin, and they had a couple of kids. Roberts had never remarried. The horses were his children, the grooms his family, and he had plenty of friends on the circuit; and when he wanted company in bed, there were always plenty of groupies eager to sleep with him. He had had casual affairs and otherwise lived alone, and had never minded it, finding the life itself enough – until Anne.

Anne Neville. He had heard of her before he met her – had even seen her around without really thinking about it, for she had worked for various members of the showjumping fraternity. She was one of those itinerant grooms who moved from stable to stable, working for a pittance, apparently for love of the horses, and since she was both a good groom and an excellent rider, she had no difficulty in getting taken on. But she was different from the usual run of mop-haired, horse-mad girl grooms, who walked like yobs, smoked like chimneys and swore like sailors: she was quietly-spoken with a cultured accent, and graceful – almost elegant – in her movements.

Her reason for taking up the itinerant and poorly-paid life was something that was always canvassed when her name cropped up in conversation, but she herself would never speak about it or answer questions about her background. Inevitably, given that she was a single and attractive woman, gossip linked her with various of the male horsemasters she worked for. John Newland had even said in Roberts's presence that she was a nymphomaniac and that her lifestyle was her way of satisfying her urges. He had added some imaginative details that had been enough to disgust Roberts and put him on her side, so that when she approached him for a job, he did not hesitate to say yes.

So, she had come to groom for him; that and much more. Whether the stories he had heard about her were true or not he didn't know, would never know – and he didn't care, either. She had found her way into his bed so naturally that he couldn't remember to this day how it had happened, or by whose initiative. But he remembered it as the happiest time of his life, the time they had lived together. She had groomed and ridden his horses, acted as secretary and bookkeeper, been a passionate lover, and had given him something new: companionship. He had not been brought up to look upon women as friends: Anne had shown him how it was done, and it was largely due to her that he was now able to hold his own in the social side of the increasingly egalitarian showjumping world.

He had loved her. No, more: he had been in love with her. For the first time in his life he had known the infatuation that makes every moment out of the beloved's presence an intolerable ache. Her pale, serene beauty had driven him wild; her ability to keep silence, so rare in his experience, had stimulated his imagination. Her unfathomable dark eyes haunted his dreams; the long curve of her lips in her curved face made it look as if she was smiling even when she wasn't, making her the enigma he could never have enough of.

He loved her still; and since she had gone he had felt prickles of loneliness and dissatisfaction that he had never felt before her. He had not expected her to leave. Though he knew she was a wanderer and had worked for dozens of people before him, he had thought their relationship so special it would naturally last for ever. He had thought she felt that way too; but one day when they were coming in after exercise she had said, 'Will you drive me to the station after tea?'

'What for?' he had asked innocently, not seeing the approaching doom.

'To catch a train, of course,' she had said.

'Where to?'

'That depends which train comes in first.'

'But . . . I don't understand. Don't you know where you're going?' She hadn't answered, and though she was looking ahead past The Iceman's ears, her eyes were focused on a more distant prospect than the lane they were riding down. It was beginning to dawn on him at last. 'You're going away?' he said.

'I'm going away,' she agreed.

'Do you want to tell me why?' he asked stiffly, offended and afraid.

But she wouldn't answer. The horses jogged, eager to get home for their feed. It was a spring evening. The tender new grass was coming in like a green mist over the paddocks, the earth smelled darkly rich, and he realised he could see the great branched vein on Freddo's ear quite plainly, proof that his winter coat was almost gone. A seasonal restlessness, he had thought, must be what was working in Anne, but he felt hugely hurt that it was enough to override all they had together. Yet at last he said, 'Will you be coming back?'

She hadn't answered that either, and later, during the many, many evenings when he went over it and over it, remembering their words and her expressions, he had wished he hadn't said it. He replayed the conversation – if you could call it that – and always erased that last question. It had made him sound needy. It had made him sound like an idiot.

He'd taken her to the station and she'd climbed out and bent to kiss him through the window, and through it all he'd managed to rein in his anger and misery and bewilderment and not beg her to stay; but at the last minute he'd let himself down again, the words bursting out of him completely of their own volition. 'Promise you'll write to me,' he'd said, and then felt a complete prat. But she looked down at him and, not mockingly, but somehow graciously, said, 'If I can.'

And then she'd left him. She hadn't written, precisely, but she had sent postcards from time to time. The last one he'd had was from Barcelona, saying, 'I'm with a circus for a change. Tomorrow we move on to Madrid. Congratulations on Geneva success.'

So much for love letters and tender sentiments!

Since she'd been gone, he'd given up on the woman business.

His emotional life was in cold storage. When he wanted sex, there were always groupies and grooms ready to accommodate him, and he loved them lightly, was careful never to raise their expectations, and left them – he felt – as happy as him with the brief encounter. Though he was friendly with the female competitors in his world – he liked women's company more than men's, really – and flirted with them, he had never made a play for any of them. There was an old adage, wasn't there, about not shitting on your own doorstep?

He thought suddenly of Polly, and the meal they had had last night. Polly was a real mate! They'd had a great time, and it would have been the easiest thing in the world for them to slip into bed together afterwards. For a moment he wondered whether, in fact, that wouldn't be the answer to both their problems. They were good friends, and there was no doubt that she was extremely fanciable, and that she looked at him not without interest. An affair with Polly . . . But he was afraid that she might not be able to take it lightly. He was too fond of her to want her to get hurt by falling in love with him, and after Anne, he was nervous of getting more than his body involved.

Anne. He brooded, seeing her in his mind's eye as clearly as if she had been with him yesterday. He'd have scorned any talk of 'hearts', but when she left him, something had shut down in him. She had gone, without warning, without giving a reason. Well, that was bloody women for you! Anger was a good way of disguising hurt. He had employed a succession of grooms, and he'd found most of them unsatisfactory in one way or another. As a groom, she'd never had to be told anything, and the horses were as good with her as they were with him. He liked to pretend that was why he missed her – because she had been a good groom. Often he believed it.

When Polly and her groom Teresa – Terry – arrived home, they found a glossy dark-blue Jaguar parked outside the front of the bungalow.

'It looks as though we've got a visitor,' Terry said.

Polly was watching the traffic, waiting for the chance to swing the horsebox across the road to park it in its accustomed place, on a mud-patch facing the bungalow. She had given the car a glance without comment, but now she sighed.

'You'd better jump down and entertain him until I get this thing parked.'

'You can't manage both horses on your own,' Terry objected.

'I'll cope. Best not to upset the Management,' Polly said lightly.

Terry stuck her lip out. 'You spoil him. Why should we run around after him just because he's a man?'

'Terry, just do it, will you? Put the kettle on.' Sometimes Polly regretted the necessity of being pally with her groom, but since Terry was a live-in and the only available quarters were the spare room in the bungalow, it was impossible to keep her at a distance. Polly was not generally at her best with other women, and her girl grooms came and went with depressing regularity, but Terry was a particularly difficult case. She hailed from the Curragh, where her father was head groom in a racing stables, and she not only tended to know it all, but was outspoken, virulently feminist, and had no reticence or respect for others' privacy. On the plus side she was a good groom, but in all probability she would go back to Ireland anyway when the hurdling started, so that was of limited benefit.

Normally, unboxing two horses at the same time would be beyond the powers of a single person, but Taggert and Mackie were wise horses, and could unbox themselves while Polly stood at the foot of the ramp to catch the ropes as they arrived. Taggert came down first, as befitted his status as First Horse – though he was only barely a horse: his height was fourteen-three, below which all horses except Arabs are classified as ponies. He was small and narrow, a dark bay gelding with very long ears, a sure sign of good humour. In fact he was the smallest horse in top-class jumping at that time. He had more 'pop' and scope than many a tall horse, and with his great wisdom and courage he had won most of the big prizes at one time or another.

Holding Taggert's rope in her left hand, Polly chirruped for Mackie, who whickered in reply and began to back down carefully. He was a younger gelding, fifteen-two in height and the colour that horsemen call simply brown, which means very dark, almost black. In fact, had not a random streak of Exmoor in his blood given him a slightly mealy muzzle, Mackie would have been classified a black. He was less bold than Taggert, less clever, but a painstaking, careful jumper, and Polly loved them both equally. The greatest sorrow in her life was that she did not own them.

They were owned, both of them, by the man whose car was doing wonders for the suburban frontage of her bungalow. Bill Simpson was an industrialist: he owned a string of factories that manufactured precision machine parts, had a large stake in an agricultural machinery business, and was getting to be an extremely wealthy and influential man. He paid all the horses' expenses, and Polly was paid a retainer to ride them for him. She also received forty per cent of the prize money, which was a generous settlement when many riders only received ten per cent; but then, Bill was in love with her. He made no secret of it, and asked her to marry him with faithful regularity, but being a man of surprisingly old-fashioned honour, he always tried to avoid doing anything that would pressure her into accepting him. It was for that reason that he did not give her one or both horses as a gift, for fear she should accept his offer of marriage out of gratitude.

But other gifts came her way, and despite her own principles in the matter she had at last grown accustomed to receiving presents, as long as they weren't too valuable, and to being taken out to expensive restaurants. Bill had never made this a bargaining point, and had never expected sex in return – though had the situation been otherwise she might well have taken him to her bed, because he was very attractive and she was very fond of him. But as it was, his restraint towards her had the effect of placing restraint *on* her. While they did not sleep together, she felt she could not, out of loyalty to him, sleep with anyone else.

Not that she often felt tempted – the life with horses was tiring – but still, a girl has urges. But though she was a pretty successful rider, she had made a hash of her private life. There was the business with John Newland, which she had fallen into out of inexperience and neediness, and felt she was lucky to have escaped from; and the only other serious relationship she had had was with a man who lived in the same village, who commuted to the nearby town where he worked as financial director of a retail firm. She had been crazy for him for a while, and he had been knocked out by the glamour of her celebrity status and what he imagined her lifestyle to be. But her way of life made a relationship with an outsider difficult to the point of impossibility. She was away so much, worked such long hours, was not free when he was and wanted him when he was at work. He didn't understand *her* needs, complained that she did not satisfy *his*; resented the horses coming before him, did not sufficiently cheer her successes or mourn her failures. In the end, temptation came his way while she was absent abroad, and she came back to find her place usurped. Things were quite embarrassing until he and his new love moved to another village nearer the town. They were married now. Polly had even seen his wife pushing a pram around the aisles of Sainsbury's one day, when she'd dashed in for something to stick in the microwave. Debbie hadn't seen *her*, and she'd made sure not to see what was in the pram, for fear of how she might feel about it.

Since then she had become wary of getting involved, and, to be honest, there were not that many opportunities. Outsiders were out, and colleagues were dangerous. It was always difficult for a woman in a closed world. Men – like Dan Roberts, for instance – could have serial relationships, or even just plain sleep around, and only enhance their reputations, but if a female did the same she was despised as a slut. And then, of course, Bill had fallen in love with her. He was so kind and tactful about it, so modest about his considerable attractions, so careful not to make her feel obligated, that she felt even more obligated than she otherwise might have, not to break his heart.

It wasn't a situation she would have chosen, but neither of the alternatives – to marry him from the position of supplicant, or to free herself from him and lose Taggert and Mackie – appealed to her more. Because the way things were was not actually intolerable or even, most of the time, uncomfortable, she kept putting off any decision. There were definite pluses to being his chosen companion: he was handsome and kind, good company, generous and tolerant, and fitted in with her way of life as she could hardly have expected anyone else to do. So, two years had passed away, leaving her, with the death of her own old horse Solo, ever more dependent on him; and the hidden frustrations seemed to be getting less hidden all the time.

She led the two horses along the track round the side of the bungalow to the stable block behind. They could smell their own boxes now and began knuckering in pleased anticipation, jogging a little and tugging at the lead ropes to hurry her along. From the paddock behind the stables Polly's young filly, Pavlova, was screaming her head off in excitement at the thought of having company after her long day alone.

Bill and Terry were standing outside the back door talking as she came round the corner.

'Hi, Bill. Is the kettle on?' Polly greeted him, and without waiting for an answer said to Terry, 'I think I'll turn these two straight out. We can feed them in the paddock.'

'What about Pavlova? She'll kick them if they've got grub and she hasn't.'

'I'll put a feed out for her, too. She needs a bit of muscle-builder.'

Bill came forward to caress the horses and kiss Polly chastely on the cheek; the familiar smell of his aftershave – light and lemony – tickled her nostrils and she felt a surge of affection for him. He was so very, very *nice*! The horses liked him too. They nudged him eagerly, associating him with titbits, which he obediently produced from his pocket: two Fox's Glacier Mints, their favourite thing. 'Well, how did my two ruffians go?' he asked.

'Oh, of course, I forgot you were out of the country. I'd been imagining you watching us on TV,' Polly said.

'I've told him about the Queen's Cup,' Terry said, taking Mackie's rope from her and turning towards the paddock. Taggert wasn't going to be left behind, and tugged Polly along too, with Bill walking beside her.

Always, for Bill, to be close to Polly was both a bliss and a pain, and he could never quite determine which sensation was uppermost. Since he had first seen her, at the age of eighteen in her first season in adult jumping, she seemed to him to have grown lovelier and more unattainable year by year.

He had been married back then, though he and his wife had inevitably grown apart over the years. He was away so much, and it was a classic case of the man, exposed to so much more experience and contact with the world, changing, while the wife, confined to the domestic sphere, did not. When he was at home he found there was less and less he could talk to Shona about. The house, what was on television, and her longing for a child, were the only topics she had, and Bill had hated himself for being bored by her. Perhaps if she could have had a child . . . But it transpired she couldn't, and though he had been sorry, it had perhaps been for the best, the way things turned out.

A business colleague – who owned the agricultural machinery firm he had later invested in – had had a stand at the county show. He had invited Bill to come to the show, both for business and pleasure purposes, and there Bill had seen Polly. He had fallen in love with her, he believed, at first sight, though he had not allowed himself to realise it for a long time. He had followed her career with interest, and when the opportunity arose a couple of years later, he became her sponsor.

But though he was known as a shark in business, he was a man of stern principle in his private life, and he'd always been faithful to Shona. He had kept such a firm rein on his feelings that he was able to convince everyone, including himself, that his interest in Polly was purely professional. He would not allow himself to draw comparisons between the confident golden girl and his insular and increasingly peevish wife. All the same, the shock of discovering Shona's illness and his deep distress over her rapid decline and death were compounded by his underlying feelings of guilt. He *ought* to have been kinder to Shona, always; spent more time with her. He *ought* to have loved and valued her more. It was a couple of years before he had made sufficient peace with himself and Shona's memory to acknowledge his love for Polly with a clear conscience.

On that day that he had first seen her she had been riding Solo, and she had seemed very small aboard the big thoroughbred. He still thought of her as a tender young girl. In spite of her way of life she seemed to him gentle, gracious – the essence of what his mother would have called 'a lady'. Inevitably over the years he had come to understand that there was a firmness under her quiet – essential to anyone handling horses – and an earthiness under her sweetness which made it possible for her to get on well with a person as different from her as Dan Roberts.

Her friendship with Roberts had caused him countless hours of spiritual wrestling, and dreadful scenes with Polly which he was ashamed to look back on. She said that her relationship with the other man was platonic, and in any case, he accepted that it was none of his business: he might sponsor her but he didn't own her. But it made no difference to his frantic jealousy, which he had learned to hide but could not conquer. Dan was younger than him, better looking, infinitely more glamorous:

the sort of handsome devil women had been falling for since Rhett Butler stood at the foot of that staircase looking up. He was afraid that it was only a matter of time before Polly became one of his victims.

After all, celibacy was not a natural state for a women any more than a man. Sometimes Simpson thought that Polly, wearied by the situation, would have accepted him as a lover now had he pressed her; but that, paradoxically, only made things worse. He didn't want her as a lover, he wanted her as a wife. He wanted her love as well as her loving.

The proper thing to do, he supposed wearily in those night hours when he couldn't sleep, would be to give her the two horses, end her dependency on him, and *then* ask her. But somehow he just couldn't bring himself to the point. Suppose she said no, and he lost her completely? Without Tag and Mackie, what sure hold would he have on her? It would be all too easy just to drift apart, both their lives being so busy. And on the other hand, suppose she said yes? How would he ever know if it was from love, or from gratitude?

And in the end he always concluded – as Polly did, unbeknown to him – that the present set-up was not impossible to bear, and the alternative might be worse, so it was better to do nothing. He had an idea that she was lonely. He was, too, of course. If nothing else, they were good company together. That had to be worth having, didn't it?

Pavlova was racing back and forth along the paddock rails yelling in a most unladylike way, and the two geldings were whickering back, their ears sharply pointed. Pavlova was Polly's intended way out of the situation. She was a very pretty, cream-coloured three-year-old, already showing great scope and promise. If she developed as planned, in a few years' time she should be earning enough to give Polly a foothold on independence.

Bill opened the gate and the two girls released the horses into the field. Pavlova rushed up to meet them, and they stood for a moment with their heads together, blowing at each other in that secretive way horses have. The filly squealed, whirled round and let fly at the other two with her heels, and then darted at them and danced back, enticing them to come and play. Taggert and Mackie were always deeply impressed with this excitable female, but at the moment they had a strong suspicion that food was in the offing and were unwilling to leave the gate. Food and sex are both strong urges; but after all they were geldings, and it was past their dinner-time.

Polly decreed they should feed all three horses at the gate by hand, for quickness; and while they stood holding the buckets, into which the eager heads plunged and snuffled, Polly told Bill about the week past, about the performance of the horses, and such odd bits of news she thought would interest him. Last of all she remembered the snippet she had from Dan.

'Oh, by the way, I heard that John Newland is selling his new horse. The story is that he's finding it too much for him, though I'm not sure whether I believe that. He's not the sort to let himself be bested by a horse.'

'As it happens, that's one piece of news I'm ahead of you on,' Bill said, picking stray oats off his sleeve and dropping them back into Taggert's bucket. 'I had it from a chap in Paris who knows the bloke who sold Newland the horse in the first place.'

'Really? I'm surprised the news travelled that fast.'

'It wasn't quite like that. Apparently Newland found the horse a handful and tried out various things that just made matters worse, until finally he had a bad fall and broke his leg, or something . . . Newland's leg, I mean.'

'Yes, I heard that, but it was his ankle, I was told,' Polly said.

'Foot,' Terry said. 'I had it from his groom. The horse trod on him trying to get up and broke a bone in his foot.'

'Well, whatever,' said Bill. 'Anyway, the first thing Newland did was to get back to the bloke in France who'd sold him the horse, and ask him to take it back.'

'No!' said Polly. 'What a cheek! I sometimes think he's completely nuts, you know. So, what did the bloke say?'

'I couldn't repeat it in front of ladies,' Bill grinned. 'The gist of it was that he wasn't in the business of rehabilitating horses Newland had spoiled, and that Newland was a so-and-so and couldn't ride for toffee. Only all in French, of course.'

'Of course,' Polly said gravely. 'I'd like to have been a bug on *that* call!' She scraped the last of the feed from the sides of the bucket, made it into a handful and fed it to Pavlova, and then released the filly's headstall and sent her off with a slap on the neck. 'All finished? Shall we go in and have something to eat, then? I don't know about you two, but I'm starving.'

They ate a scratch lunch at the kitchen table, all three of them, and then Terry took herself off to clean tack, leaving her employers spinning out a cup of coffee with desultory cigarettes. Polly had an idea Bill was going to say something embarrassing, and searched around in her mind for a subject to take his mind off it. She lit again on the topic of Newland's delinquent horse.

'So, it's going to go on the open market, is it?' she asked. 'That'll be embarrassing for John.'

'I don't expect it will get that far,' Bill said, stubbing out his cigarette. 'I had it from the chap in Paris that the horse is pretty hot stuff, and once the word gets around I daresay he'll have plenty of approaches. He'll be able to arrange a private sale.'

'What, after he's messed it about? It would have to be *very* hot stuff.'

'Well, I understand it is. Have you ever seen it?'

'No . . . have you?' He shook his head. 'Poor beast,' Polly mused. 'Spotty John must have been pretty vile to it. I wish I could . . .' She stopped abruptly and said no more.

After a moment Bill reached across the table with unmistakable intent and said softly, 'Polly . . .'

Oh God, she thought, here it comes. But all the same, she

smiled and gave him her hand, and braced herself to resist boarders.

The French lorry driver was a family man and a good Catholic, and the hitch-hiker's pale, serene beauty reminded him of the Raphael Madonna print that used to hang in his school classroom. So he required nothing of her but her company, despite taking the overnight ferry, where opportunity is rife. He bought her breakfast on the boat, and even claimed that he preferred the M20 to the M2 in order to be able to give her a lift from Dover to Folkestone. She parted from him with a sweet smile and a handshake at the roundabout, and in Folkestone soon managed to get a lift as far as Tenterden. From there it was only about four miles as the crow flew to Tom Emmerson's place.

It hadn't taken her long to decide on him as her host. His place was certainly the nearest; and she doubted that much about his circumstances had changed since she was last in England. She'd be glad to see old Sunavon again, too. She had groomed him once, long ago when he belonged to the German ace rider, Heinrich Muhl, during that long, hot summer of successes which had ended abruptly with Muhl's death in the terrible Basel air crash. Fortunately the horses had been travelling by train on that occasion, and she with them. In the disposal of Muhl's assets, Sunavon had been bought by Maurice Hayes, the Irish team rider; but he had kept him only a few weeks before deciding he was not in his style, and selling him to Emmerson. And by then she was in America, and hadn't seen Sunavon since.

Unaware of the wild card Fate was preparing to deal to him, Tom Emmerson was sitting on his dining-room windowsill, nursing a cross between a hangover and indigestion – caused, no doubt, by the whisky and ginger last night. Of necessity he had been up early, for he had three horses, who never slept in, and his finances ran only to very part-time help. He had exercised his young horse, Captain Fox, by taking him for a hack along the quiet lanes, but that still left Buccaneer to be taken out. Normally he would have ridden one and led the other, something he had learned to do in the army (all the men in his family did a spell in the Hussars) but he had been feeling too frail that morning to risk it.

But Buccaneer would have to go out. He tended to run to fat when the grass was good and had to be kept in stable for much of the time, which meant he needed more exercise than either Fox or even Sunavon. Keeping him in meant he needed feeding, too, which worked out horribly expensive. The special high-protein fodder that a jumper needed was far more expensive than the rarest delicacies Tom could have bought for himself, even had he felt so inclined.

He wasn't so inclined, of course. He lived mainly on boiled eggs, cream crackers and whisky – originally out of sheer laziness but now more out of habit. There is a kind of paralysis of will that afflicts those who live alone but were never meant to, which makes it impossible for them to do anything about the many things in their lives they hate. When his meagre appetite at last sickened of the monotony, he would walk down to the village and get a Chinese take-away, or fish and chips.

In the village his plight was not unknown, but respect for his family, and for what he had been ten years ago – when children would nudge each other excitedly when he went by or rush out to ask for his autograph – made them keep the knowledge to themselves, and refrain from offering him a sympathy that might be offensive. But he had noticed that Mrs Embley in the fish-and-chip shop looked at him oddly sometimes, and always gave him twice as many chips as anyone else. She was a large and motherly-looking female, and sometimes at night when he couldn't sleep for worrying he would think about her, and imagine himself sitting with her in the snug at the Bridge Embattled, pouring out his troubles while she nodded peacefully, nursing a gin and tonic in her lap and engulfing him with her kind eyes.

His stomach groaned, and he rubbed it and wondered if he were getting ulcers. A perforated ulcer: that would end all his worries! His teeth ached, too, sometimes, with a neuralgia pain that ran up his jaws and through his scalp like hot wires. And when he remembered to comb his soft, failing fair hair, so much of it came out on the comb that he sometimes panicked and tried to stick it back in. Stress ailments. It was money, of course, always money. If only he could be like other people, have a job: he saw himself going up each day on the commuter train with all the other 'executives' from the new houses on the other side of the village. Working in an office. Regular, safe work in a nice, clean, air-conditioned building in Town, within easy reach of the best restaurants. Lovely civilisation! Imagine having a regular income! Imagine paying income tax!

But, of course, it couldn't happen. He could never get a job because he had no skills to sell; and even if he could, who would look after the horses and the house? No job he could get would pay enough to hire someone to do what was needed to stop the manor falling to bits around his ears. He was no builder – hardly even a handyman – but at least while he was here he could do minor running repairs himself; badly of course, but it was better than nothing, enough just to hold the thing together. Old houses needed constant care. And he could never have parted with the horses, Sunavon and the others – but Sunavon most of all. He looked through the dusty window towards the field where the golden horse was grazing – and saw the oddest thing.

The old horse was excited about something. His head was up, his ears pricked hard. He trotted up the field with his tail kinked over his back as if he were a ballsy young entire approaching a mare on heat, and then made a breenge and danced away playfully, before beginning another coy approach. Whatever he was looking at was hidden from Emmerson by the height of the hedge at the top of the slope. This was where the gate on to the road stood, and he wondered if a stranger had climbed over into the field. But Sunavon's antics were not those of a horse startled by a stranger; more those of a dog greeting its long-lost master. Ulcers and dry rot forgotten, Tom got to his feet and went out to investigate, turning back at the last moment to pick up his stout ashplant, just in case. It was not unknown for yobs from the town to come out this far these days.

He slipped out of the house and went round by road to the gate in order to creep up on whoever it was and keep the advantage of surprise. But at the gate he stopped, and stood, stick forgotten, arrested by what he saw. A few feet inside the gate was a slim female, her hands either side of Sunavon's cheeks, her head tilted up and her eyes closed as the horse ran his lips over her face and hair in a display of affection, the like of which Emmerson had never seen before. They say horses don't forget, but privately he had always had a very moderate opinion of their ability to recognise old friends. There was no doubt at all, though, that Sunavon remembered her.

'If you get any closer, you two will have to get married,' he said aloud. She jerked her head round, startled, and then smiled at him. He knew her, of course. Anne something. Anne Neville, that was it. She had groomed for various people over the years, and he had noticed her from time to time in the background, a remote, even rather mysterious figure on the edge of perception. He had heard people sometimes wondering about her, why she lived her itinerant and what should be, on the face of it, unsatisfying life, but apart from that he had not really paid much attention to her, though he had always thought her rather attractive, with the sort of dark, vivid good looks he admired.

He hadn't seen her around lately – though that was not much to be wondered at, given his present state, and the fact that, down here in Kent, he was rather isolated from the rest of the horsemasters. But perhaps she had been away? Despite the hot summer they'd been having, her face was pale, as if she never went out of doors; framing the smooth oval, her hair, thick and springing, was burnished by the sun into an incredible fox-dark mane, a stunning contrast. She looked so beautiful and so full of life that he felt a stirring of something that made him forget for a moment his age, state of health and financial worries. He stood up straighter, sucked in his stomach, and smiled at her. 'Fine watchdog he turned out to be!'

'He wouldn't bark at the missus coming home,' she said.

Emmerson thought it an odd choice of words. 'Does he know you, then?'

She didn't answer, her attention on the horse again. Emmerson climbed the gate and went towards them. 'He never does that to me,' he said.

'He's a ladies' man,' Anne said, turning. Deprived of her face, Sunavon nuzzled and nibbled at her hair and the back of her neck until she was forced gently to fend him off.

Emmerson took the cheek-strap of his headcollar and only then did he stand quietly, though his bright eyes never strayed from Anne. 'So, what are you doing here?' Emmerson asked.

'I came to see him. And you,' she added.

'Why me?'

'I wondered how you were getting on.'

This seemed both unfathomable to him, and unexceptionable. He struggled to find a question that might give him a handle on the situation, but only came up with, 'And you're just back from . . . where?'

'Paris,' she said.

He waited, but she offered nothing more. He remembered that she was famously reticent about her own activities; and from a few personal encounters when she had been grooming for colleagues, that she had the unusual ability not to answer questions – not to evade them, simply to ignore them. Hardly anyone could do that. She was a mystery, and he couldn't think of any good reason why she should have turned up here so unexpectedly; but he was attracted to her, and he was suddenly aware that he was positively aching for company. So he asked, 'Are you staying?'

She looked at him with her bright, unfathomable look, and he realised that it had come out more wistfully than he had meant. He shoved his hand into his pocket and stared away across the field in an attempt to look unconcerned about her answer.

But she said, 'If you'll have me, dear Tom.'

Did she mean by that what he hoped she meant by it? Something loosened and warmed inside him. Whatever she was looking at him with, it was not indifference; and he had had his moments. Women *had* found him attractive in the past. He smiled then with something of his old Gentleman-Tom charm. 'Try and stop me,' he said, and she laughed, and Sunavon snorted at the sound.

'How about offering me something to eat, something to drink, and a bath?' she said. 'I've been living in rather a primitive way for the past few weeks, and I may not smell the way a lady should.'

Emmerson sniffed ostentatiously, and then used the excuse to put his face close to her and sniff again. She smelled, faintly but sweetly, of horses and hay. He suddenly imagined having her in bed with him in the illusive dark of a summer night. The warm grassy scent of her skin seemed just then more exotic to him than French perfume; and a sort of panicky fluttering started up in his stomach, which he recognised – part embarrassed, part surprised – as sexual desire. He drew back from her hastily.

'That bad?' she asked.

'Oh, good God, no, I didn't mean . . .' He was confused. He plucked something almost at random from his consciousness. 'I've got the pearlies. Drinking last night.'

'The dreaded pearlies? Have you eaten today?'

'I'll eat with you,' he said. 'And if I put the tank on the water will be hot enough for you to bath afterwards.'

'Lovely. You can scrub my back for me,' she said pleasantly. The words evoked images that made his blood rush hotly about his body. Was it possible she meant . . . ? Surely he couldn't be that lucky! His loins thought so, and he had to linger behind her to check the lock on the gate until he was fit to be seen again. Sunavon almost barged him aside, leaning over the gate and craning his neck to watch Anne go. Emmerson pulled the old horse's ears affectionately and murmured, 'I know how you feel, old boy.'

She sat at the kitchen table while he made scrambled eggs and coffee. He liked the way she did not feel constrained to be domestic just because she was female. She did not protest conventionally, 'Oh let *me* do that,' as his occasional girlfriends – back in the early post-Tilly days when he had girlfriends – had done, but let him wait on her without making a thing of it either way.

'Here we are,' he said, putting the plates on the table. 'It isn't much, I'm afraid, but I haven't got much in.'

'You weren't to know I'd be coming,' she said. 'It looks good.'

He took a forkful of egg and chewed it slowly. It was pleasantly easy not to wolf the food down. Already he was more relaxed than he had been in months. 'So, why did you decide to come here – rather than anywhere else, I mean?'

'Sunavon and I are old friends,' she said.

He didn't suppose she meant to be hurtful, but he was hurt. '*We're* not exactly strangers,' he said.

She looked at him briefly and piercingly. 'Of course not,' she said, and went on eating.

He couldn't leave it alone. 'I suppose horses always come first with you. Except possibly in the case of Dan Roberts. You and he were . . . pretty close, weren't you?' She didn't answer. 'Or was that really for The Iceman's sake?'

'They are alike, of course. Perhaps that's why I find him sexy.'

'Dan or Iceman?'

'Iceman, I meant.'

His eyebrow climbed. 'You find horses sexy?'

'Why do you think there are so many groupies hanging around you showjumpers?' she said. A little smile was hovering around her mouth, and he knew she was diverting the talk from her personal life; but that was her privilege, wasn't it?

'There aren't any hanging around me these days,' he said; and he oughtn't to have, because it sounded self-pitying, but he couldn't help it. The food was warming him, her company was easing a long ache in him, and he felt, for no reason he could fathom, that he could trust her. He wondered if she exuded some kind of pheremones. Maybe that was why she was so good with horses.

She drained her cup now and set it on the table with a kind of delicate precision, as if it were a full stop at the end of this passage in their unfolding story. 'How about that bath now?' she asked, standing up.

'Is that an invitation?' he said, a little shakily.

'It's an invitation.'

She was so beautiful, so confident, so . . . so *complete*, somehow. He couldn't believe his luck. He really couldn't: 'You might be disappointed,' he found himself saying. Damn!

She sighed. 'Tom, why do you make things difficult for yourself? We're both grown ups. Just be honest.'

'That's hard to do when you haven't any self-confidence,' he said. He was trying not to sound pathetic but was afraid he hadn't succeeded.

'Phooey,' she said abruptly. 'What's that if it's not self-confidence?'

He looked down at himself, and then at her, with a slow smile. 'It's what I'd call a bloody miracle,' he said.

Three

A t home in the green, quiet places of England – in neat stone farmhouses with their farmlands around them; in handsome old houses of mellow brick amid a hundred rolling acres; in bungalows of new, raw brick with thirty acres, not so rolling; in a tumbledown cottage with ten acres; in a smoke-grimed mews with three fields; in a caravan in the parental back garden – the horsemasters settled down to the normal routine of their day-to-day lives.

In the background, continual and unnoticed like the drone of the bagpipes, was the eternal round of mucking out, grooming and feeding; in the foreground the exercising and endless schooling to keep the horses fit, alert and happy. Beside all that there was the other, hated side of it all, the administrative and clerical burden, the accounts and expenses, the income tax and VAT, the insurance – a millstone, that – the bank statements, the mortgages, the vet's bills, the farrier's bills.

There were show schedules to study, entries to be made, itineraries to plan, travel arrangements to be finalised. Show reports and articles had to be read somehow – must keep up with new developments in the field, and who was winning what, who sponsoring whom, and who had bought what horse from where. Likely new sponsors had to be tracked down and beguiled, old ones kept sweet. Horses grew old eventually and new horses had to be brought on if one was to keep winning – keep earning.

Show kit had to be cleaned and repaired, tack forever

inspected and kept up to scratch – and, my God, what a saddle cost these days! The horsebox had to be serviced, new tyres in front, something was sounding nasty in the gearbox – Lord, let it not mean a new gearbox, what would that cost? The stables needed whitewashing, and how long since the yard had been relaid? There was a tile coming off the roof, and the gutters should have been cleaned out in spring, too late to worry about that now.

And at the centre of each world, the suns around which they all circled like planets, were the horses – the precious, lovely, fragile horses! Each with its own character, its likes and dislikes, its foibles and phobias and funny little ways, each like a demanding, talented but over-sensitive child that had to be coached and coaxed through his GCSEs.

Oh, they had to be wormed and vaccinated against all manner of things; their hooves attended to once a month; their coats clipped; their manes and tails trimmed and pulled once a week. A runny nose, a touch of colic – should the vet be called? No NHS for horses, the vet cost the earth, but what if it was equine flu, what if it was torsion of the bowel? So many things to worry about, a world of ailments with terrifying, Gothic names: lampas and poll evil, splints and bog spavins, thoroughpin, ringbone, strangles, laminitis, navicular disease. There was the daily wear and tear of sprains and pulled tendons, fear of overreaches, split hooves, cracked heels, saddle galls; and colic, always colic! Every horse's diet worked out like a battle campaign, small, frequent feeds weighed and mixed carefully by hand, and fed in an atmosphere of calm, to aid digestion: for horses have delicate, small stomachs. 'Eat like a horse' means 'eat like an invalid'.

It was a twenty-four hour a day job – when it wasn't thirty-six! Not a job at all, really, but a life, for there was no time off that wasn't carefully planned and liable to last-minute cancellation. You couldn't put a horse away in a garage and forget it like a car. No finishing at lunchtime and spending the afternoon playing golf, no spur-of-the-moment weekend in Paris. The life was its own justification – for after all, if you had had any spare time, what would you have done with it? Why, go for a ride, of course!

And so the year turned, from the short lay-up after Christmas through the spring and summer, competing anything up to four or five days a week, living from a suitcase, always on the road: the big counties and internationals in June, July and August, then the continental and US shows, the indoor shows in autumn and winter, and back to Olympia at Christmas – a bit of fun, that, not to be missed. A close-knit, self-sufficient group, the horsemasters: rivals in the ring, of course, but friendly out of it. One or two long-standing feuds, one or two long-standing romances, just like any group; meeting at the big shows, less frequently at the smaller ones, hardly ever anywhere else, unless they happened to live near one another. No time for socialising outside the group, no time to feel lonely, hardly any time to wonder how you would live if you had a bad accident, or when you got too old for the game, fit for nothing else and with no pension but the Government's pittance to look forward to.

It wasn't an easy life, but they hardly ever even began to want to change it for another. What on earth would you do with yourself if you did have a nine-to-five job? How would you fill all those evenings and weekends? And how could you ever live without the horses?

Polly was coming in from an exercise ride on Mackie at around ten o'clock on a Monday morning. It was still hot and dry, and Mackie was shaking his head against the flies, which made life unpleasant for Polly. He'd had a bit of a dust cough that morning, so Terry had held his mouth open while Polly smeared cough syrup on the back of his tongue. It was thick and black as treacle and had a delicious smell, and it made the horse salivate and work his bit continuously, which was all to the good, lubricating his throat and softening his mouth. The by-product, however, was a thick brown foam which Mackie had been dribbling over his chest as he went along, and every time he shook his head against the flies, he sprayed it over Polly. Once or twice a good, big gob of it had struck her full in the face, which was enough to put a person off their lunch.

So when she saw the Jaguar parked outside the bungalow again, her first reaction was irritation. 'On a Monday, too, damn and blast it! Hasn't he got a business to run?' But on second thoughts, she wondered if there was something wrong, for he never normally came on a Monday. Her real affection for him surfaced, though it sometimes lurked half-hidden under exasperation at the difficulties of their relationship. If he was in trouble she would do whatever it took to help him.

But the first sight of him put her mind at rest. He was sitting on the paddock gate (at the hinge end, she noted – her lectures on the subject had taken effect at last) smoking a cigar and looking contented, even smug.

'You've been up to something,' she called as soon as she was near enough. 'What is it, a big order? A takeover bid? A killing on the market?'

'None of the above,' he said. He squinted up at her against the sun, and put up a hand to fend off Mackie, whose nose was heading straight for his jacket pocket. 'Yeuch! Keep away with that slobber, you ruffian! I like this suit. What's he been eating, chocolate?'

'As if!' Polly snorted. 'It's cough medicine.'

'Disgusting! Why is it that colour?'

'It's made of liquorice. So he's equally dangerous at both ends.'

'Well, take him away, wipe his nose, clean his teeth, and then come and listen to my good news.'

'I was going to school him for an hour before his feed,' Polly said wistfully; and then felt mean. A person with good news needed an audience. 'All right, I'll put him in for a while and have a cup of coffee with you. Go on into the house and put the kettle on.'

'Is Terry around?'

'No, she's gone into Bedford to have her teeth rasped.'

'Good,' said Simpson, smiling at the expression.

Polly put Mackie in his box, took off his bridle, loosened the girth, watered him, and left him with a handful of hay to keep him amused. She washed her hands and face at the outside tap and went into the kitchen by the side door. Bill had laid out cups and spoons, and also – since she was often hungry by this time of day, having been busy since six – plates and knives, bread, butter and jam. His attentions were touching. She smiled at him, and though in fact she wasn't hungry today, she ate a piece of bread and jam with her coffee.

'Well, then, let's have the news,' she said. Bill reached into his briefcase, which was standing beside his chair, and took out a folder, from which he extracted a photograph and laid it before her.

'What do you think of that?'

Polly took it and studied it. It was of a chestnut horse wearing only a headcollar, being held by someone off camera – the usual sort of photo used to advertise a horse for sale or at stud. It was a gelding, and if the colour were true to life, of a particularly brilliant gold, with, unusually, no white markings. A big horse, by the look of it, big-boned with strong quarters and plenty of bone in the legs. He stood over a lot of ground, as the saying was, but for all his size, his head was neat and finely drawn, his eye large and intelligent, the ears long.

'He looks some horse,' she said. 'Could be a jumper with those quarters.' She stopped and peered more closely at the photo, and then smiled up at Bill. 'It's John Newland's horse, isn't it? The one he's selling?'

'How did you guess?'

'I recognise the buildings in the background,' Polly said, and Bill was forced to stifle a little pang, remembering she had been close to Newland once – almost engaged. So, marriage to Newland had seemed a possibility to her, but not marriage to him? That was practically an insult. Ah well!

Polly had turned the photo over and was reading what was printed on the back. 'Coppernob. Chestnut gelding. 17hh. Ten years. So old?' She glanced up. 'That won't help him sell it.'

'Horses jump until eighteen or more,' Bill objected. 'You've said so yourself many times.'

'Yes, but bad behaviour in a youngster you can hope to change. In an older horse it might be ingrained. It'll affect the price.'

'It did,' Simpson said, watching her face. 'I used that very argument, and to great effect, I might add.'

She stared. '*You* bought him?' For the life of him, he couldn't tell if she was pleased or not. 'Oh Bill, you didn't! What did you pay for him?'

'Next to nothing. I beat Newland right down.'

'Down to what?'

'Eight thousand.'

Polly looked again at the photograph. 'You're right, that is next to nothing. John's never generous without a cause. There must be something far wrong with him.'

'No, I think it's more likely something wrong with Newland,' Simpson said. 'He tried to hide it, but he was very eager to get rid of the nag, and as we've agreed on other occasions, that's not like him.'

'What did he say about it?'

'Only what we already knew. He says he hasn't ridden him since the accident, when the horse came through a jump and got a bit knocked about. Bust Newland's foot, as you know, and since then the nag's been run off in a field. No one's been near it, except for Mary . . . D'you know Mary?'

'Mary Newland? Yes, vaguely. I've seen her at shows now and then. Mousy thing.'

'That's her. Well, she spoke up for the horse . . . Copper, she calls it. She said John had handled it all wrong and spoiled its nerve.'

'She said that in front of him?'

'Oh no, she sort of tugged me to one side and told me privately . . . Though I suspect Newland guessed what she was saying. He didn't look best pleased. But still, as I said, I think he just wanted to be rid of it. He didn't put up much of a fight about the price.'

'You sound positively disappointed!'

'I didn't hone my dikkering skills in the bazaars of the mysterious orient just for an easy triumph like that!' he said.

'You've never been to the mysterious orient.'

'Hong Kong's pretty mysterious. There's a club there called the Pink Parasol—'

'That's enough of that,' she said hastily. 'I don't believe any good can come of an anecdote that starts in a club called the Pink anything.'

'Spoilsport.'

She grew serious. 'But the fact remains, you've bought a horse with a spoiled nerve that might never want to jump again, and might even be unrideable. What for?'

'I just took a fancy to it. And I thought you might like to have a go at whatsname . . . you know, rehabilitation.'

He looked at her hopefully, ready for her amazement, excitement, happiness. She might fling her arms around him and kiss him in bubbling gratitude. He was blitzed when she only frowned and shook her head.

'I don't think that's really me, that kind of job. I've never ridden anything that big . . . and if John Newland couldn't handle it, what makes you think I'd be able to?'

'You're a different kind of rider. You're gentle, sympathetic. The horse is nervy, it needs kind handling, and Newland's not the sensitive type. He handled it all wrong. Mary Newland more or less hinted as much.'

'Oh yes, she's the great expert, of course,' Polly said, and then, seeing she had hurt his feelings, added, 'Look, you may be right – she may be right – but even so, a horse that big would need physical strength as well as kindness. Someone like Alison Neave, at least . . . or a man. I'd never be able to hold it. I'm sorry, but I really don't think it's for me.'

Bill's face had fallen, and his fingers rolled a crumb of bread into a pellet. 'Well, I've bought it now,' he said at last. 'Will you at least have a look at it? You can't tell until you've seen it, tried it out.'

'Oh Bill, I don't know . . .'

'It's being delivered here this afternoon, so you could –'

'What? Here, today?' She looked up, annoyed. 'You can't just dump a horse on me like that, without warning! How can I cope with a problem horse on top of everything else I have to do? And Terry's not even here. Why on earth didn't you ask me first?'

'I wanted him to be a surprise for you. I thought you'd be pleased,' Bill said; and then his disappointment generated a seed of anger. 'In any case, where else would I take a horse? These are my stables, after all.'

Polly swallowed her annoyance and her pride in one go. 'Yes, of course, silly of me,' she said colourlessly. 'I'd forgotten for a moment that this is your place. I'm sorry.'

'I didn't mean it like that,' Bill protested.

'No, no, you're quite right. Of course you must bring your horse here. I'm sorry I spoke hastily.'

Simpson brought his fist down on the table in sudden frustration, making the cups jump. 'Damn it, Polly, don't do that to me!'

'Do what?' she said, though she knew what he meant.

He thrust his chair back and stood up and stalked to the window. 'I can't get anything right, can I? I'm caught whatever I do. This situation is the devil!'

'It's your situation, not mine,' Polly muttered. She was angry too, and upset, and she resented being made to feel guilty about hurting his feelings.

After a moment he turned back and said more quietly, 'Why won't you just marry me and have done with all this messing about? Everything I have is yours, you know that. I don't want you as an employee, I only do it because you won't accept gifts from me, but it doesn't make you happy, does it? You hate it as much as I do. Why not marry me? What can I do to make you say yes?'

'Nothing,' she said, looking down at her hands.

He stared at the top of her bent head for a moment in pain and frustration. Then he said, 'Well, that much is obvious. Everything I do or say only seems to make it worse. Don't you like me, is that it? Shall I go away for good? You only have to say.'

She looked up at that, and saw his flushed, angry face, recognised his pride, which was at least as strong as hers. He had put it aside often enough to beg her for her favour, and that couldn't have been easy for a man like him, used to command and to get what he wanted. It was something, to be the object of a man such as him.

'I don't want you to go away,' she said.

'But you won't marry me. So what do you want?'

'It's not a matter of what I want,' she said, but it was said sadly, not petulantly.

'Well, I can't do what I want,' he said. 'What I want is to marry you.' He stopped, hoping she might say something, but she only looked at him with that sad, level gaze, and the anger dribbled out of him. In a way she was right. It was *his* situation. She was the victim of it. She must hate not being in charge, just as he would. But what the hell was he supposed to *do*?

'Oh well,' he said, turning away, 'I have to go now. I've got some things to do. The horse is due at two o'clock. I'll come back then and we can sort out what's to be done with him.'

Polly watched him cross to the door, knowing perfectly well he hadn't got things to do, that he was only getting out of her way. She felt mean. He seemed to be making her feel like that a lot recently. Perhaps she really ought to tell him to go away, end it now, for both their sakes. But then, what of Taggert and Mackie? How could she bear to part with them?

Oh, but that was just mercenary, wasn't it? She shot her chair back and stood up in a violent movement of frustration, and he turned at the door, surprised. His firm-fleshed, handsome face, his well-cut hair, his good, tasteful clothes: the sheer *niceness* of him made its impact on her all over again, and she thought how many women would give their hair to have a man like him in love with them – a generous, honourable man who didn't take advantage; a man unafraid of commitment, who actually wanted proper, legal marriage. My God, she must be mad to reject him! But at all events, she couldn't be unkind to him.

'Bill, don't go like that,' she said. She smiled at him, and he smiled tentatively back, afraid of another blow to his pride. 'I'm sorry if I upset you. Let's be friends,' she said, holding out her hand.

'Friends,' he said, rather blankly.

'I was being ungracious, I'm sorry. I'm really glad the horse is coming here . . . No, honestly! I'm looking forward to seeing it, and trying it out. The horse that beat John Newland! There's fame for you.' She was trying too hard, she thought. She reached into herself for sincerity. 'It was sweet of you to think of buying it for me to ride. Thank you.'

He took her hand, and chafed it between his own, looking down into her face with a troubled smile. 'Friends,' he said again, at last, as if that was the only thing she had said. 'Uh-huh.'

Years ago Emmerson used to be out of bed and halfway down the stairs before he'd well opened his eyes. These days, he was awake long before he managed to get his head off the pillow. He had dreamt, confusedly, of sex and horses. Or was it sex with horses? What did that say about his libido? But it was wonderful to *have* a libido again. He had supposed his to have shrivelled up by the forces of evolution to the status of a coccyx or the ability to wiggle one's ears: a biological relic of former powers.

He had never understood those characters in books who wake wondering if last night were all a dream. He remembered the events of yesterday vividly: more vividly – because they were unexpected – than anything in his day-to-day life. Take the bath, for instance. His was an old-fashioned, cast-iron bath, free-standing: the sort with the curly feet and the big brass elks by way of taps. It was one of the things, the many things, about which he and Tilly had argued. She had wanted a modern set-out, a panel bath with matching suite of basin and WC – but not a bidet, which, paradoxically, she thought was disgusting. She had wanted tiled walls, tiled floor, all-white and lots of chrome – like a laboratory, he had said, annoying her. She had urged him to rip out his antique bath and throw it away; she loathed the open fireplace, quivered with antiseptic horror at the carpeted floor and the capacious armchair draped with a big, thick towel, in which one could sit and cut one's toenails at ease.

Anne knew how to appreciate a bath. She had half-filled it and then gravely, courteously, invited him to join her. Catch Tilly sharing a bath with anyone! She belonged to the squeamish generation, the age of obsessive hygiene: dedicated to the shower, panty-liners, antiseptic wipes, bottle feeding. Oh, what could be nicer, he thought, than bathing with a friend? He and Anne had soaped each other, chatted peacefully in the steam, then stood up and sluiced each other off with fresh hot water.

By the time they were out and he was towelling her dry, he had forgotten to be embarrassed about his body: blue-white, seamed, so old and atrophied, as it seemed to him; forgotten to worry about whether she could really find him attractive or whether she simply pitied him, or was doing it for a bed for the night. He wanted her so badly he didn't care about any of that. His only question was whether they would make it as far as the bedroom or whether he would have to put the old armchair to further and more energetic use.

Anne was seemingly unembarrassed by nakedness, and walked ahead of him with a towel over her shoulder as if they were going for a dip. With her mass of hair pinned up casually out of the way on the top of her head, she looked like a flower, a long slim stem supporting a prize bloom – a show chrysanthemum at least. He devoured her with his eyes as she led him to his bedroom. She was slim and well-muscled from her active life, but shapely, all the same, with soft bits where, in his opinion, women ought to have them: just the right partner for a desiccated starveling like himself.

In the bedroom, she dropped the towel and with one simple movement unloosed her hair. It was like a gift, offering him her whole self, no reservations. He backed her tremblingly to the bed, and she lay down and held up her arms to him, and he plunged in, too needy to wait.

Afterwards he said, 'That one was for me. Sorry about the haste. The next will be yours, and the next.' Her smooth-browed face, curiously unmarked, as if she had never known age or trouble, swam below him like the moon in a dark sky. He kissed her forehead gratefully, and pushed the damp hair from it. 'Thank you.'

'For what?'

'For being a good friend.'

'Greater love hath no man than this?' she suggested.

'I don't want you to give up anything for me. I'd like you to have everything you want.'

'All right, I'll give it some thought,' she smiled.

'Do.' He suddenly felt enormously cheerful. No post-coital *tristesse* for him this time! 'I'm hungry.'

'For what?' she said, laughing.

'Just food, actually. I'm suddenly absolutely starving. But there's nothing in the house.'

'Let's go out, then,' she said simply.

'No, no, I don't want to. I don't even want to get out of bed. If I had my way we'd stay here for the next fortnight.'

'I'll go, then.' She sat up. 'I'll bring something back.'

'Everywhere's shut round here. It's not like London.' He almost panicked, afraid that if she got out of bed she'd go away and not come back.

But she hauled herself out from under him with a good-natured shove, crossed the room and picked up his trousers. 'Have you got any money?' She found his last tenner in the pocket. 'OK if I take this? Right. Don't get up. I'll be ten minutes.'

Fifteen minutes later they were feasting on fish and chips and bottled beer, sitting up naked in bed and trying to keep the vinegar off the sheets. Then they made love again; dozed, woke, and loved again, and so on through the night. But it was not just sex: it was the closeness. He had thought of Anne before, in as far as he had ever thought of her, as a rather remote, silent, mysterious figure, aloof and cool; but here in his house, in his bed, close up, she had proved, despite her pale madonna face, warm and affectionate. People had said she was strange, but she seemed wonderfully normal, chatting to him in an entirely natural way, about anything that came into their heads. There were no barriers between them, of understanding or intent. When they talked, there was a level on which he was quite unaware of her being female, absurd though that seemed, considering what they had been doing together. Of course, there was another level on which all his nerve endings sang with the delicious knowledge of sex, both had and to come.

And that had been last night. Now, this morning, he was lying relaxed, with the morning sunlight on his body, feeling as if he were soaking it up, filling out the wrinkles of his fasting like a newly fortunate prune. Anne. He felt as empty as a wine skin and as full as a gander. He opened his eyes at last, rolled over, and touched her on the shoulder.

She woke instantly, and looked at him. 'What?'

'I was just thinking . . . Wishing we could have done this a long time ago.'

'The chance never arose,' she said.

'You mean because I was married?'

'And also because you never asked me.'

'I was a fool.'

She shrugged. 'Things happen in their own time.'

'I suppose you're right. My past is fast receding into a heavy fog, anyway. Best thing for it, really. The present is much more attractive.' He kissed her long and satisfyingly. 'Time for a quickie?'

'*Folie de grandeur*, that's what you've got,' she said solemnly, taking him into her arms. Afterwards she stretched lengthily and said, 'What time is it?'

'Quarter past eight.'

'That late?' She sat up, pushing the hair from her face. 'What about the horses? They'll be kicking the doors down for their feed.'

'No, it's all right, a man comes in from the village to feed and muck out. He comes early, before work. He's a gardener – used to be my gardener in happier days. He's self employed now. Just does an hour or so in the mornings for me. I can't afford full-time help any more.'

'How bad are things?' she asked him abruptly.

'As bad as they can be. Really, I'm only waiting to be made bankrupt. Welcome it, really . . . Put me out of my misery.'

'Rubbish! What's the matter with you? You've got horses, you've got a place to keep them—'

'Barely.'

'You've even,' she said implacably, 'got a horsebox. Get out there and make some money and stop feeling sorry for your-self.'

'Talk is easy,' he said, a little sulkily. No one likes to be told they're self-pitying, even if it's true. Especially when it's true.'

'Never mind talk. Let's just get out there and do it!'

61

'Us?' he said, hope reviving painfully.

'If you want me to help.'

'Want you to? Dear God!'

'I'll take that as a yes.'

'But listen, Anne, I don't want to take advantage of you. It's a bit embarrassing – I don't know what you had in mind, coming here – but I really, truly am stony broke. I can't afford to pay you wages.'

'Oh, do stop raising objections,' she said, jumping out of bed with huge, horrible energy. 'Did I ask for wages?'

He felt relieved. All this, then, was because she liked him. Still, he had to say, 'I can't even feed you properly. It'll be marching rations only, I'm afraid.'

'I don't eat much – though more than you, by the look of your ribs. Come on, let's get some breakfast, and then we'll look at all the schedules . . . You do get sent schedules, don't you?'

'Yes, but—'

'No buts. Come on, up, up!'

He climbed out under her goading. 'There isn't anything for breakfast. We ate the eggs.'

'I know how to make porrage out of the horses' oats.'

'You do? I don't know why you aren't a millionaire.'

'I don't, either,' she agreed.

Downstairs, while he cleared the decks in the kitchen, she went out, dressed in jeans with a tee shirt over her bare breasts, taking a bowl to fetch oats from the stable. She returned sooner than he expected, in a hurry. 'Trouble!' she said tersely. 'I bumped into a little old man singing a hymn. Looked daggers at me. He's on my heels.'

Before he could speak, the door was filled with the bent and irate figure of Keevey, who, Emmerson remembered belatedly, would still be mucking out at this time of the morning. Anne dived behind Emmerson in a parody of hiding for her life.

'There's been a girl stealing your oats!' Keevey cried, quivering with outrage. 'She came this way.' He stopped abruptly as he saw her in the kitchen and under Emmerson's protection. 'Oh!'

'Yes, it's all right,' Tom said. 'You see—'

'I see all right,' Keevey said, looking from one to the other with an icy glare. 'Nothing wrong with my eyes.'

'This is Anne, who's come to help me with the horses,' Emmerson said. Anne dug him in the back, which he interpreted as telling him he had no need to explain her away – and she was right, of course. It was just that Keevey demoralised him – always had done.

'I see my services won't be wanted here any more, then,' Keevey said.

'Oh, don't talk nonsense,' Emmerson said feebly, his face stiffened by the Arctic chill coming off the gardener. 'Of course you're wanted.'

'I've worked here, one way and another, since I was a boy,' Keevey said with dignity. 'Your father set down certain standards in the stables, and I've always kept to them, and what they don't include is half-naked females running about frightening the horses.'

'Anne is a very experienced groom—' Emmerson began again.

'That's as may be. But girl grooms are one thing,' Keevey said, 'and lady-friends another. People in the village look up to you, Mr Emmerson. They expect you to lead by example. If you'll pardon me, you're letting yourself down by this sort of carry-on.'

'I don't know that I will pardon you,' Emmerson said, beginning to be annoyed. 'It's none of your business, really, is it?'

'Oh, is that the way of it? Well, I'm glad I've found out. I've seen a lot of things in this house over the years, and I've stayed on out of respect for the family, but what you pay me is not enough to be putting up with this sort of caper – *or* being told to mind my own business. So if you'll excuse *me*,' he gave Anne a final glare, 'I won't be coming up again. I'll call Friday for what you owe me. Good morning.'

'Now wait a minute – !'

But he was gone.

'Well, now I'll have to stay,' Anne said. Her voice sounded odd and Emmerson looked at her anxiously, afraid she was upset. She gave up the struggle and fell into silent laughter. 'Oh dear, his face! I don't think he can ever have seen a braless woman before.'

'He's a very strict Methodist,' Tom said. 'Terribly against drink and fornication . . . Not that I've troubled him much with the latter, but he has struggled with his conscience for years over my drinking.'

'Censorious old besom! What business is it of his?' Anne said, still laughing.

'You shocked him,' Tom said. And then he began to laugh too, out of contagion. 'Oh dear, I wonder what he'll make of it. That's the trouble with country life. It'll be all over the village by lunchtime that I'm keeping a harem up here.'

'Do your reputation the world of good,' said Anne.

The big royal-blue box with *Newland – Horses* in white across the front pulled up outside just before three o'clock and Polly and Bill went straight out to meet it. They were in time to see Mary Newland jumping down from the cab.

'Hullo, Mary,' Polly said. 'Long time no see.' Mary had been just a schoolgirl in the days when Polly had been going with John Newland, so she knew her only slightly. She had felt rather sorry for the girl, with such a dominating father and older brother, out of place in that all-male world – the mother had died many years ago. Whether she was timid by nature, or whether it was the result of being sat on all her life, Polly didn't know, but it did her no favours in that fiercely competitive family.

'Hullo, Polly . . . Mr Simpson. I hope you don't mind, I thought I'd come down with Copper. He was a bit jumpy this morning, and I thought . . . Well . . .' She cast a nervous glance at the driver who was climbing out of the other side of the cab, but he was too far away to hear her. 'Only,' she went on with a pleading look, 'he needs understanding. He doesn't respond to roughness.'

The driver joined them, and Mary shut her lips tight and looked down at the ground. Polly recognised him, a beef-faced, tough-looking man, one of the older Newland grooms, trained in Newland *père*'s school of hard knocks – meaning the ones you gave to horses that misbehaved. She understood Mary's inarticulate warning, and gave her a quick smile of reassurance.

'Hullo, Jim,' she greeted the man. 'Good journey?'

'The usual,' Jim said. 'Bloody traffic. Bloody road works. Terrible bloody roads you've got round here. Bloody horse wouldn't box, either. Won't be home before dark.'

The grim lines of his face suggested life had never dealt him a better hand than this. He was ill-fortune's plaything – but, by golly, anything further down the pecking order than him was going to know all about it! Polly imagined the journey Mary had just enjoyed and thought she must be devoted to the horse to set herself up for it.

'Well, let's get him out, shall we?' she said.

'Yeah, before he kicks the bloody box down,' Jim agreed. 'Who's giving us a hand?'

'We both will,' Bill said.

The two men let down the ramp while Mary chewed her lip with anxiety. Suddenly she confided to Polly, 'We had such a job getting him in. He was so scared.'

Great sales technique, Polly thought. But of course, Bill had already bought him. 'Is he vicious?' she asked. 'Mean-spirited?'

'Oh no!' Mary said vehemently. 'He's a lovely horse, really. He's just had a bad scare, and a bit of a fall in the paddock, and – well, you know. He just wants the right handling.' She turned her pale eyes on Polly with passionate fervour. 'I know he'll go well for you. Really he will! Please give him a chance. He deserves a chance.'

Polly read between the lines. So, she thought, the horse had been threatened with destruction. That was why Mary was so anxious not to let him out of her sight, in case the evil-hearted Jim whisked him off to the knacker's yard. She was a fool, though: John least of all people would destroy a valuable horse like that. Sooner than shoot it, he'd have run it off and rebroken it himself. Money was god to the Newlands, as Polly knew very well.

'He'll get his chance all right,' she said, to reassure Mary. 'Don't worry about that.'

The ramp was down now, and she stepped closer to get her first sight of the horse. He stood in the back of the box, turning his head round and blinking in the sudden light. He was more heavily clothed up for the journey than she would have bothered with, but even so she could see that both the size and the beauty of him were outstanding. Then he laid back his ears and lashed out with a hind leg, hitting the boards with a resounding thump.

'Oops,' she murmured. 'How are you going to get him out?'

'Gerrrcha!' Jim growled at the animal. He stared, fists on his hips. 'I said we should have hobbled him.'

'You might have done better to box another horse down with him for company,' Bill said mildly.

Jim's look said precisely what he thought of amateurs telling him his job. 'We got no horses to spare for that kind o' malarkey,' he said.

'I can get him down,' Mary said quickly. 'I can go in through the loot. He'll be quiet for me.'

'You'll get yerself kicked,' Jim said indifferently. 'Ah, goo on then, if y' want to. He's got to come out one way or another. But don't blame me if y'get hurt.'

Mary scooted round the side of the box as if afraid someone

would change their mind about the whole deal. Polly exchanged an amused glance with Bill, who spread his hands slightly. Mary climbed with youthful agility through the little side door into the loot and they heard her cooing voice talking to the horse and soothing him as she climbed into his stall. Polly wondered briefly what the Newlands would say if she did get herself badly kicked; but just as she promised the horse let her untie his rope and turn him round, and then he came slithering and clattering down the ramp beside her in that alarmingly uncontrolled way horses have, and stood, trembling slightly, looking around him. Beside Mary he was massive, and Polly thought that if he decided to take off she would weigh him down about as much as a haynet.

'I've got a box ready for him,' Polly said. 'We'll put him straight in.' They walked him round to the stable block, and though his ears were working overtime and he was rather peeky, they got him into the box with only minor startles. Then Polly said, 'Bill, would you like to take Jim into the kitchen for a cup of tea while Mary and I get some of the clothes off him.' She said it mainly for Mary's benefit, since Jim's presence obviously made her nervous, but indeed the horse seemed quieter when the men had gone, too. They undressed him, talking quietly to him. He did not seem at all vicious, only nervous and uncertain, and with the gentle handling he gradually stopped fidgeting and began nosing the haynet.

'He certainly is a beauty,' Polly said when they had rolled the last rug off him. She passed a hand over him to see if he was sweating, but he was quite cool; then she looked at her hand and grimaced. 'He could do with a good grooming,' she said.

'He's been out for ages,' Mary said abjectly. 'I did give him a brushing this morning, but you know how it is.'

Polly nodded. The horse, towering above her at seventeen hands, seemed in excellent condition despite his run-off, solidly structured of bone and muscle under a fine skin and that startlingly beautiful coat. There was plenty of bone in his legs, and his quarters – so high they made him look as if he was on tiptoe – were immensely powerful. By comparison her own Taggert and Mackie seemed like beach ponies.

'How is he bred, do you know?'

Mary shook her head. 'He's not a blood horse, so of course he isn't in The Book, but John was told he was half Irish, and the other half was part Belgian.'

'I thought he had some Heavy blood in him somewhere,' Polly said. The horse turned his head to look at her as she spoke, and she exchanged a long glance with those big dark eyes. *You're* all right, they seemed to say, but keep those others away. 'There's nothing wrong with you, is there, old man?' she said, and stroked the muscled crest. The horse flared his nostrils to get the scent of her, and then turned back to his haynet.

'He likes you,' Mary said, half relieved, half wistful. Her eyes looked rather too bright.

'He'll be all right,' Polly said. 'I expect you'd like a cup of tea before you go back?' She flung a day rug over the chestnut's back and ushered Mary out, talking brightly to keep her mind occupied. 'I expect we'll be seeing you at the Manchester Show? It looks like being a grand affair, and I for one say it's about time . . .'

Simpson would have liked to see his new horse tried out straight away, but Polly said he was like a kid with a new toy, and the horse must be given time to settle down. The next morning Terry lunged the chestnut for an hour to get the travel stiffness out of him, and when Bill arrived they saddled him (with some difficulty) for Polly to ride. They took him to the small paddock, and Polly did up the chinstrap on her crash cap and wished in vain that there had been some rain recently: the earth would be like concrete to fall on.

'Well, here goes,' she said. She checked the girths, cocked up her leg, and Terry linked her hands under her knee and sprang her lightly into the saddle.

'All right?' said Terry, still holding the chestnut's head.

Polly found her stirrups and grimaced. 'He feels like an electric mountain. Yes, OK, chocks away.'

Terry let him go and climbed up on to the gate with Bill, and Polly tenderly applied the aid for a walk. The chestnut felt colossal and powerful after her own horses – a bit like changing suddenly from a pedal cycle to a motorbike – but his mouth was good, which would be the saving of him, she thought. He walked at her command, but was stiff and pauky, wondering what was going to happen, eyeing the two on the gate as if they were First and Second Murderers.

'Poor old feller, what did they do to you?' Polly murmured. He flicked his ears back and forward, listening to her, and flexed the bit anxiously. She eased him into a trot, and at once felt the measure of the power she had to control. As he dashed forward, he covered twice as much ground, even at this col- lected trot, as Taggert did fully extended. She hardened her seat and tried to loosen her wrists correspondingly, but the sheer weight of his neck made it hard work.

'He looks very stiff,' Terry said as she passed the gate.

Polly nodded. She didn't want to shout in case it alarmed the horse, so she waited until she passed again to say, 'Will you lay out some poles on the ground. Four to start with.'

Cavalettis might loosen him up a bit, she thought. She took him to the far side of the paddock and tried trotting him in figures while Terry laid out the poles, but his attention was not with her. He was watching the preparations, rather like a mediaeval prisoner watching the irons being heated. My God, Polly thought, they must have done something pretty drastic to this poor beast, because if I know anything about horses, he's no coward.

'Come on, then, feller,' she said when Terry was back on the gate, 'let's go and see what's what.'

She squeezed, but he did not move. He was like a quivering rock under her. She insisted, and he walked forward reluctantly, his ears pricked hard and his legs trembling as he laid his hooves to the ground. She talked soothingly all the time and walked him right up to the poles and let him look at them and sniff them for a good long time. Then she turned him away and trotted him right round the paddock, hoping he would come upon them and be over them before he really saw them.

He saw them. He watched them out of the corner of his eye all the way round the paddock. To him, poles were malevolent things that jumped up and struck him as he passed, and the higher he jumped, the higher they jumped too. There was no escaping them. Polly rode him strongly, expecting him to try and run out to the right – that is, towards the centre of the paddock. But he felt her intention and jigged left, though there was scarcely room between the poles and the paddock rails. She had to lift her leg sharply out of the way to avoid it being painfully scraped.

At the second approach she wouldn't let him go left or right, and at the last minute he stopped dead and then writhed right round, facing back the way he came. Patiently, she circled him again. He was beginning to sweat now, but only lightly, so she thought she'd try once more. She rode him hard, and he trotted straight until one stride before the poles, when he made an enormous leap, up and sideways, as if unable to decide between running out and clearing the lot in one jump.

'He's not having it,' Polly called to Terry. 'I'll take him down the other end. You take the poles away.'

She rode him off, but she could feel the difference in him: he was wound right up, and she realised she had underestimated his fear of jumping. Whatever John had done to him, it was more serious than simply overfacing him or riding him too hard. She had heard rumours of the Newlands doing other things, using methods that were not approved of in the mainstream. She wondered now if there had been something in the stories after all. She walked and trotted the horse in figures at the far end, and then circled him round to where the poles had been, to show him there was nothing there to fear any more; but he was hot and excited, danced and shook his head about; and then something – she didn't know what – startled him and he gave a great breenge, almost unseating her, and was off.

She couldn't hold him. His power was such that when she tried to bring his head in he simply pulled her out of the plate. She flashed past the gate, catching a glimpse of two white faces and two open mouths, and then the fence loomed up, on the other side of which was the jumping paddock. She was positive, afterwards, that he had meant to jump it: she felt him gathering himself, and though it was a five-foot fence, that was not a tremendous jump for a horse his size. But at the last moment he changed his mind: perhaps he saw the jumps in the next paddock and realised he was heading out of the frying pan into the fire. At all events he jammed on the brakes, skidded to a halt, tucked his head down, and Polly went flying over the fence and landed with a jarring jolt on the hard ground.

The odd thing was that the horse didn't run off when he found himself loose. He stood where he had stopped, his reins hanging, and the first thing Polly saw when she had stopped seeing stars was his bright face looking at her through the rails. She could almost have sworn he was laughing.

Four

'How's the juvenile delinquent?' Bill asked, telephoning one evening a week later.

'A sheep in wolf's clothing,' Polly told him. 'I took him out for a long hack this afternoon.'

'That's an advance. How did he go?'

'His gaits are superb. You couldn't see it in the paddock, he was so bunched up, but now he's relaxed he simply flows. He's like an armchair on wheels.'

'You sound smitten,' Bill said.

'I am, to the core. We went through the woods and up Pipers Hill, and we jumped several logs and hedges and a couple of brooks, and he went over them like a skyrocket. Didn't sweat up at all. Mackie looked shocked at the waste of energy: he cleared everything by about four foot.'

'No trouble, then?'

'Certainly not over natural objects, in hot blood. I haven't tried him in the jumping paddock yet, but if I was forced to bet, I'd say he'll settle down to them, once he knows he's not going to be hurt. He's got a trusting nature, and he's very bold out in the open. And there's not an ounce of vice in him, though there's plenty of high spirits.'

'That's terrific! So you think he'll be all right? When d'you think you'll have him ready for the ring?'

'Hold on, not so fast. I haven't changed my mind about him.'

'I thought you just did.' Bill sounded puzzled.

'He isn't for me. He's a gorgeous horse, and it was nice of you to think of me, and I think you did the right thing in buying him. Quite apart from rescuing him from the Newlands, I think he has enormous potential.'

'Well then – ?'

'Two things. First, I simply don't have the time, with Taggert and Mackie and only Terry to help. And Pavlova needs a lot of time spent on her at this stage of her career. I haven't got the time to dedicate myself to him. And secondly – and more importantly, really – what I said in the beginning still goes. He's far too powerful for me.'

'You managed him this afternoon.'

'Only because he wanted me to. If he took it into his head to misbehave, I'd be completely helpless. You saw in the paddock how he ran off with me. I couldn't have stopped him. I'm just not strong enough, Bill.' There was a silence from the other end. 'I'm sorry.'

'Well, what do you suggest I do with him? Sell him again?' Bill sounded almost petulant.

'Certainly not. I said you did right to buy him, and I think he'll make you a lot of money. All you need is a different rider.'

'Another rider?'

'Why not? You can have as many as you like. There's no rule that says I have to ride all your horses for you.'

There was a silence while he digested this, and then came the inevitable next question. 'Who did you have in mind?'

'You could try Alison Neave, but I know she's got her hands full at the moment, and I'm not sure the Akahito people would let her ride for anyone else. So I think the best person to ask would be Dan Roberts.'

'Ah,' said Bill sourly, 'I wondered how long it would be before his name came up.'

'Look, I can't help your personal feelings,' Polly said with remarkable patience. 'This is a matter of business, isn't it? So you should be professional about it and consider the case objectively.'

He didn't like to be called unprofessional. He said, 'All right, then, convince me.'

'Dan's very successful, as you know. He's also an excellent rider, very sensitive and capable. He's physically strong with a powerful seat, but his hands are light and he's gentle with his horses. I don't take all of Mary Newland's spiel unsalted, but one thing is sure about this horse: you won't beat him into submission. He's the kind of horse that will do anything for love, but nothing for fear.'

'What makes you think Roberts will want to take him on?' Bill asked through his teeth. No matter what Polly said, he couldn't help viewing Roberts as his rival. He had seen them together.

'Well, I don't know for certain, of course, but I think he will. He'll see what I see, a great potential being wasted. And I know something about his taste: it's his kind of horse. Anyway, you can but try.'

Bill thought a moment longer, then said, 'All right. Do you want to ring him, or shall I?'

'It had better come from you, hadn't it? It's your horse.'

'All right. I'll ring him and let you know what he says. Will he be at home this evening?'

'I should think so. He was at a show on Tuesday and Wednesday but he ought to be back by now,' Polly said unguardedly.

'I might have known you'd know that,' Bill said.

'Oh, for God's sake!' Polly exclaimed.

Roberts was at home, sitting in his favourite saggy armchair, unbooted feet up, glass of beer in one hand, statement from his accountant in the other. It made amusing reading, as long as you had a warped sense of humour. Well, horses were expensive animals to keep. Take your basic stabling costs: mortgage on the stable buildings and upkeep thereof, buildings insurance, rates, water and electricity; bedding and fodder; saddle soap, linseed oil, hoof oil and all the etceteras, plus wear and tear on tack and grooming kit and so on. Add grooms' wages; vet and farrier fees, vehicle costs and petrol; other travel costs; entry fees, professional subs, and what he paid the accountant to tell him all this baloney. On the other side put his prize money, his retainers from sponsors, and the various fees he got from endorsing commercial goods, opening fêtes, appearing on stands at horse shows, and giving interviews to the media. Take one from t'other, and it left him about twelve thousand a year net to live on. A thousand a month. Two-fifty a week for his food, clothes and fun. And that was without allowing for contingencies, such as a horse going lame or getting too old to jump. Unless prizes got substantially bigger, he would have to keep riding until he was eighty to accumulate enough money to retire on.

And the public thought they were all so rich! Well, he supposed it depended on your point of view. There were plenty of, quote, ordinary people who didn't clear a thousand a month; and there were plenty who spent that much on taxis! Of course, many of the horsemasters had farms to fall back on. One or two had other businesses, like Danny Ryan and his butcher shops, Chris Campbell and her hacking stables – though God knew *that* was a mug's game these days. But mostly they didn't do it for the money: they did it because there was no other life like it.

He remembered Anne enumerating the points that made showjumping the sport of sports: 'It's impossible to cheat; it's the only sport in which women enter on absolutely equal terms with men; it's the only sport people pursue just for the love of it . . .'

What were the other points? He couldn't remember now. He thought hungrily of Anne, and then glanced restlessly around the shabby cottage. He couldn't really say he was a lonely man. He had always been self-sufficient; and in any case, he had the company of his fellow competitors at every show he went to, to say nothing of his pick of the groupies. It was only when he was here at home that he felt solitude, and he never used to mind that. What was wrong with him these days? The cottage seemed suddenly something that did not accommodate him, merely tolerated his presence. The caravan, in which he lived at shows, was more homelike than this. Perhaps he should sell the cottage and live wholly in the caravan? But, then, what about when he retired? He couldn't live in a caravan when he was eighty.

Why in God's name had he started thinking about retirement all of a sudden? Annoyed with his thoughts he flung the paper down and was just getting up to refill his glass when the phone rang. It was Bill Simpson.

'What's up?' Roberts said. He could think of no reason for Simpson to phone him – which made it trouble.

'Nothing's up. It's a matter of business. I have a proposition for you.'

'Oh? Let's have it, then.'

'I wondered if you'd care to ride a horse for me. I've got a nag that needs careful handling, and you're the best man for the job, if you'll take it on.'

'Why me? I thought you hated my guts,' Roberts said bluntly.

'I don't know why you should think that. But in any case, this is business, and I never let my personal feelings interfere with business.'

Well, bully for you, Roberts thought. 'Why don't you want Polly to ride it? What's the catch?'

'There's no catch. But if you're not interested . . .'

'I don't know if I am or not until I know more about the horse.'

'It's John Newland's French horse, the chestnut he calls Coppernob. I bought it from him for Polly to reschool and ride, but she thinks it's too strong for her. You would seem to be the right person for the job, but if you're not interested just say so, and don't waste my time. If you feel it's worth thinking about we can arrange a trial. That's all.'

'I never turn down anything without thinking about it,' Roberts said. He was enjoying baiting Polly's keeper – though it was a bit too easy, really. 'So Polly thought I was the best man for the job, eh?'

'It's nothing to do with her.'

'You thought of me all on your own, did you?'

'This is obviously a waste of my time,' Simpson began with an air of finality.

'Hang on, don't get off your bike. I'd like to try the horse, anyway, if Polly thinks it's got potential. I've got a couple of days free at the moment, as it happens. Can you bring it over to my place tomorrow?'

'I can't get away from work until some time next week,' Simpson said.

'You and I don't have to meet at this stage. The important thing is for me to try the horse and see if I can get on with it. I can send one of my people to fetch the horse over to my place, if you like. Where is it?'

'At Polly's,' Simpson said reluctantly. 'All right. You'd better call her and arrange things.'

'OK, I'll do that. And when shall you and I meet for a discussion? I expect you'd like things settled quickly. The longer it takes, the longer the horse is costing you money instead of earning it.'

'What about Tuesday next week?'

'Next week's the Manchester Show.'

'I meant to come up to see Polly in something. I can get away on Tuesday. Is it the Grand Prix on Tuesday?'

'No, that's Wednesday. Tuesday's the Tomatsu Stakes.'

'Oh, well, that's always worth watching. I'll see you at the show, then?'

'Fine.' Roberts paused, and then added, 'Thanks for offering it to me. I appreciate it.'

Simpson, equally diffident, said, 'You *are* the best man for the job. I know that.'

What a pair of heroes we are, Roberts thought as he hung up.

Under Anne's goading, Emmerson's life was taking shape. The day-to-day things were taken care of: there were clean sheets and towels again, the kitchen had reappeared from under the avalanche of used crockery, and there was food in the house. Anne did these things somehow without seeming to. He never actually saw her clean the bath and loo or put the washing machine on, but it wasn't him, so it must be her. Food was variations on soups, stews and casseroles: things that could be left in the slow oven all day to cook themselves. The miracle was that it was there, and that he felt like eating it, both things due to Anne.

She mucked out, groomed and fed the horses, and took care of basic exercise, leaving him free to concentrate on schooling, which she made him do. Relentlessly she was shoving him into shape, and he felt the better for it. In fact, he felt pretty good these mornings, after the sound sleep that followed an active day, a decent supper and some (for him, anyway) pretty mind-bending sex.

It was astonishing how quickly she had become absorbed into his life – or had absorbed him into hers, he wasn't sure which. It seemed like a miracle that she had appeared from nowhere that day, when he was at his lowest ebb, and the miracle was fuzzed around the edges with the alcoholic blur of the past months, which made it the more wonderful and the less to be questioned. But it did seem strange to him that, though they spent every hour of every day together, and talked in such an uninhibited way, he still knew as little about her past as he ever had. It was as if she were a creature entirely of the present, spawned out of the now of his need. He would look at her when she wasn't actually speaking to him, and see her as suddenly remote as if viewed through the wrong end of a telescope. What was she thinking? Why had she come here? Where had she come from? When he looked at her as a thing outside him, so to speak, her faint enigmatical smile would have driven him crazy if he weren't already crazy with – what? Lust? Adoration? Those at least. And he had a superstitious dread that if he asked her too many questions she would disappear as inexplicably as she had arrived, so he accepted the boon of her and put his doubts to sleep.

One day, at her instigation, he accepted an invitation he would otherwise have refused, to give an exhibition on Sunavon at a local show.

'I can't,' he protested at first. 'Sunavon's been at grass for months. He's not fit. He's too old.'

'He'll enjoy it,' she said. 'He's fit enough to do a round of jumps at a village gymkhana. Anyway, if you do carve it up, what does it matter? They're only offering you a hundred quid. They can't expect perfection for that.'

'I was their last resort, I bet,' he said. 'Why else would they have asked at such short notice?'

'You should be so proud,' she said.

He was stung. 'All right . . . But his coat's in a terrible state, and his tack's dirty, and my clothes haven't been cleaned since Wembley.'

'You can leave all that to me. You just get the old boy mobile. As to your clothes, I've already had your breeches and stocks through the washing machine, and I've spot-cleaned and brushed your coat and hung it up to air.'

'You have?'

'Ages ago. I found it all lying on the floor when I first arrived. Now do stop arguing. You've got to do it,' she said grimly. 'It's all very well to pay entry fees and fodder bills with rubber cheques, but we need cash for food and petrol if we're going to get to Manchester.'

'But how can I take money for doing the exhibition? The show's to raise funds for local causes and I'm supposed to be the local squire . . . sort of,' he added when she made a grimace.

'Expenses,' she said tersely. 'They wouldn't have asked you –
even at the last minute – if they didn't expect to make something out of you, and everyone's entitled to expenses. And don't
forget to ask for it in cash. If they give you a cheque it'll just
disappear into your overdraft.'

But the local show was only part of a larger plan she had for
his future, which she laid before him the following night when
they were in bed together.

'You can't go on like this, you know,' she said out of the blue.
They had just finished making love and he thought she was
talking about that. For a horrible moment he thought she was
going to say she was leaving, moving on again. But surely this
was different? He was not her employer, they were lovers.

'What do you mean?' he asked feebly.

She sat up, the moonlight gleaming dully on her smooth face
and ivory breasts. 'Living from hand to mouth, with debts
creeping up on you like flood water. It's ridiculous for a man
like you to be in this state.'

'But what can I do?' he said. 'Don't you think I've tried to
think of a way out myself? I don't have any skills to get myself a
job.'

'What's wrong with the one you have?' she asked.

'I can't make enough money with winnings to keep my head
above water. That's how I got into this position in the first
place.'

'That's because you're not going about it properly. And
because you're starting from the wrong place. You've got an
unfair handicap.'

'Which is?'

'This house.'

He stared at her. 'What are you talking about?'

'You've got to sell this house. It is yours to sell, isn't it?'

'Yes, but—'

'Well, then. It's a millstone round your neck, and it's drown-
ing you.'

'I can't sell the house!' he cried. 'It's not just any house, it's the family seat. The Manor House. We've been here for hundreds of years. It's . . . it's—'

'It's falling down,' she said brutally. 'And burying you under it. Look, what's the point of hanging on to ancient history? You have no children. When you die it will pass out of the family anyway, won't it?'

'I might have children one day,' he said painfully.

'By that time the house will be a heap of rubble. If you care so much about the damn thing, you should sell it to someone who'll take care of it properly. Look, at the moment it's costing you everything you've got and that still isn't anywhere near enough. It's a massive liability. But sell it, and it becomes a huge asset. Country houses, especially period houses, are fetching vast prices these days. You'd have to knock a bit off for it being in poor condition but still you'd get enough to clear your debts and set up a nice little nest-egg.'

He felt numb with shock. He had always thought of himself and the house as indivisible, part of a natural order. It took a huge effort of imagination to go where she was leading. 'And what would I do then?'

'Sell the house and gardens, but keep the stables and fields. Trade in your caravan for a bigger one and live in it permanently. Change your car for a Range Rover. And tour the shows like Newland and Roberts and Baker and the other moneymakers. You're as good as them and you can make as good a living as them if you go into it wholeheartedly.'

'You've got it all worked out,' he said stiffly. But a strange thing was happening. As he thought about her appalling suggestion, he felt a weight lifting from him. Sell the ancestral home? Unthinkable . . . wasn't it? A millstone, she had called it. But that wasn't quite it. It was like some living thing, some vast incubus that he had struggled all his life to feed, and could never satisfy. It was sucking the life from him.

He thought of living in a caravan. Of living in a caravan with

Anne. How cosy that would be. How care free. Travelling to all the shows, living in the show villages, jumping sponsored horses, advertising Bisto on television, spending someone else's money.

But to lose this house! How could he do it? How could he lightly sign away the family seat? He had been born here, his father had died here, all his ancestors were buried in the nearby churchyard. Tilly had always hated it, of course; and now, staring up at the ceiling, he thought of the money – the vast fortune – he had poured into trying to maintain it, and he felt his love for the place melt away like zabaglione on the tongue.

She was right, of course: it would fetch a tidy sum on the open market, even dilapidated as it was, and even without its land. Country homes were in short supply – he had read enough in the Sundays to know that. The mortgage, the second mortgage, his overdraft on his overdraft would take a chunk out of it; but even so, there would be money left over. Maybe not a lot, but then, without the house to maintain, his living expenses would be so modest! He wouldn't need a fortune.

'But suppose,' he said, with one last qualm, 'no one wants me to ride for them? Suppose I don't get any sponsors?'

'Well, you'll be no worse off than you are now. Without this house you could probably live off the horses you've got now. And if not,' she grinned, 'there's always fruit-picking. I hear the gypsies make loads of money at it.'

'Take him round again,' John Newland shouted. 'And for God's sake, don't be so bloody feeble this time!'

Mary turned Amati, tears in her eyes and dread in her heart, and put him into a hand canter round the paddock and back towards the combination jump John had erected for her: three sets of poles at four-foot-nine, separated by one pace and two paces respectively. It wasn't such a terribly stiff jump, and Amati ought to be able to do it, but Mary believed his martingale was too tight for him to be able to get his head right, and she had 'allowed' him – as John put it – to run out at the third element.

The dun gelding turned in towards the line of jumps at her command, and at once she felt his head strain up to the limit of the standing martingale as he tried to accelerate. She held him back and he fought against her, snorting and showering her with flecks of foam.

'Now! Let him go!' John shouted. 'One, two, *three*! Go on, go on!' Amati cleared the first element, took one stride and hurled himself over the second, rapping it hard with his heels. Mary's hands went forward as he stumbled slightly. Two strides to the third element. One, two – and then again the little horse escaped her and dodged out, this time to the left. Mary almost lost her seat, recovered herself, and brought him back to a hand canter with difficulty. He was prancing on the spot, going sideways, jerking his head up and down, and she was being jolted until her teeth jammed together. This, together with what John was going to say to her, made her feel sick. She rode hopelessly back to him.

'You did exactly the same thing again,' he raged. 'What's the point of me telling you and telling you if you pay not the least blind bloody bit of attention to anything I say? How are you going to manage five-foot jumps if you let him run out over four-foot-nine? I sometimes think you must be a bit mental, Mary, I really do. That's the kindest thing to think.'

'The martingale is too tight,' she said tearfully. 'He can't extend himself.'

But John broke in. 'He doesn't need to extend himself. That jump's well within his scope. He's just plain bloody nappy . . . And you let him get away with it. And you know what happens without the martingale. Up goes his head, he bangs you on the nose, jumps flat and bolts with you. I don't have to tell you that.'

'Maybe we could try something else? A sheepskin noseband perhaps – ?'

'And have him going at everything sideways? In any case, you'd never hold him. Christ, Mary, what's the matter with you? D'you think you know better than me how to get a horse going?'

'No,' she muttered, staring miserably at the ground. Her eyes burned with tears. Inwardly she cried, 'Oh, why don't you leave me alone to ride badly if I want to?' But she didn't say it aloud; she would never defy him aloud. And in any case, she knew the answer to that one. Her father had bought her Amati, but not to potter about the roads and compete at kids' gymkhanas. Amati was an investment, he was supposed to make money, and she was supposed to earn her living. 'Everyone and everything on this place has to turn a penny,' Dad was fond of saying. She didn't want to ride in top-class jumping when it meant all this bullying and heartache, but that was what Dad and John wanted for her, and she had no chance against the two of them, no argument to present except her personal unwillingness, which was no argument at all.

She remembered what it had been like years ago, before John had really taken her on, while she was still a juvenile. She had her home-bred pony, Underhill Wildest Dreams. He was a pretty black gelding with some talent for jumping and his own brand of native-pony wisdom, inherited from his dam, who was a Dartmoor brood mare. With Dreams, Mary had hunted in winter and gymkhanaed in summer, enjoyed the freedoms of childhood and worshipped her increasingly famous brother from afar.

He had been a hero to her. She was always a solitary child, the only girl in a womanless family, but with her gymkhana friends and her worship of John she had been happy enough. Then one day John had come across her taking Dreams over some of his showjumps, put down to three feet. She had just been 'messing about' and had not noticed him watching, until at the end of the round he had called out, 'Good, now put them up a bit. You're not stretching him at that height.'

There it had begun. Wanting to please him she had jumped Dreams higher and higher until he refused, knowing himself overfaced. But John would never be thwarted, especially by a dumb animal. He had 'taken the pony in hand' in his own fashion. All the grey area on the edge of cruelty, the doubtful practices condemned by mainstream opinion, they had explored together. Dreams had changed from a happy, ordinary gymkhana pony to a fretful, nervous, white-eyed jumping pony. True, they had had successes, but at what cost? In the end Dreams had fallen in a jump-off at the County Show and broken his leg, and had had to be destroyed.

In her deepest heart, where she hardly dared look her feelings in the face, Mary blamed John for the pony's death; but he had been able to argue his way out of it as always. He had said the fall was her fault for not driving on hard enough, allowing Dreams to hesitate and muff the jump. Her fault, her fault. When she was with him, she had to believe what he told her. How she had wept! 'I'm going to take the training of your next horse into my own hands completely,' he had promised. 'We'll have no more nonsense of this sort.'

So her father had bought Amati, a compact, springy fifteen-two dun gelding, full of spirit and with the short bouncy stride which is ideal for English jumping rings. She had loved him at first sight, but her gratitude was tempered when her father said, 'Now you do everything John tells you, and no argument.' Remembering the fate of Dreams she had even dared to protest – but diffidently, of course. She had said she didn't care about competing and would just as soon be left alone to enjoy the horse in her own way. But her father had stared at her, grinding his jaw in that way that had become a habit with him, as if he was chewing and chewing on anger, and told her irritably not to talk so bloody daft. 'I didn't buy the horse for you to mess about on. That's a jumping horse. You do as John tells you, or I sell it again. Which is it to be?'

She had bowed her head and obeyed, but she thought that

given the same choice now, she might have preferred parting with the horse; for, a year on, Amati was not the same happy animal he had been, though she had certainly won things on him. And she had seen what John had done to Coppernob. Other riders managed to win prizes without resort to the nasty things John did – though perhaps they didn't win so often. John was the most successful showjumper in the country. Maybe that was it. And in any case, what could she do? While she lived here, she had to obey John. Her father backed him up and the staff were all on their side. She had no one to turn to. She longed to get away, but where on earth could she go, and what could she do?

'All right,' John said, bringing her back to the present she had subconsciously been trying to evade. 'If you can't manage him I'll have to ride him for you and show you how it's done.'

'Oh, no,' she protested quickly. She had seen John ride Amati once and didn't want to witness that again. 'No, I'll do it this time, really I will. I promise.'

'You'll do it all right,' John said grimly. 'I'll see to that. Jean!'

The groom had been watching from the gate and came over at his call. She had a lunge whip in her hand.

'Right, off you go,' John said to Mary. 'The same thing. Keep him straight and drive him on. And don't let him get his head away after the second element.'

Mary turned Amati again and rode round the paddock. As she came towards the jump she saw how it was: John was standing to the right of the third element, to stop Amati running out that way, and Jean was standing to the left with the lunge whip. Mary began to cry. She just couldn't help it.

'Now! One, two, three, hup!' John counted her over the first element. Mary felt that Amati was tiring, but he cleared the second element and landed square. She saw the white of his eye as he took in the presence of the people at either side of the jump, and felt him gathering himself as he knew he would have to jump this time. One, two small, neat strides; and then, just as he was about to take off, Mary heard a whistle and a crack and Amati flinched violently as the lash of the lunge whip landed across his quarters. Thrown off his concentration, the horse tried to put in an extra step, took off too close and crashed through rather than over the jump.

'He'll do it next time. Bring him round again,' she heard John say as Amati pecked on landing and recovered himself. He cantered sideways, shaking his head frantically. Mary turned him back to where John and Jean were standing by the jump. Almost blind with rage and pain for her horse she jerked Amati to a halt, flung herself from the saddle, dropping the reins, and rushed at John, fists flying.

'Don't you hit my horse!' she screamed, her voice skidding off the scale with her anguish. 'I hate you! You hit my horse again and I'll kill you! I'll kill you!'

John caught her wrists, holding her back from him and shaking her. 'Shut up!' His hands and arms were like iron from years of riding and she had no strength against him, but she kept struggling, maddened with frustration, screaming at him that she hated him. He let go with one hand and hit her, calculatingly, across the cheek with his open hand.

Mary gasped with pain and shock; she stopped struggling and began weeping hard with anger and misery. John let go of her hands and stood back, watching her.

'I'm sorry I had to hit you, but you were hysterical,' he said. 'You know you should never make a noise like that around horses. You were scaring Amati.'

At the name Mary looked up, knuckling tears from her eyes, looking around for her horse. Jean had caught him and was holding him a few paces off. John was proffering his handkerchief but Mary ignored it and dragged out her own, blew her nose briskly and, still wet-faced, walked across to her horse. She stroked his neck, ran her hand over his quarters and parted the hair. He flinched, but there was no mark: the lunge whip was not thin or hard enough to cut a horse's hide.

'He's all right,' Jean said. Mary took the reins from her without a word or a look, and mounted again.

'I think he's had enough now,' John said, just as if nothing untoward had happened. 'It's as well to finish with him having jumped it. Even though he hit it, he did jump it, and that's what matters. You can take him in now.'

Mary turned Amati away, giving John a look of such cold ferocity it would have made him recoil if he had seen it. But his attention was already on the next task, and he was calling to Jean, 'All right, let's have Idaho out. Fetch him, will you, while I put the jumps up. And tell Jim I'll be needing him.'

Mary stroked Amati's neck as she walked him back towards the stables. Her resolve had crystallised into two desires: escape, and revenge. She had not yet the faintest idea how she could achieve either of them, but she knew that above all she must keep silent and let John think he had won as usual, otherwise she would never get away.

'And I'll take you with me,' she said to the horse, 'don't you worry.' He laid one chocolate brown ear back for her voice, and then pricked it again, jogging a little in his eagerness to get back to his stall.

Five

P olly arrived at Moor End, Dan Roberts's place, at nine in the morning, driving the box containing Mackie, Taggert, and all the gear she would need for the show. Terry came behind, driving the car towing the little two-berth caravan. They were to travel from Moor End to the Manchester Show the next morning in convoy. It had been Dan's idea to combine travel to the show with a visit to see how the chestnut was doing, and though Terry had grumbled, Polly had fallen in with it happily.

She knew Moor End quite well, and was always amused by the contrast between the busy, immaculate, modern stable yard and the dilapidated silence of the cottage. Roberts had five horses in residence – apart from his own The Iceman and Shilling, he had two he rode for the oil company, Philadelphia and Texas, and one he rode for a private owner, Freddo – plus a couple of youngsters he was bringing on; and with three girl grooms, a part-time man, a working pupil and a part-time secretary, the yard and offices seemed as crowded and full of activity as the concourse of Euston Station. Set back from the yard behind its approach of nettles and willowherb, the cottage looked derelict and deserted.

There was a large, cinder-floored parking lot between the road and the stable yard, and into this Polly swung the box. The lot already held the Roberts horsebox, his Land Rover, car and caravan, the male groom's ancient rust-bucket and two motorbikes owned by two of the girls, so there would have to be some shuffling about before anyone could get out again.

By the time Polly had parked and cut the engine, Roberts was approaching with his senior girl – still called a girl, though she was nearly forty – the redheaded Hazel, who limped heavily with a polio leg but rode like a centaur.

'Hello! Good journey?' He reached the cab just as she opened the door and, grinning mischievously, he put his arms up to jump her down. 'Come on then . . . Careful!'

He caught her tightly as if she had been about to fall, and for a moment she looked into his sardonic blue eyes at a range of less than six inches. She felt with a jolt his strong, masculine attraction. *My God, but you're fanciable!* she breathed inwardly. It was something she had always been aware of, on the periphery of her mind, as it were: something she had tried not to acknowledge to herself. He was a flirt and a womaniser, and his path through the world was littered with the girl grooms and fans and groupies he had enjoyed and then managed only too easily to live without. But knowing all those things didn't mean she couldn't easily have fallen for him. To do him credit, he had always treated her as a friend rather than a potential victim, and she believed he really liked her as a person; but there was always, underneath their ease with each other, a sexual tension that increased, rather than diminished, the longer they *didn't* go to bed with each other. If it hadn't been for her strange relationship with Bill, she thought, it probably would have happened by now, with who-knew-what dire consequences. So thanks, Bill, the human chastity belt, she saluted him, not entirely ironically.

'Thanks, you can let me go now,' she said. Roberts gave her a farewell squeeze and obeyed. 'Hello, Hazel.'

''Ow are the 'orses?' Hazel replied. 'They box all right?'

'I think they knew they were going on a trip. They were surpassing naughty.'

'Let's get 'em down, then,' Roberts said. 'I've got boxes ready for them. Ah, here's Terry. How are ye, me darlin'? Top o' the mornin' to yiz!'

'And likewise it's a braw bricht moonlicht nicht,' Polly mocked him. 'Knock it off, Roberts. You know Terry hates that phoney man-of-the-bogs routine.'

''E's just over-excited, the big kid,' Hazel said. 'Bin up since a-pass five.'

'Now you've done it,' Roberts gasped in mock horror. 'How are you going to explain how you know what time I get up?'

'Dream on,' Hazel said with easy contempt, and went with Terry to let the ramp down.

'You see how I'm respected by my staff,' Roberts said, grinning at Polly. She suspected one of the reasons he liked Hazel was that she alone treated him as an equal – or, to be accurate, as slightly her inferior – in the human race. She was a superb groom, and knew it, and expected Roberts to behave like her grateful employer and nothing else. She had no time for his 'nonsense'. The other girls all thought he was the frog's pyjamas, and probably made up stories about him in bed at night.

Taggert and Mackie came down eagerly and the two grooms led them off, with Dan and Polly following behind.

'So how's the chestnut coming along?' Polly asked.

'Not bad at all. We'll go straight along and see him, if you like.'

'Think you'll get him in the ring this year?'

'I'm not sure. He's got some problems. I'll take him round the paddock when we've had a cup of coffee, so you can see for yourself.'

In the yard, Taggert and Mackie were renewing their acquaintance with the Moor End horses in a chorus of whickers and whinnies. Roberts led the way to the chestnut's box. He was standing looking out, calm and lordly, watching the activity of the yard with bright interest. Wearing only a light rug and leg bandages, his lines were not obscured, and he looked magnificent. Polly went up to pet him, and he tolerated her hands without showing any interest in her. Even when she produced a titbit from her pocket, he took it as if conferring a favour on her, and then looked out into the yard again, and kicked the box door a couple of peremptory times with a forehoof.

'He wants to be out and doing,' Roberts said. 'I think he's got the lowest boredom threshold of any horse I know.'

'Maybe that's part of the trouble.'

'Could be. You know, Pol, he looks familiar. I'm sure I've seen him before, but I just can't figure out where or when.'

'Really? I don't think I know him.'

'No,' Dan said thoughtfully. 'If I do know him, it was from a long time ago.'

'Ah well, of course, you're older than me,' Polly said innocently. 'A lot, lot older.'

'None of your cheek!'

'It'll come back to you when you're not thinking about it . . . Things always do,' Polly said.

'I suppose so.' He turned his fascinating gaze suddenly on her. 'You're looking very pretty today, Polly Morgan, ma little lass. So you've been let out to play for the day?'

'So it seems,' she said demurely. They turned away from the chestnut's box. 'Did you say something about a cup of coffee?'

'When you say coffee, do you mean coffee, or is that a whatsisname?' Roberts asked gravely.

'What whatsisname?'

'A euphonium or whatever it is.'

'Euphemism.'

'That's the one. By "coffee", do you really mean you want to sleep with me tonight?'

'Oh, I thought you'd never ask.' Polly pretended relief.

They were passing Terry at that moment, and she favoured the two of them with a disapproving scowl, which Roberts didn't notice and Polly ignored. Terry was anti-men, and particularly anti the sort of bed-'em-and-leave-'em, self-styled studs of which she thought Roberts a prime example. Well, that was Terry's own problem, Polly thought; and then, with an inward shiver, she allowed herself a brief thought of what it would be like if she really did slip into Dan's bed, just for the hell of it. *Whoops!* A bit too nice for comfort.

Roberts, as if he had felt her shiver, gave her a burning look from his heavenly blue eyes; and then the rampant willowherb fluff drifting over from his garden got up her nose and she sneezed, exploding the moment.

In the equestrian world the Manchester International was tipped to become the Show of Shows. Now in its third year, it had already proved popular with the American and European riders, and this year it had drawn an unprecedented number of entries for all classes.

The showgrounds were custom built, laid out like a miniature town and linked to Manchester airport by a fast road. The great International ring, where the main jumping events were held, had covered seating, sophisticated floodlighting, and an indoor collecting ring with big-screen CCTV, so that those warming up or waiting could watch what was going on in the ring. There were, in addition, two smaller rings where the children's and showing classes were held, a covered hall for exhibitions and rows of permanent shop units. The horses were stabled in two huge buildings like aircraft hangers, which housed the portable loose boxes, and there were six exercise rings laid out around them.

But perhaps the most attractive feature of the show for the competitors was what had come to be called, *à la* Olympics, Show Village. Individual cabins with running water and electric cookers had been built to house the foreign competitors, and such of the domestic competitors who did not want to bring their own vans; but to avoid segregation, the van lots were interspersed with the cabins, and there was a communal bar and lounge in the centre. The horsemasters were used to setting up their own community wherever they parked their vans, but at the Manchester International they could do it with some luxury. It was becoming their gala week, like a horse fair to gypsies: everyone was there, and it was the time to catch up on gossip and renew old friendships.

Roberts turned the big horsebox in at the gate and stopped at the security hut. 'Here we are,' he said to Polly. All their horses were in together, and they'd been sharing the driving. 'It's packed already. No chance of getting the favourite parking place now.'

'You'd need to get here early for that,' the security man said, leaning in at the window. 'They've been arriving since five o'clock.'

'They must be mad,' Polly said. 'It's not worth getting up that early, even to get the lot nearest the bar.'

'All this lot yours, sir?' the security man said, clipboard in hand.

'Half and half,' Roberts said, showing his pass along with Polly's.

'Right you are. Would you like to report to the stable manager, then? You know the way, don't you?'

The stable manager ticked them off his list and allotted them loose-box numbers.

'We're doing it first come, first served this year,' he told them. 'You want boxes together, I suppose?'

'Is it that obvious?' Polly said gravely.

'People will start to talk,' Roberts murmured to her audibly.

The stable manger was not amused. 'Here's your keys. Please remember to wear your passes conspicuously at all times. And please remember the strict no-smoking rule.'

They sent Terry and Hazel off to park the two vans in the best spot they could find, and drove the big horsebox down to the pavilions, which was what the stable hangers were called. Every few yards someone called out or waved to them. The place was seething with activity: booted riders, grooms in anoraks, owners in tweeds and flat shoes leading heavily-rugged show ponies; a steady stream of horseboxes heading slowly towards the pavilions to disgorge their valuable freights.

'I wonder what the total insurance value of everything on the site would be,' Polly said. 'There's a nice irrelevant thought. Hey, there's Alison Neave and Chris Campbell.'

'The long and the short of it,' Roberts remarked. 'Where's this idiot woman going with that pony?' as someone wandered across the road in front of him.

Polly felt ridiculously excited, like a child on holiday. 'Oh look, there's the airport box. I wonder who's in it?' The huge blue horse-transporter which ferried horses from the airport was taking up most of the pavilion access room ahead of them. Roberts pulled up thirty feet behind and watched the horses coming down.

'That's the American team,' he said in a moment. 'See the flag on their rugs?'

'That could be any flag, from this distance.'

'Anyway, I recognise the horses.'

'So do I, now. That's Slipstream, isn't it? That means Kim Gorman's here.'

'There goes your chance of the under eighteens' prize,' Roberts teased her. Kimberlee Gorman was only seventeen, and last year had won the Ladies' World Championship, the youngest person ever to win it, upsetting a large number of female riders with the consideration that her career was only just beginning.

'He's waving you past,' Polly said, ignoring the jibe. 'Come on, Roberts, I want to get these horses unboxed so I can head for the bar. I don't come here to compete, you know, I come here to schmooze.'

When they had finished bedding down the Underhill horses, Mary had lingered behind with Amati, and from the safety of his loose box was watching the American team move in next door. They still went in for big horses, she noted, but they seemed to be going for more home-bred animals, rather than the big Hanoverians they had imported for many years.

Even more than the horses, the riders interested her. The two females in the team were so young – Billie Craig twenty, and Kim Gorman only seventeen and therefore younger than Mary herself – and yet they seemed so full of confidence. She watched them striding about, hands in pockets, laughing and chatting with the males of the team, the grooms, the pavilion staff, all with perfect ease. They seemed to have no fear of doing wrong, making mistakes, being shouted at, being made to feel useless and stupid. She saw with envy the easy way Leroy Davis put his arm round Billie, and how Billie smiled without seeming awkward or overeager. Mary had only ever had one boyfriend, and that had come to nothing. She had been too shy to encourage him, and he had been scared off by the only time he had called for her at home, when Dad and John had subjected him to the Spanish Inquisition. It was another thing to chalk up against John, she thought with resentment. Not only had he killed her horse, he had driven away her boyfriend, and she would never dare bring home another – not that any man was likely to notice her, or have the chance to get near enough to ask her out, the way she was watched and practically kept imprisoned.

She was so absorbed with her own thoughts that she did not notice the young man strolling over to her until he spoke.

'Hello! Are you hiding from someone?' Mary started violently at the sound of his voice, and he said, 'I'm sorry, I didn't mean to scare you.'

She blushed. 'I . . . I didn't see you. I was watching the . . . Well, just watching.' She expected him to shrug and walk away, but he stood smiling at her in such an easy, friendly way, as if he wanted to know her. He had brown, curly hair and a very ordinary face, lightly tanned, and with that look of glowing health she had noticed in other Americans, as if they were better fed, or better groomed, or better *something*, than English people. He was still looking at her, and it was obvious she would have to say something, and she wished she could think of something smart and clever; but all that came out was a feeble, 'Are you with the American team?'

'Yes, I was picked for the first time this year. It's terrific: the whole team's under thirty. That's a first. John's the oldest – John Bryan, you know? – and he's only twenty-nine. Last year the *youngest* on the team was thirty-two. Isn't that something?'

He carried on chatting about the team selection, and Mary gazed as she listened, fascinated. For his part, he was charmed by her shyness. He had seen her peeping out over the box like a little pink rabbit and come to talk to her on an impulse. He liked her round, pretty face and her wide eyes and the way she looked at him so admiringly. Having spent the best part of every day for the last month with the self-confident, Amazonian Billie and Kim, who would have thought the less of themselves if they couldn't do everything a man did, only better, he found Mary's old-fashioned feminine helplessness a change and a relief.

'I don't think we've met before,' he said at last. 'I'm Ben Watts.' He held out his hand, and after a hesitation she shook it over the top of the box.

'I'm Mary Newland.'

'Newland? Any relation to John?'

'I'm his sister.'

He still had hold of her hand, and didn't seem to be in any hurry to relinquish it. He was looking at her with interest and pleasure, but she was afraid now that it was because she was related to John, and not because he liked *her*. Well, how could he? They'd only just met, and like an idiot she'd only managed to say three words. She wanted her hand back, but didn't know how to go about it.

'Listen,' he said at last, 'I have to go now, but how about meeting in the bar later on? I'll buy you a drink, or a coke, or something. Introduce you to the others, if you like. They're great guys. How about it?'

She'd have gladly foregone the introduction-to-the-others bit, but it was the first invitation of any sort she'd had since her one-and-only boyfriend, and she stammered, 'Oh . . . yes . . . Thanks. That'd be nice.'

'Great. About seven – would that do? Or is it too early?'

Mary would have been there in five minutes' time if he'd asked. 'No, seven's fine.'

'I'll see you there, then. Bye for now!'

He walked off and rejoined his companions.

'Who was that you were talking to?' Kim asked.

'Mary Newland. John Newland's sister. Cute, isn't she?'

Kim Gorman wrinkled her small, freckled nose. 'If you like white mice,' she said.

'I like 'em as much as cats,' Ben said cheerfully.

Tom Emmerson tightened up the haynet, slapped Captain Fox on the neck in valediction, and stepped out into the gloom of the pavilion's night lighting. Anne was standing in the shadows, her hands thrust into her pockets and her shoulders hunched. Ever since they had got here, he felt there was something different about her. She seemed in a subdued mood, as if she was brooding about something.

'The bar's still open,' Emmerson said, looking at his watch. 'Fancy a swift half?'

'No, you go on. I don't feel like one just now.'

'Is something wrong? Are you all right?'

'I'm OK. You go on to the bar . . . Catch up on some gossip.'

'Where are you going, then?' He was faintly put out. He had looked forward to being seen with her, his new lover, his pride.

'For a walk. It's a fine night.' She looked around, and he couldn't tell if she was being facetious or not.

He almost said he would come with her, but at the last

moment common sense stopped him. 'OK. You'll remember where the van's parked, won't you?'

She nodded. He hesitated a moment longer, and when it was obvious she wasn't going to move, he turned and walked off. Anne watched until he was out of sight before taking off in a direction of her own.

Roberts went down for a last look at the horses around midnight. He knew it wasn't strictly necessary, since there were staff guards on duty all night. But it was his long habit and he couldn't break it.

He was mildly disappointed that so far he was sleeping alone in his van. Terry and Hazel were sharing the double bunk in Polly's van while Polly had the single. Hazel was pleased – normally she slept in the loot of the horsebox so she'd gone up in the world – but the other part of it seemed a waste to him. His suggestive remarks to Polly were always only half in fun. He had long fancied her, but since he also liked her very much, it would have been both more exciting and more risky to embark on a sexual relationship with her. She had always treated his flirting as a joke, but he had felt recently she might be weakening towards him. He knew she had a situation going with Bill, and that it made her unhappy. Probably that was the more reason *not* to start anything with her, but his recent restlessness had brought him to the point where he was almost ready to stand the risk. He had been half hoping that Polly would do the rest herself and save him having to stick his neck out. As he walked down to the loose boxes he thought how he might phrase the final, over-Niagara question. *Would you like to see my etchings?* That was traditional and had the advantage of not being in common use any more. A bit more classy than, *Fancy a coffee?* or the horseman's equivalent, *Can you help me off with my boots?*

The horses whickered to him as he leaned over each door in turn. He spoke to them quietly for a few minutes, savouring their clean smell and aura of simple contentment, and then retraced his steps to his caravan. Halfway there, he began to get the feeling that he was being followed. Was it a rustling of grass that stopped when he did, a shadow that moved half a second too late? There were little hints that niggled at him. He switched routes suddenly, turned sharp left round the back of a caravan and stopped in the shadow. Seconds later a dark figure rounded the same corner and he caught hold of it firmly.

It gasped with surprise, and he found himself holding a female shape. It relaxed almost as once, and he heard the indrawn breath let out easily. Whoever it was, she knew him and was not afraid.

'Why are you following me?' he demanded tersely.

'What are you whispering for?' the reply came.

The hair rose on his scalp and his hands tightened involuntarily. 'You!' he said.

'Me,' she agreed, and, by moving a little to one side, allowed the light to fall on her face.

It was the last thing he had been expecting. He couldn't find any words. Her smooth face with the unfathomable dark eyes and deeply curving mouth, framed by a mass of dark hair, seemed as familiar as his own reflection. She had had her hands in the pockets of her donkey jacket; now she brought them out and put them up to his shoulders. It might have been a defensive gesture, but it made his heart beat faster all the same. Well, she'd been following him, hadn't she? Was it possible that she had come back to him? He struggled with the desire to pull her hard against him and kiss her with all the passion and anger he had been storing up since she went away. Instead, still holding her by the upper arms, he asked, 'Why were you following me?'

'To find where your van was.'

'You could have asked anyone that.'

'I couldn't,' she said, and added the deadly words, 'I wasn't alone.'

Now he let her go; took his hands back as if they'd been scorched. 'Oh. You're with someone,' he said in a flat voice.

'Obviously.'

She waited for him to speak again, and that strange ability she had to remain absolutely still and silent had its effect, as always, driving him in the end to ask the question he didn't want to ask, giving her the satisfaction of having provoked him.

'Who?'

There was a pause, as if she contemplated not telling him. But not telling him would be his preferred result, not hers. 'Tom Emmerson.' she said.

'God!' he said, and turned half away from her. Emmerson? *Emmerson?* Bloody Gentleman Tom? It made him the more furious for being unexpected. He liked Emmerson; Emmerson was old – in his eyes – and a has-been; Emmerson was from a different class, the old landed gentry. Why did all those things make him the worst possible rival? *Rival?* He caught himself up. What was he thinking? There was no question of that! Not now, not after the way she walked out on him.

'Why did you want to find my van?' he asked harshly.

'I want to talk to you.' He said nothing and she went on, matter-of-factly, 'Shall we go? Or would you rather talk in the stables?'

'What's wrong with here? What have you got to say to me that needs going anywhere to hear?' he said bitterly. She shrugged and turned away. He managed to let her get five yards before breaking and calling her back. 'All right, come on, then.'

She fell in beside him, still without a word; but when he stopped in front of the door of his van she asked belatedly, 'Are you alone?'

'You took it for granted,' he said sourly.

'Dan, don't be a pain. Open the door.'

He let them in and switched on the light. She sat down on a bunk.

'Drink?' he offered. She nodded and he poured two glasses of whisky. She took a straight sip, swallowed and began on her subject.

'I heard on the grapevine that you've bought John Newland's horse, the one he calls Coppernob. These stories can get twisted in the process, and I wanted to know if it's true.'

'Not quite,' he said. He sat on the bunk that was at right angles to hers, and studied her as he answered. 'Polly Morgan's patron, Bill Simpson, bought him for Polly to ride, but she couldn't handle him, and suggested Simpson got me to take him on.'

'Ah,' she said. 'Have you seen him?'

'Simpson?'

'No, the horse, idiot.'

'Yes, I've had him at my place for about ten days. I've to see Simpson on Tuesday to arrange things. He's coming to the show.'

'So you've tried the horse. What do you think of him?'

'Hard to say. He's got the talent, all right, but whether I can make anything of it is another matter. He's been badly frightened, and he's developed some terrible habits. I don't know whether it would be worth the effort in the long run: my time and Simpson's money.'

'He's worth it,' Anne said. She finished the whisky in one long gulp.

'What do you know about it?' Roberts frowned. 'Do you know the horse?'

'I knew him. In France he chased under the name of Le Chiffre, but before that he was a showjumper. I used to groom him, when he belonged to David Barber. The year he beat John Newland and Apache to the World Championship.'

'*Murphy?*' said Roberts. Anne nodded.

Murphy, almost a legendary horse, one of the best jumpers of all time. In two seasons he had won every big prize in the calendar, before Barber had sold him for a huge sum to an

American dealer. The horse had been taken across to the States and had disappeared from public view – no one knew why – and Roberts, like everyone else, had put him into the past tense and forgotten him.

'Are you sure?' he asked. 'Did Newland know?'

'I don't know. I don't think so.'

'Then why did he buy him? Why would he buy a racehorse?'

'Oh, he knew that the horse had been jumped. Jean-Paul Cardin jumped him for a season at Continental shows but without any success. He couldn't handle him. So he sold him to a trainer – one of these gentleman amateurs – who thought he'd do better as a chaser. That's where he got his bad habits, of course.'

'And I don't suppose Newland did anything to improve them.'

Her face darkened. 'That man shouldn't be let near a horse. One day . . .' She broke off, brooding.

'So what happened before Jean-Paul Cardin? How did he get hold of him? How did Murphy get from the States to France?'

Her expression became veiled. She shrugged. 'That's a mystery. Anyway,' she went on, 'I wanted you to know what you had. He's a great horse, and he's had a bad break. You're one of the only two riders who could bring him back.'

'Two? Who's the other?'

'Tom Emmerson,' she said.

He scowled, an unreasonable rage coming over him. 'Oh, of course, the wonderful Tom Emmerson, the greatest rider in the world! No doubt you're sleeping with him, too? How very cosy!'

She seemed unmoved. 'Don't be a fool.'

'Are you trying to tell me you're nothing but his groom?'

Infuriatingly, she would not get angry. 'We're not talking about me. And try to get a grip on reality: you know Tom's a brilliant rider. He's beaten you often enough in the past.'

'In the past . . . Before he became a no-hope old soak.'

'Think that way if you like. If it helps you.' She stood up to leave. 'It doesn't matter, anyway, what you think. What matters is what happens in the ring.'

He stood too, blocking her way, his anger ebbing in the face of helpless wanting. 'Don't go. I'm sorry, I was out of order. Just don't go. Have another drink.'

She stared up at him impassively, and he could not fathom her thoughts or wishes. It had always driven him mad, that enigmatic look of hers – but mad with wanting, not annoyance. She was dark and mysterious and unattainable, and whenever he had thought he might finally grasp her, she had slipped through his fingers like smoke.

Having her near him again reminded him of all those nights when they had lain together, breast to breast and thigh to thigh, so close you couldn't have got a cigarette paper between them. Desire surged up. He caught her face in his two hands and kissed her. For a moment he felt her response – or thought he did – but then her lips hardened and she pulled back from him. 'Anne,' he said, aching with longing. He stared down into her still eyes, only inches from his. 'Stay with me.' He kissed her again. She put her hands up over his, but it was to pull them, quite gently, but firmly, away.

He had made a fool of himself again. Desire turned to frustrated anger. 'Why did you leave me?' he demanded, the words bursting out of him.

'How can you ask me that?' she replied, and for the first time there was anger in her voice, too. He had broken through some barrier, and it surprised him so much his own anger sank.

'What do you mean? Are you saying it was my fault?'

She made a small, uncompleted gesture. 'Oh, for God's sake . . . !' And then, in her normal, impassive tone, 'Let me past now. I must go and look at my horses.'

'Emmerson's horses.'

She wouldn't rise to it. 'Take care of Murphy,' she said.

*   *   *

104

It was hard for Dan Roberts, in the days that followed, to be in close proximity to Anne and yet to be unable to be closer. She treated him with exactly the same calm friendliness as she treated everyone else, but it was obvious from the way Tom Emmerson looked at her and spoke to her and kept her as close to him as possible that he was besotted with her. He was too much of an old-fashioned gentleman to kiss or touch her in public, but Roberts hadn't the least doubt in the world that he was sleeping with her. What else could have made such a difference? Emmerson was positive and cheerful, and his drinking was moderate and social. All Roberts could do was to try to save his own face by pretending everything was hunky-dory and not staring at Anne like a hungry dog staring at a bone. Whether Emmerson was aware of any tension in the air, he made no reference either to Anne or to Roberts about their past relationship; but Polly Morgan looked at Roberts oddly from time to time, having a fair idea what he had once felt about his 'ex groom', and wondering what he felt now.

The village settled down, the usual crop of rivalries and friendships sprang up. Parties gathered in lighted caravans over packs of cards and bottled beer; others grouped and regrouped in a conversational country dance in the bar; and, in the dark of night, there were a certain number of shadows flitting quietly from one van to another. At all times, the main topics of conversation were horses and money, and for the sporting individuals, there was an unofficial book on the outcome of the major competitions.

For the public, the highlight of the week was probably the team event on Friday, and the prestige event was the Grand Prix on Wednesday; but what the riders looked forward to was the Tomatsu Stakes on Tuesday. It was a speed event, with a traditionally twisting and tricky course, and not only was it the one in which the rider could attract the esteem of his fellow competitors, but it also carried the big reward of a hefty cash prize plus a Tomatsu car. The car was on display in the entrance foyer of the big ring for the public to look at. Subtly spotlit, it turned majestically on a revolving plinth, its glass, chrome and deeply polished metallic paint winking seductively. Whoever won it, they would probably sell it immediately for cash, but it was in the rules that they would have to be photographed behind the wheel for publicity purposes, so Tomatsu reckoned to get their money's worth.

Everyone was entered for the competition, even Mary Newland, who knew she hadn't a chance in a thousand. Not that she cared. Since arriving at the show she had found she cared less and less about anything. This morning, for instance, she was grooming Amati and actually singing, while in her mind she went over every single word Ben had said to her last night. She was desperately, painfully in love for the first time, and the wonder of it was that he liked her and wanted to be with her. He seemed fascinated by her; if she had had more self-confidence, she would have dared to think he was falling in love with her, too.

How could she ever have thought he had an ordinary face? He was *beautiful*! His eyes – those long eyelashes – his hair; his wonderful skin; his voice. Last night in the bar they had held hands while they talked: she had almost jumped out of her skin when he first touched her. And then afterwards when he had walked her back to her van he had drawn her into the shadows and kissed her. Oh, it was bliss! She could think of nothing else since she woke up this morning – that and the fact that he wanted to see her again tonight, and had also hinted he might be able to have lunch with her, if there was time. He wanted to spend all his spare time with her! Life was suddenly rosy, everything rimmed with light, and even the fact that she had to do a practice round under John's critical eye in half an hour's time could not entirely quench her happiness.

In the next box Jean was grooming Apache, whom she would be warming up while John dealt with Mary. The boss was already out in the exercise ring with Greyfriar, the home-bred youngster he was upgrading. Jean heard Mary's singing with mild astonishment, and after a moment's thought put down the body-brush she was using and slipped out of the box.

Mary looked up as Jean's head appeared over the half door, and she smiled, making Jean blink. 'Finished already? I wish I was as quick as you are.' A week ago she would have been too timid to address Jean until spoken to.

'Can I have a word with you?' Jean said.

Mary's expression clouded just a little. The words sounded ominous. 'What about?'

'Well, about John, actually.' Mary looked her surprise, and after hesitating a moment, Jean plunged in. 'Have you noticed . . . Has it struck you that he's been a bit odd, recently?'

'I don't know. What do you mean?'

Jean frowned, trying to muster her thoughts. 'Take that chestnut, for instance. I mean, I know he'd had a bad fall, but it wasn't like him to give up like that and sell it. And then there were those threats he made about it . . .'

'What, having it put down, you mean?'

'Yes. Of course, he wouldn't have done it, the horse was too valuable, but he sounded so violent when he said it, I almost believed him for a minute.'

Mary looked down. 'I believed him,' she said in a subdued voice. 'I think he meant it.'

'Well, that's odd, isn't it? And then, he's been so bad-tempered recently,' Jean went on. 'He even shouted at your father the other day. And there was the way he went for you over Amati.'

Mary looked up then. 'But he always shouts at me. I hate it,' she added quietly, but with feeling. '*Hate* it.'

'It just seemed to me he was a bit more ratty than usual. I wondered if he was under stress . . . You know.'

'Under stress?'

'Heading for a breakdown or something.' But Jean could see she was getting nowhere, and gave it up. Probably Mary was too scared of John really to notice anything about him. 'Oh well, perhaps I'm wrong. I expect I'm worrying over nothing.'

'John's never ill,' Mary said.

'No, I know.' Jean was sorry she'd brought it up now. If Mary had believed her, it would only have made her more scared of John than ever, and that would have annoyed him more. He was the sort of person who was better if you stood up to him. 'I'll just keep an eye on him, anyway,' she said, as an exit line.

'I keep out of his way as much as possible,' Mary murmured.

Jean eyed her with a mixture of exasperation and pity. 'Yes, I expect you do,' she said.

Out in Ring 4 Newland was taking a highly excited Greyfriar over four practice jumps. The young horse was both strong and hot: Newland rode him in a pretty severe combination of bits and martingales, but still it was hard to hold him when he got het up. He needed a lot of exercise, but Jean couldn't ride him, so it meant he always had to wait for Newland himself to find time. And at this moment, Newland thought crossly, he ought to be concentrating on the two he was entering for the Tomatsu, the preliminary heats of which would be held this afternoon.

Out of the corner of his eye he saw Mary come out of the stable block with Amati and begin warming him up by trotting and cantering circles. A young man who had been leaning on the rails watching Newland – too far away for Newland to recognise – detached himself and went over to talk to Mary. In the moment that Newland's attention was distracted by this, the horse almost got away from him and Newland jerked its head back so hard it stumbled and almost fell. This only annoyed him more, and he leaned forward and smacked the horse across the ears and cursed it.

'Your brother looks in a bit of a stew,' Ben said to Mary. 'Is that a problem horse he's riding?'

'No, that's his youngster,' Mary said, halting Amati beside

him. The little horse flung his head up and down rapidly, and a fleck of foam hit Ben's chest. He removed it with a fingernail, and looked back towards Newland.

'You're kidding me? He's treating it a bit rough, isn't he? And that's a hell of a sharp bit for a young horse he's only just schooling.'

'Is it?' Mary said. 'I don't know, really. John always rides with bits like that.'

Ben was surprised. He watched the young horse growing more upset moment by moment, as Newland jerked again and again at its mouth. He was beginning to wonder how the greatest name in British showjumping got his fame. And did Mary really not have an opinion about it? Or was she just being loyal?

He turned and met her innocent gaze. Yes, that must be what it was. And she was very young: probably she hadn't enough experience to know whether her brother was right or not. Her innocence thrilled him, and the way she gazed at him as though he were the fount of all wisdom, for crying out loud! He loved her soft, pretty face. He loved her cool English voice – that accent drove him crazy! – and last night when he had kissed her: wow! In an American girl he would have thought it was a come-on from a hardened flirt, but with Mary he realised she was just so inexperienced she didn't know how she was affecting him. She was just being natural. It was a hell of a turn-on.

When he got back to the American cabins afterwards, Kim and Billie were sitting outside theirs drinking Cokes, and had laughed at him. 'How's Little Miss High Pockets?' Kim had said.

'Butter wouldn't melt,' Billie grinned.

'Oh, I'm not so sure,' Ben had replied loftily.

'Don't tell me you kissed her?'

'That's my business and hers.'

'Mind her brother doesn't find out!' Kim had jeered. 'He doesn't let her stay out after nine o'clock!'

'How you can fancy a little momma-baby like that I don't know,' Billie added.

'Of course you wouldn't understand,' Ben had said, goaded out of his normal restraint. 'Girls who've been round the block a few times forget what really attracts a man.' They were furious, and he was sorry afterwards he'd said it – but it was true, damn it! And Mary wasn't a momma-baby, she was just sweet and innocent and good, and he wanted to protect her against the world.

Amati was still jerking his head up and down, as far as it would go, in a way that looked like the repetitive behaviour of a caged animal, and though Ben had been trying to ignore it, the horse finally banged him painfully in the jaw with its head. 'I hope you don't think I'm interfering,' he said, 'but haven't you got your martingale too tight?'

Mary began to blush and her eyes flickered away from him and back. 'John says this is right.'

'Does he? Oh.' John again, thought Ben. That was the prime person she needed protecting against. He had to step carefully, though, given her loyalty to him. 'But, look, I was watching you circle just now, and I was thinking you'd got it so tight he couldn't balance himself properly.'

'Were you? I *thought* it was wrong,' Mary said eagerly. 'He felt all wrong to me, but John insisted and . . .' Her eagerness faltered. 'Well, he must know better than me, mustn't he? He says if I have it looser Amati will get away from me. He rushes his fences and jumps flat. And I have to do what John says.'

Ben took hold of the reins to keep the horse still, looking up. 'Don't be upset. I'm not trying to turn you against your brother. But you know, if the horse has got into bad habits, surely the right thing to do is to school him: lots of slow work to make him flex and bend his back. Tying his head down will only make him worse. It's not just me saying that: it's mainstream opinion, really. Your brother ought to know that. If you like I could have a word . . .'

110

He got no further. Unseen by either of them, Newland had ridden over to see what was going on, and had heard the last part of the exchange. Now he said furiously, 'Who the hell do you think you are, to come interfering with my sister?' His voice was so loud and angry Amati flung up his head and took two quick steps backwards.

Ben turned in surprise. 'I beg your pardon?' he said, to gain time more than anything.

Newland scowled horribly. 'What, are you deaf or stupid? I said how dare you come poking your nose in? Why don't you mind your own bloody business? What the hell do you know about it, anyway, sonny?'

'Look, I am in the American team,' Ben began, his own anger rising.

'You're still wet behind the bloody ears!' Newland interrupted. 'Half-arsed bloody kids, come over here telling people what to do, think you know it all! I was winning classes when you were still wetting yourself, so don't think you can tell *me* how to school my own sister's bloody horse. I know what your game is anyway, don't think I don't.'

'What are you talking about?' Ben said, his face reddening.

'You know bloody well!'

'No, I don't. Why don't you tell me?'

'I'll do more than tell you in a minute, you dirty-minded little—'

'John, stop it!' Mary cried, unable to bear it any more.

'You shut up! I'm dealing with this,' Newland snapped at her. Greyfriar tried to move away and he wrenched the horse's head round again, making it flinch with pain.

'Hey, take it easy!' Ben protested. 'Look, you'd better watch your step, you know.'

'Are you threatening me, sonny?'

'Stop calling me that!'

'Oh Ben, please!' Mary cried desperately.

'Don't worry, Mary, I'm going now. I see what you're up

against. I don't want to make things worse for you.' He turned back to Newland. 'But I have to say this. Showjumping is a small world, and you can't keep anything secret. If what I've seen here today is typical of your methods . . . Well, you'd better watch your step, that's all.'

'What's that supposed to mean?' Newland said angrily, but Ben walked away and did not stop or answer. 'What did he mean by that?' he demanded of Mary. 'What have you been saying to him, you silly bitch? What the hell has it got to do with him, anyway?'

Mary stared at Ben's retreating back with helpless pain, and then with growing fury. John was going to spoil it all! The first man who'd ever been interested in her, and John was going to drive him away! She turned on him, half speechless with fury.

'You leave him alone! He's my friend!'

John started at her rebellion. 'Friend, is it? We'll see about that!'

'Anyway, he's right,' Mary cried. 'He says the martingale's too tight, and I think it is too, and I don't care what you say, I'm going to ride my own way from now on.'

'Oh, are you?' Newland growled menacingly.

'Yes!' Mary cried defiance. 'And you can tell Dad, too. I don't care!'

'You will care! You bet I'll tell Dad! You ungrateful little cow, who d'you think bought the damned horse in the first place?'

Mary was beside herself now. 'You killed Dreams! You killed him! Well, you're not going to kill Amati!'

She dug her heels in, pulled Amati round and cantered away, leaving Newland momentarily nonplussed. It was like being attacked by a mouse.

Mary cantered Amati through a veil of tears. Never again, she vowed to herself, never again would she listen to anything John said! But even as she thought it, she doubted, knowing he was stronger-willed than her, and that she had no power to defy him or her father.

She halted in a quiet spot and slid off Amati to have a good cry against his neck. Only when the brief storm was spent did she remember Jean's words. *Was* John more angry and aggressive than usual? *Was* there something wrong with him? Stress, that good old standby word, the reason and excuse for everything. Or something else. Or was he just the same old John who had made her life a misery for years? It was hard for her to tell. From the inferior position you only ever saw the underside of the boot coming down on your neck.

Six

I t was, as the announcer ecstatically burbled, a truly international final jump-off for the Tomatsu Stakes, with four
countries represented. The tricky, winding course had really
sorted them out, and only five of the original fifty entrants had
survived: Sean McNally for Ireland on Cadence; John Bryan
for the USA on Franco; Franz Lohmann – the elder of the two
Lohmann brothers – for Germany on Eppi; and for the United
Kingdom, John Newland on Apache and Polly Morgan on
Taggert.

Newland and Lohmann were reckoned the favourites, Newland because of the enormous experience of both him and his
horse, and Lohmann because in the course there were several
sets of true parallels, the kind of jump the Germans never made
a mistake over. However, the jump-off was against the clock,
which always introduced an element of chaos to the natural
order; and there was a 'bogey' fence: a road closed, set at an
angle between two other fences, so that the competitor had to
thread through them to reach it, which made it difficult to get
the horse balanced in time for the take-off. A lot of riders had
come unstuck at the road closed, several of them ending up
inspecting its blue planks from very close quarters indeed; and
horses have an odd way of knowing which fences other horses
have spooked at.

The competitors' box was crowded, and behind, in the
collecting ring, the usual knot of followers had gathered around
each of the finalists: grooms, sponsors, owners, friends, rela-

tions, fans and press. Mary Newland was not at John's stirrup, and neither were any of his fellow horsemen, but he could hardly have noticed their absence, for it was to him that the press flocked, and it was he who was chosen for the pre-jump-off interview on BBC television.

Backed up against the logo screen with the mike held under his chin, he replied to the banal questions all the usual modest-but-confident things that were expected of him.

'Who are you tipping to win, John?'

'Oh, I don't know, Brian. I think we've all got a good chance.'

'You think it might be you going up for the prize tonight?'

'Well, of course I hope so, Brian, but there's some pretty tough competition out there.'

'Well, jolly good luck, John.'

'Thank you very much, Brian.'

But as he walked away to find his horse and mount up, Newland felt for the first time in years nervous, and uncertain of the outcome. He had drawn to go first, which of course put him at a disadvantage; but he had the most experienced horse, and he himself had won more than anyone else in speed competitions, had been placed twice as often as his nearest rival: so what had he to fear?

He looked at them under his eyebrows as he walked across the collecting ring. Dan Roberts was giving Polly Morgan advice which she was smilingly waving away. Bespectacled, painstaking Lohmann was checking his girth and stirrup leathers yet again before mounting to walk Eppi round. McNally was being gallant to Alison Neave and Chris Campbell simultaneously and they were helpless with laughter at his verbal gymnastics, while his groom and Bryan's were walking the two horses round together and discussing the difference in wages on either side of the Atlantic.

And where was Mary? Ah yes, there she was, in the competitors' box, cosied up to that bloody Watts kid. They had their heads so close together, mooning over each other, they practically had their tongues down each others' throats. Young bloody love! he thought with savage contempt. He'd have to see about that little situation. And the ungrateful little cow didn't even have the decency to come and wish him luck! Suddenly he felt alone and cold, unloved even in the midst of all this media adulation. He hurried to find his horse, almost as if it were a haven, one sure thing in a hostile world.

The ring steward called him at last. The spectators' lights dimmed and their voices sank to a murmur, the curtain was pulled aside and Newland rode Apache forward into the flood-lit ring. There was a burst of applause which drowned the loudspeaker's announcement of their two names and made Apache's ears flatten for a moment. The wise old horse stepped calmly across the ring, his white stockings catching the light showily, the bit rings glinting as he mouthed his bit. Silence settled over the arena. Newland saluted the box where the respective presidents of the British and American jumping federations were sitting with the Tomatsu party – the Tomatsu president had come over from Japan to present the prize – and then pushed Apache into a hand canter, waiting for the bell. He felt jumpy and on edge, and the silence, instead of exhilarating him as usual, oppressed him, as if everyone were whispering about him behind his back.

Well, he thought, if he had to go first, he would damn well give them a time to beat! His tension communicated itself to his horse, and when the bell rang Apache jumped forward as though stung. They hurtled across the ring at the first jump, and Apache took it like a hurdler. John crouched forward – he rode with the now old-fashioned Italian seat – and urged the horse on. An old hand at the game, Apache had memorised the course as he jumped it, and the sharp turns and twists did not throw him out. The bogey fence with its awkward pacing was no problem to him, and when Newland stood him off and gave him an extra kick, he went up like a rocket, tucking his feet up carefully, to clear it. Over the last fence, and then his ears flattened against the applause as he galloped the few yards through the finish.

'And a textbook round from John Newland and the veteran Apache,' said the announcer over the loudspeaker. 'A clear round in thirty-six point four, and that's really going to take some beating.'

It was fast, very fast. At that moment most people thought it was all over; and they seemed to be proved right by the rounds that followed. Lohmann went clear in beautiful style, but was six seconds slower. McNally went all out for it, as was expected of him, but had the bogey fence down, and was slower too. Bryan went clear and made a race of it, but made thirty-eight seconds dead. Then Polly Morgan went in with Taggert, with no one's money on her – except, of course, Bill's.

Taggert knew all about speed competitions, and being small and handy had an advantage over the horses that had gone before. It was immediately apparent that they were shaving inches off the course by their sharp turns, and the cheering grew to a deafening level as they hurtled through the finish, to be greeted by the incredulous tones of the announcer.

'Thirty-six point four! Unbelievable! It's a dead heat! The time is identical with John Newland's, and I don't think that's ever happened before in the jump-off of a speed competition!' His voice went off the scale, and there was a beat before he resumed. 'It remains to be seen what will happen now, whether they'll jump off again, or whether they'll share the prize.'

Polly, still breathless, and John Newland were being asked that very question in the collecting ring. Polly expressed herself happy to share. She didn't think either of them could jump the round faster than thirty-six point four, and that any further jump-off would be an anti-climax. Besides, the horses were tired.

Newland interrupted her with a cold glare. 'We'll jump off.'

'Eh? Oh, come on, John . . .'

'No, *you* come on! You know that short of a miracle you can't beat me, or even match me again over that course. That's why you want to share the prize. Not very sporting of you, is it?'

Polly gasped with surprise at his open rudeness. They had not been on particularly friendly terms at any time since she had broken off their engagement years ago, but she had never known him to be openly insulting, to her or anyone. Her face flushed slowly. 'If that's the way you feel,' she said, 'far be it from me to deny you any prize you can win by fair means. We'll jump off.'

'All right,' said the steward, and nodded to his assistant, who relayed the news to the judges' box and the announcer. 'It'll be the same course as before, and against the clock, of course. But if you should tie again—'

'There won't be another tie,' Newland said. 'I shall win.' And he strode away to mount Apache.

Polly and the steward exchanged a surprised glance, and the steward shrugged slightly.

'Shouldn't we be drawing for who goes first?' Polly asked.

'No, let him go first,' the steward said with a hint of dislike. 'The crowd will like it better that way, anyway.'

The news was travelling like fire through dry grass, and by the time Polly was mounted up again, everyone knew what had been said and by whom. 'What's up with him?' was the usual indignant reaction, to which comment Polly mostly shrugged. She had just the faintest trace of pity for him, suspecting he had come to the end of some personal tether and that she had simply been in the way when his elastic snapped. But it *was* only a trace.

Tom Emmerson came up to her stirrup and said, 'You'd better damn well win after that, Polly. I know I'm a completely impartial onlooker at this stage, but I hope the bastard falls off his horse.'

'Oh no, don't say that! You wouldn't want something awful to happen to poor old Apache, would you?'

'Anne said something like that,' Emmerson frowned. 'You don't mean you think he'd inflict cruelty on the horse?'

'What? After he threatened to have the ginger horse put down for tipping him off?'

Emmerson looked grave. 'It's too serious an accusation to repeat, even in fun.'

Polly *had* only been joking – well, mostly – but now she grew annoyed. 'Balls! Don't tell me. Go and talk to his sister. She'll tell you.'

'If you're saying what I think you're saying, it's a matter for the BSJA.'

'Try proving it.'

'That's exactly my point.'

Polly scowled theatrically. 'Oh, go away and stop trying to upset me! Do you want me to beat him or not?'

Emmerson grinned. 'Sorry. I'll make myself scarce. Good luck!'

To the knowing onlookers, there seemed something desperate about the way John Newland rode that final jump-off. His first round had been phenomenally fast, and even going all out, no one had been able to beat it. He couldn't possibly expect to go faster and still clear, especially on a tiring horse; yet when the bell went he went off hell for leather, cornering on two legs, jumping at impossible angles, anything to scrape a tenth of a second off the time. The first prize was eight thousand pounds, well worth winning – well worth not sharing – but there seemed more than that involved now. Newland himself hardly knew what it was, but he knew he had to win. Apache, brave, wise and willing, turned himself inside out to please, and as they raced through the finish the announcer said with a note almost of hysteria in his voice, 'Thirty-five point nine! John Newland has done the impossible and beaten his own time by point seven of a second! And now Polly Morgan and Taggert, and Polly has got to beat that time to win!'

'Gee, thanks for telling me,' Polly muttered, marvelling at the average sports commentator's talent for stating the obvious. She waited in the collecting ring for the curtain to be pulled aside. How could she possibly beat that? Her heart sank. She stroked Taggert's neck and thought, why should you be put through it all again? Poor old boy, you're tired out. I might as well resign. Second place is worth three thousand. Let him have his silly prize if it's that important to him.

But at that moment the curtain was drawn back and Newland passed her on his way out of the ring, and his smile of self-congratulation rankled in her mind. She sent Taggert forward with a light tap, and decided that even if they couldn't beat the time, they'd go down trying. The only place to save an extra second was between the third and fourth jumps, by turning inside rather than outside the parallel poles. But it was probably impossible. It would mean turning a right angle immediately on landing from the third, and even then you'd have virtually no run-up for the fourth. It was too tight. It was impossible. But if any horse in the world could jump from that angle and with no run-up it was Taggert. Anyway, she had nothing to lose: she couldn't be worse than second!

She set off over the straightforward first and second jumps. Tag knew the course by now and was automatically adjusting his pacing for the third, but she had to make him put in an extra stride so that he took off close and jumped high rather than wide. Two strides out she pulled him for a second and then sent him on. His ears went back to her questioningly as he popped the other foot down and took off. Too close! But no, he could manage that, he said, and did a neat vertical jump, landing close on the other side. At once Polly flung her weight over and wrenched him round with hands and legs. Taggert snorted with injured surprise, but turned on the pivot of his near hind, changing legs to dodge round the parallel poles. Two strides was all there was, and then they were under fence four.

It was too close, she thought, it was impossible. The horse had no impulsion after that sharp turn, the angle was all wrong, it was not going to come off. 'Come on!' she cried in desperation. Taggert's ears shot forward, he snorted, found an extra leg, and climbed air.

Polly went up his neck and threw the reins forward to give him head room, and the poles seemed to go by under her so close they almost grazed her nose. The landing nearly unseated her, but she knew from the audience that they had not hit it, and she drove Taggert on, knowing they had a real chance now. His neck was black with sweat, but the excitement galvanised him, and as they cleared the last jump the roar of the crowd made him flatten his ears and buck despite his tiredness.

'Absolutely unbelievable!' the announcer shrieked. 'And Polly Morgan goes clear in an unbelievable thirty-three point two to win this incredibly exciting Tomatsu Stakes jump-off, and what fireworks we've seen here tonight—'

The rest of his burble was cut off from Polly by her slightly uncontrolled exit through the curtains: Taggert was making a dash for it, and as he pulled up sharply in the collecting ring she almost fell off. At once she was surrounded by exclaiming, congratulating friends, and she sat panting and laughing, making much of her clever little horse. Not only to win, not only to beat Newland's time, but to beat it by more than two whole seconds! The best she had hoped for was to scrape in by a tenth of a second, but this was beyond anything!

She slid down from the saddle to be embraced and patted by Bill and Dan and Terry and various others, and when she had got her breath back she looked around for Newland. Ring etiquette dictated that he should congratulate her; but more than that, her win was so spectacular that she felt sure his temper would be appeased and he would say something generous, about Taggert if not about her herself. She spotted him a few yards away, already mounted, and went towards him with her hand outstretched; but he gave her a cold, angry look, pointedly ignoring the gesture, and turned Apache away with a harsh jab of the bit. Polly stopped abruptly, and there was a moment of silence as everyone saw what had happened. Then the voices resumed in an angry murmur. Polly found herself more surprised than upset. This was surely not normal behaviour, even for a competitive bastard like Newland; and in making himself so unpopular he was going to hurt himself more than her. She almost felt sorry for him.

Bill wanted to take Polly out for a celebratory meal, to which she had no objection, having lived mainly on sausages and eggs for the best part of a week; but when she suggested inviting Dan Roberts along, Bill scowled.

'I was rather hoping to have you to myself,' he said pointedly.

'Yes, that may be, but you did come down here to discuss the horse with him, and when else are you going to have the chance? Besides, I'm sure he'd like the chance of a decent meal, too, and it would be mean to leave him to celebrate alone.'

'Celebrate? What's he got to celebrate? As far as I can make out, he was equal sixth with about eighteen other people.'

Polly put her hands on her hips. 'Well!' she said. 'He's celebrating my win, of course. It's a matter of national pride.'

'Is it?'

'Yes: John Newland versus the human race.'

When it was put to him, Roberts agreed with alacrity, only asking that Chris Campbell be asked as a fourth.

'Howard's going away until Thursday, so she's all on her own,' he explained. 'I'll pay for her and me, and you can pay for you and Polly. How'd that be?'

Simpson was happier with the idea of a foursome, since the natural division that was bound to take place would separate Polly from Roberts: something that was becoming more and more his object.

'Right. Half an hour to wash and change? We'll meet at the bar and I'll drive us into town.'

It was a merry party that entered the rather exclusive little restaurant off George Street an hour later. They had all washed and changed so quickly that there had been time for a drink before they set off, which had worked on their natural propensity to relax after a hard day so that even Chris Campbell, who was normally very quiet in company, was cracking jokes. When they were seated the menus were passed round, but Polly pushed hers away and stuck her elbow on the table.

'I just haven't got the energy to read it. You order for me, eh Bill?'

'Oh, me too,' Chris agreed. Bill raised an eyebrow, and Dan Roberts shrugged and smiled.

'Go on, then, make it unanimous. Give the kitchen staff an easy time.'

The other eyebrow went up, for it would never have occurred to Simpson to consider the kitchen staff in an expensive restaurant, but he was happy enough to comply.

'All right. I usually have the steak tartare when I come here. It's a speciality of theirs, and it's a thing you can't get everywhere nowadays. Is that all right with everyone?'

'Oh, yeah, I can always eat steak,' Roberts said. 'Make mine well done, with extra chips.'

Simpson looked put out, and opened his mouth to explain, but Polly broke in, 'He's pulling your plonker, Bill. No more o' that ignorant-yokel stuff, Roberts, or you've had it.' She took him in an affectionate headlock, which, since his head ended up on her bosom, Roberts didn't mind at all.

Simpson, who had been thinking how lovely she looked in that sleeveless dress, with her thick shining plait hanging over one shoulder, and feeling quite mellow, had his balloon punctured. He finished ordering, and when the waiter left, said coolly, 'How about getting the business over with first, before the wine arrives?'

'Whatever you like,' Roberts said agreeably. Under the table his right knee was firmly pressed against Polly's left one, and she hadn't moved away. He didn't know whether it was because she hadn't noticed, or she liked it, but he was always the optimist, and was already thinking up excuses for getting her into his van later. 'I suppose Polly's told you what it is you've bought?'

'Murphy? Yes, she told me about that.'

'Actually,' Roberts went on, 'I wonder whether old John Newland's bad temper tonight wasn't partly due to me. I bumped into him this afternoon and couldn't help telling him that I'd got the horse he'd given up on, *and* what a horse it is. He didn't seem very pleased with the news.'

'I should think not,' Simpson said. 'But I wonder why he didn't recognise him?'

'Why should he? It was a long time ago, Murphy belonged to someone else, and there've been a lot of horses under the bridge since then. None of us recognised him.'

'You did,' Polly said.

'Not really. I just thought he had a faintly familiar look. I didn't know it was Murphy. No one knew.' Except Anne, he added inwardly, and then cursed himself for thinking of her again.

'Anyway,' Simpson went on, 'I've looked up Murphy's records, and he was brilliant in his day. The question is, has that day passed?'

'No reason why it should have,' Roberts said. 'He's not in his first youth, but showjumping's not like flat racing. A jumper's just hitting his form between ten and fifteen, and most of us ride horses much older than that.'

'And he's fit and healthy,' Polly added. 'The vet passed him A1.'

'So what's your conclusion?' Simpson asked. 'Can he be a top jumper again?'

'It depends whether I can break his bad habits and gain his confidence. He's had his nerve broken . . . Well, not broken, exactly, but bent, anyway. He won't obey me until he's learned to trust me. And until he trusts me he'll rush his fences, and you know what that means.'

'Well, do you think you can manage him?'

'That's for you to say . . . He's your horse.'

'I can't make a judgement on that,' Simpson said impatiently. 'I'm no horseman.'

'All right, but you have to decide if you want to put him in my hands.'

'And you have to decide if you want to take him on.'

Polly intervened, laughing. 'The pair of you!'

'What's so funny, Morgan?' Roberts said coldly.

'Each trying to push the decision on to the other. And you say women are indecisive.'

'I used to be indecisive,' Chris said pleasantly, 'but I'm not sure now whether I am or not.'

'Look,' Roberts said, trying to sound firm and manly, 'why don't you come down and watch me ride him, get an idea of how I handle him?'

'That's a good idea . . . But when?'

They wrangled dates for a while, but both were busy men, and when the suggested day and time was getting months into the future Chris, bored with the subject, cut through it all and said, 'What's wrong with tomorrow morning? There's nothing on here except some of the preliminary heats for the Grand Prix, and I know you're not riding, Dan, because you're in the same heat as me, which isn't until the after-noon.'

Roberts looked at Simpson. 'It suits me. I wanted to pop home anyway. What about you, are you free?'

He thought a moment. 'Yes, I can make it. I've got a lunch thing, but I can put that off.'

'I wish I could come.' Polly said. 'I'd love to see you ride him, now I know he's the famous Murphy.'

'Well, come then,' Roberts said hospitably.

'I can't. I must exercise Mackie, to get him loosened up for the heats.'

'Why can't Terry do it?'

'She'll be riding Taggert first thing, and then she's taking some hours off.'

Roberts rolled his eyes. 'Hours off in the middle of a show? I don't know why you keep that girl.'

'She's got some relatives in Manchester she wants to see. And I probably won't – keep her, I mean. The lure of the old sod will call her away ere long.'

'The old what?' Roberts said, with a dangerous gleam in his eye.

'Well, look,' Chris said hastily, 'If that's your only problem, I can take Mackie out for a couple of hours, if you like. If you trust me with him.'

'Would you? Oh, that'd be great. Of course I trust you. Actually, you're the only person I would leave him with. We ride pretty much alike. Thanks a million, Chris.'

'That's all right. A pleasure.'

'OK, so that's settled, then,' said Simpson.

'Thank God. Now we can have some wine,' said Chris. 'How about pouring, one of you men?'

Chris and Polly went off to the loo together. 'Why do women do that?' Bill asked, mystified.

'They want to talk about us, of course,' Dan said with supreme confidence.

In this case, he wasn't far wrong. While Polly washed her hands and Chris fiddled with her hair in front of the mirror, the latter said, 'Is there something going on between you and Dan?'

'Only the usual. Why do you ask?'

'Oh, just that Bill seems to be getting a bit upset.'

'Does he?' Polly was surprised.

'He's been giving Dan filthy looks.'

'Oh, he always does that. He's jealous of him. God knows why. I give him no cause.'

'Poor Bill,' Chris said. 'It must be a tough situation for him.'

Polly met her eyes indignantly. 'What about poor Polly? Isn't it tough for her, too?'

'But he's in love with you, so you hold all the cards. I wonder . . .' She hesitated.

'What?'

'I don't want to sound interfering.'

'Oh, go on. We don't have any secrets from each other, do we?'

'I don't know about that,' Chris said seriously. 'But, only because I'm interested in you: I do wonder what you really feel about Bill. I mean, I know you're not callous—'

'Thank you!'

'Really, I do know that; but you keep the poor man dangling. Do you care for him?'

'Of course I do. I'm very fond of Bill. He's the nicest, kindest man I know.'

'You'd miss him if he went away . . . Permanently, I mean.'

Polly looked startled. 'He's not going to go away.'

'You could lose him,' Chris said. 'Oh, don't worry, I don't mean I know anything. I'm just saying, it could happen. And how would you feel then?'

Polly stared at her own reflection. 'I don't know. I *would* miss him. If it weren't for the situation, the way it's come about . . . If only I'd met him some other way . . .'

Chris had wondered sometimes – knowing a bit about Polly's background from long girl sessions in hotel bedrooms – whether Bill wasn't taking the place for her of the father she had never been able to gain the approval of. Polly's father had died without ever saying he was proud of her. Bill was an older man, a man of authority and power; and, in a way, in authority over her, since he owned her horses and controlled the purse strings. Chris wondered if that didn't complicate what was in any case a complicated situation. But she saw Polly's troubled expression and the tense line of her shoulders and thought this was not the moment to say any of this.

Instead, she said, 'You are so lucky that he isn't married. At least that's one problem you don't have to think about.'

Polly realised, with a return of her usual warm sympathy, that she was not the only one in a tangled web. 'Oh, poor Chrissy, you're right. I'm sorry. It must be awful for you.'

'In some ways,' Chris said. 'But I'm kind of used to it, in a way. And there's nothing to be done about it.'

Polly put an arm round her shoulders. In the course of those same girl sessions, she had learned more about Chris's life than anyone, except perhaps her twin sister Phil, knew. Chris had fallen in love with Howard Meak when she was fifteen and just a horse-mad groupie; fallen in love with the distant image of him, as other girls fell in love with pop stars or film stars. He had been her pin-up for years as she rode in juvenile classes, and gazed on his wonderfulness from afar – or rather, from the ring-side of the adult competitions. She had never expected anything to come of it.

In real life, she and her twin, having left school at sixteen, joined an older friend, Keith Arnold, in setting up a hacking stables and trying to make a go of it. Keith had the initial capital, and the twins provided the hard work, while Chris contributed her prize money to the cause.

When she was eighteen she began to compete in adult classes, and occasionally came up against her heart-throb, Howard Meak, and was thrilled if ever he spoke to her, just as she would have been to be addressed by Mel Gibson – whom she thought Howard rather resembled. Two years passed in this manner. Occasionally she met young men, and occasionally they asked her out, but it was never a big thing. Her life was busy and satisfying, and there just wasn't time in it for romance. Besides, she was devoted to her twin, and would have hated to part from her, or break up the three-way friendship that underpinned the stables.

The rift came when – out of the blue, it seemed to her, which just showed how blind she had been – Phil and Keith announced that they were going to get married. They had been in love for ages; had been sleeping together, in fact, though they had kept it from Chrissy for much the same reasons.

They didn't want anything to change – but it *had* changed, and Chris felt uncomfortable with the situation. She felt she had to get out, and since she didn't earn enough as a competitor to support herself, she looked around for a job. Phil begged her not to go, was hurt that she wanted to; feelings grew tender on both sides; things were said that should not have been said. Chris was trying to spoil things for her, said Phil; no, it was Phil who was spoiling things, said Chris. Phil had been underhand, keeping secrets; Chris was jealous of her, that's what it was. Keith tried to keep the peace and only inflamed matters. A coolness developed between the previously devoted sisters.

Then in the course of a sharp exchange of words one day, Keith reminded Chris that Sunny belonged to the business, not to her personally, and she lost her temper and walked out, saying they could keep the horse and the stables, she didn't need them, and she didn't want to see them again.

She went back to her parents' house while she looked for a job, and it was then that Howard Meak stepped into the picture. He wanted a groom and rider who he could trust to exercise and school his leading strings, and hearing of Chrissy's plight and knowing her quality, he offered her a job. It was perhaps unwise of her to accept, though it was also perhaps too much to expect that she would refuse the chance to be near her idol. She went to Mitton Abbey to work his horses and bask in his presence, and in the course of so much exposure to her god, discovered he was an ordinary human being with feet of clay. He also had a wife.

Mitton Abbey was a big spread, laid out around an old house that pretty well qualified as a stately home, though it was not a family seat. The Meaks had bought it when they married, with Mrs Meak's money: they were both 'county', but his family had nothing but their name and looks. The staff lived in various flats and cottages around the estate – Chris shared a flat above the stables – and mostly they had little to do with the house or the mistress of it. But through working so closely with Howard, and because of her different status, Chris was quite often up at the house and was even sometimes invited to meals there.

It was a torment to see him in his own home, in company with his wife. Her teenage dream had become reality, and her silly, romantic infatuation with a pin-up image had dissolved: she was badly and deeply in love with a real person; and that real person was married. However hard it was, she kept her feelings hidden. She liked Mrs Meak, and it would be wrong of her to do anything that might hurt her or jeopardise the marriage; and in any case, though Howard was kind to her, and she knew he liked her, he gave her no reason to think he saw her as anything but his employee.

For eighteen months she lived with the painful situation – painful but irresistible, like touching a mouth ulcer with your tongue – until one day she and Howard brushed up against each other accidentally in a loose box, turned the same way at the same moment, and *wham*! Without knowing by whose volition, she found herself in his arms, locked in a passionate kiss. It seemed he had noticed her after all.

After that there had been nothing for it but to leave. She could not go on living in such close proximity to him, and under the eyes of his wife, feeling as she did about him and knowing he was attracted to her. She went back to her parents' house. Phil and Keith, hearing about it, hurried to her to make things up. They begged her to come back. They missed her, and Sunny was pining for her. Apologies, hugs and kisses followed, and Chris went back to the stables, where the three took up their old lives and their old, comfortable relationship.

Chris had gone back into the ring, not only with Sunny but bringing on other horses for the stables, and riding for other owners. As a fellow competitor, she was on a level with Howard, and they met as equals in the ring and on the circuit.

Since then their relationship had grown steadily more important to both of them. The natural intimacy they had built up through working closely together was augmented by her old love and his new one, and they were seen together everywhere. Probably everyone in the business except Polly thought they slept together.

But Chris couldn't do it. He was married, and he had never suggested to her that he should become *un*-married. She didn't know whether that was because he was a Catholic, or because he didn't love her enough, or for some other reason; but she loved him too much to settle for being his mistress, even if it weren't just plain-and-simple *wrong*. And in any case, she knew his wife: she even met her sometimes at shows, and was always greeted by her with friendliness. She couldn't repay kindness with betrayal.

All the same, it had been no bed of roses the last couple of years, and there were times when she thought that what they were doing was almost as bad. Even if technically they were not committing adultery, to enjoy each others' company on terms of such intimacy was practically the same thing, especially as everyone else thought they *were* lovers; and it was all still happening behind Mrs Meak's back. Chris was the *other woman*, even if she had the name without the game. And it made it no easier for her that Howard seemed to be willing to take what he could get and live with the situation. He had protested sometimes, asked her now and then, but did not press her when she refused; and never had he suggested that the solution was for them to get married. She couldn't ask him why. She was too afraid of losing him. She loved him obsessively, and if this was all she could have, then so be it.

So, with Polly's sympathetic arm round her shoulders, she shrugged and said, 'At least I can be with him. That's really all that matters. If I were never to see him again, I'd die.'

'I expect you have more of him than his wife, anyway,' Polly said, to comfort her. 'He really loves you. I'm sure theirs is just a token marriage.'

But that was something Chrissy didn't want to think about. Because if it was such a token marriage, why wouldn't he leave it?

What was meant to be a work-out turned out to be more in the line of a battle between Roberts and Murphy. The ginger horse had had several days' rest and was feeling full of himself. During the earlier part of the session he was very fresh, spooked at every shadow and threw in half a buck at every change of cadence. When the second part of the session began and Roberts tried to get him to jump, the real trouble started. At first he seemed merely unwilling, but when Roberts insisted, he became apprehensive, and then fear made him stubborn.

True to his principles, Roberts was riding him only on a very mild bit, and since the horse was very big and very strong, he was hard to hold. He twisted and baulked, ran out, and carted his rider many times round the paddock. When finally brought up to a jump he refused. Patiently, Roberts re-presented him. The fence was a substantial oxer, and he jumped it paukily, hitting it and producing a shower of twigs, frightening himself so that he took the next fence, a low pole, in a huge, unseating leap.

Simpson watched gravely, not understanding much of what was going on; Polly watched with her hands clenched, longing to intervene, to call advice, despite knowing that Dan knew better than her what to do. Roberts rode quietly and patiently, firmly correcting every wrong move and waiting for the explosion. He knew a crisis had to be reached. The horse was growing frustrated, and, like a child, would provoke a showdown in order to test the boundaries; and like a child, he would do it in the hope that the boundaries would stand firm. Roberts knew this horse, knew it instinctively as one can know a lover. Murphy was a big-hearted, bold creature whose confidence and pride had been dented. He wanted to jump, and needed to be mastered, but no cruelty would conquer him. Let him trust, and he was yours for ever, but he would sense fear or doubt in his rider as he would smell fire.

It was the wall which did it. The wall is a jump that a horse needs trust for, because he can't see the other side of it, so he's jumping into the unknown. This was not a high wall, but Murphy refused it four times, and when Roberts brought him to it for the fifth time, he broke away and started bucking. And what bucks! Polly watched dry-mouthed. As soon as his feet touched the ground from one buck he went up again, snapping like a great steel spring in an explosion of energy. At the fourth, Roberts went flying. He landed easily, shoulder and side, and got up still holding the reins. Murphy flinched backwards from him as he approached, expecting to be hit, but Roberts only stroked him. He stood to be mounted, but as soon as Roberts was in the plate he was off again.

This time Roberts came off at the second buck, never having properly got his seat. He hit the ground with an audible thud and lost the reins. Polly jumped down and caught Murphy without too much trouble, and held him while Roberts mounted again. She could feel the horse's tension like the vibration of a generator.

'He's going to go again as soon as I let go,' she warned.

'I'm all right,' Roberts said tersely. 'Just keep out of the way.'

He waited until she was back on the gate before giving Murphy the aid to walk on. Instantly the horse exploded into action, putting everything into his bucks this time, all four feet off the ground at once and with a twist in the middle that looked almost professional. Eventually, inevitably, Roberts came off. This time it was a few seconds before he got up, and Polly saw that there was blood on the side of his face. She was about to jump down to catch the horse but Roberts signalled her abruptly to stay away.

'This is getting us nowhere,' Simpson said to Polly. 'I think we ought to call it a day.'

'Be still. He knows what he's doing,' Polly said, though she wished she believed it completely. She didn't know which of the handsome creatures she felt more anxious about, but certainly it was Dan's face that was the more vulnerable. She found she minded more than she had expected about that blood.

Roberts walked up to Murphy, who stood still, watching him with a white-ringed eye. The horse's legs were trembling and his ears were going up and back in double time, but he let Roberts catch the reins. The man stroked his neck soothingly, to show he wasn't going to punish him, then mounted and turned him towards the jump. Now it was no longer fear that made him refuse, it was pride only. Almost unwillingly he ran out and began to buck again, and Roberts could have sat it out if his legs hadn't been so tired. He fell heavily, and there was an appreciable pause before he got slowly to his feet.

Polly had thought Murphy would give in the last time, and now she called out, despite herself, 'Dan, that's enough, surely that's enough?' But Roberts only shook his head.

Simpson watched in silence. There seemed to him now something horrible about this battle, but fascinating, too. Beside the huge horse, Roberts's burly frame looked almost fragile. There was blood and mud on his face and it looked as though one of his eyes was going to black; his clothes were awry and he moved stiffly, as though he was feeling his bruises. How could Polly bear to see him getting hurt? Maybe, he thought with faint hope, it meant she wasn't so very attached to him after all. She hadn't really tried to stop it – not very hard, anyway – and if it went on, Roberts was probably going to get hurt some more. In reason, the horse, being ten times his strength, ought to win.

But now Roberts walked up to the trembling animal, caught the reins, and once more petted and soothed him. For a moment more Murphy remained aloof, and then quite suddenly he broke. His ears shot forward and he dropped his head and thrust his face into Roberts's chest, as once he had done to Mary Newland.

Polly's inheld breath was let out in a sigh, and tears came to her eyes, which she rubbed quickly away before turning to smile at Simpson. 'That should be it.'

Roberts stroked the horse and murmured to it until it stopped shaking, and then, with considerable effort, gathered up the reins and mounted. The difference might not have been obvious to an onlooker, but Roberts could feel it: the flow of cooperation between them was as distinct as audible music or a visible river. He walked Murphy forward, trotted, and then put him at the low poles, something he could clear even in his weary state. They jumped from a gentle canter, cleared it easily, and then Roberts pulled up, made much of the horse, slid from the saddle and led him back to the gate.

'You look as if you've been in a fight,' Polly said shakily.

'What else would you call it?' Roberts said cheerfully.

'I've never seen an exhibition like it,' Simpson said. 'I have to tell you, I was for calling it off, but Polly said you'd master him. Is it all over now?'

'The worst. He'll never be so mixed up again.'

'Mixed up?'

'I suppose it was a bit like a nervous breakdown,' Roberts said, stroking the cheek of the weary horse who leaned very slightly against him. 'He wanted to jump but he was afraid to. He didn't want to defy me but he felt he had to. He was a crazy mixed-up kid, but he'll be all right now.'

'Well, it seems clear you're the right man to ride him,' Simpson said. 'How long before you can get him back in the ring?'

'A few weeks, no more,' Roberts said, and to Simpson's expression of surprise he added, 'After all, he's not a novice, and he's fit. I think the best way back for him is for us to get used to each other doing the real thing. Messing about in paddocks will only bore him and encourage him to misbehave. A few weeks intensive work, and then go for it, that's my view. But it's for you to say, ultimately. You'll be the one paying his expenses.'

Simpson nodded. 'Right. Then go for it. No point in keeping a potential winner out of the ring. So you'll take him on – subject to our agreeing terms?'

'Oh, I'm not a hard man to satisfy,' Roberts grinned. 'I'll take him on. I'd like to have him ready to take to the New York show: the big ring will just suit a scopey horse like him.'

Polly scratched behind Murphy's ears while he nibbled thoughtfully at her buttons. 'Wow, d'you hear that, old boy? You're back in the big time!'

'We hope,' said Roberts, and moved his left shoulder gingerly.

Seven

On their arrival back at the showground, the security guard came hurrying out from the gate, eager to be first with the bad news.

'Oh, Miss Morgan, they've been trying to get hold of you. There's been a bit of an accident with your horse.'

Polly's blood ran cold. 'What? Which horse? Not Mackie?'

'Yes, that was the one. It seems Christobel Campbell was riding him out—'

'She was exercising him for me,' Polly answered the faint question in his voice.

'Oh, right. Well, I'm afraid she took a bit of a tumble. She's in hospital with concussion and the horse is lame.'

'Oh God! What happened?'

'I don't know. I'm sorry, I haven't got all the details. But her groom would know: she was out with her.'

'Where is she?'

'Well, she was at the hospital, but I think I did see her come through about half an hour ago. Most likely she'd be down with the horses.'

'Has the vet been? No, never mind, I'll find out when I get there.' It was obvious he hadn't much information.

When they reached the stable block, they found Chris's groom, Lesley, with the vet in Mackie's box changing the cold dressings. She looked up as they arrived, and quickly came out to meet them. Polly saw at once that her face was white and strained and her eyes were red where she had been crying.

137

'Oh, Polly!' she cried. 'I'm so sorry!' .

Polly, almost as white herself, patted her shoulder. 'How's Chris?' she managed to ask.

'She's all right. She's got concussion and a cracked collar bone. They're keeping her in overnight because of the concussion, but they say she'll be fine. She was asleep when I left her. I'm going back to see her tonight. Oh Polly, I'm so sorry about Mackie!'

'How bad is it?' Polly asked. Mackie heard her voice and looked over his shoulder to whicker softly to her. She went into the box and went to his head, and he nudged her, feeling very sorry for himself. She repeated her question to the vet.

'Bad enough,' he said, without looking up. 'It looks to me as if a car touched him and he went down.'

'Jesus!' Polly breathed.

'He's lost a slice of skin on his shoulder, and there are other cuts and abrasions consistent with a fall. They're fairly superficial, though. The serious bit is that he's wrenched his shoulder, presumably as he fell, and strained his upper foreleg. I've had the portable x-ray over him and there's nothing broken, thank God. Has he had his anti-tet? Your groom wasn't around to ask.'

'Yes, of course.'

'Good. I've cleaned him up and given him an antibiotic shot, and now it's a matter of rest and cold poultices to reduce the leg. You'll have to keep him on a low diet and make sure he doesn't move around too much.'

'Oh God,' Polly said again, miserably. Mackie nuzzled her, and leaned against her, closing his eyes with content now she was back.

'He's a bit dopey at the moment,' the vet went on. 'I gave him a shot to sedate him. I'll give him another tomorrow: best to keep him lethargic for the first few days, to give that shoulder a chance.'

'How long will it be?' she managed to ask at last.

'Until he's fit? You should be able to exercise him gently after about two weeks, and with luck you might work him up to jumping in, say, a month to six weeks. But it's early to say, really. Shoulders can be tricky.' He glanced up at her. 'You're lucky. He could easily have been killed.'

'Yes, I know. Thanks,' she said. She went out again to where Lesley stood drooping, waiting for the inquisition. 'All right, tell me what happened.'

'There was nothing we could have done, honestly. We went into the woods for a hack – you know, the woods at the back of the showground. Chris was riding Mackie and I was on Cockerel. We'd got to a narrow part of the track where we had to go single file. Chris went first, and I was holding Cockie back, because he was fresh and he tried to race Mackie if I let him get too close.'

Polly nodded in appreciation of the point. 'Go on.'

'And then without any warning, this firework went off. A banger or something. It made a terrible noise. Went off right under Mackie. Someone must have thrown it at him. He went mad . . . Just took off. I had a terrible job holding Cockie. Chris stayed on at first, but she hit a low branch and got knocked out of the saddle. I thought she'd get up. I was still trying to hold Cockie back: he wanted to bolt as well. When she didn't, I realised she was out cold, and I didn't know what to do.'

Polly understood her predicament. All her instincts would tell her to go after the loose horse, while her humanity urged her to dismount and go to Chris. 'So what did you do?'

Lesley chewed her lip miserably. 'I didn't know how badly hurt she was. I didn't know what to do for the best. I didn't think I could hold Cockie if I got down so I thought I'd better get help. So I rode on to the gatehouse.'

'Which way had Mackie bolted?' Roberts asked.

'The same direction. I thought he'd be stopped there, that someone would have caught him, but when I got there the gate was open and the gatekeeper said he hadn't seen him till it was too late and he'd gone charging through on to the road. I told him about Chris and he said he'd call an ambulance and go back to her, so I went after Mackie.'

'Did you see who threw the firework?' Roberts asked.

'Well, not really. Only a glimpse. Not enough to recognise him.'

'Him?'

'I saw a man running away. But he was through the other side of the hedge, so I only just saw the shape of him through it.'

'You're sure it was a man, though? Not a child?'

'I think it was too big for a child. I know I remember thinking it was a man, but Cockie was going round in circles and I was worried about Chris . . .'

'I understand,' Polly said, taking pity on her. 'I'm sure you did all you could. Tell me about Mackie.'

'Well, I followed him as best I could. I saw his marks on the road, and there wasn't any other way he could have gone at first. But then there were some side turnings, and I couldn't tell which way he'd gone. I searched for ages, but there was no one around to ask, and I couldn't find any sign of him. And I was worried about Chris, so in the end I couldn't think what to do except phone the police. Well, they knew about Chris because of her being taken into Casualty, but they didn't know about Mackie, so I gave them a description and they said they'd make enquiries and send out a squad car. So I gave up and went back.'

She looked from face to face like a condemned prisoner, and what could they do other than comfort her? In her situation, what would they have done?

'So how was he found?' Polly asked.

'Someone rang the police, and they rang the showground, and one of the stewards rang to tell me at the hospital. He was found wandering around a housing estate about three miles away, but he was already lame. Some woman caught him and took him into her garden and rang the police. The committee sent a box for him from the ground. They don't know how he got lamed. The vet thinks he got mixed up with a car, but the police say nobody's reported an accident.'

'That's about par for the course these days,' Simpson muttered sourly. 'Never admit anything, no matter what.'

Once they had seen Mackie settled, Simpson drove Polly to the hospital to see Chris; Roberts had to get ready for his heat for the Grand Prix. They found Chris groggy but reasonably herself, though worried and feeling guilty about Mackie. She didn't remember anything about the accident so had nothing to add to Lesley's story; they reassured her that Mackie would be fine and left it at that. Her sister arrived while they were there and told them that she would be taking her home the next morning, since she wouldn't be able to ride for a few days.

'So I won't be riding in the team event after all,' Chris said, smiling faintly at Polly. 'I expect you'll be picked instead. Good luck!'

Having driven Polly back to the showground, Simpson had to take his belated departure, business calling him back to London. Roberts had qualified in his heat, which was the good news; Polly, of course, would not now be riding in the Grand Prix, with Mackie injured. Terry was back from her time off, and Polly had to go over the whole story again for her, which depressed her further.

Later, she sat with Roberts in the bar over two rather gloomy halves of bitter.

'So what do you think?' he asked at last. 'A nut? An anti-horse nut?'

'Possible, I suppose. Though in that case, why only one firework? Why not both horses? Why not all the horses who've been exercising in the woods?'

'So you think it was specific, do you?'

'Think? I don't think anything.'

'But who has a grudge against Chris? Does she have any enemies?'

'Not that I know of . . . But how can I say?'

'Howard Meak's wife, maybe?' Roberts suggested drily.

'Lesley said it was a man.'

'She might have hired a hit man.'

Polly looked reproachful. 'It's not funny, you know. Anyway, I've told you there's nothing going on between Chris and Howard. Nothing physical, anyway.'

'So you say.'

'But it's true! Chris told me.'

He shrugged. 'Even if it's true, that would seem to be the least of Mrs Meak's problems.'

Polly didn't argue. Why was it always so difficult for anyone to believe that people were *not* sleeping together? It was a cynical bloody age, that was what. And in fairness, Polly only just believed it herself, and she knew Chrissy very well. What, in that case, were they saying about her and Dan at that very moment? Or – she looked around – about Ali Neave and Michael Baker, who were propping up the bar over there; or Mary Newland and Ben Watts, snuggled up together in the farthest corner? Gossip, she thought: what a killer it could be.

And talking of killers . . . She mused in silence for a while, and then said uncomfortably, 'Dan, I've just thought. Chris was riding Mackie.' Roberts looked up but did not speak. 'Mackie's saddle cloth is a very distinctive yellow check. And Chris and I are much of a size, and both fair. From a distance – or through a hedge – you mightn't be able to tell us apart.'

She hoped he would pooh-pooh the idea, but he only nodded seriously. 'Well, but it comes down to the same question: who has a grudge against you?

'I don't know, but it's a horrible thought.'

He looked at her, and saw that she was really shaken. Well, there were a lot of nuts about. Everyone knew stories of horses that had been maliciously wounded, and any celebrity, even minor celebrities like them, knew they could be a target. Who ever would have thought, for instance, that Jill Dando would be murdered? After her, no one felt safe. He was about to give Polly some robust comforting to put her mind at ease, when it occurred to him that here was the perfect excuse for him to get what he had been thinking about all week.

'You'd better sleep in my van tonight.'

She looked at him, and any number of things went through her head, about his possible intentions and her subconscious ones, and the different likely outcomes of what might or might not be an innocent offer – *innocent? Dan Roberts? Get real, girl!* – But she really did feel scared and depressed, and as for the rest, she would just have to play it by ear.

'All right, thanks. But what about Terry and Hazel?'

'Well, they're not targets, are they? But I'll tell Hazel to keep the door locked just in case, and have a talk with the night duty guard, make sure he keeps an eye on the van.'

Polly changed from beer to scotch to fortify herself against the cold thought of perhaps having a secret enemy, and by the time they went back to Roberts's van, she had warmed up and calmed down considerably, and was more sleepy than apprehensive. In fact, she had half a mind to say her fears were silly and she might as well go and sleep in her own van; but only half a mind. The other half was fancying handsome Dan more than ever, especially with a couple of scotches to lower its inhibitions. And she was lonely. It was a long time since she had been held in a man's arms.

But first there was the dance of etiquette to get through, of pretending they were not going to sleep together, taking turns in the tiny lavatory, undressing with the lights out and their backs turned, bidding each other a polite good night and getting into separate bunks. It's really rather a farce, Polly thought sleepily; and there was Bill to think about, wasn't there? – though she had been trying hard not to. Perhaps it would be just as well to leave things as they were after all. She began to drift down into sleep.

Roberts lay awake listening to the noises of the camp around them, the throbbing of his own blood, the soft rustlings as Polly turned over a few feet away. Now he had her at his mercy, so to speak, he was suddenly nervous of taking the next step. The great lothario, Dan Roberts, with a hundred notches on his bed post! Yes, but this was Polly, his old friend, and it was hard to put a move on an old friend. Suppose he had misread her signs? He would lose not only face but probably her friendship too. One by one the outside noises died away as the village settled down to sleep, and Roberts began to feel sleepy too.

Suddenly Polly whispered sharply into the darkness, 'What was that?'

He was instantly wide awake. 'What was what?'

'That sound. I heard a sound.'

They both listened tensely to the silence. 'I don't hear anything. What sort of sound was it?'

'I don't know. It was a sort of . . . rustling. As if someone was outside, maybe, brushing against the van. I don't know. It's not there now.'

'Probably nothing. Do you want me to look outside?'

She hesitated. 'No, it's all right. It was probably just the metal contracting or something.'

There was a pause, and then he heard her sigh.

'Can't sleep?' he asked hopefully. She made an indeterminate sound. He took the plunge. 'Want some company?'

A long pause. It seemed like several hours to him. Then she said, 'Do you?'

Relief flooded through him. 'My bunk's bigger than yours. Come on over.'

In the darkness he could just see the outline of her as she crossed the small space, and then she was sliding in beside him, warm and soft and scented and female.

Polly had crossed the space still telling herself they might only be going to share the bunk as friends comforting each other; but the illusion – or delusion – did not last beyond the moment when she got in beside him. The touch of his big, hard, hot body fused the two halves of her mind again, with the reprehensible half in charge. She eased herself into his arms and felt them close round her.

Roberts kissed anything he could find to get his bearings, and then worked his way around to her mouth. He found she was smiling. 'What?' he said, startled.

'I was just counting how many years it's taken us to get around to this,' she said.

'That was your fault. I was always willing,' he said blandly.

'It had better be worth it,' she warned him.

'Trust me,' he said. He found her mouth again and they connected like sea anemones. His tongue slid into her mouth. After a few minutes she disconnected to sit up and pull off her nightdress. He'd gone to bed in underpants for decency's sake, and they were gone by the time she lay down again.

'Now then,' she said in a let's-get-down-to-business way; and so they did.

Mary Newland had jumped on the Wednesday, both in the junior class and in a heat for the Grand Prix. She'd had no hope of succeeding in the latter, but Amati ought to have got her at least a place in the former. In fact she had come nowhere. The competition was fierce, but Mary didn't think of that. She was consumed with guilt, and anxious to avoid her brother, because just before she had gone into the ring she had loosened off her martingale by a couple of holes. At the time she had convinced herself John would never notice, but since she had not been placed she was now just as convinced that he was gunning for her.

To keep out of his way she had taken Amati out for a hack with Ben instead of exercising in one of the rings. John, having given Apache and Idaho their brief work-out, was riding Greyfriar in the exercise ring nearest the leisure centre, giving him a lesson in elementary obedience. It was around half past ten, the time when the riders traditionally gathered in the leisure centre for their mid-morning coffee, and Howard Meak, just back from his business trip, paused on his way there to watch Newland. Greyfriar was very fresh, and Meak happened to arrive at the precise moment when Newland began to hand out some heavy-handed punishment for insubordination.

Meak, an urbane man whose wealthy 'county' wife's fortune underpinned his showjumping career, had been friendly all along with Newland. They were of an age and had entered first-class competition at the same time, and had been thrown together a good deal in consequence. In particular they had shared their first Olympic Games experience twelve years ago, and since the British team had been outstandingly successful that year, it was natural that their names had been linked in the minds of the public ever since.

He watched Newland for a moment or two, frowning. He believed in firmness, and it was not for one professional to interfere with another's training, but it looked to him as if Newland had lost his temper, and out of friendship he felt he ought to stop him exposing himself in this public place. So he called out, 'Hey, John! Over here a minute!'

Newland stopped, hesitated, and then rode over with a sour look on his face. 'What do you want?'

It was not inviting, but Meak was not deterred. He caught Greyfriar's reins, noting the horse's flinch, the sweat on its neck and the wildness of its eye, and said quietly, 'Time to cool off a bit, eh? I think you've got a bit carried away, haven't you?'

'What the hell are you talking about?' Newland said violently.

'Bashing the old nag about a bit, weren't you?' Meak said lightly. 'Doesn't do, old son, especially in mixed company.' He flickered a warning glance towards the leisure centre block. 'Anyone might come out.'

'What the hell business is it of yours? And take your hand off my horse.'

146

'Just a bit of friendly advice, old man,' Meak said, surprised by his reaction.

'Well here's a bit of friendly advice for you, *old man*: mind your own bloody business!' Newland wrenched Greyfriar's head away and rode off. Meak stared after him for a moment, then shrugged and went on into the leisure centre.

It was early, so many of the tables were empty, but having collected his coffee Meak saw Mary Newland and went to join her. She was sitting with that young American rider. What was his name? Oh yes, Watts, wasn't it, Ben Watts. 'Mind if I join you?'

'Oh . . . yes. I mean no . . . Of course, do,' Mary said, her cheeks reddening. 'Um, do you know Ben Watts? Ben, Howard Meak.'

Her discomposure told Meak the whole story. So, there was a spot of romance going on, was there? Well, good for her. About time too. She was a pretty little thing, if a bit milk-and-water for his taste. With an inward smile he nodded a greeting to Watts and sat down, leaned back in his chair in an attitude of relaxation and, stirring his coffee, said in a casual, unconcerned tone, 'What's bitten your esteemed brother, Mary? He seems to be in a bit of a state.'

He would have had to be blind not to notice Mary's instant start and stare of guilt. 'I don't know what you mean,' she said.

'Well, he was hauling that nice youngster of his about a bit, so I stopped and said – just in a friendly way, y'know – how about easing up a bit? And he hit the roof.'

'What . . . what did he say?'

'Bit my head off. Told me to mind my own bloody business. Well, perfect right to, of course. Just seemed a bit on the steep side to an old friend. Thought he seemed a bit agitated.'

He sipped his coffee, watching Mary under his eyelashes. She exchanged a glance with Ben, and said in an attempt at insouciance, 'I think he's just upset that I didn't do well last night.'

'Didn't you? I didn't know. Only just got back. Bad luck! I suppose John sees you as his protegée?'

Ben regarded the older man minutely, judging for himself how much shrewdness lay under that bland exterior. Meak seemed to him almost a caricature Englishman: so correct, so languid, almost effete. Yet Ben knew him to be a hard and successful professional in a sport in which the British were among the best in the world.

'But I am his protegée,' Mary said. All in a confused rush she spilled the story of the martingale. Meak listened without any change to his Lord Peter Wimsey impression.

'Forgive me, old thing, but I don't see what that's got to do with John's bad temper,' he said when she stopped for breath.

'But it's everything to do with it! John hates to be defied, and of course it's wasting Amati if I don't win when—'

'Oh bullshit!' Ben Watts broke in. 'I'm sorry, Mary, but I can't help it. You don't even know if he was watching your round, and even if he was he'd never have noticed about the martingale. You know what's wrong with him.'

'I wish I'd never told you, if you're going to go blurting it out to everyone!' Mary cried tearfully.

'Blurting what out?' Meak asked. 'Sorry, I must have turned two pages at once. Don't know what you're talking about.'

Ben seemed about to answer but Mary jumped in to stop him. 'It's nothing, really it's nothing. Just something someone said. Or suggested. It's nonsense though.'

'Whether it is or not,' Watts said steadily, 'the fact remains you've got to get away from his influence.'

At this interesting moment the door burst open and John Newland came in, looking hot, flustered and decidedly stormy about the brows. He glared around, spotted them, and came over like a tornado. Mary shrank down in her seat, but it was Meak who was the object of his anger.

'Now I know where you've been getting your ideas from. My

whimpering bloody sister and that smart-mouthed kid she's knocking around with!'

'What ideas are those, old man?' Meak drawled; but Ben noticed that despite the lazy tone and lowered eyelids, his body was tensed for action.

'You know what I'm talking about. First he comes round interfering with my sister, putting ideas into her head, and now I find the three of you together, talking about me behind my back. Plotting!'

'Plotting? What sort of talk is that?' Meak said, as if amused. 'Have we strayed into an old B movie, by any chance?'

'Oh, you think you're so bloody funny! But you'd better not start making allegations you can't prove, or you'll find you've bitten off more than you can chew!'

Meak said softly, 'Are there allegations *to* be made, that's the question. You tell me.'

'I'm warning you!' Newland shouted, incensed by the quiet tone. 'I know how you like to operate, always grovelling to the committee, arse-licking the suits, going behind people's backs! Bloody old boys' network! All boys together – public school bum boys if you ask me!'

Meak moved so quickly that Mary didn't see, as Ben did, what he had moved to prevent. She screamed. 'No, don't hit him! He isn't well!'

There was a hard smacking sound as Howard Meak's hand closed over John Newland's fist. It was neatly done, and only a man who had fielded at slip for varsity could have caught and held the fast-moving missile, but the force of it sent him backwards even so. The back of his legs caught his chair, knocking it over, and he fell, taking Newland, who was off balance, with him. Mary, overwrought, flung herself on top of them, trying to pull John away and interpose herself between him and Meak's supposed attack, while Newland tried to get another blow in and Meak tried to keep hold of him to prevent it.

149

'Ow! For Christ's sake, get her off me! Ben, get her off!' Meak howled from under the double onslaught and Newland's panting curses. Ben grabbed Mary round the waist and hauled and for a moment all was confusion before she suddenly came loose, Newland desisted, was released and rolled away, and Meak sat up, unusually dishevelled, and gingerly fingering his face.

'Bloody hell! I don't know which of them it was, but someone landed me a smack,' he said. There was a red mark around the outer edge of his eye socket. 'If I get a black eye, I shall sue. I'm nothing without my smooth good looks, y'know.'

Mary had taken refuge in tears, flinging herself into Ben's arms. Over her shoulder Ben looked in admiration at the man who could still joke at a moment like that. 'Boy, that was really neat,' he said, 'the way you caught his fist. I've never seen anyone do that in my whole life.'

'You'll never see it again, either,' Meak said with infallible good humour, flexing his fingers. 'It bloody hurts.' Newland was getting to his feet, and he added in a low voice, 'If I were you I'd get her out of here.'

'Yes, you're right. But are you OK?' Ben asked urgently.

'Sure. Reinforcements arriving, anyway,' Meak said, as the door opened. It was Polly and Dan Roberts, and they paused in surprise at the sight before them.

Ben hustled his weeping charge out past them. 'Don't worry,' he murmured. 'He's never going to upset you again, I promise. I'm going to take care of you from now on.'

'What's going on?' Polly asked as the door closed behind the young pair.

Meak got to his feet, brushing down his clothes. 'Oh, just a bit of horseplay that got out of hand. Are you all right, old man?' he added to Newland, who was on his feet.

Newland made a snort of disgust and walked out without a glance at any of them. Meak, still massaging his hurt palm, eyed the two newcomers with interest equalling theirs. They did not quite have their arms round each other, but they might as well have had, for the aura hanging round them. Polly had the unmistakable glow of accomplished love-making. Roberts, however, had scratches on his face and a purple bruise across one cheekbone.

Meak opened his eyes wide at Polly. 'Blimey, you put up a fight for your honour, didn't you? Or has he been scrapping with John Newland as well?'

'Of course not. A horse did mine,' Roberts said with dignity. Howard and Polly met each other's eyes, and after a brief silence they both burst out laughing.

Ben Watts felt a little out of his depth with Mary's tears, and eventually bethought himself of his female team members. Having left her in their cabin to be comforted, he sought audience with John Bryan and the *chef d'equipe*, Mike McNaught.

'All right, sad story,' McNaught said when he'd finished, 'but what d'you want us to do? Buy her a box of kleenex?'

'I want her to come back to the States with us. Obviously she can't go on living with him . . .'

'Oh, obviously,' Bryan said drily.

'Well, it seems to me that he's unbalanced. She's got to get away from him. And if she stays in England he'll go after her and make her go back home. She's got to get right out of the country, and if she comes back with us on Saturday she'll be safe. I can keep an eye on her till then, make sure he doesn't get at her. I thought she could sleep in with Billie and Kim.'

'Oh you did, did you?'

'Look,' said McNaught, not unkindly, 'don't you think you've got this out of proportion? OK, so the brother pushes her around a bit. So what? What brother doesn't bully his kid sister now and then?'

'It's not now and then, it's all the time, and it's getting worse. She's desperate to get away from him. It isn't just this week, you know. It's her whole life.'

151

'And her family's just going to let her leave the country, just like that?'

'They can't stop her, legally. She's over eighteen.'

'Well, then, let her do it. Why do you have to be involved?'

'Because they *would* try and stop her, even if they've got no right. That's what I've been trying to tell you!' Ben said, frustrated. 'If she goes back home at the end of the week she'll never get away. She has to come with us. It's her only chance!'

McNaught rolled his eyes. 'You're so young! She can't just jump on a plane, one-two-three. What about a passport, luggage, money? What's she going to do when she gets there?'

'I've thought about that.'

'The hell you have!'

'She's got a passport and she can go in on a visitor's visa – you can get a form to fill in at the airport – and apply for a work permit when she's there. She'll easily get work as a groom. You know everyone always wants an English girl groom. It's status. Like an English nanny.'

'Where's she going to stay? You have to give an address even to get a visitor's visa.'

'She can live with my folks to start off,' he said with a blush.

McNaught and Bryan exchanged a glance, and Bryan said gently, 'Look, Ben, I can see you want to help this girl, but I don't think it's something we should get involved in. I don't see what you want us to do.'

'Let her come with us on the team plane. We've got empty seats. It wouldn't make any difference to us.' He saw the negatives forming and pleaded, 'Give her a break, please. Just give her a break!'

'You don't understand. Even though the seats are empty, it wouldn't be free. We have to pay for every warm body, not just the plane itself. And besides, she has to have some money. The good old US immigration department won't let anyone in even on a visitor's visa unless they've got their return air fare. In fact, I think you may even have to have the return ticket. It's not going to work, Ben.'

152

'I'll sort it out,' he said, pleadingly. 'I'll sort everything out. My folks will back me. I've got some money, and if it isn't enough, I'll get them to cable me some. If she has to have a ticket, I'll buy her one.'

It was evidently a bad case of first love, and Bryan had some sympathy. If the girl was over age, there couldn't be any legal problems this end. He said to McNaught, 'If Ben's parents are willing to take responsibility—'

'Oh they will, I know they will!' Ben said eagerly.

'Well, I suppose it's nothing to us if she's just using an empty seat,' McNaught said. 'As long as everything's above board with the airline. She'll have to take her chance at immigration.' He looked sternly at Ben. 'There's no question of the team sponsoring her or anything like that.'

'No, I know. I'll sort it out, I promise.'

'And it's to be kept secret. We don't want the press getting hold of it. Can the girl keep her mouth shut?'

'It's her life at stake. Of course she will. Thanks! Thanks a lot!' He was turning away when another thought struck Bryan.

'Ben!'

'Yes, sir?'

'She can't bring the horse, you know that?'

'I know. It's not hers anyway. It belongs to her father.'

'Just as long as she knows.'

The two men watched him go, and a thoughtful silence followed. Then McNaught sighed. 'I hope this isn't going to mean trouble.'

'Oh, I don't see why it should,' Bryan said.

'He's in love with her now, but what happens when he wakes up? Which he's apt to do soon enough.'

'He's a nice kid. He won't leave her stranded.'

'She'll never get a work permit.'

'Ben's parents know everybody. If anyone can swing it, they can.' Bryan shrugged. 'Anyway, if not, she can always come back, can't she?'

Eight

A fine rain began when they had been on the road about half an hour. Tom Emmerson switched on the windscreen wipers, and watched the amazing accumulation of dust turn into mud. He pressed the washer and made himself a space to look through.

'Well,' he said conversationally, 'one way and another it's been quite a show.'

Anne, sitting beside him, didn't answer. She hadn't spoken since they left the showground, seeming to be deep in thought, or very far away. It bothered him. He had spent too long alone to relish being alone when he was actually with someone at last.

'Not only have I personally done well,' he went on, 'but look at all the excitements we've had. Howard and John Newland fighting; Chris Campbell being sabotaged; Polly snatching the Tomatsu from right under John's nose. And Dan Roberts turning up with a black eye, too! I wonder who he's been fighting.'

That roused her. She gave him a glance which, for reasons he couldn't fathom, seemed not exactly friendly. 'No one,' she said tersely. 'He had a fall.'

'Oh?'

She looked away again. 'You've missed out one item of news. Mary Newland's run away.'

'Run away?'

'To America. Packed her bag and gone off with the Watts boy.'

154

'I didn't know that.'

'It's only just happened. I got it from Jean, the Newland groom. Apparently Mary's been having quarrels with John for weeks now, and Jean's only surprised that she was willing to leave her horse. She doted on Amati.'

'Well, that's a turn-up for the books,' Emmerson said, watching in his side mirror a truck thundering down behind him. 'What on earth will she do in America?' The truck belted past, and a whack of wind and rain hit the cab side window. 'Is she going to marry the boy? Or does she hope to get work?' Anne did not answer. He tried again. 'Old John seems to be getting himself into a lot of trouble these days. Funny how he seems to be at the bottom of everything.'

'Not Dan's black eye,' she said expressionlessly.

'Or the attack on Chris Campbell, I suppose? You can't allow me a bit of sociable exaggeration, can you?'

She made a small restless movement, and frowned, and he thought she was going to say something, but didn't. A little later, however, she said in a normal tone, 'The most amazing thing about the show for me was the Belgians winning the team event.'

'I don't know why all this fuss about the Belgians.'

'They ride such peculiar-looking horses: long-backed, ewe-necked screws with terrible gaits. They seem to jump like kangaroos, from a standstill. Still, they proved effective this time.'

'You're always more interested in horses than people, aren't you?' he said, with a sidelong, affectionate smile.

'Horses are nicer people than people,' she said.

'Except in one respect,' he said provocatively, laying a hand on her knee. She refused to rise to the bait, but the corner of her mouth nearest him curled briefly upwards.

'Concentrate on your driving,' she advised.

Of the topics of conversation the show provided, that of Mary Newland's flight proved the longest lasting, as everyone speculated on why she had left in that particular way – whether it was love, ambition or fear – and what she would do and how long she would stay away.

The mysterious attack on Chris Campbell was canvassed only in private between Chris and Howard, and between Polly and Dan. No new ideas occurred to any of them. Chris was riding again within a few days, falls and minor injuries being part of the natural hazard of riding, but Mackie looked like being out of action for the rest of the season. Polly was angry and bitter about it: Mackie was half her team.

'The police haven't come up with anything,' she told Dan when they met at a local show.

'You didn't really expect them to, did you?'

'I thought they'd show a bit more interest. I mean, someone could easily have been killed. But they didn't seem to take it seriously at all.'

'Because someone *wasn't* killed. They've got other things to do.'

'They asked me if I knew anyone who had a grudge against Chris,' she went on, disgruntled, 'and when I said what about a grudge against Mackie, they thought I was joking.'

'Well, what did you expect?' He could see his apparently taking the police side was annoying her, so he said, 'It's a damn shame about poor old Mackie; but one good thing came out of it.'

'What do you mean?' She looked at him, caught his meaning, and went a bit pink. She had not quite got used to her new status as – what? – his mistress? Well, it didn't really amount to that, did it? In fact, she didn't see that anything much had changed between them. They hadn't slept together since the show, no opportunity having presented itself, and he didn't behave any differently towards her when they met at other events. They were still friends, as they had always been; but looking at him now she remembered their love-making and it made her go hot and weak. She knew he was remembering it, too, and his sidelong look and slightly crooked smile made her want him again, right there and then. Someone to hold the horses, and for two pins she'd happily retire with him to the long grass behind the tea tent.

He seemed to be reading her thoughts, and his smile became a touch complacent. 'How is old Bill, anyway?' he asked. 'He must be upset about Mackie.'

'Not really. He's sorry he's hurt, of course, but it doesn't bother him that we're out of competitions, if that's what you mean.' She turned worried, blue eyes up to Roberts. 'He couldn't find out, could he?'

'Find out?'

'About us.'

'What if he did?'

'I don't want to hurt him,' Polly said; and refrained from adding the other, ignoble matter of her depending on Bill for her living. Now Bill was linked to Dan through Murphy, too, which complicated matters even more: not only would discovery threaten Murphy's future and Dan's pocket, it would make her 'betrayal' seem all the worse. Bill would think she had conspired with Dan behind his back – and she had, hadn't she? The fact that Bill had no right to mind what she did wouldn't alter his pain or her feelings of guilt. Oh, the situation was infuriatingly complex, as it had always been, and it was all Bill's fault, which made her mad. But still, it was true: she didn't want him to be hurt.

'Oh, come on, Pol,' Roberts said, 'You're a big girl now. You have to face up to things. After all, nobody made you do it.'

'The phantom firework-thrower did,' she said darkly. 'I'd never have done it otherwise.'

'Oh, thanks a bunch!' Roberts said.

John Newland had to get used to hearing the subject of his sister's absconding discussed, and answering questions as to why he thought she did it. Howard Meak cornered him at a show and tried to talk to him about it. There was even some press interest, though the reporters who phoned or doorstepped him seemed to assume it was love that was behind it, and that she was running *to* rather than *from*. He answered questions, when he had to, as briefly as possible, saying he had not been in his sister's confidence; he never spoke to anyone about his feelings on the subject.

His father's distress on receiving the letter Mary had left behind showed itself at first as anger. For a couple of days he strode around the house in a fury, cutting her off without a shilling and swearing she'd never darken his doors again. The dogs cowered out of his way with their ears and tails down, and the staff crept about in unaccustomed silence and cleaned and polished everything above and beyond the call of duty. But after that Mr Newland relapsed into a gloomy silence, and only lost his temper if anyone mentioned Mary's name in his hearing. He locked the door of Mary's room and pocketed the key. When the cleaner asked if she should do the room, he bit her head off.

John took over the schooling of Amati at first, but his heart did not seem to be in it, and after a week or so he told Jean to exercise him daily, and otherwise ignored the horse's existence. Jean could not decide whether that meant he thought Mary would come back, or that he thought she wouldn't. She kept a worried eye on her boss, but though he seemed quieter, the symptoms of oddness that had worried her seemed to have disappeared – or enough so, at least, for her to forget about it in the busyness of her days.

John Newland had no intimate friends, nothing nearer than the casual acquaintances of the ring, and he had always been a secretive kind of person; so if he changed at all in his private life, no one would have noticed. Not that anyone was interested. Since Polly, there had never been anyone who cared for him that way.

* * *

For Tom Emmerson, life had changed radically, and it was all, he felt, for the better. He and Anne now lived in his new caravan which was parked just behind the stable yard. The house was up for sale, and there had been so much interest that the agent was in seventh heaven and had advised an auction to maximise the price. Even given the dilapidated state, it was an important building, and he was talking in terms of a price far beyond anything Tom had imagined. On those expectations, the bank had been willing to advance him enough to trade in the small caravan for the present bigger one; and the sale of the furniture had provided some living capital.

It surprised him how little he minded parting with the home of his ancestors. It should have been a huge wrench, but all he felt was relief. Perhaps he would feel it more, he thought, when the sale was done and there were strangers living in what had been his home. On the other hand, when the sale was through there would be enough money to clear all his debts, and some over, and it was hard for him to see beyond that.

Of course, his position would be precarious. At the moment he had plenty of fodder in stock, and the good summer grass in the paddocks as well, but if he didn't make some money before he had to restock – if he hit a bad patch or had a big vet bill to pay, if he was injured and couldn't ride, if he failed to find a sponsor – if any of these things happened, he would quickly find himself in queer street.

But at the moment he was completely happy. Anne was more at home in the caravan than she had been in the house, and there was something both cosy and liberating about having only one room to live in. All his responsibilities seemed to have fallen away overnight; he knew they were talking about him in the village but he just didn't care. He had stopped drinking, and he both felt and looked years younger. It was all thanks to Anne of course; all her doing. He loved her – worshipped her, practically – but she would never allow him to talk about his debt to her.

'You gave me a job, that's all. You don't owe your life to every girl groom you employ, do you?'

He hated her to talk in those terms of what seemed to him the great love, as well as the great renewing experience, of his life; and in any case, he could hardly be said to be employing her, since he had never paid her anything.

'If you're my girl groom, I owe you six weeks' wages.'

'Wait until you've earned some hard cash before you talk about wages,' was her answer to that.

It was not long, however, before a new topic of conversation ousted all others: who was to be picked to represent Great Britain at the New York Horse Fair. This was the great equestrian event of the non-Olympic year. There were big money prizes, and lots of other perks to be picked up, such as advertising contracts, broadcasting fees, gifts of clothing and saddlery, and even non-horse-related stuff like perfume, sports gear, holidays and cars, which came the way of the celebrities of the moment. And, of course, it was a chance to visit the States, and most of them tried to work a few extra days at the beginning or the end of the show for sightseeing and relaxation.

John Newland and Dan Roberts were pretty sure to be chosen: sure enough for everyone to discuss only the other two team places. Polly Morgan, who otherwise might have been picked, was out of it: with only one horse fit, she would not even be considered as a reserve. She was very sorry. Quite apart from the financial aspects, she had never been to the show before, and viewed it rather as a child might view a trip to Disneyland.

A friendly, noisy group discussed the possibilities in the competitors' beer tent at Hickstead. Howard Meak was strongly for his friend and favourite Chris Campbell.

'She's bound to be picked, y'know, now Polly's out of the running.'

Polly, wanting to show she was a good loser, asked him, 'Which horses? Cockerel for one, obviously, but who else?'

'Sunny, of course.'

'Too old,' Alison Neave said brutally.

Michael Baker, sitting beside her, broke in to defend Sunny. His horse Magnus was even older. 'He's still a top-class jumper. Age has got nothing to do with it, as long as he's fit.'

'The plane journey would be too much for him.'

'He'd take it more calmly than a young, inexperienced horse. It's panic and stress that make air journeys hard on horses.'

'Bollocks. His heart wouldn't stand the strain. He's decrepit.'

'He can still gallop on, which is more than can be said for some of our so-called top horses.'

'Meaning what, exactly?' Alison said dangerously.

Howard Meak saw Chris coming back from the loo and held up his hands. 'Peace, peace my children. It's all settled anyway. I have to have Chris along. Couldn't go to New York without her.'

'Howard, don't,' Chris protested quietly, thinking of his wife.

'For the good of the team,' he added firmly.

'Oh, come off it, Meak,' Alison said in her blunt way. 'Everyone knows you two sleep together.'

'We do?' he said, raising an eyebrow.

'You're not exactly the archetypal faithful husband. I'm sorry to dent your fantasy, but it's just about the worst-kept secret in the country.'

'The ones who talk about it never do it,' Polly said.

'You'd just better hope the corollary isn't true,' Meak replied, and she made a face at him.

Michael Baker was not interested in all this. 'Well, I think it's going to be a young team,' he announced loudly.

There was a chorus of groans and dissent. 'Young this, young that. We're up to our ears in Yoof,' Meak said.

'You wait till the Olympics next year for a young team,' Roberts said. 'That'll be your stamping ground. Leave the big cash shows to us hoary old professionals.'

'What do you mean? Are you saying I'm not professional?' Baker said, turning red.

Alison patted his hand. 'Never take anything Dan says seriously. That's the first rule of survival in this biz.'

'You're absolutely right, Ali,' Roberts agreed, straight faced. 'And I was just going to say that you're a brilliant rider and ought to be first one picked.'

Alison said a rude word.

'It wouldn't be fair to pick Alison,' Meak said. 'She's rich enough to go under her own steam.'

'You can talk!'

'Me? I'm just a poor farmer.'

'Nobody's mentioned one obvious choice,' Chris Campbell said. Her voice was quiet, but she spoke so rarely that she generally commanded attention. She was so small and fair and shy-looking that almost everyone in the equestrian world, in common with Meak, felt the urge to protect and encourage her, though she was – and in fact self-evidently – as tough a professional as any of them.

'Who do you mean?' Meak asked her.

'Tom Emmerson.'

There was a silence while everyone pondered this, and wondered why it was that his name hadn't leapt to mind. Of course, everyone had got used to mentally writing him off and thinking of him as a has-been, but – as Meak summed up for them all – 'He has been going very well this season, and there's no doubt he's got two good horses.'

'He's the kind of rider who does well in big rings,' Polly added generously. 'Forward-going and scopey.'

'Well, if they pick Tom Emmerson, John Newland and Dan,' Alison concluded, 'it'll have to be a man for the fourth.'

'Why?' Polly demanded indignantly.

'Because none of us females are old enough to qualify for a veterans' team like that.'

'Talking about me?' Tom Emmerson said, coming in at that moment. 'I heard someone mention veterans.'

'We were just picking a team for New York,' said Meak.

'And you picked me? How kind. I just hope the selectors are as kind. I must make sure to show myself at my best today.'

'Today?'

'What d'you mean?'

'Are they here?'

Emmerson smiled around at the impression he had made. 'I have it on impeccable authority that the selection of the team will be not unconnected with performance in the Derby today.'

'Who told you that?' Alison Neave asked, always scornful of rumour.

'I cannot reveal my sources,' he said. 'Anyone want anything while I'm up?'

When he had gone to the bar, Dan said, 'It doesn't matter, anyway. Everyone knows how he knows. Anne told him.'

Polly glanced at him, surprised and concerned at the bitter tone of his voice. But no one else seemed to have noticed anything. Perhaps she was oversensitive.

'Anne who?' Michael Baker wanted to know.

'His groom, Anne, of course. Anne Ashley Neville,' said Alison. 'The name says it all, mate. She has friends in high places.'

'What, his groom does?' Baker protested, puzzled.

'She knows everyone from the president of the FEI downwards, and they all fall over themselves to give her classified information.'

Chris added, 'Fortunately for us, she falls over *her*self to pass it on.'

'Well, in that case, my children,' said Howard Meak, standing up and brushing non-existent crumbs from his perfectly-cut breeches, 'I think I'd better go and do some work on my horses. Polish the odd hoof. Maybe comb out Ploughboy's rollers. Coming, Chrissy?'

'Yes, I think I'd better.' She added, with a perfectly seraphic expression, 'I have to warm Sunny up . . . old as he is.'

The atmosphere in the collecting ring was always much less formal at Hickstead. The collecting area was merely roped off from spectators, and there was no fixed seating on that side of the ring, so the competitors sat on the grass or on a pile of jumping poles just under the timekeeper's box, where they were out of range of the BBC camera which was mounted on a platform at the ring entrance.

John Newland was in the ring waiting for the starting hooter, Apache's distinctive white socks flashing in the sun. At the ring entrance Alison Neave waited for her turn, towering above everyone on her huge half-Clydesdale, Balinasloe. Polly was walking Taggert about to keep him supple, relying on second-hand reports about what was going on in the ring. Since she had only Taggert with her this time, she had left Terry at home with the other two and was grooming for herself, so she could not go and sit at the ringside with the others. She listened to the oohs and aahs and tried to sum up the round from them, until Dan Roberts came to put her out of her misery, shouldering his way through to her.

'How's he doing?'

'Four faults at the double ditch. I think it must be the way the sun's shining: flashes on the water and makes them shy. Never mind him, anyway. What about me?'

'What about you?'

He grinned. 'I've just been told that I've definitely been picked for New York. Me and old Newland. The other places will depend on today's performance. But I had it that Chris Campbell's a possible.'

'Don't tell her, then, or she'll get stage-fright and make a hash of it.'

'It makes me wonder if old Howard's got influence somewhere. Hey, John! Heard the news?' This as Newland rode out of the ring, having completed the round.

'What news?'

'You and me are picked for New York. And Chris is a possible. I reckon old Howard's pulling strings somewhere—' But Newland had ridden past him without stopping, and without comment. Roberts stared. 'What's the matter with him?'

'Dunno. Maybe it's because you're with me. He's never forgiven me for the Tomatsu. Or maybe he thought you ought to have asked him how he did.'

'I know how he did: four faults. They just announced it.'

'What ears you have! Never mind him, anyway. He's just a rude bastard. I'm really glad for you, that you've got picked. I just wish I was going. Poor little Mackie.'

'Well, listen, Pol, I've had an idea about that,' Roberts said, leaning on Taggert's obliging wither and squinting up at her against the sun. 'Why don't you come with me as my groom? I have to take someone, and there's no law about who it has to be.'

'Are you kidding me? Hazel would kill me,' she said, not taking him seriously.

'She wouldn't care. Really, I mean it! Why not? It'd be great.'

'Oh, I don't know,' she hesitated. 'I hadn't thought . . . I mean, it'd be ten days away, I'd be missing shows.'

'Well, you've only got Taggert anyway, and he could probably do with a rest.'

'He'd get unfit.'

'Terry can ride him. Or if you don't trust her, you can take him over to my place and Hazel can ride him. A few missed shows is neither here nor there, is it?'

'Yes, but it's not really my decision, is it? I mean, he's supposed to be earning money. What do you think Bill would say about it?'

'Bill would say about what?' They both jumped in ludicrous and very revealing guilt as Simpson came up behind Roberts. Taggert demonstrated his clear conscience by whickering a

165

wholehearted welcome to the sugar provider and shoving Roberts aside to get to him.

Polly tried to regroup. 'How nice that you made it! I didn't think you were going to be able to come today.'

'Sudden change of plans. Thought I'd pop over. Yes, Taggert, old friend, I have got something for you. Mind if I give him something?' he asked Polly, a courtesy he never forgot. 'I've got his favourite acid drops.'

'Go ahead,' she said, slackening the rein so that Taggert could investigate Simpson's pocket. 'I'm sure he doesn't really distinguish one sweet from another, though. It's all just sugar to him.'

'You'd be surprised,' said Simpson, sliding an acid drop into Taggert's mouth and allowing the horse to suck his fingers. 'Us chaps with superior taste have to stick together, don't we, Tag?'

'How was your weekend? How's Maureen and the boys?' He had been spending the weekend with his sister and her sons, who regarded him very much as the favourite uncle, a cross between a stand-up comic and a cornucopia.

'Fine. It was exhausting though. Apart from having to romp with the boys practically non-stop, there was a dinner party Saturday night that went on until all hours, and then I got roped into the cricket match on Sunday. I had to go back to work to get a rest.' He gave Taggert another acid drop, and without looking up asked again, devastatingly, 'What Bill would say about what? What were you talking about as I arrived?'

Polly exchanged a look with Roberts over his head. Roberts shrugged and turned a little away, as if to say, this is nothing to do with me.

'Um . . . well . . . I was just saying how disappointed I was not to be going to New York,' Polly said. 'Mackie not being fit.'

She hoped to leave it at that, but Simpson looked up, his expression contained, and said, 'You mentioned my name.'

Now her guilt prodded her anger into action. It was ridiculous for a grown woman to be in this situation, unable to please herself what she did, jumping like a child caught with its fingers in the jam pot. 'Dan said would I like to go along as his groom,' she said baldly. The words seemed to tremble on the air almost visibly. Too late to take them back now.

'I see.' Simpson caressed Taggert's ears, and looked at Roberts. 'You're definitely picked, then?'

'Yes. Iceman, Shilling and Texas. I thought I'd take Murphy too, with your approval. I think he's ready, and they've said there's room for him.'

'Good idea.' His eyes came back to Polly. 'You'd be missing shows if you went,' he said mildly. 'You thought about that, I suppose?'

'That's what I was saying when you arrived: that I didn't know what you'd think about Tag missing shows.'

'Oh, that's what you were worried about, was it?' The mask slipped off then, and there was a world of hurt and anger in the next sentence. 'You weren't wondering what I'd think about your going off for a fortnight's holiday with Dan Roberts, by any chance?'

Polly, though flinching inside, had no choice but to brave it out. 'It wouldn't be a holiday, I'd be grooming.'

'You know that's not what I'm talking about.'

'Look, why should people working together have anything more than a working relationship?' And the knowledge of her own duplicity made her angry. 'In any case, do you think it's any of your business?'

Simpson took a deep breath, and then let it out slowly. 'No,' he said in a brittle way. 'Of course it isn't. You sleep with whoever you want, Polly. I just thought I deserved a little better than that.'

'Oh, for God's sake!' Roberts muttered.

Simpson looked at him. 'In case you're thinking of denying it, my friend, I might as well tell you that I've had a poison pen letter. I suppose that's what you'd call it. Normally I wouldn't take any notice, but from the way you two are acting it seems it was right on the button.'

Polly felt pale. 'What are you talking about?'

'I had an anonymous letter saying that you were sleeping with Dan Roberts at the Manchester Show. And I presume it didn't end there.'

Polly saw his hand make an involuntary movement towards his pocket. He had it with him! Somehow that made her angrier still. 'Show me!' she demanded.

He hesitated no more than a moment, and handed it up to her. She read it, and then with a grimace of disgust passed it to Roberts. It was made up of words and letters cut out of a periodical – *Horse and Hound* if she was any judge of typefaces – and postmarked Manchester on the last day of the show. Nothing to show who had done it.

'Have you told the police?' Polly asked.

'What for? There's no threat, no demand for money. Just a piece of unwelcome information – though I must have been blind not to have worked it out for myself. My God, the evidence was in front of my nose for long enough!'

'Now look here,' Roberts began, but Polly stopped him with a gesture.

'No, Dan. Look, Bill, my relationship with other people, unless it affects my riding, is not a thing I'm prepared to discuss with you. Equally, my relationship with you is not a thing I discuss with anyone else.'

'So . . . What are you trying to say?'

'*So*, all that we have to discuss here is whether from a *professional* point of view you object to my going to New York. Anything else is not in the province of our relationship.'

'Is that what you really think?' Simpson began.

But at that moment one of the ringside spectators screamed, and a babble of voices rose in shocked comment and protest.

'Something's happened!' Polly said. She stood in her stirrups to try to see over the crowd; but Captain Fox, being held just in front of her, flung up his head at the noise, blocking her view. 'What is it? I can't see. What's happened?'

The mass of people between them and the ring entrance was eddying to and fro as everyone tried to see round or over everyone else. The loudspeaker commentator said, 'And Christobel Campbell and Sunny have fallen . . .' and then stopped and vouchsafed no more.

'It must be bad,' Polly said whitely.

'Stay here, I'm going to see,' Roberts said tersely. He was big and strong, the best person to force his way through a crowd. He made it to the front to see, a few yards inside the ring, the golden horse, Sunny, lying flat on his side, unmoving. Chris, hatless, knelt beside him, stroking his cheeks. Someone's groom – not Lesley – was also there, kneeling with her. Some people had linked arms across the ring entrance to keep everyone else back.

Cries of 'Vet!' and 'Let him through!' caused the crowd to part. As the vet passed him, Roberts saw Howard Meak close behind, and attached himself to them and was able to slip through the self-appointed guard chain into the ring. Meak did not even glance at him, seeming to take it for granted he would be there; and as a close friend of both of them, it was not a cause for comment.

Chris looked up as they reached her, her face a mask of terror. 'He just collapsed,' she said. 'He didn't fall. He just went under me, as if he'd been shot.'

Meak took her in his arms. The groom – it was Michael Baker's lad, Gordon – said, 'I saw it. It was as he landed. He just sort of crumpled.'

'He didn't seem quite right earlier on,' Chris said, gripping Howard's coat with clenched hands like monkey's paws. 'But it was nothing I could put my finger on. I thought he might be getting a touch of colic, but I didn't . . .' She stopped, shook her head as though to free an impediment. 'Is he dead?'

'No, he's still breathing,' Roberts said quickly, and then, to the vet, who was examining the horse, 'What is it, do you know?'

The vet rolled back one of Sunny's eyelids, and then bent to sniff at his breath. He peeled back a lip and with a finger removed some yellow foam. 'It's my opinion,' he said, in the voice of an official pronouncement, 'that this horse has been drugged.'

'Drugged!' Roberts said, shocked.

Chrissy stared, her eyes round with shock. 'Oh no!' she whispered. 'Oh poor Sunny!'

'We'll have to get him back to a box and take a blood sample,' the vet said. 'I have to warn you there may be an official enquiry. I advise you to say as little as possible about this to anyone.'

He addressed this principally to Chris, but she made no response, white-faced and seemingly numb with shock.

'I don't think there's any doubt that she'll be acquitted,' Meak said much later that day as he sat with Polly and Roberts in the private bar of a village pub – not the nearest to the ground, where they would have had no peace, but one a mile or so away.

'Well, of course she will,' Polly said, shocked. 'Poor Chrissy! As if she'd ever hurt Sunny in a million years. She dotes on him.'

Meak glanced over his shoulder to see they were not being overheard. Chris had gone to the loo, giving them their first chance to discuss the business. It had taken some persuading to make her leave her horse, but it was the only way to get her away from prying eyes, gossiping tongues and the press.

'You don't understand,' he said. 'Obviously they must suspect she was the one who did it. Who else benefits?'

'What do you mean? No one would be crazy enough to nobble their own horse,' Polly protested.

'It was a gee-up drug, not a slow-down drug,' Roberts

170

explained kindly. 'It was the overdose that made the old horse collapse.'

'He's rising twenty,' Meak said gloomily. 'There's still some danger of heart failure. I don't know how she's going to take this.'

'Whatever the drug was, you know Chrissy would never do a thing like that. Not to any horse, but especially not to Sunny,' Polly persisted.

'Yes, of course he knows, and I know, and you know,' Roberts said. 'The thing was intended to impress strangers, not us.'

'You mean . . . someone drugged Sunny to make it look as if Chris was trying to improve her chances illegally?'

'She's there!'

'And whoever did it overdid the dose and made Sunny collapse?'

'I think the overdose was intentional,' Meak said.

'Why?'

'Well, think about it: if the dose had been just right and Sunny simply did extra well, maybe no one would ever have known he'd had anything. The perpetrator would have had to come forward and make an accusation, and that would be giving himself away.'

'He could have sent an anonymous letter to the committee,' Polly suggested, a little tenderly.

'He could have, but that would be risky. They might just ignore it; and in any case, by the time they got round to testing the horse, the stuff might be out of his bloodstream. No, I think the overdose was calculated to make sure she'd be found out. She's lucky it didn't kill him. Though I suppose the perpetrator wouldn't have minded that outcome particularly.'

'But who would do such a thing?' Polly said, horrified.

'It had to be one of us,' said Meak gravely. 'A competitor or a groom: someone who could go in and out of the stable yard without being challenged.'

'Oh, great!' said Roberts. 'That narrows the field to a couple of hundred people!'

'It's better than—'

'Ssh!' Polly warned as Chris appeared behind them.

She was white faced, as if she'd been sick. 'It's all right,' she said. 'I know what you're talking about. I don't mind if you want to discuss it.'

'We've finished now,' Howard said, pulling her chair out for her.

'I want to go back soon,' she said. 'I don't like leaving him.'

'I suppose this puts paid to you being selected for New York,' Roberts said, hoping to alleviate one misery with another. 'Sunny will hardly be fit again in time.'

Chris shook her head vaguely, seeming not to have taken in what he said. 'It's horrible,' she said. 'Who has such a grudge against me? First the firework, now this. Someone wants to see me hurt.'

'The firework may not have been meant for you,' Polly said, not because she believed it any more, but to comfort Chrissy. 'It may have been meant for me. We do look alike at a distance, and you were riding my horse.'

'But that doesn't make it any better,' Chris said, looking up. 'That would mean there was a lunatic around attacking all of us. Who will it be next? A random killer.'

'Oh come, on . . . Killer?' Meak said robustly. 'Who's been killed?'

'No one *yet*,' Chris said, and began crying. Meak put an arm round her and looked across at the others.

'I think I've given her too much brandy. Perhaps we'd better go back now. The walk in the fresh air will clear her head.'

'We'll come too,' Polly said.

The night was dark – only a quarter moon – and quiet, and the air was fresh and cool. They walked back through the country lanes, talking about anything they could think of that was unconnected with the accident. It was hard work with two of them virtually out of action, Chris numb with shock over Sunny, and Polly preoccupied with the unfinished business between her and Bill. What the incident in the ring had interrupted had not been resumed before Bill had taken himself off, pleading business; and though Polly was angry with him for provoking a scene, she felt guilty too, and miserable, and worried. How hurt was he? What would he do? She remembered Chris's words: *you could lose him.* She didn't want to think about that. Oh, damn the situation! She didn't want to think about anything just now.

Howard Meak had dipped into his excellent repertoire of vulgar jokes, and now Roberts had gone into a rambling monologue of a story that Polly guessed would end with the feeblest punchline in history. They were walking along a narrow lane edged on either side with steep grassy banks and high hedges when it happened. There was a sudden roar, and a beam of light cut through the darkness from behind them. For an instant they didn't realise the danger. Then Roberts grabbed Polly, yelled, 'Look out!' and jumped, bundling her and himself up the bank. Meak was an instant slower to realise what was happening, but in his spare time he was a rally driver and his reactions were sharp. He grabbed Chris and jumped the other way.

With a deafening roar of over-acceleration the car shot through the space between them, slewed wildly from one bank to the other, then straightened out and disappeared into the darkness. A few early leaves were sucked along in its wake, and their rattling and the rustling of the disturbed hedgerow were the only sounds left as the noise of the engine died away.

Polly managed to push Roberts off her and remove her face from the damp grass. She felt as if she'd been kicked in the back by a carthorse, but as Roberts rolled over and asked her if she was all right, she was able to say, 'Yes, just had the breath knocked out of me. What about the others?'

'Are you two all right?' Roberts called, jumping down the

bank and crossing to them. Polly followed, to find them both sitting on the bank, Chris nursing her right leg and Meak his left.

'What happened? Are you OK?'

'I twisted my ankle trying to get up the bank,' Chris said. 'It's nothing. It's Howard who's hurt.'

'Something caught me . . . The car I suppose,' Howard said through gritted teeth. 'Hurts like buggery. Knee. Hope to Christ nothing's broken.'

Roberts squatted beside him. 'Let me have a look. Pull your trousers down a minute. Oh, don't be so modest, the girls can't see anything in this light. If they weren't so tight I could roll the leg up. Your own fault for being so vain.' Talking soothingly as he would to a horse, he felt around the knee with fingers that knew injury from years of caring for horses. 'Good job you were wearing thick cords. Luck of the bloody wicked,' he said as Meak winced and sucked his breath in pain. 'All right, put your kecks on. You'll live,' he said at last. 'Nowt broken, just a nasty bruise.'

'That's what I thought. Thanks,' Meak said, pulling his trousers up.

'Don't thank me. It'll swell up enough as it is.'

'You'd better come between Dan and me and let us support you,' Polly said. 'Chris can keep an eye out in case he comes back.'

'He won't come back,' Meak said, more certainly than he felt. 'I don't suppose anyone saw the registration number?'

'I was too busy getting out of the bloody way,' Roberts said.

'I didn't see the number, but it was a Range Rover,' Polly said.

'Big help. Practically all of us drive Range Rovers,' said Meak.

They looked at each other. 'I suppose it *was* another attempt?' said Chris uncertainly.

'It might have been just a drunk,' Polly said. 'Or a bad driver.'

'Pigs might fly,' said Roberts. 'Come on, let's get the wounded home. Who's stupid idea was it to come out for a drink anyway?'

'*Mea culpa*,' said Meak, wincing as he put his weight on the wounded knee. 'The interesting question is, which one of us was it meant for this time?'

Nine

H oward Meak's knee was badly bruised and swollen, but there was no serious damage, and he was not likely to be off riding for more than a few days. The news was not as good about Sunny. He was an old horse, and the vet thought his jumping days were probably over. Certainly he would not be fit again that season, and Chris Campbell's chances of going to New York were finished.

The team was finally announced the following day, and the news was brought by Alison Neave to the tea tent.

'The news you've all been waiting for, guys and gals,' she announced at the door, and her rather penetrating, 'county' voice had all heads turning her way. 'No real surprises, though. John Newland with Apache and Idaho.' Newland had looked up from the morning paper which he was only just getting round to reading, but finding her eye on him quickly looked down again so as not to appear interested. Alison shrugged and went on, 'Dan Roberts and his three. Well, you knew about that, didn't you?'

'I deny it!' he called, and there was laughter.

'Howard Meak with Ploughboy and Vibrant.'

'Alias Long John Silver. How's his limp?' Dan called over.

'Limp what?' someone shouted.

'He denies it,' Alison came back.

'Why only Ploughboy and Vibrant?' Polly asked. 'Why not Vixen?'

'Too old,' Alison said. 'This ain't a welfare trip.'

'Could have fooled me,' Michael Baker muttered. 'Old folks' outing so far.'

'And number four is Tom Emmerson with Buccaneer and Captain Fox.'

'Good for you, Tom,' Polly said. There were murmurs of agreement, but some of the younger set did not look so pleased.

'Who's reserve?' Baker wanted to know, riding on a hope.

Alison met his eye, not without sympathy. 'Me,' she said. 'Come on, they've got to have some leaven to the lump.'

She left the doorway and headed for the tea urn, and Roberts, in a fit of kindness, went off to telephone Howard Meak with the good news, in case he hadn't heard it yet. He would not be competing for the rest of the week, and had left that morning, as had Chris Campbell, who had taken Sunny home. Roberts put in a bit of thought on the way to the telephone, and instead of ringing Meak's home number, tried his mobile. When Meak answered, from the background roar Roberts guessed he was in his car.

'I'm on my way over to Chrissy's. I dropped the nags home first; now I'm going to make sure she's all right. She's taken this drugging business very hard.'

'I'm not surprised,' Roberts said. 'I've got some good news for you, though.' He told him about the team.

'That's great,' said Meak.

'You don't sound over the moon about it.'

'Oh, I was just thinking it's a shame Chris won't be picked now. I think the selectors had their eye on her.'

'Maybe.'

'I think I'll ask her if she wants to come with me, as my groom. That might cheer her up.'

'What about your wife?'

'She doesn't need cheering up.'

'Seriously, Howard – as an old friend—'

'That's right, Chrissy and I are old friends. As everyone knows,' Meak said, 'including my wife.' Roberts's silence spoke his disbelief. 'Taking Chrissy to New York won't change anything, old boy. Those who believe there's something going on between us will go on believing it, and those who mind their own business will go on minding it, and my wife will go on trusting me, or not, as the case may be.'

'It sounds just like poetry when you say it, old boy,' said Roberts ironically.

'Yes, well, you can talk. You're going to have to face the same problem . . . You and Polly.'

'What?'

'I'm not blind. And I'm rather good at arithmetic.'

'Yeah, well . . . I'm not married. And neither's she.'

'I wonder if Bill Simpson will see it that way.'

'Oh, bugger Bill Simpson.'

'No thanks,' said Meak.

Roberts rehashed the conversation with Polly, and she sighed and said, 'I wish I had his brass neck. What am I going to say to Bill when he comes back tonight?'

But as it turned out, she didn't need to worry. He didn't return that evening as expected. Instead, a letter came for her from him.

> I don't know how you feel at the moment, but I feel confused. Maybe it's my fault. I don't know. Maybe our whole relationship needs overhauling. Perhaps it would be a good thing for both of us to have a little time to think about this. So have your trip, and enjoy it – you deserve that much – and when you come back we'll talk again, and let's try to be honest with each other.
> Yours, as always,
> Bill

'Bill's given us his blessing,' Polly said to Roberts when they met again.

'He's a bleedin' prince.'

'He is. On the whole, I wish he'd been nasty about it. I feel so rotten.'

'Feel away, then,' Roberts said. 'Don't expect me to join in.'

There was one more big show before the New York trip, at Lutterworth, for those who thought it worth the effort and the risk of injury so close to the departure date. Of the horse-masters, only John Newland, Dan Roberts and Tom Emmerson went. Emmerson went because he was missing nothing that might make him money, Newland because he felt sure of winning. Roberts wanted to give Murphy an outing before New York. He did not risk his picked horses, though. As well as Murphy, he took Philadelphia and Freddo, and one of his youngsters for the novice class. Newland brought Idaho and Greyfriar. Roberts had a good show: Murphy jumped extre-mely well, and he had the pleasure of beating Newland to first place in all the classes they shared, a rare occurrence.

The only other incident of interest, as he told Polly afterwards, was John Newland's fall. 'Though it wasn't so much of a fall as a stunt. He was coming over the triple bar on Idaho in the speed competition and his stirrup came off and he went flying. Com-plete somersault. Triple lutz with a double salco thrown in. If he'd been wearing tights he could've auditioned for the circus trapeze.'

'Your metaphors are somewhat mixed, but I get the point,' Polly said. 'Was he hurt?'

'Bumps and bruises,' Roberts said, 'but it could have been a lot worse: he really did come a purler.' He gave her a significant look. 'It seems as if someone might have sabotaged him.'

'What?'

'Well, I went over to see if he was all right, and he and that groom of his—'

'Jean?'

'That's her. They were examining the stirrup leather practi-cally through a magnifying glass, and she asked me what I thought of it. Newland said he thought the stitching had worn and then broken, but Jean said it had been cut deliberately.'

'No! Really?'

'Well, I couldn't tell. I mean, I looked at it, but I couldn't tell, and I wasn't that interested really. Newland was bloody rude, as usual, said if I hadn't got an opinion on the subject I could piss off and leave him alone, so I left him to it, ignorant sod. But I thought afterwards that given how much weight goes on the stirrups over a jump, if someone had cut the stitching nearly through—'

'If they had, surely Jean ought to have spotted it.'

'It was apparently a saddle he doesn't use very often.'

'Oh? When was the last time?'

'Well, I don't know! What am I, Inspector Morse?'

'All right,' said Polly, 'I just thought if we knew when, it might give an idea as to who did it. You see, if it was deliberate, it must have been done by someone who knew how dangerous it would be. Your average punter wouldn't be likely to think of a stirrup leather, would they? So it would seem likely that it was done by one of us. The phantom menace, in fact. But,' she short-circuited herself, 'if he hadn't used it for months, the damage could have been done any time, couldn't it? Though it would have to have been done at one of the shows where we stay over, like Manchester or Hickstead, or the menace wouldn't have been able to get access to the tack.'

'Dunno,' Roberts said. 'I wouldn't make too much of it, Pol. It could happen to anyone. Probably it was just worn, and Jean didn't want to admit she hadn't checked the tack properly, so she punted this idea of sabotage.'

'Perhaps,' Polly said. 'If it was sabotage, it puts John in the clear, along with you and me and Howard and Chris. So who does that leave?'

'I wouldn't think about it,' Roberts said firmly, and changed the subject.

*   *   *

180

Mary's first week in America – or the States as she had now learned to call it – was like being in a dream, or in a movie. Everything was so luxurious, so immaculately clean. Everyone's clothes seemed new, expensive, and chosen to match, down to the last detail. The women's hair seemed fresh every day from the hairdresser, their nails from the manicurist.

Ben's parents were kind to her: so unfailingly polite, anxious for her well-being, so flatteringly interested in everything she said. Despite the awkwardness of the way she had suddenly been foisted on them, they seemed really glad to have her, treated her like an honoured guest, and never once let it appear that they thought anything about the situation was strange.

Their house seemed enormous to Mary, and looked as if it had just been newly decorated and carpeted, though it hadn't. She was given a bedroom bigger than their living room at home, with fitted wardrobes and an en suite bathroom – every bedroom in the house had an en suite. Their living room was so big it exhausted her walking across it, and it had a round, raised fireplace right in the middle with a great, grey stone chimney like a funnel going up through the ceiling. This being summer, of course, it was not lit; instead there were french windows on to a terrace, beyond which were acres of rolling lawns. Ben's parents had servants, too, just like in a movie; and when once she wandered into the kitchen – itself as big as a whole English flat, with a fridge the size of *two* wardrobes – she found they had a cook, too.

Everything was as different as it could be from home; and when in the course of the week she was taken to the Watts' friends' houses, to restaurants and to the golf club, she discovered that everywhere else was as luxurious as their house and everyone else as polite and kind as they were. For a week, perhaps a little longer, she was very, very happy – apart from anything else, it was wonderful to be able to be with Ben – but then the very things that had entranced her at first began to depress her.

The apparent luxury of everything, the relentless smartness, made her realise how poor and untidy and shabby everything was at home. No matter how she tried with her appearance, she always felt scruffy alongside her hosts, and though they never so much as looked sidelong at her, she could not believe they did not notice. Her clothes were cheap and nasty compared with theirs; her hair never looked as if she had just come out of a salon: more as if she had just got out of bed. She even started worrying that she wasn't clean enough: everyone in the States seemed to be so clean they were practically sterile!

And though their polite and kindly attentions did not fail, the very unvaryingness of their exquisite manners began to make her feel like an outsider. She almost longed for a little homely neglect, a friendly insult. It wasn't that the politeness was put on for her: they were just as polite to each other, it seemed. The worst thing was that Ben was polite to her, too. Not that he had ever been *dis*courteous, but here at home there was more formality to his manners than in England. And though he had kissed her once or twice, he had never, as she had half expected, half hoped, come to her room; or even gone in for those long snogging sessions like in Manchester. It did not occur to her that the presence of his parents inhibited him. She was afraid that she had mistaken him, and that what he felt for her was not undying passion after all, but mere disinterested kindness.

Little by little she became bored, lonely and homesick; and there was her future to worry about, too. The Watts parents had begged her to consider their home as hers, but she could not believe they would be willing to keep her for ever. She must get a job; she longed for a job. She needed to do something that she could do well before her morale sank beyond recall.

She raised the subject at dinner one evening. Owing to her quiet voice and shy hesitancy, she was misunderstood at first.

'Of course, dear, you can ride any time you like,' Mrs Watts said, bending her elegantly curled grey head courteously towards her. 'There are plenty of horses in the stables, and one of the grooms can go out with you if you feel you don't know the way.'

'Mary rides very well, Mother. I'd trust her with any of mine,' Ben said.

'There you are, then,' Mrs Watts concluded.

'Oh, yes . . . Thank you . . . You're very kind,' Mary said breathlessly, 'but it isn't just riding. There's never anything to do in the stables – everything's always so spotless – I never even clean the tack. I know I can never repay you, but—'

'There's no need even to think about it, dear,' Mrs Watts said. 'We love having you . . . Don't we John?'

Mr Watts, who had just cut a corner off his steak, put down his knife and transferred his fork from one hand to the other in that exhausting way Americans have, and said, 'Mm? Oh, yes, yes, of course. Delighted.'

'Thank you . . . You are so kind,' Mary stumbled on, 'But you see I have to get a job of some kind. I can't stay for ever. I mean . . . I have to *do* something, don't I?'

The Watts parents met each other's eyes down the length of the table. 'Well, now, this needs thinking about,' said Mr Watts. 'What sort of job had you in mind?'

'Something with horses,' Mary said promptly. 'It's . . . it's what I'm good at. Riding, grooming . . . Even teaching riding, I think, as long as it was to children.'

'But Mary,' Ben jumped in eagerly, 'it's not long till the Horse Fair. You'll be sure to hear of something while you're there. *Everyone* will be there . . . won't they, Mother?'

'Yes, dear, that's true. It really is the social event of the season,' she explained to Mary, 'and if the word is passed around to our friends and acquaintances, I'm sure something will come up. You must be careful, after all, who you go to. I'd feel happier if it was someone we knew. We are *in loco parentis*, to an extent. Much better wait until the show, I think, all in all.'

'But . . . what about a work permit?' Mary asked, rather flattened by the Watts family confidence.

'Oh, I'm sure that can be sorted out,' Ben said quickly. 'You could ask Uncle Jack, couldn't you, Dad? I'm sure he could pull the right strings. Senator Richardson. He's not really my uncle,' he explained to Mary, 'but Mother and Dad have known him for ever, and I used to call him Uncle Jack when I was a kid.'

'Well, now, I don't know,' Mr Watts began slowly, but his wife wagged her exquisite head at him down the table.

'Yes, John, that's the best idea, I think. Have a word with Jack.'

Mr Watts raised his eyebrows, shrugged his shoulders a little, and went back to his steak.

After dinner Mary and Ben went for a walk round the grounds. Later still Ben proposed walking down to the stables to say goodnight to the horses, but Mary was feeling cold in her sleeveless dress and said she would go back to the house for a cardigan first.

'All right, I'll see you there,' said Ben.

Coming back along the terrace towards the open french windows, Mary heard the Watts parents talking, and paused out of their sight to listen, realising at the last moment what they were talking about.

'I wish you wouldn't bounce me into these things, Gilda. You know I hate asking Jack for favours,' Mr Watts was saying.

'But it's such a little thing! Jack won't mind.'

'Maybe he will and maybe he won't, but *I* mind.'

'Oh, don't make such a fuss! Besides, it's better that than the alternative.'

'Which is?'

'Ben means the child to stay on here one way or the other, and the sure way to keep her here would be if they were to get married.'

'He hasn't said he wants to *marry* her?' Mr Watts exploded in what sounded like horror.

'Well, he hasn't said it in so many words, but I've seen how he looks at her. He's got a crush on her, and we don't want him to do anything hasty. So the sooner we get the girl a work permit and a job the better.'

'But it would only be a permit for a couple of years at best,' Mr Watts pointed out.

'A job will get her out of his orbit, that's the thing, and out of sight is out of mind. They're so young, they'll have forgotten all about each other in two years, but I don't want him stampeded into marriage just because this girl's only got a couple of months on a visitor's visa.'

'You're dead set against her, aren't you?'

'As a daughter-in-law, absolutely! Oh, she's a harmless enough little thing, and quite pretty in her way, but we know nothing about her family.'

Mr Watts began in his slow rumble, 'Well, she's the sister of—'

Brisk Mrs Watts interrupted. 'Yes, but all we know of the brother is his record in the ring. And frankly, dear, they must be odd people if they let her go like that, without a word or the slightest attempt to get her back. And you've only got to look at her clothes to know there's no money or taste in the family. I want Ben to marry a girl of his own sort, and . . .'

Mary crept away, not wanting to hear any more, and entered the house by another door. She got up to her room before giving way to the tears that were burning in her throat. Her cheeks were hot with shame and hurt, and her first thought was to pack her bags and run away, as far and as fast as she could; but second thoughts reminded her that that would not be very far, given that she had no money and was in a strange country. Oh, how could they be so horrible, so two-faced, so snobbish! She hadn't thought there could be anything like that in America, the land of equality.

Ben didn't think that way, she comforted herself. Or did he? But no, even Mrs Watts admitted that Ben was attracted to her. But what use was it, if his parents were against her? She had never felt so alone, so afraid, so rejected. What could she do?

Where could she go? She hadn't even the money to run away back to England, little as she wanted to do that.

When her tears slowed enough for her to think coherently, she realised that her best – no, her only – hope lay in staying here and doing what Ben had already mapped out for her: to go with him to the Horse Fair, groom for the team, and hope for a job to come up. Let Mrs Watts find her a good position, let Mr Watts get her a work permit; and if their reason for wanting to help her was an insulting one – well, help was help all the same.

And, she thought, sitting up on her bed and blowing her nose, they couldn't stop Ben marrying her if he really wanted to. He was of age and so was she. Mary had been squashed all her life by those around her, but her fighting spirit got up on its hind legs at last. She would get the better of the horrible Watts parents! She would get a permit, get a job, stay in the States, and, if she had any say in the matter, she would marry Ben too! She'd be as nice as pie to his parents until then, but as soon as she was Mrs Ben Watts, she'd tell them what she thought of them!

Polly had been up since before dawn. She had driven her two horses over to Moor End, unloaded them and seen them settled while Dan and Hazel were loading up his four. She was still giving instructions to Dan's rough-rider, who was to have special charge of Taggert and Mackie – leaving Terry at home with only Pavlova to worry about – when she was almost forcibly dragged away.

'Come on, woman. Don't you realise how far we've got to drive?'

'Don't fuss. There's plenty of time.'

'And I want it to stay that way.'

'Ooh, you are masterful,' she mocked him.

'You wait till I get you to the States!'

'You'll be lucky! You know how strict the committee is over

186

there. You won't be able to indulge in any hanky-panky with your groom.'

'Oh my God, you're right. I'd forgotten. We're segregated, aren't we? Why didn't you remind me when I first asked you?'

'You might not have taken me. I wasn't going to risk missing out on the trip.'

Roberts sighed and shook his head. 'I'll have to sign you in as my wife.'

'You will not!'

They drove steadily, taking turns at the wheel, and stopping twice for breaks, mainly for the sake of Hazel, who was travelling in the loot. They bypassed the main entrance of Heathrow and skirted the airfield, heading for the quiet corner where the team's special plane would be waiting.

'It always makes me feel I'm sneaking out by the back door,' Dan said.

'Must be your guilty conscience. I wonder how the beasties will travel?'

'As well as you. They've done it before.'

'What about Murphy? Oh, I'd forgotten, he went to the States, didn't he?'

'And now he's going back, on his way up the ladder again,' Roberts said confidently.

They needed to leave about eleven, and so Anne was surprised when Tom disappeared at half past ten. The horses were groomed and ready, the clothes packed, so there was not much left to be done, but it seemed an odd time to slope off even so, and without a word to her. All was revealed when he arrived back at a quarter past eleven with whisky on his breath. He must have been down to the village pub.

He made no reference to his absence, however, so she did not mention it either. They closed and locked the caravan, took a last look around, and boxed the horses. Anne pushed the tail pins home and was heading for the passenger side when Tom caught her arm and said abruptly, 'You drive.'

'OK,' she said. As she turned the box out on to the road she noticed that his hands were shaking; he saw her look, and stuffed them between his knees to hide them. But as the journey continued he seemed to grow more and more nervous, shifting about restlessly in his seat. She waited for him to explain, but he did not speak at all. At last she was driven to say, 'What's the problem?'

'Eh?' he said, as if jerked back from some distant train of thought. 'Problem? What d'you mean? There's no problem.'

'All right, I'll mind my own business. But for God's sake sit still. Your fidgeting distracts me from my driving.'

'Don't give me orders,' he snapped.

Anne said no more. A few miles further on he sighed and said, 'I'm sorry.'

She shrugged. '*De nada.* But what *is* wrong with you?'

'If you must know,' he said reluctantly, 'I'm afraid of flying.'

'What!'

'Yes, I know, I know. It's totally irrational but I just can't help it. I've always been like it. Every time I go on a plane I have to get plastered before I can even get up the steps.' He glanced sideways at her. 'All right, you can laugh now. Mock away. I'm ready.'

She only frowned a little, and drove in silence for a few miles. Then she said, 'When we get to Heathrow, you'd better leave me with the horses while you go to the VIP lounge and tank up. Only try to keep out of the way of any press lurking about.'

'Is that all you're going to say?'

'What else did you want? I can't lend you any money, if that's what you're hoping.'

'No, that wasn't what I—'

'I dare say there'll be someone around you can touch for a fiver. That little runt of a photographer that's always hanging around, maybe.'

188

He laughed, sounding much more his old self, and reached out to squeeze her knee. 'You're a marvel.'

'What did I say?' She pretended surprise, but smiled slightly, her eyes on the road ahead.

Chris, travelling separately, arrived at the airport ahead of Howard and was waiting in the shadow of the big potbellied plane when the Mitton Abbey horsebox arrived. She went forward eagerly to meet it, and saw Fred, the elderly head groom, get down from the passenger side, while one of the younger men was behind the wheel. They both nodded a greeting to her.

'Hullo! How did they box?' she asked.

'Quiet as lambs,' said Fred. 'The guv'nor's coming in the car with Mrs Meak.'

'Yes, I know.' She found that Fred was looking at her curiously, and wondered suddenly how much he knew and what he thought.

'The Guv'nor said you were going along as groom,' Fred said. 'Be a nice trip for you, won't it?'

Chrissy only nodded. His face was a cat's cradle of wrinkles, and it was impossible to tell what he was thinking. She had known him since she first went to Mitton with stars in her eyes and a teenage crush on Howard. Probably, she comforted herself, Fred hadn't noticed that she had grown up a bit since then.

'Not the last, are we?' Fred asked.

'No, the Newland horses haven't arrived, and the others aren't all on board yet. Tom Emmerson's are still in the box over there. I don't know why: they were here early enough. He and his groom both seem to have disappeared.'

'Well, I'm supposed to hand the nags over to you,' Fred said, 'so we'd better get 'em ready, hadn't we? I got all their rugs and bandages and folderols in the loot. Get it open, Mike, will you?' As the groom walked away, Fred said, so softly she was hardly sure she had really heard him say it, 'With a bit of luck, you'll be out of sight by the time she gets here.'

Returning to the Emmerson horsebox, Anne Neville began cladding up Buccaneer. It was a lengthy job, for every inch of the animal had to be protected during the flight, in case of bumpy weather or any other misfortune that might knock some part of the horse's precious, fragile body against the walls of his stall. When all the bandages, boots, caps and shields were in place, she added the final touch, the leather flying helmet that was held in place by straps under the cheeks. It always struck her as slightly whimsical to put a hat on a horse; but of course, poll evil – a disease caused by a blow to the poll, the delicate part between the ears – could kill.

Hearing another motor draw up, she walked to the ramp and looked out to see the Underhill horsebox a few yards away. Mr Newland senior was getting down from the driving cab. He looked ten years older than when she had last seen him. Well, everyone's here now, she thought, and went back to start dressing Captain Fox. She wondered how Tom was getting on.

The atmosphere in Howard Meak's car struck him as somewhat frigid, and he couldn't quite account for it. It was, after all, very kind of Felicity to suggest coming down to see him off. It meant he could come in the car instead of travelling with the horses, because she would then drive the car back. He had said more than once, 'You don't need to, darling,' but she had merely smiled and said she wanted to. It was the smile that bothered him. There was something rather tight about it.

She hadn't volunteered a remark since they set off, and had replied very briefly to his, so it had been largely a silent journey. It was as they were approaching the airport that she finally spoke, and said, 'You can drop me off at the terminal before you go on to the plane.'

'Drop you off? What do you mean?'

190

'Exactly what I say. Drop me off at Terminal 3 where I shall be catching my plane.'

'What plane? What are you talking about? Where are you going?'

'To New York,' she said with icy sweetness. 'Do close your mouth, Howard, you look like a fish. Yes, I'm coming to New York too, and I shall be at the show most days, though I shall have lots of other things to do as well, so you'll never know when to expect me. I shall keep you guessing, as you've kept me guessing all these years. A delightful game, don't you think?'

He couldn't take his eyes off the road, but he flicked a white glance sideways at her, like a nervous horse. 'I don't understand. If you wanted to come with me, why didn't you say? You could have travelled with the team.'

'Oh, no,' she said, with a little theatrical shudder. 'I like my comfort too much for that. I shall be travelling first class on a scheduled flight, with a limousine waiting for me at the other end. I don't intend to slum it. Besides, I think it might make me nauseous to see you and your little *friend* together.'

'Fliss, what's going on?' he said angrily.

'I think you know that better than me,' she said with controlled fury. 'I ought to have known long ago, but I suppose it was a self-protecting blindness.'

'If you're talking about me and Chrissy, you know very well that there's nothing—'

'Oh, spare me that! No more lies, Howard, please. Our whole marriage has been founded on lies. Your lies, and my money.'

'I didn't marry you for your money, if that's what you're trying to—'

'Yes, that touches your pride, doesn't it? I know you very well, you see. You wouldn't look good in your own eyes if you had to admit to yourself that you married me for money, so you pretended to be in love with me. It didn't last long, but then it didn't have to. Men do fall out of love with their wives. After a decent interval, you could tell yourself that you'd done your duty and it couldn't be helped.'

'This really isn't the time for this,' he said desperately. 'How can you be going to New York, anyway? You haven't got any clothes with you.'

'Two suitcases in the boot. I had them put in while you were seeing the horses off.'

'The devil you did! How long have you been planning this?'

'Only since I finally realised what was going on. When I heard you were taking your slut to New York with you.'

'She *isn't* my—!'

'I was such a fool not to guess before. When she had that accident and there you were on television, going into the hospital to visit her. The camera caught your expression just for a moment before you realised it was on you. You looked so harrowed. Would you have looked like that if it had been me in that hospital bed? Don't bother to answer that. But then I received that convenient letter. You had better indicate if you're turning in here for Terminal 3.'

He turned in helpless obedience. 'What letter?'

'I've told you, the one that said you were taking her to New York. One of your chums is not so much of a chum as you thought, it seems. Unless *she* sent it. It's the sort of pathetic thing females like that do.'

He said, 'You're as wrong as you can be. There's nothing going on between Chrissy and me – nothing wrong, I mean. We're friends, that's all.'

'Thank you, I prefer to believe otherwise.'

He almost tore his hair. 'But if you're so convinced about it, why on earth would you want to come to New York?'

Her control broke at last. Until now she had spoken with frozen calm. Now she spat venomously, '*To spoil your fun!*' The car swerved and straightened as his hands jerked on the wheel in surprised reaction, but at once she brought herself back in hand and said calmly, 'You'll never know when I might come round the corner or knock on your door. You'll never be able to relax. That'll put a crimp on your jolly little holiday, won't it? Because, I tell you this, Howard, if I catch you in the act, you are out. You can go and spend the rest of your life with your slut and see how you like living without my money. I don't think you'll like it one bit. Stop here. I'll walk the rest.'

'Fliss—!'

'Press the boot release, please. No, don't get out. I don't want you to help.'

A last thought occurred to him. 'What about the car? What am I supposed to do with it, if you're not taking it back?'

'That is entirely your problem,' she said.

Tom Emmerson was making his slightly unsteady way back to the plane, well warmed with whisky courtesy of the airport photographer Anne had mentioned, who, true to form, turned up at Tom's elbow almost as soon as he entered the building. As he came in sight of the plane he saw that there was something wrong. Those members of the team already aboard were disembarking hastily; various members of airport and airline staff stood around talking, gesticulating and using their cell phones with an air of agitation. Tom broke into a run, and accosted the first person he reached, which happened to be Alison Neave.

'What's up? Is something wrong?'

'Oh, Tom, there you are.' She sounded calm, but there was a tension in her that he could sense even through the drink. 'There's probably nothing in it, but there's been a telephone call to say there's a bomb on board. It's probably a hoax, but the airline's saying we've all got to get off. It's a bastard, just when we've got the horses settled.'

'Get off? Horses too?'

'Of course – where've you been, anyway?'

'In the lounge. Yes, you're right,' he read her eyes, 'I am a bit drunk. Truth is, I'm—'

'Scared of flying. I remember now. This bomb scare's really going to delay us. By the time we've got the horses out and the police have come and the plane's been searched . . .'

She broke off as Anne Neville appeared at the top of the ramp which led down from the belly of the plane. She had Captain Fox. She led him carefully down on to the tarmac and said clearly, so that everyone could hear, 'There's a briefcase in stall No 1, in the corner against the partition. If it doesn't belong to anyone, it could be the bomb.'

'No 1? Good God, that's Bali!' Alison exclaimed. 'That's what I get for being punctual. Let me by, I've got to get him off. Thank God he's a quiet horse, but still . . .'

'It might be someone's,' one of the cabin staff said hopefully.

'In a stall? Don't be daft,' Alison said, striding towards the ramp.

'You can't go up there,' said another member of staff, putting out an arm. 'You have to wait for the police.' Alison brushed him aside as easily as a fly.

'Ali, wait!' Polly called. 'We ought to unload the horses from the back first. You'll make them nervous taking Bali past them.'

'Too bad!' Ali shouted back. 'I've got to get him out before he kicks the bloody thing accidentally.'

The whole group surged forward automatically as the thought struck home; but from their ranks, someone gave a little shriek, and ran after Alison. It was the airport animal welfare officer's assistant, a young girl new to the job, whose previous experience as a veterinary nurse had all been with small animals. She knew little of horses or the handling of them, but the idea of them being blown up was horrifying, and obviously the urgent thing was to get them out of the plane as fast as possible. She ran into the stall nearest the door – Alison had already gone past towards her own horses further in – and grabbed for the head rope.

Unfortunately it was Idaho, who was a nervy, irritable horse in stable at the best of times. Horses are easily startled and the first rule of the stable is never to run or make sudden movements. When the girl flung herself suddenly under his nose, Idaho jerked his head up, flattened his ears and then bit her hard, his big yellow teeth sinking into the tender flesh of her upper arm. She screamed with pain and surprise, and that, together with the sense of anxiety she was giving off, threw the horse into a panic. He jerked backwards, tightening the knot of his rope, and finding himself held, began to plunge, throwing his weight back again and again on the rope, which flattened and creaked like a ship's timber.

Alison meanwhile had got Balinasloe loose and was leading him towards the door, but the sounds were making him nervous, and he stopped and put his head up, trembling. Another horse caught the atmosphere and whinnied; they were all shifting uneasily at their tethers. Alison, her hand on Balinasloe's neck, peered into the stall and saw the girl cowering there.

'What the hell are you doing?' she hissed quietly, but with venom. 'Get out of there!'

'We've got to get the horses out!' the girl cried in the high voice of fear.

'Shut up! You'll set them all off! Are you mad? Leave him . . . Get out! Get some of the grooms up here!'

The girl seemed too frightened to move, but to Alison's enormous relief, Anne Neville appeared at that moment and summed up the situation at a glance. She stepped into Idaho's stall and slipped her fingers through his headstall. 'Get out,' she said tersely to the girl, and then, like a monument of calm, began soothing the big horse who towered above her.

'Can you hold him while I get Bali past?' Alison said.

'I've got him. Hoo, there, hoo, there, big feller.'

Alison judged her moment, when the black's swinging rump was in rather than out of his stall, and got Balinasloe past, and then he was slithering and sliding down the ramp to safety.

The next ten minutes were a nightmare. More and more people seemed to be arriving, police, bomb squad, airport security, dog handlers, airline officials, the press. The grooms and riders went back and forth leading out the increasingly nervous horses as quickly as they could. Fortunately, the Underhill box was still on the tarmac, as well as Tom Emmerson's, and they were able to load most of the horses into them and drive them to a safe distance, while the last ones out were led away at a hand trot. Only when the horses were safely away were the police able to force the team members to vacate the area while the suspect briefcase was examined, and the rest of the plane searched for other objects. The grooms all went with the horses; the team was herded off to a lounge, and Emmerson saw Anne disappear with a feeling almost of despair. He didn't think he could cope without her.

'I knew I was right to get drunk,' he said to Alison, who was beside him.

'Well, nothing's happened yet,' she pointed out with brutal honesty, 'and you're sober again.'

'Don't remind me! Much comfort you are to a friend,' he complained.

'Never mind, maybe there'll be free drinks in the lounge,' she said.

Ten

'Apparently,' said Polly as she rejoined Dan, Howard and Chris, 'it was a hoax. Nothing in the briefcase at all. It was just a very heavy case – one of those reinforced executive jobs with a combination lock.'

'They have to say that,' Dan said. 'Otherwise everyone would give up flying.'

'Oh, come on!' Howard protested. 'Why would the police lie about it?'

'Because we – and everybody who read the story in the paper – would start thinking what would have happened if it had gone off.'

Chris shuddered. 'Don't. It doesn't bear thinking about.'

'Yes, well it was only a hoax in the end,' Polly said reassuringly.

'*Only* a hoax?' Howard drawled, knocking ash off the tip of his cigarette with his usual lazy gesture. 'Whoever did it nearly achieved his object even so.'

'What object?' Chris asked.

'To sabotage the team. There was very nearly a nasty accident when the horses started to panic. Can you imagine the damage they might have done themselves?'

A waiter approached and he stopped.

'Can I get you anything more, ladies? Gentlemen?'

'Let's have the same again all round,' Howard said.

When the waiter had gone, Chris said, 'The panic, as I understand it, was caused by that airport animal welfare girl. You surely can't suspect her of wanting to sabotage us? What would she have to gain?'

197

'No, no, as I see it she was just a random element in the plot,' Howard said. 'She just happened to help it along. A useful idiot, if you like. The panic would have been caused by all of us trying to get our horses out at once, and setting them off by our own nervousness.'

'Which I suppose is only too likely,' Polly sighed. 'Look how Alison behaved, dashing in to get her nag without waiting for the police or the bomb squad . . . and she's usually the sanest, calmest person.'

'It was the person who put the briefcase there and phoned in the hoax call who's the real villain,' Dan said. 'And that had to be one of us.'

'Why? Because of the other attacks?' Polly said.

'You got it.'

'But we don't really know they were attacks . . . Not all of them. After all, that car business at Hickstead could just have been a drunk or even a normal, stupid driver. Practically everyone in Sussex has a Range Rover, and you know how country people all drive like maniacs.'

'True . . . And thank you,' Howard said with a bow in her direction. 'But what about the attacks on Chris?'

'Well, the firework might just have been a kid's prank,' Polly said.

'And it might have been me that drugged Sunny,' Chris said tonelessly.

Polly reddened. 'I didn't mean that.'

'I know. But it has to be said.'

'Nobody thinks you did it,' Dan said warmly, and laid a hand briefly over hers, resting on the table.

'This is all speculation anyway,' Howard said, trying to defuse the atmosphere. 'There may have been four attacks on members of our group—'

'Five,' Roberts said. 'Maybe. There was John Newland's fall at Lutterworth.' He told Howard and Chris the story.

'All right, possibly five,' Howard said. 'Five attacks—'

198

'Six.'

They all started and looked up, to see Anne Neville standing just behind Howard's chair.

'What?' Dan said.

'Six attacks. Don't forget the letter,' she said, looking straight at him.

'What letter?' Howard asked, screwing round in his chair so sharply he ricked his neck.

'Poison pen,' she said, and looked at Polly.

'It was just a stupid letter, nothing important,' Polly said.

'*You* got a poison pen letter?' Meak asked. He hadn't told anyone about Felicity getting one.

'It was nothing,' Polly said again. 'I don't want to talk about it.'

'How the hell did you know about it, anyway?' Dan asked Anne. She merely shrugged and walked on.

'How long had she been standing there?' Howard asked, watching her walk away.

'I don't know,' Dan said. 'I didn't notice her. I was concentrating on you lot.'

'It couldn't have been long, anyway,' Chris said.

'You realise that she's Prime Suspect Number One,' Howard said quietly. They all looked at him. 'All the trouble has started only since she came back on the scene.'

'Oh, that's ridiculous,' Polly began.

'And she was the one who "found" the briefcase. That vet girl might be a useful idiot, but I can't believe Anne is.'

'But the firework-thrower was a man,' Polly objected.

'Lesley only caught a glance,' Howard said. 'It could have been a woman in trousers.'

'Let's stop it!' Chris said suddenly. 'This is all so horrible. I can't believe she'd ever deliberately harm a horse.'

'But the same goes for all of us, surely?' Meak said. 'And yet it must have been one of us.'

'Well, let's look at who's eliminated,' Polly said. 'Newland's out after Lutterworth. Dan and me because of the letter. You were hit by the car.'

'That could have been meant for Chrissy,' Meak said. 'She might have been victim of each of the attacks.'

'Unless the firework was meant for me,' Polly added.

'But you notice nothing's happened to Tom Emmerson or his horses,' said Meak, 'and who's grooming for him?'

'Yes, but—' Polly began.

'Stop it, stop it!' Chris cried, interrupting. Her voice was a little too high. 'I can't bear this. I don't want to hear any more about it. Don't you see, it does no good talking about it like this. It's poison. We'll end up suspecting each other. If the hoaxer wants to break up the team we'll be doing his work for him.'

'She's right, y'know,' Howard said.

'She's not wrong,' said Dan, and Polly looked at him, realising that he had contributed no single word to the debate about Anne Neville as suspect. He caught her gaze and made an enigmatical grimace. 'Ah, here's the drinks. Just in time,' he said, seeing the waiter approach.

'All right, let's drop the subject,' Howard said. 'But let's keep our eyes and ears open, all the same. We may have been lucky so far.'

Dan gave him a warning look, and lifted his glass. 'Let's have a toast. To the New York show: beauty ashore and prizes galore!'

'Pothunter,' Polly said witheringly.

'And what are you here for? The honour of your country?' Roberts asked cynically.

'I'm a groom, this is my job.'

'God, I'd forgotten!'

'So had I,' Chris said. 'Can I come in with you, Polly, if it's shared rooms in the barracks tonight?'

'Bars on the windows won't keep us out, will they, Howard?' said Dan.

'Bras, did you say, or bars?' Polly asked.

Howard was about to join in with a bit of badinage, and then remembered the interview with his wife in the car, and closed his mouth again.

Everyone had to give a statement to the police, and so it was very late that the plane finally took off. As soon as the seat belts light went off, people began swapping seats, walking up and down, standing in the aisles chatting, and the drinks flowed extra fast to make up for lost time. Naturally everyone talked about the bomb hoax, except for Tom Emmerson, who had reached a state of alcoholic euphoria which prevented his fear of flying but effectively prevented conversation, not to say movement, as well.

When Polly came out of the loo at one point she found Howard Meak and Alison Neave standing in the space by the rear door, in discussion about the bomb. She paused to hear if they had anything new to add.

'The problem with your theory,' Alison was saying, 'is that we all had horses on the plane. If the hoaxer was one of us, who would put their own horse at risk to start a panic with the others?'

'Someone who hoped to get their own nags off before anything happened, perhaps,' Meak said. 'Whose horses were in the stalls nearest the exit?'

'Apache and Idaho,' Alison said. 'But surely you don't—'

'It can't have been John,' Polly joined in. 'He was a victim of the prankster at Lutterworth. He could have been badly hurt.'

'If that was an attack,' said Meak.

'If any of them have been attacks,' said Alison. 'And the other two by the exit were Captain Fox and Buccaneer.'

'Which brings us back to you-know-who,' Meak concluded.

'But that was pure chance,' Polly said. 'The stalls weren't reserved, they were allotted on a first come basis. The last to arrive loaded last.'

'John was late, wasn't he?' Alison said thoughtfully. 'Surprisingly late. I've never known him unpunctual before.'

'Even more suspiciously,' Meak said, 'the Emmerson box was there for ages before the horses were unloaded. It wasn't until the Underhill box arrived that Fox and Buccaneer were put on board.'

'Oh, but this is all wrong,' Polly said anxiously. 'I think Chris is right. I don't believe' – she glanced around and lowered her voice – 'Anne would do anything that would hurt a horse.'

'I'd believe it sooner than that it was one of us,' Alison said. 'She's an outsider. Nothing happened until she came back on the scene. And you must admit she's a bit strange.'

'But what could possibly be her motive?' Polly said.

Alison shrugged. 'Maybe she hates us all. Jealousy *because* she's an outsider. I don't know. I don't know the woman.'

'The trouble is,' said Polly, 'no one knows anything about her: who she is or where she comes from or anything.'

Alison gave Meak a strange look. 'Oh, I think Howard knows a bit more than nothing . . . Don't you Howard?'

He looked uncomfortable. 'I don't know what you mean.'

'Don't you? Isn't she a cousin of yours?'

'How the hell did you know that?'

Polly stared in astonishment. 'Is she?'

Meak shifted his gaze away and back. He lowered his voice still further. 'She is a sort of cousin, but only by marriage. Not a blood relative. She's actually my cousin's wife's daughter by her first marriage, but I've never had anything to do with her. She ran away from home when she was pretty young, and I don't think anyone's had any contact with her since.'

That explains the accent, Polly thought, if she came from a posh home. 'Why did she run away?' she asked.

'*I* don't know,' Meak said, as if goaded.

'I bet you do,' Alison said remorselessly. 'Come on, Howard, spill the beans. You know something about her. We've got a right to know if she's a bad lot. It's our horses – maybe even our necks – at stake.'

'Oh, all right,' he said reluctantly, 'But don't make a big thing of it. I don't know why she ran away from home, but she was in a mental institution at one time.'

Neither woman said anything, but Alison looked grimly satisfied.

'It's probably nothing, and it was a long time ago. I don't like fingering anyone for something in their past,' said Meak, 'but . . .' He let it hang, thinking resentfully of the letter Fliss had received. And how had Anne known about the letter to Polly? It was all a bit rum. 'We must all be on our guard, that's all,' he finished.

'We'll be that all right,' Alison said.

Polly only nodded and went away. She felt a bit sick. It was all so horrible, suspecting someone who might be perfectly innocent. But what if she wasn't? As she went back down the aisle and passed Anne's seat she couldn't help glancing back at her, and, finding her disconcerting eyes on her, faced front again hastily. Anne always knew everything, Polly thought. Whether or not she was the hoaxer, it was tanners to tenners she knew more than she was saying about a lot of things.

Like the Manchester Showground, the New York Horse Fair's grounds had been purpose built, but the difference in budget was readily apparent. The Horse Fair was so vast it had to be served by its own public transport – mini-buses, with electric 'trams' for the main routes – and at the eastern end was the Horseman's Rest, a hotel-motel complex of glittering aspect, with the usual complement of bars, restaurants, conference facilities and a large, heated swimming pool and gym.

The competitors and grooms were put up in one wing of the hotel, and the team were pleased to find that segregation had died since last time. The rooms were allocated more or less along team lines, and the English crew were all on one floor, with the exception of the *chef d'equipe* who had an executive suite: tucked away with the big nobs, was how Polly put it.

She was enjoying herself enormously. On their arrival they had, of course, tended first to the horses, settling them in and making them comfortable after their long journey. Then they had had quick showers and changes and hit the high spots. Polly thought privately that they had overdone it, but Dan assured her with globetrotting confidence that it was only jet lag. Whatever it was, they all looked rather haggard in the morning. An early call, a stimulating shower, and a lavish breakfast chosen from a menu so vast one had to hold it in both hands and prop it on one's knees, and Polly felt on top of the world again. She was looking forward to riding Dan's horses.

There was ample exercise room, so she chose herself an empty corner of the tan and began to school Shilling gently on both diagonals to loosen him up after the journey. It was a strange experience for her: firstly because Shilling was an old horse, set in his ways and with very odd gaits; and secondly because Dan rode him in a hackamore – a bitless bridle. It was not something of which she had much experience, and she found she was using her seat much more than usual: so much so that at the end of an hour she was aching like a beginner and was glad to give Shilling a rest, and rode over to the ring where Dan was working Murphy.

The big ginger horse was going beautifully, and had already collected an admiring audience of fellow horsemen and early spectators. Amongst them Polly noticed Anne Ashley Neville. There was nothing abnormal looking about her this morning, she thought. She looked like any other horse groupie. In fact, Anne's expression of longing as she watched Dan and Murphy canter past made Polly smile with mixed amusement and sympathy.

'What's the joke?' asked Anto, Alison Neave's Irish groom.

Polly looked down. Anto had stopped in passing and was

leaning on Shilling, who had dozed off, enjoying the sunshine. The old horse had cocked one hind foot comfortably, his long white ears were drooping, and his whiskery, white lips trembled rhythmically with his deep, steady breathing. He looked nothing like a top showjumper, she thought; more like a greengrocer's horse.

'I was watching Anne,' Polly said. 'She looks like the Little Match Girl.'

'The little what?'

'Gazing at Dan with hopeless longing,' she translated.

'Goway with you,' Anto said scornfully. 'That one doesn't know he exists. It's the horse she's watching, and stars in her eyes the way you'd think it was Sean Connery in the buff!'

'Oh, come off it! Polly laughed. 'She's a normal human female, y'know, with all the normal urges.'

'She's not, y'know,' Anto said. 'I speak whereof I know. Didn't I try me luck with her last night, and nothing doing?'

'You think that not fancying you makes a woman abnormal? God, you're conceited!'

'I am not. It's the bloody horse she's in love with,' he assured her earnestly. 'I'm telling you.'

'Yes, you're telling me. And here's your missus looking for you,' Polly warned him, seeing Alison bearing down on them. 'After your blood by the look of her. What have you been up to?'

'Jaysus, I was supposed to be tacking up Bali,' Anto yipped, and scooted.

Roberts brought the chestnut from a canter to a square halt, and then walked him over to where Polly was sitting on Shilling. Murphy was still cool and scarcely even breathing quickly. He looked magnificent, curving his neck and flexing his bit, and for a moment Polly had no eyes for his rider. She could quite understand Anne's being in love with the animal, even if it was only in Anto's fertile imagination.

'Problem?' Roberts said.

'No, just taking a breather. I've ridden more comfortable bicycles.'

'Do you want to swap, take Murphy round for a bit?'

'God, no! Thanks all the same, but he looks like dynamite. I'd never be able to hold him.'

'He's a smasher,' Roberts said, running his hand hard down the great curve of muscle from Murphy's ears to his withers. 'I've never had a horse like him. He's a bloody king!'

Polly was surprised at the tremor of emotion in his voice. She had never known him so moved by a horse. He cared for all his animals and ruled them by love rather than fear; but this seemed love of a different order.

'He is beautiful,' Polly agreed, and sighed. 'Well, I suppose I'd better get back to my circling.'

Roberts grinned at her suddenly. 'Tough being a groom, isn't it? You can't foist the dull jobs off on to someone else.'

'It's not the dull of it I mind,' she said, 'it's the agony. This beast has got the gaits of a mule on stilts.'

'Don't you insult my horse,' Roberts said, 'or I'll make you ride bareback!'

'God forbid!' Polly shuddered. 'I'd be cut in two. Come on, then, 'orrible!' And she woke Shilling up and hauled him off to school some more.

Mary was happy again, and busy; happy because she was busy, perhaps. Her future looked more assured, too. She was glad she had run away to the States: even if ultimately she was not able to settle here permanently, at least for as long as she was here, no one would browbeat or bully or humiliate her. She would have a job, a job that she could do well, where her skills would be valued and rewarded. Above all, she would be herself, for whatever that was worth, and not merely John Newland's sister.

For the duration of the show she was helping Ben and the other members of the American team, not doing the menial grooming – though she wouldn't have minded that in the least, for nothing she did for horses was distasteful to her – but the exercising and schooling. Ben had fixed it up. Ben said she had light hands and a good seat, and a natural sympathy with horses which made her invaluable. *Invaluable!* She had glowed with pleasure at his compliment. Now he was away from his parents' house, he was like his old, Manchester self again, and they had had a satisfying session in the back of a loose box last night – so satisfying that Mary had thought for a bit they were going to go all the way. But someone had come along and disturbed them. Still, there was the rest of the show to go. She thought if it happened, she wouldn't try to stop it. She loved Ben, and she knew he would look after her.

Mike McNaught had warned her he couldn't pay her for her services during the show because she was only on a visitor's visa, but she didn't care about that. It was a privilege to help. John Bryan had watched her ride the first day and said in her hearing that she had been very well taught and that all English riders seemed to have good seats, better than their own girls. That had pleased her too; and Ben had said that both Mike and John Bryan were putting out the word that she was looking for a job, and recommending her if anyone asked, which was wonderful of them.

The work permit business was not going to be so difficult after all. Senator Richardson – 'Uncle Jack' – had been appealed to and had explained that if she got a job offer from a respectable family, and if they wrote to the Department saying that she had special skills which made her uniquely suited for the position, and that they wanted her and no one else, she would be able to get a working visa for up to two years.

That was wonderful, but even more wonderfully, Ben had explained to her – a little diffidently – that if while she was on a valid visa she married an American citizen, she would automatically be entitled to resident status.

Mary had not, of course, repeated to him what she had heard

207

his parents say; though it did occur to her that it might make him so angry he would propose to her right there and then, just to show them. But if they did marry, she thought, it would make it awkward if there was bad blood between them and his folks. Better to keep quiet. If Ben loved her, in time they would come round to it. They'd have to. Besides, until the job materialised, she depended on them. Ben said it would not be long. She would be flooded with job offers in no time.

She was in no hurry. A job might take her away from Ben, and at the moment what she wanted most in the world was to be near him. And the show was going to be so exciting. She loved being part of it, feeling that she really belonged for the first time in her life, that she was liked, that she was useful. And she loved to see the horse-mad little girl spectators staring at her with bug-eyed envy as she rode by on the big team horses with their national rugs folded back over their quarters. That had been her, she felt, all her life: on the outside looking in with helpless longing. Now she was on the other side of the glass.

Only one more thing was needed for her happiness. She wanted to see Jean and ask how Amati was. But she wasn't sure how she could do it without John seeing her or knowing about it. Her great fear was that she might bump into him. She believed that Ben would protect her, and that he wouldn't allow John to force her to go home, but all the same she didn't want to see or speak to her brother. It would spoil her perfect happiness if there was a row.

Polly was just getting changed when the letter was pushed under her door. Had she not been struggling at that moment through a rather clingy little black number, she might have been able to get to the door in time to fling it open and see who was responsible, for as soon as she saw the folded sheet of paper lying on the carpet she had no doubt of it's being something undesirable. However, by the time she did get the door open, the corridor presented a vista of identical closed doors. No one was in sight; there wasn't even a breath of air movement to hint at hasty departure, just the stuffy stillness and white noise of air conditioning.

There was nothing to be done, of course. She could have knocked at the other doors to see who was home, but being in the room or not being in it could equally be construed as suspect. The staircase was just a few doors down – the perpetrator could have gone that way – and both lifts were in use, as they generally were. She sighed and went back into her room.

A glance was enough to take in the poison pen letter, created, as was the other one, with cut-out letters and words, sellotaped this time on to a sheet of hotel writing paper: glue or paste, she supposed, were harder to come by when you were not at home; or perhaps merely harder to conceal.

'Stay away from him. Remember your horses.'

Economical, she thought. No doubt who 'he' was, of course, but what exactly was the threat? Stay away or I'll tell Bill and he'll take your horses away from you? Or was it stay away or I'll get at you by hurting your horses? Either way it was as misguided as it was nasty. Someone's mind was sick, and a sick mind could be dangerous in all sorts of ways.

Polly set her hands to the middle to tear it up, and then hesitated. It was evidence, after all, and if – God forbid – the sick one did carry out some act of vandalism, or worse, the note might be useful to – she hesitated to say the police, even in her own mind, but to whoever wanted to investigate the matter.

Perhaps she ought to show it to Dan, see what he made of it. She put it into her handbag and continued getting ready. Who *could* it be? The question teased her as she stared into the dressing-table mirror, putting on her make-up. She met her own eyes, rather wide and in a face that looked a little pale, and thought, unwillingly, that Howard had been right about who the prime suspect was. Who, after all, would mind about her and Dan? Who watched him longingly from the ringside – whatever Anto said? It did fit, didn't it? The troubles had only started since she came back, and she was the outsider who no one really knew much about. And yet, like Chrissy, Polly hesitated to think that Anne Neville would hurt any horse. Horses were her life and her livelihood. But then, what if she had become mentally unbalanced again? That might override both deep instincts and self-interest. She *was* a strange person; and she lived an odd sort of life, wandering from place to place and bed to bed. And then there was that odd way she had of knowing everything. That would go with being a snooper and leading a secret life.

Polly blinked and drew back from her image and her thoughts. Snooper, blackmailer – and worse: potential injurer of people and horses? Was that possible? And did she *really* care so much for Dan? There had been others – lots of them, according to rumour – though one could never be sure about rumours like that. But she was 'with' Tom Emmerson now, that was a fact. Could one really assume that Dan was so different in her mind from everyone else?

But she had found the 'bomb'. What had she been doing in Balinasloe's stall anyway? Planting the thing in the first place? On the other hand, wouldn't that have been rather an obvious thing to do – too obvious?

How had she known about Bill's poison pen letter? Had Dan told her? Perhaps even Bill had told her – she seemed to know everyone. Or maybe she'd just overheard them talking. It was quite possible she'd been near enough in that crowded ring to hear without them seeing her – and Polly's attention had been firmly on the situation in any case, so she would hardly have noticed. Come to think of it, the nearest horse to her had been Captain Fox, hadn't it? She hadn't seen Anne, but who else would have been holding him?

A knock at the door made her jump. 'Who is it?'

'Who would you like it to be?' Dan's voice came.

'I'm not quite ready,' she called back, bending forward to address her mascara. She'd only done one eye.

210

'Coom on lass, stop fiddling with yerself. I'm bloody starving.'

'You really do know how to woo a girl,' Polly said. She went and opened the door, and went straight back to the mirror as he lounged in, looking handsome and dangerous and – it would never do to tell him – worth a poison pen letter or two.

'Are we going to eat in one of the hotel restaurants?' he asked.

'What's the alternative?'

'A taxi into town. Which'll cost a bomb unless we share.'

She smiled privately. Talk about Hobson's choice. 'Let's eat here. It'll be a chance to see all those celebrities.'

'What celebrities?'

'Didn't you know? There's a horse show on. We might get to sit next to someone really famous, like John Newland.'

'Less bunny, woman. Get yourself moving,' Dan said.

She straightened up and examined her eyes for evenness. 'You don't have to put on this macho act for me, you know. I'm already hooked.'

'My mother said women liked men to be masterful.'

'That was back in the dark ages, darling.'

Very shortly they were seated at a table with the obligatory glasses of iced water in front of them and the vast menus propped on their knees. The drinks they had ordered came: a gin and tonic for Polly and a whisky for Dan. Both were in tumblers filled to the brim with cracked ice. Dan stared at his morosely. 'Can't tell if it's a proper measure with all that ice.' He sipped. 'And the ice waters it down. They could be giving you anything.'

'Order it without ice next time. You're so reactionary. If everyone was like you, the wheel would never have been invented.'

'What's the wheel got to do with ice?'

She was about to answer when Gentleman Tom Emmerson came into the restaurant with Anne Neville on his arm. He looked every inch his sobriquet, and fitter than he had done for years. Anne was in a dress, for once, and with her hair shiningly arranged and a touch of make-up on eyes and lips. She looked very beautiful. She was smiling at something Tom had said and she didn't look odd just then, but kind and happy, not like a nut, a poison pen, a saboteur.

Polly glanced across at Dan, and her stomach did a somersault. He had noticed the new arrivals too, and was staring at them with such an expression of suppressed anguish that Polly turned her head away, feeling embarrassed to be seeing so much that he would presumably prefer to keep concealed. She didn't want him to know she knew. And it gave her her answer about whether or not to show him the letter. It would just be too unkind. She would get rid of it the first chance she had.

Before she had time to consider the mental process that brought her to this conclusion, Dan had recovered himself and was saying, 'Well, have you decided? What d'you fancy?'

Polly smiled and said brightly, 'D'you know, I think I fancy a hamburger. Unadventurous of me, I know, but there it is.'

'Have what you like, lass. I'm having a steak. You can't go far wrong with a steak, can you?'

Later on, when she went to the loo, she fished out the letter, tore it into little pieces, and flushed it down the pan. She wished she could flush away her suspicions with it. Chris had been right not to want to canvass the matter: it was, as she had said, poison.

The restaurant loos were out in a corridor of their own at the side, and later when Roberts went, he met Anne coming out of the ladies. They were alone there and out of view of the tables and he stopped in front of her, looking at her hungrily.

'You look very nice,' he said at last.

'Thank you,' she said. Her face was white and expressionless, her eyes fixed on him fathomlessly.

He couldn't help himself. He burst out, 'You know what

they're saying about you. That you're the one . . . who's doing these things.'

'The hoaxer,' she said flatly.

'Only it's not just hoaxes,' he said. 'Anne, you wouldn't . . . wouldn't . . .' He couldn't find the words. 'Would you?'

She gave him a bitter look. 'Do you have to ask me that?'

'No! I don't think it was you. I mean . . . I don't think the person I used to know would do those things.'

She looked at him a moment longer and then her eyes moved away and she began to walk past him. It enraged him that she wouldn't even argue her case. He caught her arm and stopped her.

'Let me go,' she said quietly.

'Anne, why did you leave me? *Why?* I thought we had something special. Christ, I *loved* you! Why did you just walk out like that?'

She looked down at his fingers digging into her bare upper arm, and obedient to the look, he released them slowly. There was a red mark. He had held her more tightly than he meant to. It must have hurt. He thought she would walk on without answering, but she said, 'You asked me that before. Do you really not know?'

'No!'

'You betrayed me,' she said. He stared at her, uncomprehending. 'With that girl at the Yorkshire County Show. You had her in the loot of her employer's horsebox. And then again in the hotel that night. Did you really think I didn't know?'

He still stared, and very slowly, memory came back. He was aghast. He didn't even recall the girl's name. 'You don't mean it was *that*? But she didn't mean anything to me.'

'When you were doing it, neither did I,' Anne said. 'I thought we were special to each other. Your idea of special turned out to be different from mine. I trusted you. You betrayed me. That's all.' And now she did walk away.

'It's not all,' he said. 'Anne!' And then, more urgently, '*Anne!*' He moved to the archway after her, but she didn't turn back. He watched her cross the restaurant. As she passed behind John Newland's chair she paused a moment and bent forward as if she was going to say something to him, into his ear; but then she moved on, and it was obvious he hadn't noticed her presence. It was only a momentary check, and by the time Roberts had followed she was back in her seat, *à deux* with the undeservingly lucky Tom Emmerson.

John Newland and Howard Meak went out on the town together. They had been friends for a long time before their upset at the Manchester Show, and Meak had always been anxious for the breach to be healed; for his part, Newland had already had several drinks when Meak came upon him alone at one of the bars, and perhaps that had softened him. At all events, he had received the overture with equanimity if not warmth and agreed to take a taxi into town. Chrissy had gone early to bed, so Meak was able to exert all his considerable charm on making the evening go. He sensed a reserve in Newland that he didn't remember on past jaunts; but then he himself had things on his mind.

His life seemed to be on a knife edge, and he dreaded having to make a decision, yet it seemed to be that Fate – or someone else beginning with an F – was pushing him steadily in exactly that direction. He didn't want it. He liked his life. Everything had been so comfortable before, and if it had been a little of a juggling act, surely he had managed it with supreme skill? Keeping plates in the air – keeping everyone happy – surely he deserved some credit for his dexterity? And yet, of course, if he applied his mind to his own problems as he applied them to other peoples', he would have to realise that nothing stays the same for ever. Life is change. And women in particular always seem to believe that if something isn't getting better, it's getting worse. They would want to make him choose between them, whereas that was the very thing he had been trying to avoid, for all their sakes.

What John Newland's problems were at this specific time he couldn't begin to guess, and didn't want to. His mind wanted an evening off, and a bit of light-hearted, ordinary jollity. Newland wasn't the world's jolliest at the best of times; but still, enough to drink on both parts, and an avoidance of any personal topics of conversation, and they managed to create at least a decent semblance of it.

When they got back to the hotel, they stopped off for one last one in the hotel bar, and then took the lift up to the ninth floor and fell out of it together almost in their old companionable way. As they turned, Meak saw someone come out of a room at the far end and disappear through the staircase door. It was only a glimpse, but his intellect, which had been on standby, snapped to attention and partly sobered him at once.

'Wasn't that your room?'

'Wasn't what what room?' Newland asked, much the drunker of the two.

'Isn't your room down there on the left?'

'I don't know. Can't remember the number.' He fumbled in his pocket. 'Where's the key? If you can call it a key. Plastic bastard. Had two of the buggers somewhere.' He produced one at last, and with it the cardboard ticket with his room number on it. 'Here's one, anyway. 9057. Wouldn't think they had nine thousand rooms in this hotel, would you?'

Meak ignored the feeble joke, busy calculating. 'It was your room. Someone just came out of it.'

Newland goggled a little, trying to think. 'Couldn't have.'

'I'm pretty sure it was yours. I'd better come with you, just to check. There've been some funny things going on.'

Now Newland seemed to sober abruptly. He straightened and walked down the corridor purposefully. Meak went with him, apprehensive as to what sight might greet them when Newland opened the door. A wild imagination remembered

The Godfather and hastily cancelled the thought as tempting fate. Burglary? A little vandalism? Glancing sideways at Newland's face, he saw that he was worried now. Despite his drunken state, his nostrils were flared and white with tension.

At the door he fumbled with the oblong of plastic that served these days for a key, dropped it, retrieved it, put it in upside down, rattled the handle frantically. 'Bloody thing! I miss proper keys,' he moaned. Meak took it from him, inserted it, waited for the green light, and pressed the handle. Newland pushed him aside and flung the door wide. The room stared back at them, innocent, tidy; the sheet corner turned neatly back, a pair of pale blue pyjamas, striped with crimson, lying ready on the bed.

Newland went across to his suitcase, opened the lid and looked in, checked in his bedside drawer, and then his breath escaped with a sigh as he straightened up. 'You had me worried for a minute. You must have been imagining things.'

'I'm sure I saw someone come out of this room.'

'Must have been the maid, then, turning down the beds.'

'Yes, I suppose so.'

'Got me worried for nothing, blast you,' Newland said, swaying; seeming to sink back into the drunkenness from which he had briefly emerged.

'Sorry and all that. Best intentions. Well, I'll push off to bed, then. See you at breakfast. Must say I don't admire your taste in pyjamas, old man. Bit gaudy!'

Meak backed out and closed the door behind him. He stood for a moment in thought, staring down the corridor. Of course maids don't turn down beds at that time of night, but perhaps it was as well Newland should think so. Meak thought he had recognised the distant figure, and if he was right, it added fuel to several fires. If it was her, what had she been doing in Newland's room – and how had she got hold of a key? Surely hotels didn't give them out just for asking? But perhaps he had been mistaken about the room. Perhaps she had been innocently visiting someone else in *their* room and was just leaving as they came out of the lift. But then why had she gone down the stairs when she saw them?

Well, maybe he was mistaken and it hadn't been Anne after all. He'd only caught a glimpse. He would much rather believe he was mistaken, because he didn't want to have to take action, having no idea what action would be appropriate or even possible. He went off to bed, but not to sleep for some time.

Emmerson was awake when Anne got back into bed beside him.

'What's the matter?' he murmured.

'Nothing. I've just been to the bathroom,' she whispered. She slithered down, tucking her head into the hollow of his shoulder. She stretched one arm and one leg across him, hugged him briefly, and settled for sleep.

Tom almost held his breath. He cradled her tenderly, long after both she and his arm had gone to sleep, afraid to move in case he woke her. They had had a lovely evening together. She had been affectionate and happy; they had made love; and now he was holding her in his arms as he had not held a woman for so long.

He knew what the others were saying about her. No one had said it directly to him, but he was not blind or deaf, as some people seemed to think. They thought Anne was the prankster, apparently on the old adage of 'here comes a stranger, let's heave a brick at him'. But it wasn't true, it wasn't true! She was a strange person in some ways. Sometimes when they were together she would be so warm and normal, chatty and funny, so absolutely human. At other times she would go all still and remote, and not answer, perhaps not even hear him, when he spoke; staring at nothing, far away in her thoughts. Her face would take on that madonna look, and her eyes become like deep pools, opaque to him. Then he would feel cold and shut out, almost afraid of her.

217

But everyone was entitled to their own thoughts. And one thing he knew for sure, absolutely for certain: she would never have drugged Chris Campbell's Sunny, or thrown a firework at Mackie. He had seen her with Sunavon, witnessed how all his horses loved her. He might believe her capable of playing a trick on a human, but not on a horse. She was not the prankster, and he was not even going to wonder why she had left the room, and why she had said she had only gone to the bathroom.

Tonight she was folded warm and soft in his arms. And tomorrow he would be competing in the big international ring and he would do well, he was quite sure of it. Life was wonderful, thanks to her. He was just being glad he hadn't died of a perforated ulcer back in his nadir period, when he, too, fell asleep.

Eleven

Mary Newland and Jean met at last by chance, bumping into each other at one of the stalls, and when Mary had stammered an incoherent greeting and half an explanation, Jean invited her to have a cup of coffee with her and talk.

'Don't worry, I won't tell John you're here,' she added, reading the terror in Mary's eyes, 'Though I can't see how you can keep it secret for ever. You're bound to bump into him sooner or later.'

'I'll take later,' Mary said, with a flash of wit that was new to Jean. When they were seated in a quiet corner with their cups before them, she asked, 'How is everything?' Despite her new found freedom and confidence, she kept her eyes on her revolving spoon. The habit of shyness came back to her now she was confronting this figure out of her old life, one who was so much bound up with John in her mind.

'Oh, OK,' Jean said. 'Your father was very upset, you know.'

'Was he?' Mary said. 'I suppose he was angry.' He had never liked to be crossed in anything. That was where John got it from, she supposed.

'I didn't say angry, I said upset. He doesn't talk about it, but you can see it. It's really knocked him for six.'

Mary said nothing. She had never thought anyone would *mind* about her, not in *that* way. Perhaps – bold thought – Jean was wrong, and Dad was only angry after all? 'Is . . . ? I suppose . . . suppose John's angry with me?'

Jean shrugged. 'Hardly expect him to be glad about it, can you? He did everything for you.'

Mary kept her eyes down. 'I expect he thought he did.'

'Well, he wouldn't have bothered with you if he didn't care about you, would he?'

'I don't think he cared about me,' Mary said bravely. 'I think he just cared about John Newland's sister. He didn't want me to let him down.'

Jean shrugged. The difference to her was no difference. 'Well, you did, didn't you? Big time.'

'I'm not doing anything wrong,' Mary protested, looking up at last. 'Just . . . just trying to do things my own way.'

Jean met her eyes with a hard look. 'Did you cut the stitching on John's stirrup leathers?' she asked abruptly.

Mary looked startled. 'What do you mean?'

'He had a fall at the Lutterworth show. His stirrup leather broke. Only when I came to look at it, it looked to me as if someone had cut the stitching nearly through.'

'He actually came off!' Mary said wonderingly, and then added hastily, 'But I wasn't even there!'

'It could have been done any time. It wouldn't go right away.'

Mary blushed vividly. 'It wasn't me.'

Jean watched her face with hard eyes. 'Bloody stupid, child-ish thing to do. He could have been killed.'

'Not John,' Mary said with absolute certainty. 'He could never have been hurt. Did . . . did John think it was me?'

'He said he thought it was just wear.'

She continued to stare thoughtfully at Mary, who, finding the scrutiny uncomfortable, sipped her coffee, and then changed the subject to what she really wanted to talk about. 'How's Amati?'

'He's all right.'

'Who's riding him?' Mary asked eagerly.

'Nobody. John told me to exercise him at first, but once we got busy I just didn't have the time. So we let him down, and turned him out to grass.'

'He's out all the time?'

'We couldn't keep him up with no one to ride him. But he's hardy enough to live out. Don't forget he's part native.'

'Oh, I know. That wasn't . . .' Mary stopped.

'What then?'

'I thought he . . .' Mary had been going to say she was afraid he would be lonely, but she was wary of Jean's scorn and sharp tongue. In the end she said, 'I sort of expected Dad to sell him.'

'I think he thinks you'll come back,' Jean said. 'Well, everyone does.' She fixed the girl with her eyes. 'What *are* you going to do?'

'Get a job,' said Mary.

'You?'

Mary saw the scorn and disbelief in Jean's eyes and stuck her chin out a bit. 'I've already been offered one. A very good job with a family in Connecticut.' The Marriotts were old friends of Mrs Watts, and she was gently urging Mary to take the position. Mary liked the sound of it, but thought it was rather a long way away from Ben. 'They're very rich and they keep two horses and three ponies, and I'd look after them and help the youngest girls who want to start competing in shows.'

'You, a groom?'

'Yes, and teaching and schooling. Anyway, what's wrong with being a groom? You're a groom.'

'I'm not Mary Newland.'

'Neither am I, any more. I'm just me,' Mary said defiantly. 'No more being John's sister. I'm free now, and I'm going to be happy. I can make lots of money here, grooming. The wages are fantastic, and I'll be living in so there'll be no expenses. I can get a permit for two years, and by that time, I'll have saved enough to go off travelling, unless . . .' She couldn't mention her hope of marrying Ben, not to Jean. She changed track hastily. 'It's what everyone does over here: all the young people. They work and save up, and then travel. Real freedom.'

Jean studied the pink, excited face and thought how young

221

she seemed. Rebounds did not only happen after unhappy love affairs: Mary was on the rebound from her brother, and after that complicated affair, everything seemed glamorously simple to her. Jean felt faintly worried for her, but there was no reason why she should: Mary was no charge of hers, and no concern either. Yet she felt she ought to warn her that life was never that easy, and that the past never really lets you go.

And families that you go and work for, especially live-in, are never the freshly-painted, smiling façades you see. Like the Newland family, they conceal, on first acquaintance, a lot of darkness and cobwebs. Free? Only money makes you free, and even then, only if you've been born to it, or you're lucky enough to have the perfect personality.

But Jean said nothing. A great part of her wished Mary well. I hope you make it, she thought. I never did, and nor did anyone else I know, but I hope you prove me wrong. You didn't have much of a life at home, God knows: bottom man on the totem pole. I don't blame you for trying to get out.

The mere sight of Mary, so full of innocent hope, made Jean feel faintly wistful. She was thirty-two and had never been pretty, naïve or in love like Mary. She didn't think she had ever even been that young. 'Well, good luck to you,' she said gruffly. 'Send me a postcard when you're settled, let me know how you get on.'

Mary smiled with pleasure at the approbation. 'Yes, of course I will!' she said eagerly. And then a cloud crossed her face. 'You won't tell . . . Dad or . . . or John? I mean, I know they can't stop me, or make me go home, now I'm eighteen, but . . .'

But it would take the shine off it if they tried, Jean thought. She shrugged. 'Your business, not mine. I won't talk.'

'Thanks,' said Mary fervently. In a warm surge of gratitude she almost reached out and touched Jean's hand, but didn't *quite* have the nerve.

*   *   *

At mid-morning break time, Howard Meak made his way
cautiously into the coffee shop least used by the team, hoping
to find no one he knew. Fliss was still playing cat and mouse
with his nerves, and it was – as she meant it to – spoiling his time
with Chrissy. He had left her with the horses to sneak a quiet
cup of joe and have a think; but he was not too unhappy to find
Polly Morgan sitting alone at a table, trying to make a house of
cards with the sugar packets.

'Hullo,' he said as it collapsed. She looked up. 'No Dan?'

'He's gone for a swim in the pool. I didn't bring a costume
with me.'

'They have them for hire.'

She gave a faint smile. 'Yeah. I know.'

He sat down. 'Have you two quarrelled?'

'Of course not. I haven't worked out yet how it's possible to
quarrel with Dan. No, he's having a moody and I'm having a
mope, that's all.'

'Ah.' Howard offered Polly a cigarette. She shook her head,
and he lit one for himself. 'Any reason in particular?'

'For which?'

'Well, we all know what Dan's problem is. I was more
interested in yours.' She didn't answer, turning a sugar packet
round and round in her fingers. 'Life with Superman not all a
bed of roses?'

'Oh, Dan's all right,' she said with faint discontent.

'Yes, he is. He's a great bloke and I love him like a brother,
but he's not right for you.' She looked up, one eyebrow raised
enquiringly. 'He's not exactly your intellectual equal, is he?'

'I hadn't exactly thought about him in those terms,' she
riposted. He smoked in silence, watching her, sensing she had
something she wanted to say. After a while she said, 'I'm a bit
mixed up.'

'You can say that again!'

'You're a rude bugger! What do you mean?'

'No, you tell me what you mean.'

223

She sighed. 'I was watching the news on CNN in the room this morning while Dan was in the shower. There was an item from England, some science and technology awards ceremony. A Yank boffin had won the big prize for innovation or something. It was only a short item . . .'

'Obviously. Not exactly the Oscars, is it?'

'They wouldn't have had it on at all if it hadn't been one of theirs winning it. But anyway, they showed him walking up to get the prize: past the big round tables up to the platform, you know the way these things go?'

'Only too well.'

'Some geezer at the top table handed the prize. And there in the background, also sitting at the top table . . .' She hesitated.

'Was Bill Simpson?' She nodded. 'With?'

She looked startled. 'How do you know?'

'My dear idiot, it didn't take the mind of an Einstein. So who was he with?'

'That's just it, I don't know. But she looked pretty glam. A bit of a blasted babe, if you want to know.'

'How do you know she wasn't with the bloke on the other side?'

'The way they were sitting, it didn't work that way. Anyway, she was practically in his lap,' she said fretfully. 'Low cut dress leaving everything to be desired. Tarty make-up.'

'Sounds delish.'

'Yes, but the point is, he didn't ask me.'

'You're not around,' Howard pointed out.

'But I'm only just not around. He must have known about it for ages. These things are arranged months beforehand, aren't they? But he never mentioned it to me or asked me to go with him. And if I wasn't free, why didn't he take Maureen?'

'Who's Maureen?'

'His sister. That's who he took when he had tickets for the ballet and I couldn't make it.'

Howard laughed. 'Maybe he fancied a bit of glam instead. What's your beef?'

She stopped frowning, with an effort, and said lightly, 'Oh, I haven't got a beef. It's just made me think . . . about things in general.'

'About Dan?'

'Partly.'

'Hmm,' said Howard. He watched her face a moment, and then said, 'Y'know, there's a saying: there's more to marriage than four bare legs in a bed. Sometimes the best person is not the one you fancy most.'

She smiled. 'I wasn't thinking of marrying Dan.'

'What are you doing it for, then?'

'Fun. It's just a bit of fun.'

'And is it fun?'

She didn't answer that. After a moment she said, 'And a bit of rebellion, maybe.'

'I see.'

She sighed. 'I'm very fond of Dan.'

'I've known him a long time, and there's only ever been one woman he cared about.'

'Yes.'

'And now all this stuff's come up . . . It's bound to make him fractious.'

'Fractious? What a lovely word,' Polly smiled.

'You see, you couldn't have had a conversation like this with him, could you?'

'I wouldn't try.'

'Bill Simpson's a pretty smart man. You don't run big companies single handed without having a lot of furniture in your attic.'

'Yes, yes, he's got a brain the size of a planet,' Polly said testily. 'Thank you Howard, I get the picture. Blimey, you're as subtle as an enema.'

'Elephant, did you say?'

225

'You're a lovely man, Howard Meak, so you are,' she said in brogue.

'I've always been able to give advice to everyone but myself,' Howard confessed contritely. 'Cup of coffee?'

Probably the first sensation of the show from the spectators' point of view had been the sight of Murphy bounding godlike into the ring and robbing all the best native horses – champions like Slipstream and Franco – of the Texaco Trophy. Now that he was officially called Murphy, commentators remembered that he had been David Barber's in his World-Championship year, history was researched and old photographs dug out. The Horse Fair had its own daily newspaper, pushed under every door before anyone was awake, and on the morning after the Texaco its front page was decorated with Dan's and Murphy's handsome faces.

But for the riders the first sensational event was not a pleasant one. It was Polly who raised the alarm, white faced from the shock the discovery had given her: when she went into Shilling's box first thing, she found the grey gelding's night rug had been slashed. The fact that it was still in situ had caused her to fear the worst until, with trembling legs, she had managed to get close enough to examine him and find his hide intact. Further examination showed that The Iceman had received similar treatment. Murphy's rug was almost in ribbons.

'So the phantom strikes again,' Howard Meak said to the group that gathered round the stable door. There was no humour in his voice.

'Thank God it was only the rugs,' Roberts said, and Polly caught his hand and pressed it. She didn't want him even to say the words, in case thinking about the evil gave it power.

'How many have been damaged?' Chrissy asked quietly.

'Five,' Polly said. 'At least, I've only heard of the five.'

'But all in our team?'

'Oh yes. Our three and Tom Emmersons' two.'

Chrissy's eyes widened and she looked at Howard.

'Our phantom's growing more random,' he said.

'Doesn't this rather let off who you were suspecting before?' she said.

'Well,' Polly began, and then stopped. Meak looked at her shrewdly and wondered if she'd thought the same thing as him. It would be a good ploy for the phantom to divert suspicion by an attack aimed at themself.

The stable manager came up to them along with Harry Parkinson, the *chef d'equipe*.

'We're going to ask you all to keep absolutely quiet about this,' Parkinson said, even at this hour and on this occasion a spotlessly turned out and utterly calm figure. He was an ex-cavalry colonel, and so much the epitome of what Americans would expect an ex-cavalry colonel to look and sound like that some of the British team suspected it was a conscious act. All the same, it was reassuring at a shivery moment like this. Just a glimpse of his perfectly groomed hair and neatly clipped moustache made you feel he was on top of things. 'I'm sure none of you would feel like spreading this story around anyway, but I'd like you to avoid talking about it even amongst yourselves, if you'd be so kind.' His calm grey eyes moved around them steadily. 'You appreciate that if any of this leaks to the press it will cause a very unpleasant sensation. I'm sure you all want to avoid that at all costs.'

'We won't talk,' said Meak abruptly, 'but it will leak out anyway. These things can't be kept under.'

'Maybe so,' the stable manager said, his hostility just apparent. 'But with your *cooperation*,' he stressed the word ironically, 'we might keep it down until the end of the show, by which time it will be too stale to make big news.'

'And while you're playing ostrich, what's being done to catch the lunatic?' Roberts snapped.

'We'll be proactive, I can assure you,' the stable manager

replied. 'But you'll appreciate that since the perpetrator may be one of you, I'm not going to tell you exactly what we're doing.'

'Thanks a bunch,' Polly muttered.

'We'll co-operate all right,' Howard Meak said. 'Just you make sure none of us gets murdered in our bed. Now that *would* be sensational news, wouldn't it?'

The damaged rugs were taken away and new ones provided, and it seemed that the attempt to confine the news to the team was successful. No one had any desire to gossip about it, especially outside their own numbers. It had been an extremely unpleasant incident, not least for bringing to mind what had *not* happened, but might so easily have.

But while the incident and the secrecy drew the team together as a team, it simultaneously held them apart as individuals. They all knew the phantom had to be one of them, and that he or she must be unbalanced. But to escape notice so far, they must also appear to be normal, and it was a nasty thought that anyone with whom you might be chatting, having a cup of coffee, or going up with alone in a lift, might have a secret life that they were able perfectly to conceal. Suspicion and apprehension made them uneasy in each other's company. Each rider trusted only his own groom, and the pairing off that was to an extent natural was emphasised by each pair's avoidance of the others.

Even the previously close foursome of Roberts, Morgan, Meak and Campbell drew apart somewhat. Roberts knew that Meak suspected Anne Neville of the acts of sabotage, especially since he had come back late at night and seen her – he *thought* it was her – prowling about, and he resented it. It was easy to avoid each other, for there was the exercising and schooling to be done, as well as the preliminary heats for the McDonalds' Speed Competition that evening; and they took their coffee and lunch breaks alone and avoided conversation.

Had they discussed the events of the day, they would have discovered that each of them had been unobtrusively interviewed by one of the plain clothes detectives who had been called in by the show committee. They would be on duty near the stables during the night, in addition to the usual security team, to make sure there were no other incidents; but their presence did nothing to relax the team. The horsemasters walked softly that day, and their tension communicated itself to the horses, who were jittery in their turn, whinnied to each other from their boxes and kicked out at each other while on exercise.

The Roberts-Meak conflict flared up in the afternoon, proving that their instinct to stay apart had been sound. They met by accident at one of the bars. Roberts had ordered a beer and a snack when Meak walked in alone. The two found themselves stranded face to face on a sandbank of politeness, and felt obliged to sit down together at a small corner table.

'So, how's tricks?' Meak asked at once, as if to stave off any tactless leap into the subject that Roberts might have been going to make.

'So-so. You?'

'Fine.' He sought around for something to say. 'I've just been riding Vibrant. He's in top shape. Didn't mind the plane journey at all. We're going to give you a run for your money tonight, even on your present form. Have you decided which horse you're going to jump?'

Roberts had qualified both The Iceman and Murphy for the speed competition, but competitors were only allowed one entry. As it was not a team competition, he had a free choice. 'Oh, Murphy, without a doubt.'

Meak raised an eyebrow. 'Surely Murphy's a puissance horse rather than a speed horse. And you're not forgetting that Vibrant cleaned the board here last year? Just a friendly, disinterested warning . . .'

'What else?' An unwilling grin tugged at Roberts's lips. 'Kind of you to worry about me. But you won't get out of facing Murphy that easily. In a ring this size there's not much difference between speed and puissance. It's a kind of Hickstead, if you like, and Murphy's yer ideal Hickstead horse.'

'You're telling me. I wish I'd been offered him before you got your word in. How's he settling? All the beasties seem to be seeing spooks today.'

'They sense the atmosphere,' Roberts said, and then his heart sank as he realised he had brought them round to the forbidden subject. His eyes met Meak's and what he read there drove him to say, 'You're wrong about her, you know, absolutely wrong! Listen, I know you think I'm just stuck on her, carrying a torch or whatever, but I do know her, and she'd never put a horse in danger.'

'You *did* know her once, but do you now?' Meak asked.

'What's that supposed to mean?'

'She'd never endanger a horse while she was in her right mind, but—'

'What are you saying? That she's nuts?'

'Don't get hostile. All I—'

'Hostile? Of course I'm bloody hostile! You sit there telling me to my face that she's off her head, that she's turned into a sadistic nut overnight—'

'Keep your voice down,' Meak pleaded quietly. One or two heads had turned. 'Didn't Polly tell you?'

'Tell me what?'

Meak told him what Alison Neave had coaxed out of him on the plane, about Anne's having been in a mental home. Roberts listened in pained surprise mixed with disbelief. 'Look, I've got no personal axe to grind,' Meak continued. 'I've got nothing against her. All I'm interested in is self-preservation. And you have to admit that it does make her the most likely suspect.'

'I don't see that,' Roberts said angrily. 'I don't accept that.'

'Oh, come on! I'm no more keen than you are to pin this on anyone, but you've got to look at the evidence, and look at it coolly.'

'Evidence? What evidence? You've got nothing! It could still

230

be any one of us. In fact,' Roberts added with the triumph of having just thought of it, 'the evidence is that it couldn't be her. What about the slashed rugs? She'd hardly do that to her own horses, would she?'

'They're not her horses. And besides, what better way to throw people off the scent?'

Roberts clenched his fists in frustration. 'Well, by that token you can't suspect anyone. I mean, it's just ridiculous! Are you saying Chrissy drugged Sunny to throw people off the scent?'

'No, of course not!'

'Then why pick on Anne, for God's sake? You're just mud-slinging because you don't happen to like her. She's an outsider and not one of your class.'

'Oh for crying out loud! Don't bring class into it.'

'In any case, you've got no right to speculate. You aren't involved. Nothing's happened to you.'

Howard Meak had spent the day looking over his shoulder, wondering what was going to face him when he got home, feeling wretched that Fliss was upset for no reason, feeling guilty about Chrissy being brought into it, feeling most of all the fury that comes with being wrongly suspected and being unable to make oneself believed.

'God, when you set out to be blind, you really make a good job of it, don't you!' he snapped.

'You mean something *has* happened to you?' Roberts began slowly.

'None of your damned business.'

'I'm sorry. Why didn't you tell me?'

'I don't like to broadcast my private business. And, to keep to the point, I'm not slinging mud. I'm trying to keep an open mind and examine the evidence, which is more than you're doing.'

'And I said you've got no evidence!'

'Then we'd better hope we get some before the phantom – whoever it is – escalates the action,' said Meak grimly.

*   *   *

Tom Emmerson was sitting, dressed for the ring in all but his stock and coat, in one of the chairs by the window when Anne came out of the bathroom. A glass of amber fluid was in his hand, and on the round table beside him were three of the miniature bottles out of the mini-bar, all empty. She eyed them as she passed, wrapped in a towel, her hair skewered on top of her head, but said nothing. Emmerson's eyes followed her across the room. She sat down on one of the beds, unlatched her hair, took up a brush and began to untangle it.

Their eyes met at last and she said, 'Nerves?'

'About going in the ring? Never. That's never been what made me drink.'

'I didn't think it was. So, what, then?'

He took a long time summoning the question. 'Is it true?'

She sighed. The hand holding the brush fell into her lap and her face took on its remote look, a pale, expressionless oval marked by two black pits of eyes.

'I know you don't like answering questions,' he went on, a little desperately, 'but I have to know. You do see that I have to know.'

'I see nothing,' she said remotely.

'Anne, you know how I feel about you. God, I've never known anyone like you in my life. And I owe it to you that I'm here. But they're saying . . . it's going round . . .'

She waited, patient as death, for him to say it.

'They say you were in a mental home. Is that true?'

He didn't think she would answer. For a long time he looked at her, waiting without hope, and only when he raised his glass to his dry lips again did she say simply, 'Yes.'

'Yes?' A pause. 'Is that all?'

'What else do you want?'

'What else? Christ, I want to know *why*, of course. What were you in for?'

'Does it matter?'

'It does to me.'

She stood up. 'A nervous breakdown, Tom. I had a nervous breakdown.'

Relief flooded over him. 'Is that all? Oh, thank God! I thought . . . I was afraid . . .' He was babbling. Anyone could have a nervous breakdown. That didn't mean anything.

She was looking at him oddly. He stopped babbling. She said, 'I have a certificate to say I'm sane. How many of you can say the same?'

He thought she was making a little joke, and he smiled broadly. 'Well, put like that, of course . . .' She hadn't been joking, and her expression cut him off. It chilled him.

She turned away. With her back to him, she said, 'You shouldn't have asked me that.'

'I'm sorry,' he said feebly.

She picked up her nightdress from where it lay on the bed they had been sharing, and with an eloquently economical movement placed it on the other bed. Then she gathered up the clothes she had put out ready to wear and took them into the bathroom with her to get dressed. He heard the small click as she locked the door behind her. It was the first time since she had come to him that she had ever done that.

The competitors' box was packed, as all those who had failed pressed in eagerly to watch the third and final jump-off of the McDonalds' Speed. It lay between four hoary old professionals: John Bryan for the USA on Franco, Gerhard Bruna for Germany on Orly, John Newland with Apache, and Dan Roberts with his new wonder horse, Murphy.

They had drawn for the all-important order, and Bruna went in first. It was always a challenge, not knowing how far to risk accuracy for speed, and he went clear, but in no remarkable time. Bryan going after him went a little faster but had a brick out of the wall: just a careless flick of a hind hoof that could happen to anyone, any time.

John Newland had gone in with the expectations of most of

the crowd – if not the wishes of his fellow competitors – and true to form he stripped eight seconds off Bruna's time, only to have a pole off at the very last jump, leaving him with four faults. He arrived in the competitors' box, panting, as Roberts rode into the ring, and shoved his way down to the front. The others let him through, pardoning his manners out of sympathy, giving him the best spot from which to watch whether Roberts would leave him with second place or push him down to third. Newland's face was still red from his exertions, and he was sweating with the heat and effort and tension, his hands, resting on the top of the barrier, clenched into fists.

The Murphy who came out into the ring was a different creature from the horse who had plunged around the Underhill paddock a few months ago. The spotlights picked up his golden coat and turned it to flame as he paced calmly forward, holding his head as delicately as if the bit were an egg he had to carry in his mouth without breaking it. His flexible lips worked, his long ears flicked forward and back and then forward again, taking in the scene and listening for the voice of his rider.

The rider sat so apparently relaxed that he might have been a mere passenger; but the great muscles of his thighs lay against the horse from knee to buttock, holding him in a grip that was both commanding and reassuring. A straight line could have been drawn from the horse's mouth through the reins and the rider's forearms to the delicate hinge of his elbows. As his flexible body and strong legs made a spring that controlled the horse's great quarters, so his flexible hands and strong biceps made another spring against which the horse's forward motion was delicately buoyed.

The horse leaned ever so slightly against this precision restraint, needing it as the wind needs the resistance of the sail to make the boat skim along. He weighed almost half a ton, yet his hard round feet hardly dented the tan as he walked. He was ten, twenty times more powerful than the man he carried, yet had the reins been merely silk threads, they would not have snapped. Horse and man moved forward in utter accord, and it was a beautiful thing to see. Polly felt almost hollow with desire: she had never fancied Dan as much as at that moment. A slight movement made her turn her head, and she saw Anne Neville a little way away, watching with her hands unconsciously clasped. She looked as if she was holding her breath at the sight, and her eyes were shining with what Polly had no difficulty in recognising as pure love.

Roberts's position was a hard one, as hard in its way as Bruna's. He could take it slowly and precisely to try to make sure of a clear round; but then he might not be fast enough to beat Bruna's time, and if he had a pole off he would certainly not be fast enough to beat Newland's. But if he went all out for speed he might knock something down – or even several somethings – and end up fourth. It was a problem he was well used to facing, but this time he had no hesitation. He no more made a conscious decision than he did when he was about to make love. He and this horse were in utter accord, and he felt its confidence and its power as if it were an integral part of his own body. The competition was between them as an entity, and the jumps. Newland, Bryan, Bruna were not in it. The bell went, and without any conscious command given or received, horse and man went forward into a rocking hand canter.

Polly watched, entranced, swaying a little, unconsciously, as she followed the horse's movement. As Murphy passed a few inches from her she felt his weight and warmth as he pressed the air aside, heard his snorting breaths like the sound of ripping silk, felt the vibration of the tan under his feet. He would do it – the thought came to her with the simplicity of truth. She turned her head to follow him over the next jump, and her eyes lit on John Newland, so tense his whole body seemed to be trembling, his face as white as if he was going to be sick. His eyes were fixed on the ring in some kind of anguish, and he chewed his lower lip painfully. What made this so important for him? she wondered. Every contest matters, of course – they would not be here, any of them, if they did not have the competitive spirit. But, as with that time when she had snatched the Tomatsu from him at Manchester, this seemed something more.

Well, who could care about John Newland? And yet he had loved her once, though it seemed so long ago now she could not remember how she had felt about him. Still, she felt a stirring of concern, or pity. There was something magnificently inevitable about Murphy in the ring, and John was pinned by it like something helpless and insignificant, a rabbit transfixed by headlights, about to be mown down. When Dan and Murphy cleared the last jump, undoubted winners, faster than Bruna, faster even than Newland – when the crowd erupted with wild applause and cheering – she heard Newland's indrawn breath, like pain.

Roberts rode out of the ring, and Polly's first instinct was to push through the crowds to get to him as quickly as possible with her congratulations. Others obviously felt that too, for a general movement was sweeping back towards the exit, and amongst those hurrying to acclaim the winner Polly saw Anne Ashley Neville, her face taut with pleasure. But John Newland had struck at her consciousness like a wounded animal, and she could not leave him so abruptly. He was still where he had been, staring at the empty ring, his chewed lip showing bloody now.

'John,' she said. 'John, bad luck. It was a good competition.'

He turned, but didn't seem to see her. His eyes were angry, his face set in grim lines. He seemed to be staring at someone or something beyond her. She put out a tentative hand, but he pushed by her without a word and shouldered his way through the crowds. Polly turned to see what he had been looking at, but could pick out nothing of significance from the massed bodies behind her.

She shrugged the matter away and went to find Dan.

The evening's drinking was lavish, and Dan got pretty ripe; and with ripe came a touch of maudlin. Polly, to her own disappointment, couldn't get much of a glow on, and there's nothing more irritating than to be sober in the company of a sentimental drunk. Eventually, tiring of having him slop over her while his eyes were unmistakably fixed elsewhere, she removed his massive, heavy arm from across her shoulders and said she would go and take a last look at the horses.

'I thought Iceman was looking a bit off earlier. I want to make sure he hasn't got a touch of colic.'

'You shouldn't have to go, Polly, ma little lass,' he said. 'I'll do it.' But he didn't move to get up; if anything, he sank a little further in his seat.

'You forget, I'm the groom. It's my job,' she said lightly.

He gave her a rather crooked grin. 'S'not what I brought you all this way for.'

'Don't let Harry hear you say that,' she said, dropping a kiss on the end of his nose. He tried to grab her but his arms were moving even more slowly than his brain and she evaded him easily and slipped away.

Outside, it was a moonless night, and the starry sky was partly obscured by veils of hazy cloud. Once she had passed out of the circle of muffled light cast by the hotel, it was quite dark, but the shrub-bordered way to the stables was lit by lamps on sticks down at ground level, which showed the path, though they illuminated nothing above it.

The air felt fresh after the fug in the bar, and the gravel crunching under her feet made a cheerful sound. She breathed deeply and got her equilibrium back. Poor old Dan, she thought. Poor old her, too. What a muddle it all was. Who *was* the woman with Bill at the awards ceremony? Had she driven him away once too often, and finally lost him? She had thought she was pretty level headed about Bill, and was taken aback at the strength of her feelings about the mystery woman. Bill was too nice a person to be 'caught' by such an obvious bimbo! If he was going to love anyone but her – and she had to admit that it surprised and hurt her that it could even be

237

possible – it ought to be someone she could see the point of: someone she could respect, if not actually like. But then why, if she didn't want to marry him, should she care?

Pondering this phenomenon, she reached the stable yard. One of the security guards was walking across it, on a routine circuit, she supposed, and stopped on seeing her. She waggled her identity badge at him and called, 'Just going to look at one of my horses.'

He came a few steps nearer and examined her face and noted her name. 'Gotta stick you on the log. You gonna be long? I was just gonna put the night lights on.'

'No, I just want to check on a horse. He didn't seem quite well earlier. I want to make sure he's not sickening for something.'

He looked her up and down – checking her for weapons, she wondered, or admiring her figure? – and then said, 'OK.'

The Iceman was actually lying down when she went in, looking very comfortable and absurdly like an enormous white cat. He blinked his long eyelashes and drew a huge sigh, which ended in a rattle of the nostrils that was almost a sneeze; but he didn't offer to get up.

'Well, there's nothing much wrong with you, is there?' she said, reaching down to rub his forehead. He grunted in reply. 'You're so sweet,' she told him, and he flapped his lips at her and then rested his chin on his knee, half closing his eyes in a manner that said as plainly as words *close the door after you.* Polly took the hint and left him.

The security guard was further off but still in sight, and she waved to him and made a forefinger-and-thumb circle to say everything was all right. He raised a hand in reply, and turned away. Fabulous security, she thought. I could have done anything in there. But she supposed he couldn't be everywhere all the time. She set off down the path back to the hotel.

The path, probably in the interests of landscaping and such artistic considerations, was laid out in two generous curves, like a backwards *S*, and the central section was out of sight both of the stables and the hotel, cut off by the shrubbery. She was walking at the edge of the path, watching her feet displace the gravel and looking at the moths dancing around the low, tubular lights, when suddenly her plait of hair seemed to catch in something. She was pulled backwards with a jerk that hurt her neck; but before she could put her hand up to release herself, an arm came round her from behind and a hand in a leather glove was slapped over her mouth.

Panic struck her like a bolt through the heart. Behind the leather she gaped for air, eyes wide in fear. The arm and hand tightened, pulling her backwards. A knife came into her line of sight, flashed dully in the faint light, and was pressed against her neck as she was dragged backwards off the path into the bushes.

Terror froze her brain. She was too frightened to struggle. Gagged by the hand, she couldn't breathe properly; she felt the coldness of the knife pricking the skin over her carotid artery. Despair joined terror. She was going to die.

Then she remembered someone in a self-defence lesson long ago saying *don't resist; use your weight.* There was no time to think about it, or whether it was a good idea. Already off balance, she dug her heels into the earth and used the leverage to fling herself backwards against her assailant.

She felt the body behind her teeter, and then they both went over. Twigs scratched Polly's face; she flailed; the leather-clad hand was gone from her mouth and she gasped in air. They hit the ground, Polly on top; then it was all confusion, thrashing arms, legs; a wild struggle to get away. Polly lashed out, hitting something soft, scrambled over on to hands and feet, wood bark under her fingernails, her hair snagging on a bush. Something grabbed her ankle and she jerked herself free with a mad effort, and screamed. Yes! She could breathe now, and she could shout! '*Help! Help me!*'

A yell answered her. She staggered forward. Sound of feet

crunching the gravel. Stumbling madly for her life, she shot out
on to the path and cannoned into someone, shrieked again, and
then realised it was Dan.

'What is it? What's wrong? Are you all right?'

'He tried to kill me!' she gasped, clutching at his broad chest.
She flung a hand back. 'The phantom! Grabbed me . . .
Knife . . . Thank God you came!'

'Where?'

'Bushes!'

'I'll get the bastard!'

She was put roughly aside, but went after him, afraid to be
alone. She thought of the knife, and of the phantom jumping
out on them from the dark; but there were two of them now. It
must have been because the phantom heard Dan coming that
she had been let go. It surely wouldn't have been so easy
otherwise.

Dan was beating the bushes like a gamekeeper. 'Bastard!' he
kept saying. 'Bastard!'

'It's too late, he's gone,' she said, tugging at his sleeve. 'It's no
use.'

He pulled away from her for a moment, then saw it was true.
The dark shrubbery was silent and motionless. 'Goddammit,'
he growled with frustration.

Polly was trembling. 'I feel sick.'

He saw that she needed him, and abandoned the hunt.
'Shock,' he said. 'You need a large brandy. C'mon, back to
the bar. We'll call out security.'

He put his arm round her. She leaned gratefully against the
huge heat of his hard body and they headed for the hotel.

'I was coming to find you, of course,' Dan said. 'As soon as you
left, the party broke up and everyone else went off to bed. I
hung around for a bit hoping you'd come back. Then I came to
find you.'

The bar was empty apart from them, and the barman was

looking not a little cheesed at having to stay on duty. But Roberts had insisted with all the force of his personality that he guard Polly while he went to raise the alarm. On his return he found she had stopped shivering, but administered a second brandy just in case.

Dan, Polly noted, had been plunged into absolute sobriety by the shock.

'Are you really all right?' he asked her, more than once.

'Yes, now my heart's stopped racing. Just a ricked neck and a few scratches on my face and hands from the bushes. But thank God you came along when you did.'

'I'll never forget hearing you scream like that. Blimey, I nearly had a heart attack. What happened exactly?'

'He grabbed me by my pigtail and pulled me backwards. He had a knife.' She shuddered.

'He?' Roberts said eagerly. 'Did you see him?'

'No. It was all so quick. I didn't see anything.'

'But it was a man?'

She understood his purpose. 'I don't know,' she said slowly. 'I just assumed it was. But I honestly don't know.'

He glared at her a moment as though he could make her remember. 'It must have been a man. A woman wouldn't have been strong enough.'

Polly didn't want to upset him, and she was in no state for an argument. 'It's more likely it was a man, I suppose.'

The search of the shrubbery produced nothing, which was only to be expected. The detective took down Roberts's account, then interviewed Polly, but there was little she could tell him.

'Can you remember anything, anything at all that might help identify the attacker?'

'It was all so quick,' Polly said. 'Really, it was all over in a second. There was a leather glove, and a knife. That's all I know.'

'He didn't speak?' She shook her head. 'How tall was he?'

'I don't know. I was in a state of panic. Please, I'd help if I could. I just don't remember anything else.'

She was almost tearful, and Harry Parkinson intervened before Dan could blow a fuse. 'Maybe something more will come back to you later, when you've had a sleep. I think she ought to get some rest now,' he said firmly to the detective.

Polly stood up, and Dan with her. 'I suppose you'll have to find out where everybody was at the time,' he said.

'It's a pity everyone had left the bar and gone up to bed,' Parkinson sighed.

Roberts met his eyes defiantly. 'Tom Emmerson's in the clear, anyway. He and Anne Neville are sharing a room.'

'Yes,' said Harry, perfectly well aware of what he meant. 'It would appear that way.'

Twelve

I t was a subdued group that gathered in one of the small conference rooms the next morning, to be addressed by Harry Parkinson. There was none of the usual joking and badinage; everyone sat quietly, avoiding everyone else's eyes.

'It would appear that the stakes have been upped somewhat by this latest incident.' Parkinson gazed around them, calm as a lion on the veldt. 'I don't want to upset anyone unduly, but I think you should all try to be on your guard. In particular, I am making it a rule that after dark no one should go down to the stables alone. Keep at least in pairs.'

'Yeah, that's all right as long as your pair isn't the phantom,' Anto muttered audibly.

'Thanks,' said Alison. 'I needed that.'

Parkinson raised his voice a little over them. 'Our phantom seems very keen to avoid identification, so I think it unlikely that anything will happen in daylight; and the hotel and most areas of the grounds are too populous to represent any danger. If you all take reasonable precautions, there should be nothing to worry about.'

'So what was the result of last night's investigation?' Howard Meak asked.

'Nothing conclusive was discovered,' Parkinson replied smoothly.

Meak looked angry. 'Look here, Harry, this is not the time for Cabinet secrecy. We were all dragged from our beds to be interrogated last night, and the outcome affects us all.

So don't give us that "nothing conclusive" crap. What did you find out?'

'If there were anything to tell you, I would tell you,' Parkinson said, unmoved. 'I think it best if we don't discuss this, even among ourselves. The more it is talked about, the more likely it is to leak out, and the last thing we want is to have a general scandal. That would be to play into the hoaxer's hands, wouldn't it?'

'Hoaxer?' Meak exclaimed, but Parkinson raised a magisterial hand and ended the meeting by walking out. The group broke up and people left the room, talking in low voices or hugging their thoughts in silence.

Later that morning, Howard Meak was sitting on Vibrant in the collecting ring, waiting for his turn in the preliminary heat of the Duracell Time Test, when Dan Roberts came up to him.

'Well,' Roberts said, after a quick look around to see there was no one within hearing range, 'that shoots your bloody fox, doesn't it?'

'What are you talking about?'

'The attack on Polly last night.'

'How so?'

Meak's cool tones and his choice of words annoyed Roberts. 'How so? How bloody so? Because it couldn't have been Anne, that's how so! For a start, it had to have been a man to overpower Polly; and for a second thing, Anne was tucked up safe in bed with Tom Emmerson at the time. So suck the pips out of that one!'

Meak looked down at him with a frown, wondering whether to respond. He had no desire to pick a fight with Roberts, especially on this issue, but he was short of sleep this morning. He was worried about Chrissy's safety. Whatever Harry said, he thought she and Polly, at least, were vulnerable, and he couldn't be with her every minute of the day. Like now, for instance: could they really be sure the phantom wouldn't attack in daylight? Then there were his own private problems nagging at the back of his mind; and besides, oafishness was his particular *bête noir*. His resolve snapped.

'To answer your first point, Anne is not exactly a weakling. All our women are pretty strong; and if you are attacking someone of near your own build, the best way is to get them off balance, by catching them by surprise and from behind.'

'My God, you'd say anything!' Roberts said in disgust. 'Do you really—'

'And secondly,' Meak went on across him, 'she wasn't tucked up in bed with Tom Emmerson, as it happens. Harry wouldn't come across, but I had a word with the detective bloke, and got it out of him. She and Emmerson got as far as the lift, then she said she'd left her jacket behind in the bar. The lift had just arrived so she told him to go on up and she'd follow. So at the appointed time, she was God knows where and unaccounted for.'

Roberts stared. 'Well, she *could* have left her jacket,' he said at last, trying to speak calmly. 'Why not?'

'You stayed on in the bar after we all left. You'd have seen her if she came in.'

This was uncomfortable. 'Maybe she left it somewhere else. Anyway, she couldn't have been away for long. How long did Tom say she was away?'

Meak shrugged. 'He's in love with her. He's not going to give her away. But I've seen the way he looks at her. He's not sure about her any more, and neither should you be.'

'You're just bloody prejudiced!' Roberts almost shouted in frustration.

'Look, I've no time for this now. I've got to go in the ring any minute.'

'That's right, run away. You know you're wrong.'

'I'm just trying to be objective.'

'Then put your money where your mouth is.'

'What do you mean?'

'All this uncertainty is driving me nuts. Let's do something about it.'

'You've got a plan to uncover the phantom?' Howard was unable quite to conceal his scepticism.

'Maybe not that, but to clear Anne of suspicion, anyway.'

'So what is it?'

'Keep watch tonight. Tom Emmerson's room is nearly opposite the staircase, and there's a glass panel in the staircase door. We can stand out on the landing and watch. If she comes out, we'll follow her.'

'Are you serious?' Meak stared. The thought of spending a night standing on a cold staircase staring at a closed door appealed to him so much!

'I'm dead serious.'

Meak saw that he was. 'It's ludicrous.'

'No it's not. It's simple. But if you're not man enough to put your money where your mouth is . . .'

'It's not a matter of that.'

'Isn't it? You're free enough with your accusations. It's different when it comes to proving it, isn't it?'

'Oh, all right,' Meak said, goaded. 'I suppose you're right. But I don't think it will prove anything. And you don't expect me to stay out there all night, I hope?'

'For just as long as it takes,' Roberts said grimly, and Meak shuddered.

Keeping watch on Tom Emmerson's hotel-room door hadn't seemed like the best idea in the world when it was first put to him, but by three o'clock in the morning, Howard Meak was sure it was the worst. Why had he ever agreed to it?

After the show, the inevitable drinking session was still going on when at about a quarter to one Anne and Tom Emmerson got up, said goodnight and headed for their room. At that point Meak would have avoided Roberts's eyes altogether had he been allowed to. He had enough on his mind as it was, without mounting ridiculous surveillance exercises. Surveillance was the dirtiest of dirty words as far as he was concerned.

Felicity had shown up. She might have been at the complex all along, of course, for all he knew, but that evening after the show she suddenly appeared, waylaying him in the side foyer of the hotel – the one the team used to get to their annexe – just as he was coming in with Chrissy. Though he had been expecting her ever since they left England, it was still a shock, like being hit over the heart with a heavy stick. From the expression on her face, he knew she had seen his reaction and interpreted it as guilt. He stopped dead. Chrissy stopped. The three of them stared at each other through an atmosphere as thick as pea soup.

'Well, this is nice,' Felicity said. 'Cosy, almost. Domestic.'

'Hullo, Fliss,' Chrissy said with an attempt at normality. 'I didn't know you were going to be here.'

'Oh, didn't you?'

'No, she didn't. I didn't tell her,' Howard said quickly. 'What do you take me for?'

'Very protective, aren't you?' Felicity said nastily. 'It's quite touching, really.'

'What do you want?' he asked, trying to sound patient, adult, innocent. 'Have you just come here to insult me, or did you want something?'

She turned and beckoned to a man who had been standing by the lifts, pretending to be nothing to do with the scene. 'I came here to put an end to things,' she said. 'This is George Stanford. You may have seen him around quite a bit lately.'

Meak stared at the man, who had a face quite devastatingly ordinary and unmemorable. 'I don't think so. But there are lots of people in this wing . . . and thousands at the show.'

Fliss gave a triumphant smile. 'You weren't supposed to notice him. He's a private investigator.'

Chrissy stirred at that, flung a look up at Howard that he couldn't quite interpret. He said, slowly, outraged, 'You put a private detective on me?'

'How else was I going to catch you out? I gave you fair warning, Howard. Most wives wouldn't do that, but I wanted to play fair with you. But you' – her voice took on a quiver of rage – 'didn't even respect me enough to take my warning seriously.'

'Now look here . . .'

'I think I'd better go,' Chrissy said in a small, pale voice.

Fliss rounded on her. 'No, you stay right where you are, Miss! You aren't going to run away from it! When I think how kind I've been to you over the years, welcoming you into my house, treating you like one of the family . . . !'

Chrissy put out her hands in helpless anguish. 'But Fliss, we haven't *done* anything!'

'Oh, save me that! Spare me the pious lies!'

'I'm not lying!'

'You're in love with my husband!' Felicity raged suddenly. 'Aren't you? Admit it! You see, you can't deny it. You little slut! Home wrecker! *Deceitful bitch!*'

Chrissy reeled back from the words as if each was a slap across the face.

At that point Stanford spoke for the first time, in tones so even and matter-of-fact they were almost shocking. 'Perhaps we should take this somewhere quieter. Less public.'

None of the other three had any words just for the moment, and followed in silence as he led the way to a quiet corner of the foyer, where there was a round table and chairs. They all sat with the uneasy air of people who have come to a party on the wrong day. Howard and Felicity were glaring at each other; Chrissy avoided everyone's eyes, staring down unhappily at her hands.

'The situation is this,' said Stanford. 'Mrs Meak hired me to mount a surveillance on you, with special regard to this young lady.' He flicked a not unsympathetic eye at Chrissy. 'I have a copy of the hotel registration list which shows that you occupy room 9041 alone while Miss Campbell officially shares room

9010 with a Miss Morgan. In actual fact, Miss Morgan has not been to room 9010 at all. You, on the other hand, have visited that room on several occasions, and Miss Campbell has been on several occasions in your room, both during the daytime and at night.'

Howard felt rather sick. He wanted most of all to run away as far and as fast as he could, but he had to play the endgame, for Chrissy's sake if not for his own. 'We're friends. How many more times? We are *friends*. Friends visit each other's rooms. We haven't done anything . . . Haven't done what you're suggesting, I mean.'

Felicity spoke, holding up a hand to silence Stanford. 'I don't care. Don't you understand that? I don't *care*! I'm sick of your disgusting, endless, *platonic* affair! Do you think that not actually dipping your wick . . . Oh, too crude for you? Well, I've got news for you, Howard: it *is* crude, the whole thing, crude and vulgar and disgusting! And d'you really think that not dipping your wick would let you off the hook while you were unfaithful to me in every other way, day in and day out? God, I could almost have liked you more if you'd boasted about it! At least it would have proved you had some red blood in you! But no, you're like one of those horrible overbred pedigree dogs, one of those shivering things that's had all the life bred out of it. You're welcome to him,' she turned suddenly on Chrissy, 'and his limp, white, overbred, bloodless cock! Much joy may it bring you!'

'Mrs Meak,' Stanford warned quietly. She looked at him and closed her mouth. He continued, as unemotionally as if he was reading the weather forecast. 'The incontrovertible evidence I have that you have been in each others' bedrooms, along with photographs showing you continually together, and the anecdotal evidence of a long-running affair from various friends and acquaintances, will be quite enough in court to convince the judge to grant the divorce.'

Felicity gave a little nod of satisfaction. Howard stared

hopelessly from her to Stanford and back. 'What do you want, then?' he asked.

'Want? Nothing,' she said. 'I'm going to divorce you, that's all. You will get nothing. I will keep everything. You're finished, Howard. I just wanted to have the satisfaction of seeing you caught and telling you this to your face. You're *finished.*'

She stood up, and Stanford stood up with her. 'You will receive an official communication in due course,' he said. 'Goodnight.'

They left without another word, leaving Howard and Chris in the sort of shattered silence that might have followed an earthquake.

When at last he pulled himself together and tried to speak to Chrissy, she stood up too, shaking her head. 'No, please, don't talk. I know we have to talk about this, but not now. I couldn't bear it now.'

'All right, I won't talk, but let's go to my room.'

'No,' she said, still not meeting his eyes. 'I'm going to my own room . . . *alone*. I can't bear anything more now, not tonight. Please, Howard. Please understand.'

She went, alone. He felt exhausted, miserable, sore, lonely, mistreated, guilty, angry. He went straight to the bar and ordered a double brandy, no bloody ice, and knocked it back, and was ordering a refill when the others came in, full of bonhomie and cheer, and he was trapped. The drinking session ensued and he was called upon to play his part. Yes, everyone looked to Howard Meak for entertainment. I'm the court bloody jester, he thought bitterly; when's it going to be my turn to enjoy myself?

When Anne and Emmerson said goodnight and left, he tried to avoid Roberts's eye, and contemplated slipping away soon afterwards, but his wrist was seized in a great ham of a hand, and with a wink at Polly, Roberts stage-whispered, 'This is it. Come on, let's go.'

Howard felt irritation rising in him and said, 'She's not going to go anywhere while we're all still up.'

'Yes, but we must check she goes into his room, otherwise we won't know we're watching the right place.'

'Oh, really, I don't think—'

'*Come on*! You promised.'

So he was let in for it.

Now, much later, he was exhausted and miserable, and longed for sleep as the way out of his own repetitive thoughts, but sleep was not to be his. Staying up all night was no new experience for him, but he had never before spent the early hours of the morning standing on a cold concrete staircase landing with a large, bristle-chinned man, and he was not eager to prolong or repeat the experience.

Enough was enough. At last he said, 'Oh, come on, this is a waste of time. Obviously nothing's going to happen.'

'Shh!' hissed Roberts. And then, 'This is it!' He shifted a little so that Meak could join him at the glass panel, and he looked across at that hated door in time to see it open, just a crack. Then it opened fully, and the dark, narrow figure of Anne Neville came out. She was wearing a black cotton roll neck and tight black ski pants. Her hair was tied back, and she held something in her right hand down at her side.

Meak felt his heart trip and accelerate. In spite of everything, he really hadn't expected this; and he had certainly not wanted it. Not Anne. In the deepest places of his soul, he hadn't really, not *really*, believed it was her. But here she was, creeping out, dressed for dark deeds. Oh God, he thought miserably, I wish I hadn't agreed to this. What the hell is she up to? She looked guilty. Oh, surely this couldn't be it? He wished himself anywhere but here, a witness to evil.

She eased the door shut behind her so that it would make no sound, and stood for a moment looking down the corridor, away from them. Faintly, transmitted through the fabric of the concrete walls, they could hear the lift shuddering into action.

She lifted her right hand and did something to whatever it was she was carrying; then as the hand went back down to its previous position, Roberts gasped and gripped Meak's arm painfully, and at the same moment Meak saw the faint glint as the corridor light glanced off the blade of a large Swiss Army knife.

She had been opening it. Oh Jesus, no! She was going to hurt someone. Or some horse. But everyone was in bed. God no, surely not the horses? She wouldn't – she mustn't! But the knife, the knife was a fact. Polly had been threatened with a knife. Anne said she had gone back for her jacket last night: she could have left it stashed somewhere, with the gloves and knife in its pocket. It must have been her after all! She must really be mad. Unbalanced. His hands were damp now, and he had ceased to notice the pain in his arm where Roberts was gripping him, though the latter's breath was whistling in his ear like a gale.

Then she seemed to make up her mind and moved, coming straight for them. Stupid. Stupid not to think that she might use the stairs! If she was guilty, she wouldn't risk the lift, which came out into the foyer where there was always a member of staff on duty. These thoughts flashed through Meak's head even as he and Roberts, with scrabbling haste, ran up the stairs and round the turn of the flight. They stopped, pressed back against the wall, trying not to breathe. The sound of the door opening made Roberts clutch him again, pressing them both harder back against the wall. Had she seen them? Heard the movement? The door sighed shut. They waited, wide-eyed, half expecting her to creep up on them. Was it a trick? Was she waiting for them to let out their breath? Roberts craned cautiously over the banister rail.

'She's gone down,' he whispered. 'Christ, she moves quietly!'

'We should have stopped her,' Meak whispered back.

'No! We've got to find out where she's going.'

'But she's got a knife, you idiot!'

'I know, I saw it. But it might not mean anything.'

'Oh, for Christ's sake . . .'

'Shut up!' Roberts hissed fiercely. 'If she's the one, we have to catch her in the act, or we'll never know for sure.'

'Come on then,' Meak said, 'or we'll lose her. Let's get this over with.'

Roberts gripped his arm again, and Meak turned to meet the most miserable face he had ever encountered. The poor bastard was really suffering. He was shaken himself, and bitterly sorry, but Roberts was hurt to the core. He really had loved her.

'You'll do as I say?'

'Sure. You're the boss. Go on.'

Roberts nodded, and led the way, going quietly down the stairs, keeping to the wall at each turn, listening, though there was nothing to listen to. Everyone but them must be in bed at this time of night – though who had been using the lift? A late reveller? Three o'clock was bloody late! Far below there was the familiar muted clunk of push bars: the external door was being opened.

'She's gone out,' Roberts whispered.

So that eliminated one innocent possibility, that she had just been slipping out to someone else's room, Meak thought. Bed-hopping. After all, it happened. And maybe Tom Emmerson was not all that much fun at his age. Oh, but wait, there was the knife. He shivered. He had been forgetting the knife. No, there was no way out: she was the phantom all right, the nutcase. What the hell were they doing trailing a lunatic with a knife? What if she'd seen them, knew they were coming? But surely the two of them could restrain her if necessary? Unless she jumped them, as she'd jumped Polly. There was a nice thought. His palms were really wet now. Maybe she was lying in wait for them right now. His fertile imagination offered him the swift, silent rush and the sting of the blade. There was something particularly unnerving about a knife: worse, to a man who shot regularly, than a gun. In a struggle, in the heat of the moment, a bullet, after all, might go anywhere, but a blade was pretty well sure to go somewhere.

The last section of the stair was in darkness. Either the bulb had gone, or someone had removed it. Roberts was oozing quietly but steadily down and barely hesitated, buoyed perhaps by his determination, but all Meak's hairs were standing on end as they turned the last corner.

But there was no one there. The stairwell was empty and the external door was standing open, wedged to stay open – it was a fire door – with a wad of paper. She had gone out, but left herself a way back in.

'It's the horses, then,' Roberts said; and there was something like grief in his voice.

'We'd better call security,' Meak suggested.

'No! I want it over. I have to know, one way or the other.'

Meak shrugged, resigned, like a good lieutenant under orders. Outside they set off down the dark path through the shrubbery towards the stable, stepping on to the grass to avoid making any sound. Anne must have been well ahead of them by now. There was no sound or shadow of her.

The bend in the path came, leading into utter darkness. This was the section where Polly had been attacked. Meak had been feeling more normal out in the open with the smell of grass and earth, but now he shivered with apprehension and wished he were anywhere but here. His feet lagged of their own accord, his eyes swivelled madly from side to side, trying to see through the darkness. He was glad of Roberts's bulk ahead of him: God bless his happy lack of imagination!

Roberts stopped suddenly, freezing, his head turned. He seized Meak's arm, almost stopping his heart with shock.

'What?'

'Listen!'

The silence sang against Meak's ears. The dark seemed a physical thing, pressing against them, menacing.

'I thought I heard something.'

For an instant the night held its breath, and then there was a scream. It seemed to rip the air like fabric.

Meak's stomach contracted, his hair lifted so that he actually felt the cold air against his scalp. 'Oh shit. Oh shit,' he heard himself say. Both men started forward as though jerked by a string, running, the adrenalin pounding into their bloodstreams. Was it a man, woman or horse that had screamed? Meak didn't know, but the image of the knife blade flashed in his mind, and there was a taste like blood in his mouth.

And now there was the unmistakable sound of hooves on a concrete surface – panicky hooves, clattering and slipping. They raced round the curve of the path and into the stable yard. It was under night lighting only, a sort of dim pinkish illumination, which made everything look unnatural, like a stage set, throwing deep and unexpected shadows. The upper doors of the loose boxes were kept shut at night for security, and they looked like row upon row of closed eyes, denying everything. No one was in sight; but there, over there in the British team block, one door was open, still swinging slightly on its hinge.

'It's one of ours,' Meak said. No need to whisper now. His heart hammered as they ran. What would they find? But he had heard hooves. 'I heard hooves. The horse must have got away. Maybe—'

'It's Murphy,' Roberts interrupted. 'That's Murphy's box.'

'Oh God, I should have guessed,' Meak said. They had almost reached the box. The door was open and there was no horse in there, they could see straight away. 'Which way did he go? Maybe she didn't have a chance to . . .'

He stopped dead. Through the door he could see that though there was no horse, there was something in the box: something dark crumpled up in the bedding. A human being, limp and motionless.

'Anne!' Roberts cried in a terrible voice, and flung himself down beside the still figure.

It was much darker in there, in the shadow, out of the faint night illumination. Meak held back from the door, not to block what little light there was. 'Is she hurt? What's happened? The horse must have knocked her down, or something,' he said.

'It's not Anne,' Roberts said with relief. 'Thank God! It's not Anne!'

Not Anne? But they'd seen her face! They'd followed her here! What the hell was going on? 'Well, who is it?' Meak said impatiently. 'For Christ's sake . . .'

'It's a man.' There seemed a very long pause, and then Roberts's face turned towards the door, gleaming very whitely in the eery light, his mouth like a black hole in a piece of paper. His voice came cold, with a creak of desperation, like the lid of a tomb lifting. 'It's John Newland. For God's sake, go and get help. I think he's dead.'

One or two of the horses had woken and were whickering and moving about in their boxes as Meak ran in the direction of the security hut. He'd only crossed the first yard when a dark shape jumped out in front of him from behind the next stable block, and a voice barked, 'Freeze! I mean it, buddy! Hands up! Stay right where you are!'

Meak's heart contracted so violently it hurt him. He stopped as though nailed to the ground, his hands went upwards in a convulsive movement. He had seen that pose, heard that command on a thousand TV shows; but this was real. A man was pointing a gun at him. 'Don't shoot!' he cried, his voice breaking with genuine panic.

'Keep 'em where I can see 'em. Who are you?' said the voice of authority.

'Howard Meak, one of the British team. For God's sake get the lights turned on! We need help. There's a man injured back there in one of the boxes. We think he may be dead.'

'Did you kill him?'

'Oh don't be stupid! Call for help!'

Either his accent or the tone of his voice carried conviction. The security man inched forward and stared briefly into Meak's face, and then said, 'OK.' The gun was lowered. Meak's hands faltered downwards. He found his legs trembling.

'Where is he?' the man asked, holstering his gun and unclipping his radio at the same time.

'This way,' said Meak.

Hurrying beside him, the man put the radio to his mouth and it made a barnyard noise before he said, 'Get the full lights on will ya? We got a man down.' Squawk. 'No, I'm OK.' Squawk. 'Yeah, I got it. I'll let you know if we need the paramedics.' He switched off and said. 'Bill'll get the other one.'

'Other one what?' Meak asked.

'The one that went after the horse. What the hell are ya doin' down here anyway? How many of you?'

'Dan Roberts is back there with the injured man, that's all I know about.'

As they reached the still-open door of the loose box, the full lights came on, flooding the yard and making Howard screw up his eyes. Inside the box, Newland lay face down, still motionless.

Roberts hunkered beside him, his face turned towards the door and now masked with resignation. 'He's dead,' he said.

'OK, let's see.'

The guard gestured Roberts to one side and took his place. He felt in a professional manner for a neck pulse, then laid his hands under Newland's shoulders and lifted him over. Newland was wearing trousers and a dark-coloured cardigan over his unbuttoned pyjama top, and two things struck Howard Meak about him particularly. The first was how young and vulnerable he looked in his thin, stripey jim-jams, tenderly white up to the bottom of his throat where his suntan ended. The second thing was the hypodermic syringe that jutted out rather obscenely from his marbled chest.

'He's dead all right,' the guard said briefly and superfluously, and he stood up.

Meak heard the click as Roberts swallowed with a dry throat. 'God,' he said. 'Poor old bastard.'

Meak said nothing. He was staring in awful fascination at the body, whose eyes – horribly – were still open. How the hell did Newland get here? *Why* was he here? He couldn't think what had happened. Couldn't think at all. Didn't want to think what had transpired between Anne and John Newland in those moments before they arrived.

Roberts stood up too, and the guard moved a pace to block the doorway, his hand going to his gun. 'You two've got some explaining to do. What the hell's going on here?' They didn't answer, too shocked to think. 'Christ, what a night! I never liked horses, but this was s'posed to be a cushy number,' he moaned to himself. 'I never expected crap like this.'

There was a sound of hooves outside, and Anne Neville appeared, leading Murphy by the forelock. His light summer rug was askew, but he seemed unharmed. They were flanked by another two uniformed security guards, who were looking both nervous and confused.

'Where am I to put the horse?' she asked, seeing the guard blocking the door.

'Not in here, lady. It's occupied.'

'Anne, are you all right?' Roberts asked from behind Meak.

But she looked at Howard, and she said, 'It was an accident.'

'Cops are on their way,' one of the newcomers said at the same moment, his voice overlaying hers. 'Do we need the paramedics?'

The first guard glanced down at John Newland briefly and gave a little shrug.

'No hurry.'

'So you were following her?' Howard and Dan exchanged a glance. The detective turned to Anne. 'And *you* were following *him*? Quite a little party game. D'you wanna tell me why you were following him?'

'I wanted to know what he was up to. I thought he might hurt one of the horses, so I was keeping my eye on him.'

'And what *did* he do?'

'Went down in the lift to the first floor, then down the rest of the way by the stairs. That's what he did before when he slashed the rugs. Safer that way. No one on the first floor would know him if they happened to come out and see him. Out by the fire door – wedged it open so he could get back in the same way. I followed him to the stables. When he went into Murphy's box I knew he was up to no good.'

'Murphy?'

'The horse.'

'The horse. Yeah. Go on.'

'As I got to the door I heard Murphy cry out and he plunged out past me. I tried to grab him – the horse – but I only got a hand on his sheet and he pulled away. I couldn't hold him. I saw John fall, just out of the corner of my eye. I was going after Murphy.'

'You went after the horse?'

'Of course.'

'Why of course?' The detective seemed surprised.

Howard Meak broke in. 'It's second nature. To a horseman, a loose horse is like – I don't know – a live wire to an electrician. You have to secure it before you do anything else.'

'Uh-huh,' the detective said, reserving judgement.

'You wouldn't even think about it.' Roberts roused himself to add his weight to the point. 'You'd just do it.'

'OK, what did *you* see?'

'We heard the horse running loose, but we didn't see it. By the time we got there the yard was empty, but the box door was open. We went to look and saw John Newland lying there.'

'You knew who it was?'

'Well, no, it was dark. I went in to see who it was and if he was hurt.'

'Is that right?' This to Meak.

'Yes. He went in and said, "It's John Newland, I think he's
dead," or words to that effect. So I went to get help, and ran
into the security guard. And that's all I know.'

'OK,' the detective said, stretching until his shoulders
crackled. 'You guys can have some coffee now, and then my
officers will get your statements down while it's all fresh in your
minds.'

'Fresh?' Meak groaned. 'I think old Newland must feel fresh
compared with me at this moment in time.'

It was only his way of relieving the tension, but Roberts
glared at him and snapped, his voice sharp with hysteria, 'Shut
up! You hear me, shut up! Haven't we got enough trouble
without your stupid jokes?'

'All right, break it up, break it up!' the detective said
soothingly. He pushed his loose piece of side hair, which he
trained to cover his bald top, back into its rightful position.
'One death in a night not enough for you? Christ, you British!'
he muttered, half amused, half resentful.

The police surgeon.

'A massive dose of equine tranquilliser, injected directly into
the pericardium, having the effect of paralysing the heart. He
would have died instantly.'

'Would it have killed the horse?'

'I'm not an expert, of course, but I imagine not. I should
think it was intended to make the horse too groggy to perform
in the competitions. Dosage for a horse would naturally be
bigger than for a human being.'

'What about the blow to the head?'

'Superficial. Wouldn't have killed him. Could have made him
dizzy enough to fall, possibly knocked him out briefly. My
guess is that the horse reared or kicked and caught him a
glancing blow, and he fell forward.'

'On to the hypo?'

'The position of the needle is consistent with his having fallen on it, yes.'

Anne Ashley Neville, to the detective.

'I knew he'd been performing various acts of nuisance over a period of months. I knew also that he drugged his own horses sometimes – or at least, that he had done so when I was last in England.'

'What made you think he was going to do it tonight?'

'I saw his face when he looked at Dan Roberts after he beat him in the speed competition. And I'd been in his room, so I knew he had the gear with him.'

'How did you get into his room?'

'Each room was issued with two keys. It's standard. John was on his own in that room. I took one of them out of his jacket pocket when it was hanging over a chair in the restaurant.'

'Did you indeed? And what about the knife?'

'Self-defence. And just generally "in case". I didn't know what I'd find. It's an all-purpose penknife. Most of us carry something like that all the time at home.'

'Well you're not at home now. You've put yourself in a difficult position, you know that?'

She shrugged. 'I knew he was going to do something really bad. I had to stop him.'

'You could have reported him. Why didn't you report these other . . . acts of nuisance, you called them?'

'To the police, you mean?'

'Why not?'

'I had no evidence.'

'You had no evidence this time. So what was different?'

'They were minor things. And anyway, they weren't acts against me. If the victims didn't report them, why should I interfere?'

'But you interfered this time.'
'That was different. I couldn't let him hurt Murphy.'

Howard Meak to Dan Roberts, over another cup of coffee.

'When you come to think of it, I suppose it could only have been him. He's the only one among us who could think of deliberately hurting a horse. I don't say he was vicious, only . . . a little careless in his methods.'

'You say that now,' Roberts said bitterly. 'You didn't when you thought it was Anne.'

'Come on, old man, don't hold that against me. She did behave oddly. And I had reason to think—'

'Yeah. I know. I suppose there was even a time when I had my doubts.'

'No, you held out for her. You've got nothing to reproach yourself with. You were a real friend.'

'Tell her that.'

'Maybe I will . . . If I get the chance. I'd like the chance to apologise myself.'

The medical examiner, after the post mortem.

'I don't know if it has any bearing on the situation, but it seems he was in the early stages of a brain tumour. I'll be able to demonstrate it better when I've done some tissue slides, but it's unmistakable.'

'How would that have affected him?'

'At this stage? Hard to say. Symptoms vary a lot. Headaches, dizzy spells, double vision perhaps. It might well have affected his personality, too. Mood swings. Feelings of depression, bouts of unfocused aggression.'

'Persecution complex? Paranoia?'

'Quite possibly.'

'That fits,' said the detective, staring at his notes. He

remembered the groom Jean's hesitant testimony. 'Yeah, it fits.'

Howard Meak to Chris Campbell.

'Well, that's it. That ought to clinch it, if anyone still has any doubt. Poor bastard. I suppose he suffered. I thought he was behaving rather oddly back at the Manchester Show. You know when he tried to slug me for interfering with his sister?'

'No, I was in hospital, remember?'

'So you were. And when I say interfering with his sister, I don't mean . . .'

'How can you joke at a time like this?'

'How can I not? My dear, it's the only way I can cope. Everything's as bad as it can be.'

He stared gloomily at his hands. Without Fliss he had no money, and his lifestyle was going to change drastically. He'd always had money – or access to money, anyway. He'd never had to earn a living. He thought of Mitton Abbey: the spacious house, the lovely grounds, the well-trained staff; of shooting, polo, rally driving, Goodwood, a box for Wimbledon – all the apparatus of his expensive lifestyle. He was used to the comforts, the finer things of life. Then he thought of Chrissy's pokey flat over the stables and winced inwardly. Assuming she'd have him. He might not even have that. How would their relationship cope with the drastic change in circumstances?

Speaking of which, what had happened to his tact? 'Except for you and me, that is.'

Chris didn't pick up on it. She was still thinking other thoughts. 'Poor Anne, everyone assuming it was her, when she knew all the time it was John Newland. It's awful to be wrongly accused.'

'Yes,' he said feelingly.

She looked up. 'I'm glad it wasn't her who sent the letter to your wife.'

'What difference does it make? Sent is still sent.'

'I don't want to think badly of her, that's what. Poor Anne!'

Despite knowing that the culprit had been John Newland, he still felt an obscure irritation at Anne Neville. He couldn't help feeling – irrationally, he acknowledged – that somehow none of this would have happened if she hadn't come back on the scene. Bad pennies turning up and so on. It was an uncomfortable thing to think so many people now knew she was a distant relative of his, even if only by marriage.

'Don't waste your sympathy on her,' he said tersely. 'It's Mary Newland you should feel sorry for.'

Mary Newland to Jean, in tears.

'You were right all along. You knew he was ill.'

'I didn't know. Nobody knew. It was only a . . . a kind of feeling that everything wasn't right.'

Jean's eyes were bleak. The darkness that had been uncovered was overwhelming, seeming to reach out for her, too. Everything was tainted by it. And she dreaded the thought of going back, of facing Mr Newland. Underhill would not be a pleasant place to work; but what if she lost her job now? That was a worse possibility. She was not so young that she could just waltz into another one.

'I wonder what caused it,' Mary said. 'Do you think it was that fall he had in the paddock with Copper . . . Murphy, I mean? The blow on the head?'

'You don't get it that way.'

'Oh, poor John! Poor John!'

'He's out of it now,' Jean said grimly. 'You ought to think about your father, how he's going to feel.' Mary seemed to shrink like a salted snail at the thought. 'You'll come home now, won't you? You'll come back to England?'

'No!'

'But you must.'

'I'm staying here.' She lifted her flaming eyes to Jean's with sudden determination. 'I'm sorry John's dead, and I'm sorry Dad'll be sad. I mean, they were my family, even if they were mean to me. Of course I'm sorry. But I was practically a prisoner back there. They made me so miserable. John killed my horse and drove away my boyfriends, and Dad backed him up in everything, and neither of them ever cared a jot about me. I never had anything of my own: not even room to breathe. I've got a life here. I'm free, and even if I can't stay in the States, I'm never going back to Underhill.'

Dan Roberts and Polly Morgan sat alone in a corner of the coffee room. Even the waitresses didn't come over to disturb them, so dense was the atmosphere around them.

Everyone was subdued, naturally, by the tragic event, and by the decision that had been made to scratch the team from the rest of the events. They were only waiting now for all the police business to be finished so that they could get the all-clear to go home. It meant a lot of hanging around with nothing to do, and nothing to think about but the Newland business. It meant that it was almost impossible for anyone to talk about anything else.

'So the first attack – at the Manchester Show – was meant for me?' Polly said.

'We'll never know any of it for sure, of course, but it's logical. And Anne thinks so.'

'Because I'd beaten him in the Tomatsu? Well, he's never liked me beating him in anything, that's true. And I remember his face, and his behaviour. He snubbed me good and hard.'

'Yes. And remember also that you and I had just got together. We weren't exactly discreet.'

'Are you saying he was jealous about me? But he didn't still care for me.'

'He'd never had anyone since you, had he?'

'True – as far as I know. But he's always treated me coldly since then. I mean, if anything, it was animosity, not heartbreak.'

'All right, that works out the same. He was bitter at losing his woman. And he resented someone else having you when he couldn't.'

'Yes, dog in the manger I can believe. That's more in his line than everlasting love,' Polly said, and then remembered. 'Oh, poor bugger, I keep forgetting he's dead. God, this is a terrible business!' She brooded a moment. 'So what was the second thing? Sunny being drugged at Hickstead? But what beef did he have against Chris?'

'He had a beef against Howard. Howard tried to stop him bashing up Greyfriar at the Manchester Show, and then John thought he was interfering over Mary and Ben Watts, and they had that fight. And several times after that, when he met him at shows, Howard tried to talk to John about Mary running away and got his head bitten off. He was only trying be nice, but suppose John still thought he was interfering and resented it? And what would be the best way to revenge yourself on Howard?'

'By hurting Chrissy? Yes, and hurting Sunny was the sure way to hurt her.'

'It was that that put Anne on to him in the first place. She knew he'd used stuff on his own horses in the past, and she reckoned he was the only one of us who'd do something like that. So she started to watch him.'

'What about the car incident? Who was that aimed at?'

'Could have been both of them. Or even all four of us. He had a big beef against me by then, didn't he?'

'Did he?'

'I'd got the horse he couldn't manage and the woman he couldn't marry. Remember the poison pen letter?'

'How could I forget? How *did* Anne know about that?'

'Overheard us.'

'That simple?'

'We weren't exactly whispering.'

'And then there was the bomb hoax.'

'Newland's horses were closest to the door.'

'Yes, I remember talking about that with Ali and Howard, though of course Tom Emmerson's nags being by the door as well confused the issue. And I thought it couldn't be anything to do with John because of his accident at Lutterworth. How do you explain that?'

'Jean was sure it was deliberate, but it might have been just wear and tear. Or it might have been him being cunning, hurting himself to make sure he wasn't suspected. I'm not sure about that one.'

'Who was the bomb hoax supposed to hurt?'

'Me, you, Howard – I don't suppose by then he cared who else got hurt in the process if the paranoia was really starting to take hold. Remember how ratty and solitary he'd become?'

'Yes, poor bastard. And then there was the slashing of the rugs, and the attack on me in the shrubbery.'

'Anne deliberately left her jacket behind and slipped back so she could follow him.'

'Where was her jacket, by the way?'

'On the hooks in the lobby by the loos. That's why I didn't see her.'

'Ah!'

'She was afraid he was going to do something. She saw his face after I'd won the McDonald's. But she couldn't find him. He was already out in the bushes, lying in wait for you, of course, but she thought he'd be after me, so she was looking in the wrong place. She says she thinks he was actually going to hurt Murphy, then saw you going down the path ahead of him and changed his mind, decided to jump you on your way back.'

'He did look furious about the McDonald's. I saw his face

267

too. I suppose getting at me to punish you killed two birds with one stone.' She shuddered. The memory of those terrifying few seconds would be with her a long time yet.

'And the thing that really bugged him most – maybe what tipped him over the edge – was that I won it on Murphy. Murphy and David Barber beat him and Apache to the World Championship, the only time he might have won it. Then he couldn't handle his new horse and sold him, and I got him, and he turned out to be the very same Murphy, and I *could* handle him. That must have burned him up! And of course Anne had been Murphy's groom that championship year. It was all tangled up together in his twisted little mind.'

'Murphy was really at the centre of it all, then,' Polly traced a pattern on the table with some spilled sugar. 'I'm sorry I suspected Anne. You held out for her all along, didn't you?'

'I knew her better than the rest of you.'

'No, I don't think it was that.' She looked up now. 'You still care about her, don't you?'

He didn't answer, which was her answer.

'I had a phone call from Bill, did I tell you?' She looked up and caught the flicker of hope in his eye that he didn't mean her to see. 'He'd heard about John, of course, and thought I might be upset and need comforting, so he rang to see if I wanted him to come over.'

'Nice of him.'

'I could get a plane straight over, if you like,' Bill had said.

'No, don't. I'm all right,' she had replied. 'Of course I'd like to see you, but we'll be coming home soon. It'd be silly for you to go to all that trouble and expense when, really, I'm quite OK. It was awful, of course, and I think we all wonder whether we ought to have realised how sick he was and whether there was anything we could have done. But I don't think there was. He never was a man you could talk to.'

'Some people got on all right with him. You did, once.'

'Don't remind me. Poor John.'

'How's Dan Roberts?' he had asked with what seemed to her an edge.

'Oh Bill, please, no jealousy. I couldn't cope with it now.'

'No, I'm not being jealous. I've done a lot of thinking. I realise I've treated you abominably. I've no right to tie you up with gratitude and try to run your life . . .'

'You haven't! I *am* grateful – I mean, you've been very good to me, and more than generous, and I'm not grateful because you expect me to be. Oh hell, you know what I mean,' she said, getting in a tangle.

'All the same, I'm not going to impose on you the way I have been. When you get back, I'm going to give you the two horses. I should have done it long ago. I'm going to sign them over to you legally, and back out of your life. Then if you want to contact me, it will be your decision. I'll be your friend, your escort, whatever you want. Or nothing at all. Up to you. No pressure.'

Back out of her life? Her heart contracted painfully. 'Are you trying to tell me – is there someone else?'

'What?' He seemed startled.

'Look, you can tell me the truth. God knows, I don't own you. I'd just like to know.'

'Why on earth should you think that?'

'I saw you on television.' She laughed nervously. 'Banal, isn't it? That awards ceremony. It was on CNN, and there you were with . . .' She hesitated to say 'a bimbo'. She didn't want to come across as catty. 'Someone,' she finished. 'Well, I couldn't help noticing you hadn't asked me to go with you.'

'I didn't know about it until the last minute,' he said with the calm, sure voice of absolute honesty. 'Sir John Pearson fell sick the day before, and they asked me if I could take his place. We're both on the same committee. I had to give a speech – it wasn't a pleasure outing, I can promise you.'

'No – I see. I just wondered. The – er – your companion? I wonder why you didn't ask Maureen.'

269

Now he laughed. 'To the Sci-tech Awards? She wouldn't have thanked me! She'd have been bored stiff.'

'So who was she?'

'Lady Pearson.'

'Really – Lady Pearson? Sir John lent her to you, did he? He's doing well for himself. She looked a bit of a babe.'

'She is the *second* Lady Pearson.'

'Oh, I see. Trophy wife.'

'She also has a double first from Cambridge in chemistry and engineering, and she's the head of the res and dev department at Monson Chemicals. *She* gave the speech before mine.'

'You're enjoying this, aren't you?' she said tersely.

'I'm enjoying the fact that you seem to have minded my going to the dinner with someone else.' She was looking into the confusion of her thoughts, and didn't answer. 'That's a very expensive silence,' he said at last. 'Were you, by any remote, wonderful chance, jealous?'

'I don't know. I don't know what I was. My head's in a mess, Bill. I can't discuss it all now, over the telephone.'

'I don't expect you to.'

'No, but listen – don't do anything – *anything* – until we've talked, right? I don't want you to back out of my life, as you put it. I don't know exactly how things are going to be between us, but I've treated you badly, too, and you've been nicer to me than I had any right to expect – no, don't interrupt for a minute. Things are not absolutely simple, but I want you in my life, I do know that. So when I get back, we'll talk it through, and see where we go from here.'

'You think we might . . .'

'I don't know, Bill, honestly I don't know, but . . .' She searched for the right words. 'I feel as if I went to sleep in midsummer and woke up in November. The world seems very chilly and bleak just now, and I'm really glad to know I've got you to come back to. I – I really *care* about you, you know.' She hesitated, and added in a small voice, 'Maybe I was jealous.'

'Oh Polly,' he had said, and there had been a lot of expensive transatlantic sighing.

She remembered all this as she looked at handsome Dan Roberts across the table. Dan the Man. It had been fun, it had been an exciting fling, and as long as they went back to being friends they would have lost nothing by it. But she had seen the way he looked at Anne. He had never looked at her like that. And, frankly, she didn't think she wanted him to. She wanted something a little more substantial, more sustaining to life than the cappucino froth that was her relationship with Dan. Being with him had not stopped her feeling lonely. And she guessed that perhaps he was beginning to realise that he was lonely too.

'I'm very fond of Bill,' she said at last. 'And not just because he owns my horses.'

'I'm glad to hear it.'

'Dan, it's been great, but I think we've come to a natural end, you and I. Don't you think?'

'Because of Bill?'

'And Anne.'

'Yeah,' he said sighing. 'You could be right.' He looked up. 'I want to get her back. I treated her badly, and I don't know if she can forgive me, but if I do get her back, I know it's got to be different this time. Exclusive.'

'So I should think.'

'I've been a bit of a bastard in the past. Not worrying how other people felt. I think I've been a bit of a bastard to you.'

'No, no, it's all right. We were using each other,' Polly said hastily. She didn't want him beating his breast over her.

'But you could have got hurt, and I never wanted that. I really like you, Pol. I swear I never meant you to get hurt. I just wasn't thinking, I suppose.'

She suppressed a smile. 'Dan, my love, I promise you I'm not hurt and was never likely to be. We were having fun together, that's all. No harm done.'

271

'You're sure? Well, thank God.' He reached across the table and clasped her hand. 'Friends?'

'Always that.'

'You're a star.' He grinned. 'And tell Bill if he ever makes you cry I'll break his neck.'

Since the night Newland had died, Tom Emmerson had scarcely spoken to Anne. She had withdrawn not only from his bed, but from his company and conversation too. Of course, at first she was being interviewed practically non stop, by the police, the show management, the *chef d'equipe*, the police again, the press, and Uncle Tom Cobbley and all. In between she slept like the dead at any odd hour she was able, sprawled face down across the second bed. He saw her only when they happened to bump into each other, or when he sat and watched her sleeping.

And then when the interviewing came to an end she spent long hours in the stable. She took care of Fox and Buccaneer in her usual efficient manner, but she seemed also, by some tacit common consent, to have taken over care of Murphy. She seemed reluctant to leave the horse for a moment, as if afraid someone would wreak vengeance on it in her absence – though who there was to do that he couldn't think, unless it was Mary Newland. Nobody blamed the horse, as far as he knew. There was no question of its being destroyed. If the blow to Newland's head had been caused by Murphy rearing, he had provocation, and it was plainly an accident. Still, she couldn't seem to bear to be parted from the horse, he didn't quite know why.

But he knew she was going to leave him. It wasn't only the events of that night: he had broken something when he had asked her that question. He saw it now, in retrospect, though he didn't fully understand it. If not here in America, then as soon as the plane touched down in England, she would walk away. It was over.

The pain of that was terrible. He didn't know how he would live without her. If she had not come into his life that day, like a miracle, he would just have wandered slowly down the gentle path to bankruptcy, alcoholism and death, and hardly noticed his progress. But she had brought him back to life, made him feel passion again, and hope. He tasted power and self-determination, he had won again in the ring, and in bed. So he could not go back to the gentle decline he had left. If he went down now, it would be hard and painful.

Well, he was not going to go down. He stuck his hand down into his soul and pulled up resolve. He was not going to go back to stagnation and failure. And he was not going to be pathetic, either. He knew she was going to leave him, so he would make it easy for her, and leave himself with some dignity.

On this determination he stood up, and then paused with a little smile, and told himself that it was all very well to plan a noble gesture, but the first thing he had to do was to *find* her, in order to be noble to her, and he hadn't the least idea where she was.

Epilogue

The horses, muffled in their flying gear, were all aboard, securely tethered and with full haynets to keep their minds occupied during the long flight. Among them, his fame and his notoriety sitting with equal ease upon him, the big chestnut stood with his head bent to receive the caresses of the woman who was now a familiar figure to him. She had groomed him long ago, in his youth, and perhaps he had a dim memory of her to add to his instinctive knowledge that she was quiet and good. At any rate, he nudged her comfortably, and turned his head as far as it would go to watch her retreating back as she went to take her seat for take-off.

In the cabin the mood was still subdued and thoughtful, and even when the seat-belt light went off and they could move around again and ask for drinks, they stayed in their seats, absorbed with their silent thoughts. Howard and Chris held hands openly now, but that was the only difference in their behaviour. They had always been best at comforting each other, and the rest of the team left them alone to get on with it. It was accepted that Howard must be the most upset about Newland's death, having been the nearest thing John Newland ever had to a friend. If there were any other cause for his gloom, they didn't know about it.

The other bit of pairing off happened after take-off. Tom Emmerson and Anne Neville had been seated together, as had Polly and Dan. Once the plane had stopped climbing, Emmerson got to his feet and said, 'I need a drink.' Anne said nothing, staring straight ahead, at her most impassive. Emmerson walked down the aisle until he reached Polly. 'How about coming and sitting with me, and cheering me up?' he said. 'Anne won't mind swapping seats. She and I have exhausted each other's conversation.'

Polly looked at him a moment, and then smiled with ready understanding. 'Of course.'

'I'm going to get myself a drink. Can I get you one while I'm up?'

'I'll take a gin and ton off you, thanks.'

As he passed Anne on his way back, he caught her eye and jerked his head backwards, indicating the exchange. She stood up, and laid the fingers of one hand lightly on the back his for a moment. He twisted his hand over, caught her fingers and lifted them to his lips.

'God bless you,' he said, and walked on.

Polly, behind him, flattened herself to let Anne out. The two women looked at each other.

'Gentleman Tom,' Polly remarked.

'He's a good man,' said Anne. She turned her head, looking towards the seat where Dan waited, and she seemed a little hesitant.

'He's got a lot of things to say to you,' Polly said quietly. 'I think we've all learned something in the past week or so. It's changed us all in one way or another. We've had to adjust our values.' Anne met her eyes questioningly. 'For what it's worth,' Polly concluded, 'you have my blessing, too.'

And Anne smiled suddenly. Polly thought it was the most natural and human smile she had ever seen on Anne's face.

There was quite a press presence at the airport, but it was for Harry Parkinson and his assistants to field that, and save the team from having to give interviews. Fortunately the intervening days spent in the States meant the news was now fairly stale, and various political rows had blown up in the meantime, to blunt the pack's teeth.

More welcome people were at the airport to meet them, too. Bill Simpson was there with the Jaguar, and had a brief word, man to man, with Roberts about the travel arrangements.

'I'd like to take her straight home. She looks done up.'

'Emotional strain,' Roberts said. 'We've all felt it.'

'Are you . . . and she . . . ?' Simpson hesitated. It was not a question he could properly ask.

'Hazel's come down with the box; and Anne's coming with me, so there's plenty of help with the horses. We can manage without her.'

'Ah,' said Simpson, understanding. 'Well – good. That's all right, then.'

'I hope so,' Roberts said, with a faint smile. 'Terry can come over and fetch your nags any time, can't she?'

'Not my nags any more.'

'So I understand,' said Roberts. He offered his hand, on an impulse. 'Take care of her,' he said, as they shook.

Phil and Keith were there for Chris Campbell with the Land Rover, and a hasty conference brought them up to date on the Meak situation. The Mitton Abbey box had come for the horses, and a stern but uneasy Fred told Howard that Mrs Meak had said he was to take them home and on no account to allow Howard to accompany them.

So there were four warm bodies in the Land Rover as it drove off round the perimeter road towards the M4. Chris's first enquiries were after Sunny, who was doing better than expected. Then Phil said, 'You look tired, Twin. How was it?'

'Dreamlike,' Chris said.

'More nightmarish, I should have thought,' Keith said.

'Not real enough to be a nightmare. More Gormenghast, really. I have the most peculiar unfinished feeling about the whole thing.'

'Poor old John,' Phil said shortly. She met her twin's eyes in the rear-view mirror, and then shifted her focus to Howard. He was looking both gloomy and hangdog, but she supposed that was inevitable. Apart from Newland's death, he had his marital strife to think about. He had always lived the high life, and it would be a shock to have to face the future without life's little luxuries, like a vast house, several cars, expensive restaurants and first class flights.

But at least there would still be horses for him, she thought, if he and Chris made a go of it. Not the same kind of horses, perhaps: apart from Chris's jumpers they were solid riding-school nags, that was all. She tried to imagine the glamorous, ultra-smart Howard Meak escorting lumpish, bumping beginners in jeans and trainers out on hacks, and failed utterly. It was a bit of a joke, actually.

'Never mind,' she said. 'Soon be home.'

Much later, that night, Dan Roberts was lying in his own bed in his seedy little cottage, too happy to sleep, despite being dog tired. Anne was with him again, in his arms, in his bed. They had made love with a hunger and passion which had surprised even him, and now she was curled against his shoulder, her arm and leg across him, and his chin was resting on her hair. He sighed with contentment, and she squeezed him slightly in response, as a cat clenches its paws with pleasure.

'You will stay this time?' he said after a long silence.

'That's up to you,' she said. 'It was up to you the last time.'

'I'm different now. Blimey, that was years ago! I'm not like that now.'

'What about Polly?'

'That's all over. I told you. Anyway, there would never have been Polly if I'd had you.'

'No more groupies? No more grooms?'

'I don't want anyone but you.'

She was silent. After a bit, he said, 'Can I ask you something?'

She stirred. 'Be careful. There are some questions that can't be forgiven.'

'I *always* believed in you,' he said. 'I never thought it was you. But it's this business of the mental home. I know there's nothing in it, but I'd like to know how the story got started.'

She sighed and rolled out of his arms, and lay on her back, staring up at the ceiling. He lifted himself on one elbow to look at her, to see if she was angry. But she seemed only sad.

'I was in an institution for a while,' she said. 'It was a nervous breakdown.'

'Well, anyone can have one of those,' he said, rallying. 'That's nothing. What caused it?'

Her eyes were remote. 'My father died when I was thirteen. My mother married again.'

'To Howard's cousin – Polly told me.'

'No, he was her third husband. There was one in between. The second one took quite a fancy to me.'

Something about the way she said it warned him. He felt a chill. 'You mean – ?'

'I couldn't tell Mummy. She loved him. Why do women fall in love with bastards? Anyway, I stuck it out for two years. Then I ran away. They brought me back of course, and it all came out. Mummy never forgave me. So as soon as I was sixteen I left home. I struggled on for a couple more years, then I cracked up.'

She closed her eyes, squeezed them tight a moment as if against memory, and then opened them.

'In a way, what he did wasn't the worst thing. People are always hurting each other without necessarily meaning to. He knew what he was doing was wrong, but he didn't set out deliberately to hurt me. He was just sick.'

'You forgive him?' he said in amazement.

A glance flashed at him. 'Not quite,' she said with brief irony.

'So what was the worst thing?'

She paused, as if assembling her words. 'Having been inside – in a mental home – is something you never escape from. Sooner or later people find out, and then they look at you differently, avoid you, blame you for things. They never forget. So you have to move on. That's the cruelty I can't forgive.'

He didn't know what to say, and it was probably for the best that he said nothing.

She went on, 'It makes it hard to trust people after that. Animals are much easier. Horses especially. They don't judge you. It took me such an effort to trust you, Dan, and then you went and betrayed me.'

'I'm sorry,' he said quickly. 'I'll never do anything like that again. I swear it.'

'It's funny,' she mused, 'my step-dad did time in jail for what he did, and he'll never live it down. They hound people like him. Pillar to post. But my sentence was just the same. We were both punished the same way for the same act. We both had to keep moving on.'

'Not any more,' he said, half plea, half statement. 'I'll take care of you. I'll never let you down.'

Her eyes moved from the ceiling to his face. 'You followed me that night.'

'Because I *knew* you were innocent. I followed you so that I could prove it.' He held her gaze steadily, and then drew her back into his arms, and she came without resistance. 'Everything will be all right,' he said. 'It's all over now, and everyone knows the truth about what happened. You'll never have to move on again.'

Howard Meak was still up, sitting alone in a shabby armchair in the sitting room of Chrissy's flat, nursing a whisky. Chris had gone to bed, exhausted, and he had promised to follow, but he was postponing matters. The ride back from the airport had been uncomfortable. The riding-school Land Rover was exceedingly shabby and dirty, and seemed to have no springs whatever, and Chris's twin and her husband had kept eyeing him and being shatteringly tactful.

Back at the stables there had been work to do settling the horses, and then up in the flat they'd had a supper of the sort of nursery food – sausages and beans – that he'd found rather charming when it was part of his secret life with Chrissy, but the prospect of which as a permanency appalled him. And Phil and Keith had left them at last to an uncomfortable silence, which Chrissy had broken by taking herself off for a bath and to bed.

To bed! There was a thing. After almost two years (for him: he had a suspicion it had been longer for her) he was going to be able to go to her bed. They could become lovers. There was nothing to stop them any more: Fliss was going to divorce him anyway, and he was free to take everything from Chrissy that she wanted to give. Well, and how did he feel about that? He loved Chrissy, was in love with her, and had he been a free agent they would have been lovers long before this. But from having held off for so long, the thing had become something of a precipice, and he had to admit that under the fluttering excitement there was fear – definite fear. He imagined that a fledge-ling bird, sitting at the edge of the nest in the high tree, about to launch itself for the very first time, might feel something like this. It was all very well believing you could fly – *knowing* it was a different matter; and getting it wrong could bloody well hurt.

He had been pondering the bed thing so long she was probably asleep by now anyway; and his mind had ranged on, over many other topics. Now as he swirled his whisky absently round and round his glass, he was not, in fact, thinking of Chrissy, sex, his terminally ill marriage, or of his grim and penniless future. He was thinking of Anne Neville.

When they had landed at the airport she had gone with the other grooms to see to the disembarking of the horses. She had been sitting with Dan Roberts since just after take-off, their heads together in earnest conversation, and he assumed that things had been settled between them at last. She had paused on passing Tom Emmerson, presumably to arrange matters about his horses, and in straightening had caught Howard's eye, and given him a long, thoughtful, and not entirely friendly look.

There was something that bothered him, had been bothering him all along. The explanations about John Newland's sickness and activities were perfectly convincing, and he was satisfied that Newland had indeed been the prankster, nuisance, whatever you liked to call it. It all made sense. But there remained to disturb him that moment down in the stables, when Anne had come back leading Murphy, and the thing she had said which, because the security man spoke at the same time, only Howard had heard.

You had to take into account her background, her strange lifestyle, her history of mental illness, he thought. You had to give those things due consideration when weighing up her account of what happened that night. No one would ever know for sure; all there was to go on was logic and probability.

According to Anne's story, she had only seen Newland fall out of the corner of her eye as she was trying to catch Murphy, and running out of the box after him. So as far as she knew, Newland had merely fallen over – knocked off balance, perhaps, by the escaping horse. There was no reason for her to think he was hurt, far less dead. And with the first guard and Howard himself standing in the box doorway, she couldn't have seen the body lying there from where she was.

But she had said, 'It was an accident.'

That was what bothered him. *What* was an accident?